Mai Tai
to Murder

ALSO BY CANDY CALVERT

Dressed to Keel

Aye Do or Die

A
Darcy
Cavanaugh
Mystery

Mai Tai
to Murder

Candy Calvert

MIDNIGHT INK
WOODBURY, MINNESOTA

FIRST EDITION
First Printing, 2007

Book design by Donna Burch
Cover design by Kevin R. Brown
Cover illustration © Kun-Sung Chung / www.kschung.com

Midnight Ink, an imprint of Llewellyn Publications

Library of Congress Cataloging-in-Publication Data
Calvert, Candy, 1950-
 Mai tai to murder / Candy Calvert.—1st ed.
    p. cm.
 "A Darcy Cavanaugh mystery."
 ISBN 978-0-7387-1074-7 (pbk.)
 1. Cavanaugh, Darcy (Fictitious character)—Fiction. 2. Cruise ships—Fiction.
 3. Nurses—Fiction. 4. Murder—Investigation—Fiction.
 I. Title.
PS3603.A4463M35 2007
813'.6—dc22

                                                          2007013606

Midnight Ink
Llewellyn Publications
2143 Wooddale Drive, Dept. 978-0-7387-1074-7
Woodbury, MN 55125-2989, U.S.A.
www.midnightinkbooks.com

Printed in the United States of America

This book—though liberally poking fun at the literary world—is dedicated to those same folks: agents, editors, and publishers, whose vision and talent put great books into the hands of eager readers. And to my fellow writers (published and pre-published) to honor the unique combination of guts, heart, and tenacity that it takes to pursue this craft in the face of daunting obstacles, not the least of which is self-doubt. You are my friends, mentors, and the only people who truly understand this crazy calling—go for the dream!

ONE

"I'm serious," I said, waggling the knife, "one more word and I'll whittle your horny heart out." I raised the blade and eyed my target, a tanned expanse of well-defined masculine chest muscle. I did a speedy medical assessment: *a four-inch blade plunged through the pectoralis minor, between the anterior ribs and directed down toward the heart's ventricles, ought to ...* "Hey," I warned, raising my eyes to the smug smirk on my victim's handsome face, "if you dare laugh, I swear I'll—"

In an instant, Luke Skyler's hand shot out to grab my wrist. The plastic picnic knife slid from my fingers and into our warm, rumpled nest of bed sheets. Behind him, the Florida morning sun peeked through a gap in the hotel's bamboo shades, closed in haste during the crazy rush of last night's reunion. Haste being the key word. After the Bureau moved Luke to Boston last spring, we'd burned up the air miles whenever our hectic schedules allowed. But it was never often enough.

"You stab like a girl, Cavanaugh," Luke said with a slow smile. The autumn sunlight played across his dark blonde hair, and those amazing blue eyes crinkled at the edges with the widening of his dimpled smile. He leaned close, his breath tickling my ear. "Besides, I'm pushing thirty-six and weakened by six damned weeks of celibacy; if you want to kill me, let's just go for the big heart attack, okay...?" His faint Southern drawl dissolved into a deep chuckle as warm hands slid beneath my mango silk chemise. "God, I've missed you, Darcy."

"Wait ... *wait*," I said, shaking my head and sending my long, and stubbornly curly, tangle of red hair sweeping across my shoulders, "you *promised* to help me with this, remember? Stabbing, strangulation, poison, bludgeoning... my whole deadly spreadsheet." I glanced toward my laptop in the suite's business niche. A leather office chair was heaped high with Luke's clothing and paraphernalia: tweed sport jacket, starched oxford shirt, Levis, Oakley sunglasses, ID badge, shoulder holster... and the gun, of course: 9 mm Glock. Try stuffing that sucker in your beach tote when your man wants to play volleyball bare-chested. Dating a federal agent—especially one working undercover as a lawyer—gets creative, trust me. "You know, the outline for my 'Nurse's Guide to Murder' workshop. I brought the notes and all my cute little props." I fumbled with a fold of bed sheets, trying to locate my pink plastic knife, and—

Ooh. I tried not to weaken as Luke's mouth moved into the hollow of my neck, his warm tongue snaking across my collarbone. I peered over his head at a digital clock perched atop the office desk. "I'm serious, Luke. I've got to board that cruise ship in exactly two hours, and I have no clue what to say to a bunch of romance and mystery writers." I groaned and rolled my eyes. "I could choke Ma-

2

rie for talking me into this. I mean, we're ER nurses, for godsake! We *save* lives—took a friggin' oath for that. And now we're hooked into teaching a bunch of writers how to murder people? Why did I agree to do this?"

Luke sighed and scooted back against the headboard, lifting me up into his arms until my head rested against his chest. He reached to pull up the sheets, and I caught a glimpse of the ragged and still-pink scar on his left shoulder from the gunshot wound he'd suffered six months ago—the last time I'd been aboard a cruise ship. It still freaked me out to remember all of that. This man could teach a murder class himself.

Luke laughed softly. "Why did you agree to do this workshop? That's a no-brainer. You're doing it for the comped vacation, five days in the Caribbean and away from Northern California fog. I'd go with you in a hot minute, but you know how many strings I had to pull just to come here to Canaveral." His lips brushed the top of my hair. "And you're also doing this workshop because Marie Whitley is your best friend, and she's a complete pushover for all of Carol's artsy-fartsy whims."

I nodded and then smiled at the image of my cigar-smoking lesbian pal and her long-time partner, strangely the most traditionally committed couple I knew. Right down to a white picket fence and strawberry pancakes on Sunday mornings. Face it: they had Ma and Pa Cavanaugh beat by a long shot. And it hadn't been hard for Carol to convince Marie to do the writers' workshop because normally Marie *worked* when she was aboard cruise ships—as an infirmary nurse. This mini-vacation promised sunshine, snorkeling, and umbrella drinks without the pesky interruptions of *stat* pages for emergency nursing stunts. I could hardly argue with that logic.

"And most importantly," Luke said, tightening his arms around me, "you're doing this for the opportunity to spend some quality time with my mother."

Oh... man. I bit my lip and stifled a groan. If Marie were here, her gray eyes would be bugging out of her head. I hadn't exactly shared this ugly tidbit of information with her yet. I took a deep breath and lied through my teeth.

"That's right," I said sweetly. "It was so great that your mom was able to take the time off from her... work to come along on this cruise." Right. However will Judge Lucas Jefferson Skyler II survive without someone to oversee the ironing of his honorable boxer shorts? And—horrors—what if there were a Charlottesville Garden Club emergency? Chrysanthemums were at risk.

I forced the image of my divorced parents, Bill "the Bug Man" Cavanaugh and a novice nun turned Vegas blackjack dealer, from my mind, not wanting to conjure up the inevitable oil-on-water comparison with Luke's family. And admit that I'd somehow managed to fall into a yearlong relationship with forbidden (and Roman-numeraled) fruit. Forbidden fruit according to Angela Barrett Skyler, that is. Luke's mother hated me like chiggers in her pantyhose.

"That's because she likes you so much, Darcy," Luke said, nuzzling my earlobe. "Really, I *sense* that."

Mm-hmm. Right. It was pretty obvious that, right this minute, all of this man's senses were focused somewhere below his navel.

"Well," I said, smiling because I knew how much Luke wanted to believe that his mother and I could find some common ground, "I do think she was impressed that I was able to snag her an ap-

4

pointment with that hotshot literary agent." I shook my head. "Although I had no idea that your mom is a writer."

Luke laughed. "Well, supposedly she's been working on that; all I can remember are things like the Ladies' Club Cookbook and six-page Christmas letters. Let's see…can we count all her long-winded notes on morals and social etiquette? She hid them in my suitcase every time I came home on college break."

My jaw dropped. "She *didn't*. Morals?"

"On the Judge's letterhead paper, folded up and slipped between layers of my boxers." Luke's voice dropped to a whisper as he traced a fingertip up my inner thigh. "I'm a true product of proper Southern breeding. Haven't you noticed that I always remember to say…" his fingers continued their teasing climb, "'*Please may I, ma'am*'?"

I sneaked one last look at the clock. There was still an hour left before I had to catch the port shuttle. And this federal agent *was* asking politely, but first…I spotted the plastic picnic knife and lifted it from the sheets. "First explain why I 'stab like a girl.'" I batted my lashes when Luke groaned. "C'mon. Just humor me with a couple of tips, so I don't make a complete ass of myself in front of those writers. And *your mother*?"

"Okay, okay." Luke took the pink plastic knife from me and grimaced. "But if the Bureau gets wind of this, I'll be laughed out of Boston." He sighed and nodded toward my suitcase near the desk. "Exactly what are these other 'cute props' you brought?"

I grinned. "Rope for strangling—or maybe I'll use pantyhose. That's more interesting, don't you think? And a plastic baseball bat, a jar of almond potpourri—"

"*Potpourri?* What…murder by air freshener?"

I narrowed my eyes. "Cyanide. I'm covering deadly poisons, and cyanide smells like almonds, so I'll pass the jar around and—"

"Got it. And by the way . . ." he leaned away and reached into his wheeled carryon case near the bed. "I brought you something else to take along."

I raised my brows with curiosity, not the mixed-emotion panic I'd felt six months ago when I thought Luke was chasing me with an engagement ring. I had no idea then that Mama Skyler would see hell freeze over before she let that happen.

"Comfort food," he said, grinning and handing me the blue-on-blue box adorned with a likeness of SpongeBob. I smiled—Kraft Macaroni and Cheese, my secret pig-out.

Luke tapped the box. "I figure there'll be a microwave in your room, and water. In an emergency, Marie could mix it up in a Styrofoam cup. Would that work?" He laughed at the look on my face. "Five long days with the Judge's wife, Darcy. That could make for a meltdown, trust me."

I didn't know whether to laugh at the image of Marie cooking a batch of mac and cheese like a heroin fix or cry because—hey—there's something pretty mushy-wonderful about a guy who can love you despite your pathetic quirks. I decided to kiss Luke instead, but before I could do that he brandished the plastic knife.

"Now observe," he said, as seriously as if he were giving a Bureau briefing. "A woman typically grabs a knife and swings in a downward arc, like this." Luke demonstrated, grazing the plastic tip across the front of my chemise. "Not always effective, because the blade can be deflected by the ribs, which protect vital organs."

I nodded and then saw a smirky smile tug at the corners of Luke's mouth. His dimples deepened. "A man," he said, slowly lifting a spaghetti-thin strap of my chemise with the plastic blade, "does it more like this." He watched the strap slide down my arm and then repeated the tactic with the remaining strap, until the chemise fell to my waist, leaving me bare. His gaze moved appreciatively to the tiny tattoo above my left breast. To say the man was intrigued by that Mardi Gras mishap would be an understatement. Mrs. Skyler would have a stroke if she knew that her son's thirty-foot classic sailboat, the *Shamrock Tattoo*, was named after a redheaded Yankee's left boob. You can bet she wasn't going to hear it from me.

Luke's smile spread, and he changed his grip on the blade as I squirmed and struggled to sit still—A Nurse's Guide to Murder was suddenly the last thing on my mind. "A man stabs with an upward cut, more like this," he explained. The tip of the knife moved slowly across my bare skin from navel to ribcage, making my skin quiver. "Leaving the victim's body vulnerable to ..." The blade followed the lower curve of my breast and moved upward to touch—

"Got it," I said, interrupting before I spontaneously combusted. "Now drop your weapon, Skyler, and let's get back to that 'please, ma'am' thing. I've got a boat to catch."

I tossed the box of mac and cheese onto the floor alongside the plastic knife, and we got back to our reunion. But I knew that when I packed up, I'd be sure that both of those items were safely tucked into my suitcase, along with the rope, baseball bat, and that little jar of faux cyanide. Jeez, it sounded like I was drawing cards for a game of Clue. But after all, I was headed to the tropics with a bunch of artsy and imaginative women who wanted to learn about murder. Along with one very moral and very proper Southern matriarch—a woman I thought I might want to kill before this week was through.

7

A few hours later, we were preparing to sail, and I'd finally come clean with Marie—who already had her own ideas on how to handle my surprise guest.

"Well, hell," she said, watching her cherry-scented smoke ring drift beyond the polished deck rail. "Simple solution: what does Mrs. Judge drink? We'll get her snockered and then—" Marie's gray eyes blinked wide and she jabbed her little cheroot in the air, pointing down the sun-drenched Lido deck. Her husky voice rose to compete with the steel drums of a reggae band tuning up next to the pool. "Did I just see a guy with a ponytail and a plaid skirt, carrying a sword?"

"Brandy," I said, pulling my eyes away from the dwindling line of passengers filing along the palm-lined dock below. We would set sail for the Bahamas in less than twenty minutes. Where *was* Angela Skyler? Cruise ships didn't hold up a launch for late passengers. I frowned and then completed my answer to Marie's question. "Angela drinks *brandy* from a set of crystal glasses that probably cost more than my Subaru." I nodded toward the guy with the sword. "And that's a *kilt*, not a skirt."

I brushed some specks of coconut prawn from the front of my beaded tunic and then pointed to the blonde, bare-chested man now surrounded by an admiring covey of women. "See?" Then I pointed toward another man with shoulder-length dark curls and a hint of a beard. "There's another Highlander over there, talking to the werewolf and that woman with the pinstriped suit and a parrot on her shoulder." *Aagh.* I knew as soon as the words left my lips that I had just proven what fools we were for being here. I cleared my throat. "The guys in the kilts are *models*; at least that's what it said in the Writers Afloat brochure. You know, for those romance book covers—historical suspense, paranormal mystery…" I bit my lip before I could add "erotica." I needed another drink before I could go down that steamy road, even after my morning's strip-search by the FBI. "But then," I narrowed my eyes and shot a look at my best friend, "this cruise was *your* idea."

"Carol's idea," Marie corrected quickly, reaching for a couple of piña coladas as a deck steward stopped beside us. She handed the man her shipboard charge card. "Carol owed that favor to one of her writers' groups. And it was only natural that when they were organizing this cruise-conference, she sort of…" Marie hesitated, peering up at me through her dark fringe of bangs.

"Offered us up like sacrificial lambs," I said, filling in the blanks and taking a frosty umbrella-topped drink from Marie's hand. I turned away for a moment and offered a quick apology after bumping against a middle-aged woman, with heart-shaped sunglasses and a feathered sun visor, standing at the rail beside me. She was loaded down with tote bags and fumbling with brochures, and her freckled shoulders were already crisp with sunburn. A plastic ID badge hung from a ribbon around her neck and was so studded with multicolored stickers and logo pins that I could barely see the woman's name—Vicky, maybe. I had no problem, however, reading the huge button on her orange tank top: *Indulge Your Inner Vixen.* One of the Writers Afloat, I'd bet, and maybe even registered for our murder workshop tomorrow.

I turned back to Marie. "And so Carol is just basically cutting us loose in her writing world without a road map or a guide. Like

Alice in Wonderland. That psychotic Cheshire cat could pop up any second." I shook my head slowly, remembering the last time we'd cruised, the trip that left Luke with the scar on his shoulder. "Or *worse*," I said. "With our bad-juju cruise record, I'm surprised Carol trusted us with this at all. Two cruises, two dead bodies, and—"

"Don't go there," Marie interrupted, lifting her palm quickly. "I'm trying really hard not to obsess on that. It's past; it's done. The point is that Carol's a national-level officer in that writers' association now, and she's responsible for some of the event planning. This workshop needed *medical experts*, so …" Marie winked at me. "'Who ya gonna call?'" She lifted the paper umbrella from her drink and aimed it at me. "Besides, it's giving you this great opportunity to bond with your lover's mom."

I frowned and glanced down at my watch. "Yeah, well, if she doesn't hustle it, Angela Skyler's going to be left standing on the dock with confetti curls on her head. We're sailing in ten minutes."

"She's not on board?" Marie asked, glancing toward the pool, where a raucous crowd was gathering. They seemed to be closing in around that woman with the huge red parrot and around another woman who had joined her. From the level of frenzy, you'd think they were royalty. Even the two Highlanders and the werewolf had joined the group. Cardboard cameras, held overhead, clicked rapid-fire.

"I don't think so," I said, watching the escalating commotion. "I've left messages in Angela's suite, and I tried the cell number that Luke left me. A bunch of times. No luck."

I moved out of the way as Vicky the Vixen lifted a camera and pointed it toward the group at the pool, adjusting a large and complicated-looking lens. There was a metallic tick-tick and whir as she snapped a series of shots. I shook my head, clueless. Nobody over there looked remotely like a celebrity to me.

"I don't think there's anything else I can do," I said, feeling a little guilty about my surge of relief. It's not that I didn't want to please Luke; that was certainly climbing high on my priority list. But suddenly, minus Angela, it seemed like my little vacation could be a *real* vacation. Workshops and cruise juju worries aside, it would be fun spending time with my pal Marie away from the chaos of our ER jobs. With no pressure to impress a woman who'd perfected the art of looking down her nose at me.

I took a substantial sip of my drink, letting the rum and the warm Florida sunshine wash over me as my spirits rose. "Well, if Mrs. Skyler missed the launch, so be it. Although you'd think if she were really serious about getting her book published, she'd jump at the chance to show it to that hotshot literary agent. Trust me, I had to do some fast-talking to get her that appointment. I think I promised somebody they could use my cousin's neighbor's boyfriend's beach house."

"Who is this agent?" Marie asked. "Carol told me, but I can't remember."

We both slid down the rail a couple of feet to accommodate another pin-laden and camera-toting comrade who had joined Vicky. This one was younger and dressed in what looked like a Renaissance-era velvet gown. Her face was dripping with perspiration in the Florida heat. A calligraphy nametag read "Renee."

"The agent's name is Theodora Kenyon," I said. "All I know is that she's from New York and that every writer onboard wanted to pitch a manuscript to her. Her appointments have been booked for weeks. Her name meant nada to me, but Luke said his mom knew who she was and that she got totally excited. She's sure this woman will read her manuscript and know she's the next Nora Roberts." I shook my head. "Plenty of ego there."

Marie raised her dark brows. "Not if she doesn't get her ass on-board." She twisted the band of her Kermit watch to see its face. "The engines ought to be starting up any second now. And as a ship employee, I can tell you that the time schedule is everything and..." Marie's voice was drowned out by the series of overhead blasts from the PA system.

Renaissance Renee lowered her camera and smiled at us. "They're going to announce a departure delay," she said, swiping a hand across the sweat trickling over her brow. "I know somebody who works in the Purser's office, so I get the inside scoop on things."

"A delay?" I glanced sideways at Marie and smirked. "Well then, maybe Angela will have her chance to get onboard, meet that agent, and become the next *New York Times* bestseller." I lifted my index finger. "One point for the Yankee redhead."

"Don't count on it," Vicky said, wrinkling her nose in the shadow of her feathered brim. "See that woman in the red suit, next to the woman with the parrot? The blonde with the face so tight it looks like she's battling G-forces?"

I raised my brows and nodded, watching the red-suited woman jab her finger in the air to make some sort of point. In her other hand, she held what looked like the slim, leather case of a laptop computer. The pinstriped woman with the parrot nodded her head up and down like a puppet on strings. "Yes, I see her. So?"

Vicky sighed as she watched the entourage in the distance. "That's Theodora Kenyon; she goes by 'Thea.' She's brilliant, well connected, and her clients make millions of dollars in royalties. You know that heiress Paris Hyatt, the one who just wrote the great tell-all? Thea brokered that deal." She turned back to me. "And see that parrot?"

I nodded, fighting a sudden unnerving sense of foreboding as I watched the huge red and green macaw nip at its human perch.

"Thea's parrot," Vicky explained. "The assistant carries it wherever they go, perched right there on her skinny shoulder. Let me tell you, I couldn't afford those dry cleaning bills." She lowered her voice. "I heard Thea feeds little pieces of rejected writers to that bird." Vicky stared through her heart-shaped lenses and into my eyes. "This agent is the scariest woman in the publishing business. You'd better hope your friend survives that appointment. She could be eaten alive. Overblown ego or not, she's no match for Kenyon."

I jumped as the PA system crackled again and the launch delay was officially broadcasted. A fifteen-minute delay, the polite British voice announced. Terribly sorry for the inconvenience. There would, however, be a complimentary round of cocktails. Please drink up and enjoy.

My skin prickled and I turned to Marie. I didn't like the way I was starting to feel. "I wonder what that's all abou—"

Renee tapped me on the shoulder, interrupting. She blinked again, a rivulet of perspiration dripping into her left eye, and smiled knowingly. "The delay is for a VIP passenger, according to my inside source." She lowered her voice to a whisper. "She got someone high up in Virginia state government to pull some strings because of a late appointment at the beauty salon. Can you imagine the nerve?"

The woman shook her head in quiet amazement as a bead of sweat dripped from her chin onto her embroidered velvet bodice. "Some judge's wife."

Aagh. I had a sudden, all-consuming hunger for macaroni and cheese. My bad cruise juju was holding.

TWO

No MACARONI AND NO SpongeBob SquarePants.

What I got instead was grilled asparagus with smoked salmon tartar and wasabi cream, and a melon montage sprinkled with port wine ... as a warm-up for seared ahi tuna. Swear. I wasn't complaining. The mandatory lifeboat drill was behind us, and the fading sun painted the sky gold, pink, and lavender beyond the Vista Dining Room's vast expanse of windows. A tuxedoed pianist sat at a grand piano on a balcony above, sharing space with a collection of artwork—giant, colorful abstract canvases—and played a lively medley for the enjoyment of the several hundred assembled passengers. With the Atlantic dipping gently beneath my turquoise beaded sandals and the promise of the Caribbean to come—and, okay, after nearly two generous glasses of Chardonnay—I was starting to lose that earlier sense of doom. Except for the facts that the well-coiffed Mrs. Judge was seated across from me, and that I'd just picked something that looked suspiciously like a small green parrot feather from my ahi. Could that be possible? I looked quickly around: no nasty agent, no indulgent assistant. No bird. Good.

I ordered a third glass of wine regardless of the fact that Marie had shaken her head *no* and discreetly poked my left thigh with her shrimp fork. So much for the trust she had in Cavanaugh Cool. But I needed a tad more liquid courage to accomplish my mission; I could fix everything by simply convincing Angela Barrett Skyler to cancel her appointment with Kenyon. No way I was going to be responsible for Luke's mother being shredded and fed to a mite-infested parrot. The biggest trick would be to keep her from being swept up in the yada-yada writer chit-chat swirling amongst the other passengers at our dinner table. A rogues' gallery for sure: Vicky the Vixen and Renaissance Renee, the writers we'd met on deck, one of the Highlander models—now wearing at least a gauzy shirt with his kilt, thank God—and Sarah Skelton, a thirty-ish blonde who identified herself as part of the Readers Afloat group. Great. Readers, writers, cover models, and a Charlottesville queen of etiquette and morality. I was more comfortable with trauma victims and psych patients. I needed to take control of this situation with Angela. Now.

I swallowed the dregs of my second glass of wine a little too quickly and coughed, barely stopping before it dribbled from my nose. Angela Skyler's eyes, blue as the ones that had lingered on my tattoo earlier this morning, swept over me. I saw her take in my hastily top-knotted hair, beaded mocha tunic, and California-minimal makeup, as analytically as if she were inspecting the teeth and hocks on one of her show horses. And if the look in her eyes was any indication, I was headed straight for the glue factory. *Doesn't matter what she thinks of you, Darcy. Doesn't. Matter.* I tucked an errant curl behind my ear, ran my tongue over the tiny split between my front teeth, and then plunged ahead with my plan to save this woman's well-bred ass.

"You know," I said to her, lowering my voice and hunching forward over the remains of my tuna, "Marie's friend, Carol, says that these face-to-face appointments with agents are a waste of time for new writers and—" I winced as the shrimp fork did a double jab into the drape of skirt covering my thigh. Okay, it *was* pretty chickenshit to use Carol as a scapegoat, but I was desperate. I cleared my throat and ignored the fork. "And, for *beginners*, the best bang for the buck would be to skip the agent appointments and concentrate instead on going to the workshops. Since there's a huge waiting list for Thea Kenyon, it wouldn't be a problem to cancel your appointment and—"

"Oh my God!" Vicky dropped her fork and tried to speak around an alarming wad of garlic mashed potatoes. Her face flushed. "Oops." She apologized and swallowed several times. "Sorry, but is it true? You've got an appointment with Thea?"

Mrs. Skyler patted her mouth and returned her napkin to the lap of what I would have bet my grandmother's beloved goldfish was a Chanel suit in soft oyster gray. "Yes," she said, smiling at Vicky and then turning back to me. "Darcy was a dear to arrange that for me. Although," she shook her head and I noticed that not a single strand of her highlighted ash blonde hair shifted out of place, "it does sound as if she's trying to talk me out of my appointment." She raised her glass of wine, and her diamonds caught the light, nearly blinding me. Her perfectly shaped brows rose. "Why is that, Darcy?"

Marie cleared her throat. "It's not that she's trying to talk you out of it, exactly, Mrs.—"

"It's *Angela*. Please, let's not be formal," Luke's mother corrected. She glanced down the table to include Vicky, Renee—now wearing a fuchsia tee shirt boasting *Yes, I write romance. No, you can't help me do research*—Reader Sarah and the blonde Highlander, Barth, lustily devouring his dessert. "I think everyone here can understand my position. We're all here for the same reason: a passion for things literary. Isn't that so?"

There were answering murmurs of agreement, and then Barth spoke up from the end of the table, spewing a fine spray of tartlet crumbs down his plunging shirtfront.

"You bet," he said. "And if you want my opinion, go for that meeting with Kenyon. She couldn't be half the bitch my makeup woman is. *You* try and lie still with someone waxing your chest hairs." The Highlander's dark eyes moved slowly over the jacket of Angela's impeccable Chanel. "What sort of stuff do you write, Angie? I'm guessing…hot?"

Oh God. I glanced sideways at Marie and considered the merits of sliding under the table and crawling on my hands and knees toward the door. SpongeBob was waiting.

The Judge's wife blinked several times. "Women's fiiiction," she said, her soft drawl stretching the words with a kind of reverence. She gave a confident nod. "Southern locales. Well researched, right down to the culture and social mores. I'm sure that Ms. Kenyon—"

"*Hates* it," Sarah blurted, giving the air a little jab with her butter knife. The little Reader nodded toward an attractive older woman in a lavender suit at the next table, who seemed to be signing an autograph for a passenger. "See the author over there? That's Carter Cantrelle." Sarah sighed. "She's the best. The cream. I've read her Atlanta Allure series three times—family sagas, delicious, poignant…*perfect.* But when Kenyon was a reviewer, she completely trashed them. Said she would only consider buying Miss Cantrelle's series—" Sarah's voice hissed through her teeth as she quoted, "*'to line the bottom of my parrot's cage.'* I tried to get an appointment with Thea Kenyon myself, just to give her a piece of my mind. She's worse than a beast. She's—"

"Brilliant," Vicky said, cutting Sarah off. "And excuse me for being frank, but if you were a *writer* you would understand that what we call 'voice and tone' can be very individual, and that it sometimes rubs a reader the wrong way. Even a prominent literary figure like Thea Kenyon. It isn't easy for any of us, published or not, to hear criticism of our work. But we suck it up and we learn from it. I've been trying to find an agent for six years, and I would kill to have an appointment with Thea. No such luck." Vicky shot me a mildly accusing look. "Or connections."

Renee lifted a cherry from her drink and nodded. "Me, either, but I've got a backup plan. I've been practicing my Elevator Pitch." She giggled. "I've even managed to include that funny bit about the earl and the barnyard "

"Elevator Pitch?" Marie asked, pulling out one of her cheroots and playing with the cellophane wrapper. I could tell that she was dying to wind this dinner up and escape to the Cigar Lounge.

"In case you're lucky enough to get into an elevator with an agent or editor," Vicky explained. "You try to give a two-minute pitch for the idea of your book. It's all considered fair game. The publishing people really don't mind." She shook her head. "Unless you're tacky enough to slip a manuscript under the stall door in a bathroom, that is. That's a no-no."

19

"The bathroom?" I grimaced and then glanced around the room. "Where is Kenyon anyway? I thought someone said she would be at this dinner seating."

"She was," Barth said, pausing over a forkful of his second dessert, "but she walked out after a few choice words to the table stewards." He shrugged. "Don't know if it was because they were going to seat her near Carter Cantrelle," he glanced sideways at Sarah, "or because they wouldn't let her parrot stay in the dining room. She was furious; said she'd filled out all the papers, done the quarantine, and 'Nobody's going to call my bird a health risk.'" The man rolled his eyes. "You should've heard that bird squawk. Cusses like a sailor."

I peered down at my tuna. Great, it *was* a feather. I'd probably get mites. And, worse, I wasn't any closer to keeping Luke's beloved mother from becoming part of that bird's diet. I'd promised to keep an eye on her although, Lord knows, even Chanel and perfect manners couldn't hide the fact that Angela Skyler was one tough broad. On my single, regrettable visit to the Skyler farm last summer, I'd seen this woman reach elbow-deep into a horse's womb to haul a foal out by the hooves. Hell of a risk of losing your tennis bracelet.

"Well," Renee said, smiling warmly down at Angela. Girlish dimples appeared beside her mouth. "I'm thrilled that you have an appointment with her, Angela. From what I've seen, you've got what it takes to make a *great* first impression. I love your suit. I saw it at Target in green."

Angela opened her mouth and then closed it, a smile of obvious amusement lingering on her lips. "Thank you," she said. "But I'm sure that 'good impressions' only go so far. What matters is the writing. The well-honed craft. In the end, *our work* is the only legitimate way to influence that special agent or editor and—"

Angela Skyler halted mid-sentence as a woman arrived at our table, hefting a magnum bottle of—if my eyes weren't lying—Dom Pérignon champagne. Two hundred bucks a pop, minimum. *Who...?*

The woman was about sixtyish, I'd guess, probably close to Angela Skyler's age, although that was as far as the similarity went. Slim and angular, she had straight, mousy brown hair in a chin-length, wash-and-wear style, wire-rimmed glasses and thin, colorless lips. Her pantsuit, navy with a narrow pinstripe, looked like a synthetic blend, and modestly priced, I'd guess, from the hint of shine and those tiny puckers at the shoulder pads and ... *hey, what's that on top of her shoulder?* A glob of white and gray like ... *oh jeez, parrot droppings?* My eyes widened. This had to be Thea Kenyon's assistant.

Marie must have come to the same conclusion that I did, if her nudge to my ribs was any clue.

"I'm sorry to interrupt," the woman said, her face pink with a sudden blush. Warmth spread to her brown eyes as she smiled, and I was astounded at the change that made in her appearance; I started thinking Diane Keaton, *First Wives Club.* "Is there an Angela Skyler here?"

"I'm ... Mrs. Skyler," Angela said with a sudden wariness that I thought was strange for a woman being presented with a fabulous bottle of bubbly. The table chatter died down and all eyes focused on Luke's mother. I heard Vicky whisper, "Omigod, that's Thea Kenyon's assistant. What's this about?"

21

The assistant cleared her throat. "Mrs. Skyler, I'm Barbara Fedders, and I work for Miss Kenyon. She's asked me to bring this to you."

Angela's face blanched and her lips tightened into a grim line. I glanced sideways, flashing Marie my *"What the hell?"* look. Our tablemates leaned forward on their elbows, straining to hear.

Barbara Fedders set the champagne on the table, flushed again, and then lowered her voice. "First, may I say that I know you were being kind and that I can completely understand your desire to . . ." She cleared her throat and her smile disappeared. "Miss Kenyon said to tell you that she only drinks mai tais and that she buys those *herself.* She said to make it very clear that gifts have no influence on her." She glanced up and Marie and I discreetly pretended interest in our dinner plates.

The assistant sighed. "I'm sorry. But she insisted that I say, 'Your champagne is the same as a manuscript shoved under a bathroom door.'"

*   *   *

Forty minutes later, I stood beside Marie, peering out through the glass-and-brass elevator that rose smoothly alongside the ship's marble staircase. Five decks below us, full-size palm trees stretched above beds of ferns, snowy potted cyclamen, and speckled mauve orchids. Cruises. Unbelievable. I was a third-trip veteran and the fairytale opulence still blew me away. I smiled, watching as a cluster of formally dressed stewards, as diminutive as Snow White's dwarves from this height, marched across the expanse of peach and aquamarine carpeting carrying huge trays of champagne glasses aloft. I unfolded our ship events brochure, skimmed it, then nodded.

"'VIP' party," I explained to Marie as I pointed to the scene below. "Says right here that the captain's hosting a reception for those artists whose work was displayed in the dining room. Um … Bill and Frankeen Price. From Houston." I glanced at a photo of an attractive sixty-ish couple sitting in a golf cart and holding a small white poodle. Then traced my finger down the printing. "'By Invitation Only,'" I added with a sigh. "Angela's going, of course."

Marie peered up at me through her bangs, her expression making it very clear what she thought of art in general, and of VIP parties in particular. "Well, what a shame we can't make it."

"Right." I scrunched backward an inch, to avoid being stepped on by a pair of book-laden Readers Afloat. We'd learned that their group numbered more than fifty, most of them climbing the gangway for the chance to meet author Carter Cantrelle. She was a big deal, all right, with the readers and writers alike. But even if Marie and I were way down on the Writers Afloat celebrity totem pole— and the VIP party list—we still needed to go over some plans for our upcoming Nurse's Guide to Murder workshop. If we could combine that with a couple of drinks, all the better.

"So where *are* we heading?" I asked, giving Marie's twill blazer a nudge with my silver-studded leather handbag.

She patted a fanny pack that I knew was stuffed with cherry cheroots and her pink Volkswagen Bug–shaped lighter. "Anywhere I can smoke"—she grimaced as the crush of passengers pressed us both back against the glass—"and not have to listen to any more scintillating discussions of metaphors and the correct use of italics." She peered up at a brass ship schematic near the elevator doors. "Crow's Nest Bar sounds pretty safe to me."

But it wasn't. Our first clue was when a snowy-haired woman in flowered capris, pink bifocals, and high-top Keds leaned across the bar—and nearly on top of me—to shout a husky, breathless order for "Another … penis colada, please!"

Marie choked on her beer nuts and I thumped her on the back.

"Oops—I think you mean *piña* colada," I said, nodding at the woman with encouragement and thinking of my sweetly demented grandma back in California. She'd been a nurse, too, although nowadays she mostly dispensed fish food "medicine" to her neighbors at the Care Home. Harmless koi pellets from a woman who meant well—not that the Home's administrators had a sense of humor. I hated to think of the legal battles I still had to fight because of that big mess.

"No," the older woman said, grinning with what appeared to be great pride, and a lot of dental work. "*Penis.* And I'm not shy about saying that word anymore, honey." She nodded briskly and continued, her voice scratchy and low. "Isn't it great? I attended this writers' clinic in Vegas last summer and it was *so* liberating." She extended her hand, "I'm Gertie, by the way." I took her hand and it was then that I noticed the logo button on her cardigan, fastened right beside a perky petunia appliqué: "*Senior Erotica—decades of smoldering.*"

She winked at me. "And there's lots of other great words, too, hon'. I've got a notebook full and I'm collecting more every day."

"Well …" I wasn't sure what to say, but it didn't seem to matter because there was no stopping this woman now. Within moments, I began to think my grandma's fish-food obsession was a blessing. Marie pressed her forehead flat against the bar and groaned.

"As a matter of fact," I explained as quickly as I could wiggle in some words of my own, "my friend and I are presenting our own workshop tomorrow, A Nurse's Guide to Murder, and we should really go now, *right now*, and start doing some—" I grimaced as Gertie continued on without blinking.

"Pecker, peter, dick, Admiral Blinky—*love* that one," she said, her eyes glinting behind her pink bifocals, "hot link, hunk o' love, happy rocket, trouser trout—" she halted when, by some act of a merciful God, a horrific series of guttural squawks split the air. Followed by a blue streak of profanity. Marie's head shot upright and all three of us turned to stare at the Crow's Nest's teak-trimmed doorway.

"What the…" my voice trailed off as I spied the silhouettes of the familiar threesome, Thea Kenyon, Barbara Fedders, and, on her shoulder and flapping its nasty red wings, the infamous writer-eating parrot. I mouthed a thank-you prayer that Angela was attending the artists' reception and then going on to her appointment at the ship's Sunny Isle Spa. I hoped she'd spend some of that time rethinking the wisdom of proceeding with her very dicey agent appointment.

Gertie shook her head and whistled softly with open admiration. "Isn't she something?"

I raised my brows.

"Thea Kenyon," Gertie said. "I've followed her to six conferences now and finally—hot diggity—got myself an appointment."

"You're not scared?" I asked, noticing that the pair of Highlanders, blonde Barth and his dark-haired cover-model counterpart, had risen from their table by the ocean-view windows to offer the agent and her assistant seats. Thea Kenyon, dressed in a fabulous ivory suit and what I'd bet were a killer pair of metal-heeled Manolos, gave the backside of Barth's leather pants a lingering squeeze before settling down into her chair. In just moments, she'd whipped her laptop from its case and was tapping at the keys. Apparently the woman needed to be connected at all times, whether by Wi-Fi or simply by pressing her palm against a fine masculine ass.

Barbara sat down opposite Thea and immediately hiked her shoulders as the parrot made a grab for her earlobe. The dark-haired cover model—who, I couldn't help but notice, had the most *incredible* eyes—came to her rescue by distracting the bird with a pretzel.

"Me? Scared of Thea Kenyon?" Gertie laughed, sloshing some of her drink onto her petunia cardigan. "I'll be seventy-four on my next birthday, honey. I've got emphysema and I've survived a hip replacement, the Alaskan quake of '64 and three colonoscopies. *Nothing* scares me anymore." She nodded sharply, and I thought I saw her upper denture slip a tad as she took a raspy breath. "I've got a manuscript that I want shopped in New York City, and Thea Kenyon is just the woman to do it. Sure, she's got a reputation for being tough and critical, but she knows this business inside out. And she's one agent who doesn't leave you hanging, either; reads a manuscript and makes a decision fast. Black or white, yay or nay, loves you or *hates*—" Gertie's sparse brows shot up. "Holy joystick!"

"What?" Marie asked, as we both turned to look where she was pointing.

"Carter Cantrelle," Gertie said, nodding toward the far end of the Crow's Nest Bar. Settling onto the barstool was the author we'd seen signing autographs in the dining room. Gertie looked quickly from Cantrelle to where Thea Kenyon was sipping her mai tai. "Those two women hate each other. The last time I saw them face off, it was one bloody cat fi—" She yelped, and the three of us ducked frantically as the huge red parrot swooped overhead, dropping feathers and damp bits of something I didn't want to think about. Its squawking came to a stuttering halt as it settled on the bar in front of Carter Cantrelle. It whistled shrilly enough to make ears bleed and then found its voice.

"Goddamn hack," the bird screeched. "Ya write shit! Shiiit. Flush it, flush it! *Aaawk!*"

I peered under Gertie's armpit, caught Marie's eyes, and tapped my copy of our Nurse's Guide to Murder notes. *How can we get out of here?*

"Right," Marie whispered, tossing me a wry smile. "And let's put one more thing on that list. Strangulation, shooting, stabbing, cyanide, and ... death by literary rejection."

I nodded, my eyes widening as the parrot opened his beak for a second assault.

THREE

"Oh my God," I said, watching the squawk-fest in utter disbelief. I turned to Marie. "Did you hear what—"

"*Shiiit!* Burn it… goddammm *triiipe!* Re-jeck-ted, re-jeck-ted …aaawwk!" The parrot screeched again, tried to scramble across the polished bar, and slipped, tipping forward onto its beak. It righted itself and then clung to the bar's edge with its claws, flapping its wings. Beak opened wide, it threw its head back and screamed, "*Gimmee a damned mai tai!*" Then it whistled, arched its back, and pooped on the bar.

Carter Cantrelle rose from her stool and, with more dignity than I could ever have mustered, stepped calmly aside to let the hunky, dark-eyed cover model and an obviously embarrassed Barbara Fedders recapture the parrot. A silver-haired gentleman rose from a nearby table to lend a hand. I was pretty sure I recognized his face—even without a pith helmet—from the head shots of those shipboard lecturers. A flora and fauna expert, maybe. I turned my head as I heard the bartender issue orders to remove the parrot from the bar.

The room fell silent as we watched the bestselling author, holding her cocktail napkin and a glass of white wine, walk across the short stretch of carpet to Kenyon's table. The agent, fishing the orange slice from her second mai tai, looked up and shrugged, a smug smile teasing her lips. "Carter, how very nice to—"

"I see, Theodooora" Cantrelle interrupted, a soft drawl stretching her words, "that you can't manage that traashy bird any better than your daddy did." She smiled sweetly, and I saw an unmistakable twitch at a corner of Kenyon's mouth. "Small wonder, though. Perhaps you should have your assistant get a bar of soap and wash its mouth out." She smiled again and raised her wine glass, almost as if she were making a silent toast. "Now if you'll excuse me, I promised to stop by the Prices' party before my book signing begins."

With that, she turned and walked toward the door, managing, somehow, to walk gracefully erect even though the Crow's Nest Bar had begun to roll and dip with the movement of the sea. I noticed that blonde Sarah, the author's devoted Reader Afloat, rose from a table by the window and began following Cantrelle toward the door. I also saw the very icy glare she tossed at Thea Kenyon on her way out.

The cover model, his dark hair brushing his muscular shoulders as he walked, left the lounge moments later, followed by Barbara Fedders and the now mercifully quiet parrot. The port lecturer trailed after them.

Marie and I turned as Gertie began to cough and sputter, dabbing at her mouth with a napkin.

"Hey, you okay?" Marie asked, sliding off her stool to stand beside the elderly woman.

"Oh … sure—" Gertie was racked by another cough, and I heard a mild wheeze as she inhaled. I met Marie's gaze and scrunched my brows. Our nursey antennae were twitching.

"I'm fine," Gertie said, voice steadier now. "It's the emphysema. I left my inhaler in the cabin, but it's easing now anyway." She shook her head. "Thank goodness I have a nonsmoker roommate. Smoke's the worst." She smiled and nodded toward where Thea sat tapping at her laptop next to blonde Barth. "That was pretty close to a hair-pulling match over there, wasn't it?"

"Sure was." I took a sip of my Long Island iced tea. "What was that crack Carter made about Kenyon's father?"

"Yeah, I was wondering about that, too," Marie said, reaching down to pull up a sagging sock. I glanced downward and smiled. Argyle, with green Kermit faces to match her watch. The woman had more socks than she knew what to do with.

Gertie glanced toward Thea and lowered her voice to a husky whisper. "The parrot—his name is Artie after Arthur Miller, the playwright—belonged to Thea's father, Theodore Kenyon."

Marie peered up through her bangs. "Theodore and Theodora?"

"Right," Gertie said. "Daddy's girl all the way. He was her hero."

"Was?" I asked, trying to balance my drink as the ship dipped again. A three-piece jazz combo had begun to play in the far corner of the lounge. One of my grandma's favorite tunes.

"Theodore Kenyon died several years ago. Shot, as a matter of fact."

"God," I said, grimacing. "How awful. And that name sounds familiar—wasn't he a journalist or something?" For some reason, I remembered a photo on a column in one of the numerous stacks of *San Francisco Chronicle*s my less-than-tidy mother left piled on kitchen chairs—along with her countless packs of playing cards.

"Theatre critic," Gertie explained. "And with a real caustic tongue." She chuckled and her upper denture did that little dip. "I guess you can imagine that by listening to Artie-bird."

"So he was killed by someone whose work he reviewed?" I asked, suddenly thankful my disgruntled ER patients did little more than spit, curse, or occasionally flash body parts. Artistic rejection seemed far more hazardous.

Gertie shook her head. "Nope. Jealous husband. Old man Kenyon was quite the ladies' man." Her brows rose. "You might say he couldn't keep the trouser trout—"

"Got it," I said, just in time. "But why would Carter Cantrelle make a crack about someone's dead father? She seems too classy for that cheap shot."

Gertie sighed. "Right. Except that her father was a playwright."

Marie scrunched brows over the rim of her beer. "Thea's father trashed Carter's father's play?"

Gertie nodded. "Yes, and it closed just days after opening. Taking his dream, the two mortgages on his house, and the money for his kids' educations." She pursed her lips. "I heard he drank himself to death in some bayou town outside New Orleans."

"And then Thea became a literary reviewer and went after Carter's work," I said, remembering what Sarah Skelton had told us at dinner. I shook my head. "Two generations of rejection?"

"Maybe three soon," Gertie said, polishing off her piña colada and yawning.

"Three?" Marie asked. "What do you mean?"

31

Gertie began to gather her belongings. "I heard Carter has a daughter who's writing now, too. Second-year college student." She clucked her tongue against the roof of her mouth. "You know how a girl can be at that age. I was that way myself, back in the Dark Ages. Bright and determined, but damned rebellious. Doing just the opposite of what her mother advises."

I was confused for a moment, and then I suddenly got it. "Carter's daughter sent a manuscript to Thea Kenyon?"

"That's right," Gertie said, "and rumor has it that she's reading it onboard this ship. You can bet that Thea *loved* encouraging the spread of that bit of news."

There was a peal of braying laughter, and we turned to see our infamous agent nip a dangling cherry from the fingers of Barth, the leather-pants Highlander. Three empty mai tai glasses flanked her ever-present laptop.

Marie and I reminded Gertie to take a shot of her inhaler before she went to bed and watched as the senior headed off to the Internet Café for "research." I hoped to goodness she wasn't planning a search for more penis euphemisms. I'd had all I could take.

"Okay," Marie said, pulling a pencil, a cigar, and her Volkswagen lighter from her fanny pack. "Let's grab a table and go over our workshop agenda for tomorrow morning. We need to review those questions that were sent in by the participants, too. Then we can firm up our plans for the shore excursions on Grand Turk and Half Moon Cay." She chuckled and ran her fingers through her short hair. "Suddenly, your crazy 'Swimming with Stingrays Adventure' sounds pretty tame, kid." She picked up her cigar and glanced over at Thea Kenyon. "Not nearly as scary as this publishing business. That looks like murder."

*   *   *

An hour later, I'd hit as many of the Galleria shops as I could on Promenade Deck, weighing my need for a Burberry charm bracelet watch against the ER overtime it would take to pay for the splurge. I touched a fingertip to a wine bottle charm and smiled. I'd work half of Marie's next Sunday shift—piece of cake. A woman needed a reliable watch. And who knew when I'd get a chance to browse the shops again, what with doing the murder workshop and the requisite bonding time with Luke's mother? What time was I meeting her?

I raised my wrist to squint at the face of my dangling timepiece and then headed down the lush carpeting toward a door to the outside deck. Angela was going to be in the spa for another half-hour and Marie had opted to hit the ship's casino, something I was never tempted to do. I have this strange Pavlovian response to anything related to gambling; it makes me ravenously hungry. I'm fairly sure it was because of the fact that my brothers and I had eaten all of our childhood breakfasts on a green plastic gaming cloth; Mom's Vegas practice table, stenciled with hearts, diamonds, clubs, and spades, and always sticky with spilled milk and pancake syrup. I'd bet three Fruit Loops, and raise it by seven Cocoa Puffs, that I could gain three pounds just by smelling a deck of cards. Much better to be outside letting the ocean breeze frizz my hair, especially after that chaos in the Crow's Nest Bar. Pure Jerry Springer. We were only a few hours into our cruise, and I was already tired of these literary folks. Some alone time wasn't a bad idea at all.

Of course, it wasn't meant to be. I pushed open the door and nearly fell over a guy crouching on the deck directly in front of me. The butt view, though only for a split second, was pretty impressive.

"Oh, *jeez*, sorry," I blurted as I stumbled sideways, scrambling not to twist my ankle in my wedge sandal.

He rose quickly and took hold of my arms to steady me. I looked up—way up, maybe six foot three inches—past a broad expanse of white shirt, to the face of a man with close-cropped black hair and ridiculously chiseled good looks. Sort of a *GQ* magazine photo, tapped into existence by that fairy godmother who transforms pumpkins.

"Whoa," he said, letting his warm hands linger on my arms for a few seconds longer than was necessary. He smiled slowly. "I'm the one who's sorry. My fault." He let go of me and held up a cocktail napkin that fluttered in the balmy breeze. "I was chasing this." He laughed and a cliché-perfect cleft dotted his chin. "Mom was a stickler about littering. You okay?"

"Sure," I answered, smiling back, "I'm fine. I guess I was in too much of a hurry—had to get out of those shops before my credit card combusted." I laughed at the look on his face. "Retail therapy. And, trust me, it's not as risky as sitting in some of the bars on this boat."

He lifted his dark brows. "You mean the one with the parrot act?"

Huh? I scrunched my brows. I studied his handsome face, aware of some vague familiarity. "How did you know that?"

"I saw you in the Crow's Nest Bar with the other writers." He slid a sleeve back to expose several fresh scratches on his forearm. "Damned bird nearly drew blood." The man lowered his arm and shrugged, smiling down at me again. His incredible dark-lashed eyes were warm, boyish, and ... *oh jeez, familiar.*

"You're that cover model!" I said, tilting my head to stare. The man who had hurried to help Barbara Fedders after Artic the parrot swooped at Carter Cantrelle. How could I have missed those eyes? "But your hair was all long and—"

"Wig," he said quickly, and I swear I saw his face growing pink in the deck lights. "And please call me Keven. I'm Keven Brodie." He extended his hand and I saw no reason not to take it.

"Darcy Cavanaugh," I said, turning my head for moment as a trio of passengers stepped from the doorway onto the deck. "And I'm not a writer. I'm just here to present a loosely related workshop, or at least that's the general plan." Somewhere on the deck above, reggae music had begun. I withdrew my hand, stepped toward the rail and then walked on for a few more yards. Keven followed.

"So, you're a Highlander?" I asked trying not to tease, though I was tempted. The ER had nothing on the weirdness of this publishing business. And now I was just plain curious. After all, the man obviously had some insights into the world Marie and I were about to enter via our workshop.

"Four days and counting," Keven said, "and then I hang up my broadsword. I'm finishing out the last of an old modeling contract."

"Oh?" I asked, studying his face again. A string of colored party lights shone down from overhead and were reflected in his dark eyes. I would guess his age to be about early thirties. Maybe a couple of years older than me. "And then what?"

"Actually," Keven said, smiling again, "I'm a literary associate with a Los Angeles agency. Started about six months ago." He chuckled.

"Got dared into the cover model job a few years back, and I've done it off and on since. Embarrassing, but it helped repay my student loans, you know?"

"I do," I said, honestly. "My brother has done some … acting, to help out with college costs, too." I bit my lip softly, stopping myself from adding the rest of it—that the college Will Cavanaugh attended was Disney University. And that his temporary "acting" job was now permanent; my little brother had started out to earn college credits toward a business degree and then found his true calling inside an enormous Goofy costume. He was very content with floppy ears, buckteeth, a cluster of kids hugging his ankles—and the occasional clandestine rendezvous with the newest Snow White. He was happy and I was glad. But it wasn't something I planned to share with Angela Barrett Skyler. No shamrock tattoo and no Goofy brother. I looked up at Keven. "And now you're working at an agency? Representing writers?"

"Mostly by way of the 'slush pile,'" Keven said, his brown eyes warm. "That means that I read a lot of the manuscripts that come to our agency unsolicited." He smiled when he saw my confusion. "We require writers to send a letter to introduce their work before we'll offer to read a manuscript. It's called a 'query.' But sometimes—"

"They slip one under a bathroom door," I said, remembering the discussion among the writers at our dining table. And the nasty remark that Barbara Fedders relayed to Angela from Thea Kenyon. *Your champagne is the same as a manuscript shoved under a bathroom door.*

"Right," Keven said. "And of course I'd like to believe that I'll find a diamond in the rough." He shook his head. "The interesting thing is that I probably have more of a chance to find potential clients by parading around in that damned kilt." His beautiful lips twisted into a smirk. "Especially since Thea Kenyon loves to chew writers up and spit them out so quickly. Trust me, she's made some mistakes that she regrets. I tend to give writers a little more benefit of the doubt." He shrugged and smiled. "Especially since I do some writing myself—crime drama, mostly TV scripts. So I know how tough the process is. But Thea ..." The look in his eyes hardened, and I sensed that this man could never be gentle enough to make that final cut at Disneyland. "Hell, I'm not opposed to scooping up her leftovers or doing whatever it takes to ..." the reggae music swelled overhead and Keven glanced up, his words trailing off.

But I wanted to know more. "Do you know them well, then?" I asked. "Thea Kenyon and her assistant, Barbara?"

Keven smiled. "I know enough, I guess," he said. "From being thrown together at a half-dozen writers' conferences a year for the last few years." He laughed. "Barbara knows I'm an agent. But Thea doesn't." He frowned. "Not that Thea would feel threatened by someone like me. But I have to say that she's damned lucky to have Barbara. Who else would put up with all that"—Keven hesitated, obviously censoring himself—"stuff she pulls? Did you know she bathes with that idiot parrot?"

My mouth gaped. "Barbara has to bathe with him?"

"God no!" Keven laughed and I was struck again with how beautiful he was. "I mean that *Thea* bathes with Artie." He shook his head. "Barbara got a little sloshed at the Vegas conference last summer and told me the whole thing. She said Thea likes to sit in a tub sprinkled with sea salt, typing rejection letters on that laptop while downing her mai tais. And that the stupid parrot nibbles on the orange slices and then takes a few dips in the tub himself." He grimaced. "I wish to God she hadn't told me. That's enough to . . . wither a guy. If you know what I mean."

I nodded, struggling with my own image of the spiteful agent half snockered and naked, getting pruney in a tub while typing away to drown the dreams of aspiring writers. I also wondered how much alcohol a bird could suck out of an orange. What was in a mai tai, anyway? Rum? I didn't want to think about the vocabulary of a drunken parrot. "How does Barbara stand it?" I asked.

Keven shook his head. "She idolizes Thea. And prides herself on being the 'right arm' of the best agent in the country. For about five or six years now, I guess." He shrugged. "And, hell, I can't blame her. It's an exciting business, Darcy. Last year, one of the Kenyon Agency clients wrote a screenplay that got an Academy Award. Barbara was sitting there right beside Thea. Who, by the way, sprang for Barbara's gown." He nodded and I saw that hard glint return to his eyes again. "I can understand wanting to hang onto coattails like that." Keven winked. "Although I'd think of a way to strangle that damned parrot."

His voice trailed off and his eyes swept slowly over me, making me blush unexpectedly. If they ever added "bedroom eyes" to Webster's, a sketch of this Highlander's face would be printed right beside it.

"How about if I buy you a drink, Darcy Cavanaugh? And then maybe we can find someplace to . . . dance?" Somewhere behind us I heard a deck door open and close. Keven took a step closer and raised his hand to touch a loose tendril of my hair. "You've got such great hair. So wild and red."

"Thanks," I said, taking a step backward. "But no. I've got that workshop in the morning." I laughed, a little self-consciously I'm sure, as I glanced away from his too-intent gaze. "A Nurse's Guide to Murder. Can you believe that? I've spent my career saving lives, and now I'm supposed to teach people how to commit murder. I've got to talk about strangulation, gunshot wounds, poison, stabbing, and…" I was pretty sure I was babbling, but I kept going. "And after I've taught CPR enough times that I could do it in my sleep."

"Yes," Keven said, taking a step toward me again to close the gap. He leaned closer and his voice dropped to a teasing whisper as he took hold of my arm. "You look like a natural for mouth-to-mouth to me."

Oh for godsake. "Hold it," I said, moving my arm away and deciding how blunt I needed to be with this guy. Before I could do that, a woman's voice, dripping with sarcasm, rose from behind me.

"I'm so *awfully* sorry to interrupt, Darcy dear," Luke's mother said.

*   *   *

So much for my initial stab at the bonding process. But we'd moved to the Rumrunner Lounge, a small mirrored and palm-lined bar outside the Captain Cook Theatre, and I was determined to be sweet and patient. I was going to do my darnedest to—as my grandma would say—"make nice" with Angela Barrett Skyler. Especially since I was certain that she'd been thoroughly humiliated by the champagne incident in the dining room. For godsake, everyone within earshot of that table knew she'd tried to bribe her way into an agency contract. But after a couple of hours in the Sunny Isle Spa, I was sure she'd devised some face-saving way of wiggling out of her doomed appointment with Thea Kenyon. I took a breath, smiled, and reminded myself that this was *Luke's mother*. And I was all about helping her to save face. Even if it meant ignoring the way that particular—and well-moisturized—face was looking at me right this minute. Like I was the slut sister of Goofy, eating Cocoa Puffs on a blackjack table.

"And so," I said, blowing on my café mocha, "are you coming to the workshop that we're presenting tomorrow morning?" I caught her gaze and then noticed her woven scarf, ecru boucle, shot with gold. A hand-loomed "Lovisa," I'd bet; each design one of a kind, and mostly draped around the necks of movie stars. I smiled and resisted the urge to stuff my own improvised scarf—the beaded silk belt from my beach boutique blouse—into my purse. It was tied around my ocean-frizzed ponytail and the only thing keeping my red hair from exploding outward like Medusa's head of snakes. "Should be fun. Or as much fun as shooting, stabbing, poisoning, and …" I watched Angela's fingers play with the knot on her Lovisa, "strangulation can be. I even brought these great props to use in demonstrations."

Angela let go of the scarf and picked up her coffee, lifting her brows as she smiled indulgently at me over the rim. "Props?"

"For the murder demonstrations," I explained. "I've got a baseball bat for bludgeoning, a jar of fake cyanide, and a plastic knife." My face warmed as I remembered that pink plastic weapon in Luke's hands early that morning. "Marie and I will sort of choreograph the various assaults for the writers." I scrunched my brows. "I need to practice more, though. I guess it's the nurse thing, but murder doesn't come naturally to me. Anyway, I think you'll en-

40

joy the workshops, Angela." I hesitated, cleared my throat, and then plunged ahead, determined to reassure her. "Since you don't have to worry about keeping that agent appointment anymore, you'll have time to attend the workshops and mingle with the other writers and—"

"*What?*" Angela asked, interrupting and setting her coffee down on the table. "Not keep my appointment with Theodora Kenyon? Why on earth would you assume that, Darcy?" Her blue eyes swept over me and I sensed that I'd just stuck my foot in my mouth. In fact, I could taste the cork on my wedge heel. I'd seen that same determined look on this woman's face another time—right before she'd reached inside that horse to grab the foal.

"I'm absolutely keeping my appointment," Angela said, her fingers moving to the ends of her scarf again. Her just-waxed brows drew together. "I accept the fact that this agent, no matter how well-connected in the literary world, quite obviously has *no* appreciation for genteel manners and social etiquette. She's basically a bohemian." She allowed herself a small, unladylike smirk. "But then, who could expect anything better from those people in New York and California?"

Those people? California? I opened my mouth and, by some miracle, closed it again without saying a word. But I did reach up and pull my very-California scarf from my hair, not giving a damn that I had no doubt transformed myself into a West-Coast hippie gypsy. Goofy would be proud.

Change in plans; helping this woman save face wasn't working. I would head to the casino and snag Marie. We needed to practice for that workshop. I smiled placidly at the Judge's wife as I knotted the beaded scarf in my lap. Then I pulled the ends and stretched it taut.

We'd start with strangulation. Suddenly murder didn't feel unnatural at all.

FOUR

"Um ... would you repeat that question, please?" I set the plastic knife down on the table and stared at the pretty, twenty-something writer, certain that I'd misunderstood her question. Man, I must have. I smoothed the front of my watercolor batik jacket and glanced sideways at Marie. She was holding our strangulation demo pantyhose and there was a weird look on her face, half smirk and half impending doom. Kind of like she knew something that I didn't. She set the pantyhose down and reached for a stack of colored index cards.

"Yes, Miss Cavanaugh," the young writer said, reaching up to adjust the metal studded frames of her trendy glasses. She smiled and tapped her stylus against the screen of the little PDA in which she'd been furiously typing. Notes. Like everything I'd said was gospel. Frankly, I was flattered. When I'd been talking CPR or TB precautions to health givers, no one had seemed this interested. Now, ironically, here I was proposing *murder* and I was suddenly a freaking genius—with a podium and microphone, PowerPoint capability, and a plate of those great little sausage rollups from the Lido Deck buffet. Unbelievable. And in just another hour, Marie and I would be free to enjoy our "Day at Sea," complete with suntan oil and umbrella drinks, lolling poolside as our gleaming ship continued its course toward the even more intoxicating promise of Bahamas beaches. Life was good.

In fact, I was having such a great time that I'd even started to rethink my approach to handling Luke's mother—less emphasis on strangling her and more of an accent on working *with* Angela in her attempts to woo an agent. After all, I'd promised Luke that I'd keep his mother safe and entertained. And even if she was a godawful snoot, Angela Skyler didn't deserve the punishment Thea Kenyon could dish out. She hadn't seen that filthy parrot in flagrante like I had. And I wasn't at all sure that she would have handled that situation with the same cool composure as Carter Cantrelle. So, I was actively percolating a new idea. And, meanwhile, this whole workshop gig was turning out to be an ego-boosting experience. I had my audience in the palm of my hand and things were going great. Except for the acoustics in this conference room, which made it sound like this young woman had actually asked me—

She repeated the question. "Could you please explain the sort of wound a *fang* would make, and what kind of bleeding to expect from that?" The woman traced a fingertip in a tidy line beneath her jaw. "For instance, a fang sunk deep in the neck."

"Fang?" I glanced helplessly sideways at Marie again. *Fang?*

"Yes," explained a middle-age redhead, rising to her feet in the front row of the fifty-or-more occupied chairs. "Basically a wound inflicted by a *vampire*." She glanced down as a blonde in a fur-trimmed vest tugged at her jacket sleeve. The redhead nodded quickly and then looked back up at me. "Or a werewolf."

Her penciled brows lifted as she pointed toward the stack of index cards in front of Marie. "We detailed those questions on the cards, exactly the way you asked. The ones relating specifically to the plots in our Paranormal Romantic Suspense Group?" There was a vigorous nodding of heads in the clutch of writers surrounding her. "Didn't you get them?"

Oh jeez. I opened my mouth, closed it and smiled weakly as Marie tossed me her infamous "I told you so" look. She reached over and pressed a paper-clipped chunk of cards into my palm. No doubt the cards she'd been hounding me to read last night, when I was ranting on about Angela Skyler. And then had to drink two medicinal Mojitos to calm myself down. Which made me fall asleep in my clothes. And is the reason why I never exactly ever … read the question cards.

"Well, sure, I got them," I lied, "and we abso-lute-ly …"

"Wait. Excuse me." A figure I recognized as our dining tablemate, Renee, stood up on the opposite side of the room. Sitting next to her was Sarah, the Reader Afloat.

"I've got a question card in there, too," Renee explained, "but I didn't know you were going to talk about murder as it relates to specific genres. In that case, I'd love it if you could cover crossbow wounds, and maybe dagger …" Her voice was drowned by a rising rumble of whispers around her, followed by a flurry of raised and waving hands. I saw Keven, the Highlander-agent, slip from a back row seat and exit out the door.

"Ooh, yes, Miss Cavanaugh," a heavyset woman called out, "sword gashes, too, if you don't mind. That would be so helpful."

I leaned toward the microphone, but before I could respond, another woman stood, clutching a clipboard against her crisp khaki blazer. "Hold it. No swords. That's going too far off track. Half the people in this room write contemporary thrillers. What we need is information on trauma by assault weapons, ligature, dismemberment, or—"

"Poisons!" Some shouted from the rear of the room, "we're supposed to go on to poisons according to your outline. I *need* cyanide!"

"Cyanide's wussy and overdone," a male voice shouted back. "Let's cover anthrax. Or Ricin—now that's a poison with balls!"

Balls? For godsake.

"Psst, Darcy! Over here!" Gertie waved her inhaler frantically overhead, hailing me for a question that I was very sure I didn't want voiced. Death by trouser trout figured nowhere in my outline. I stared at Marie. *How do we get this back on track?* Our murder class was turning into a lynch mob at warp speed. I needed to do something. Fast.

I cleared my throat, tapped the microphone and grimaced as electronic reverb screeched across the room. The crowd covered their ears and a few people openly glared. I clutched the microphone again. My hands were sweating and my stomach began to rebel against all those fancy breakfast sausages. The queasiness intensified as I caught a surprise glimpse of Carter Cantrelle sitting in a far corner of the room. A few chairs behind her, was Angela, now sitting with arms crossed. I pried my tongue from the roof of my mouth. "Please, may I have your atten—"

Marie tugged at my sleeve and I turned. Standing beside her was Barbara Fedders, sans parrot, dressed in classic gray herringbone and radiating pure confidence. She stepped alongside me, gave my arm a reassuring pat, and then leaned toward the micro-phone, raising her arms like Mother Theresa before the troubled masses. Damn, she looked better than macaroni and cheese. The room magically hushed.

"Thank you for your attention," she said warmly. "Miss Cava-naugh and Miss Whitley have asked the stewards to provide cof-fee and goodies outside in the foyer. Let's all take a twenty-min-ute break." She smiled and winked at the writers from behind her wire-rimmed glasses. "And then we'll come back to plan our devi-ous murders."

*   *   *

"I could absolutely kiss you," I said, groaning softly and leaning against the polished deck rail. The midmorning sun warmed my face as I glanced sideways at Barbara Fedders and grinned. In the distance, salsa music mingled with playful shouts from the Sports Deck basketball courts. A bar steward passed by holding a tray aloft, and I caught a tantalizing whiff of pineapple. My stomach rum-bled; the earlier queasiness was gone. "You saved my ass in there, Barbara. If you've got any secrets about how to survive the rest of my morning, I'm all ears."

She laughed softly. "It's your first workshop and my," she rolled her eyes and sighed, "*fortieth*, maybe?" That fleeting, but amazingly warm, smile spread to her eyes and I wondered why she didn't do it more often. It transformed her like an Oprah makeover. "And don't worry," she said, nodding vigorously enough to make her bobbed hair swing, "you're doing just fine, Darcy." She reached up, flicked her fingers across her shoulder pad and stopped, then caught me watching, and blushed. "Whoops, phantom parrot syndrome. Can't take me anywhere."

"Where is he, anyway?" I asked, remembering what Marie had said after I relayed the juicy tidbits Keven told me about Thea, Barbara, and Artie. About how loyal Barbara was. Marie had looked at me like I was nuts. *The woman has bird shit on her shoulder, Darc'. Loyal is not the word.*

Barbara smiled. "Sleeping, with a ship's terry bathrobe covering his cage. I gave him a dose of the sedative we carry for traveling. The poor guy gets so frantic in crowds. Thea's still sleeping, too. But that's because she stays up half the night editing her clients' work, developing their marketing lists, posting writers' tips to her blog…" She shook her head. "Mornings are the only time I can pry that laptop away to check the power source. You wouldn't believe how fast she drains a battery."

And a mai tai. I tried to squelch the image of the naked agent swilling drinks and typing in the tub. Too late. I forced an incredulous smile. "Wow. Workaholic. Must make it tough on you."

Barbara shrugged. "It's not so bad, really. The only hard part is running all that interference." She shook her head and sighed. "Thea Kenyon is a highly successful woman. She didn't get that way—and doesn't stay that way—without stepping on some toes. She'll fight for her clients, she'll hold their hands when they need it, and she's incredible with contract negotiations, but…" Barbara smiled, "day-to-day tact is not her strong point. Some days all I do is soothe ruffled feathers, if you'll pardon the pun."

I nodded with empathy, remembering a brilliant but implacable surgeon who'd hurled more than one scalpel across my Morgan Valley trauma room. He was a huge former college football star who hosted a savage paintball club on Sundays. I always half expected to hear he'd smuggled his weapon into the OR to take aim on one of the surgical nurses. Still, if I were ever unlucky enough to wrap my Subaru around a tree, I'd want that nasty brute to be scrubbed and waiting. But, damn, he pissed a lot of people off.

"So why do it, Barbara?" I asked, grasping the deck rail as the ship's deck dipped beneath our feet. "Why work for someone like that?"

She looked at me like I'd lost my mind. "Because it's *wonderful*. Working alongside Thea gives me the chance to learn so much about this business—how all the elements fit together, the writing, representation, publishing, marketing, sales…" Barbara paused, and her smile crept back and this time it was accompanied by an excitement I hadn't seen in her before. "Dreams. I'm seeing dreams come true, Darcy. That's worth everything." Her eyes were intense behind her glasses. "A good writer has to dig down deep, sometimes into very secret and painful places, to dredge up the necessary emotion it takes to make his story come to life. He puts little pieces of himself into every book. And then he takes the risk to send those very personal feelings out to agents, editors, and critics, all for the chance to realize a dream of being published." She shook her head. "Can you imagine the courage that takes? It's like going naked in public."

Naked? I widened my eyes and nodded, wondering about Angela Skyler and her book. I couldn't believe the Judge's wife was into public nudity. "It sounds like you can really relate, Barbara. You're a writer, too?" I asked, remembering something that Keven, the cover-model-turning-agent, had said. That he was doing some writing himself.

"Me? An author?" Barbara pressed her fingers against her herringbone lapels and choked on a laugh. "Lord no. You won't find my name on the cover of any novels. The closest I came was when I wrote for a small newspaper. You know, obituaries, lost and found ads; the kinds of things that line the bottom of Artie's cage." She reached down for her attaché case. "But thanks to this job, I've had the chance to read so many aspiring authors' work and learn what it takes to produce good stories. It really is exciting."

Exciting? I watched her reach into her embossed vinyl case to retrieve some papers, and realized I'd never understand this whole literary thing. Swimming with stingrays, on the other hand, sounded *very* exciting. And if Marie and I could manage to get through these murder workshops alive, then we'd have time for that and a whole lot more.

"Here," Barbara said, handing me a copy of my Nurse's Guide to Murder outline. I could tell by looking that it was an earlier version, the one I'd submitted to the Writers Afloat chairperson months ago. It now had neatly penciled notes in the margins.

"What's this?" I asked, not understanding.

"Some of those tips you mentioned," Barbara explained. "I made some suggestions on where to tighten your presentation. How to focus things to keep your audience interested and less apt to pull you off track with," she smiled, "too many questions about 'fangs.' I've sat in on enough of these workshops to know that's quite a challenge when you're speaking to a roomful of bright and multifaceted people." She tapped a fingertip to her forehead. "That 'right brain phenomena.'"

"Um, sure." I glanced down at all the careful notes she'd made with tiny, precise handwriting and penciled asterisks. I looked back up, raising my brows. "This is great, Barbara. I can't believe you went to all this trouble." I tapped the paper with my fingertip. "Where'd you get this old copy? I passed out the new-improved version today."

Barbara hesitated for moment and then rolled her eyes. "Thea," she explained. "Workaholic *and* micromanager. She always asks the conference people to forward the workshop proposals. She likes to know ahead of time what's going to be presented. Sometimes she even sits in on a few of the workshops. You know, to take part in the discussions and hear the writers bouncing book ideas around. Candidly, not under the pressure of an eight-minute agent appointment." Barbara laughed. "Watch out, maybe she'll show up for your stabbing practice."

I glanced down at my charm bracelet watch and added, "Which is starting up in about five minutes. Guess I'd better get back in there." I waggled the edited outline in my hands. "Really, thanks again for this; I'll show it to Marie, too."

"Glad to help," Barbara said, her tone sincere. "I meant to give it to you earlier, but I got stuck back at our suite." She frowned. "Handling some complications."

I smiled knowingly. "Charging the laptop battery, I assume."

"No," Barbara said, chuckling. "But thanks for the reminder. And please cross your fingers that the battery hangs on; it's been dropping the charge. I forgot to pack the second battery pack, and Thea will have a *fit* if she has to sit by outlets to plug in." She sighed. "Actually, the reason I didn't get that outline to you earlier is that I was trying to handle a complaint about Artie."

I wrinkled my nose and nodded, finding it easy to imagine that there would be complaints after the bird's revolting behavior in the Crow's Nest last night. The damned thing had pooped on the bar. "Ouch," I said with sympathy. "Carter Cantrelle, I'll bet."

"No," Barbara said quickly. "Carter is amazingly tolerant. I can't imagine she'd do this, even though her name *was* mentioned." Her lips tightened. "The note was anonymous, but I'm fairly sure it came from one of Carter's fans." She nodded. "There was a book signing event last night, you know. Several authors took part, and maybe thirty or more participants in the Readers Afloat program. Most of them are very loyal to Carter."

"Yes, I heard." I scrunched my brows, remembering Cantrelle leaving the bar to go down to Lido Deck for the signing, followed by Barbara, Keven, the ship lecturer, and ... "So you think one of the Carter's fans got mad enough about Artie's behavior to write a complaint?"

Barbara's lips tensed. "Mad enough to make a threat against Thea."

* * *

Apparently a strangling and stabbing demo isn't quite the draw as napkin folding, poolside Yahtzee, or watching some guy carve a porpoise out of a three-hundred-pound block of ice.

"Ice sculpture, for godsake?" I whispered to Marie, after glancing around our conference room. We'd spent the past hour re-hashing the subject of strangulation and then reviewed diagrams of a human torso, with the location of vital organs and the estimated quantities of blood loss from wounds to the various sites. We'd fielded additional questions about how fast a victim would die, what it looked like when intestines protruded from the belly, how purple and puffy a face might get, and ... well, a smorgasbord of pre-lunch trauma. I was fairly certain there'd be a run on the vegetarian lasagna.

Our audience, now divided into pairs, was busy assaulting each other with L'Eggs pantyhose and pink plastic knives. We were missing quite a few of our original workshop participants, though, including Gertie, Keven, Renee, Sarah, Carter, and Luke's mother. I shook my head. "We lost a quarter of our class to a frozen porpoise?"

"Pair of porpoise," Marie said, tapping her unlit cheroot to the ship's daily program. "And the ice sculpture is part of the galley tour—you know, a behind-the-scenes glimpse into the ship's kitchen. A chance to see the chef do his fancy slice-and-dice show. No plastic knives there, kid. And then they get to check out those big walk-in coolers with," she traced her cigar down the columns on the program, "twenty-three thousand eggs, thirty-eight hundred pounds of poultry, sixteen-hundred bottles of wine and—"

"Saw that," I said before Marie could quote the exact stats for the veggies, ice cream, and sugar packets. "So at least it wasn't because learning how to commit murder is too boring." I sighed. "But I kind of hoped that Keven and Angela would stick around so I could introduce them."

"Ah," Marie said, after popping open a silver egg container to hand a pair of pantyhose to the woman who wrote vampire romances. We watched as she headed off to team up with Vicky. Marie turned back to me. "So that's your new idea? Diverting the Judge's wife from Thea Kenyon to the cover model?"

"Well, don't you think it's safer?"

"*Safer?*" Marie asked, grimacing as she watched the writer couple nearest to us swinging wildly at each other with the plastic knives.

I sighed. "I guess what I mean is, that she'd have less of a chance of being openly humiliated." I shook my head, remembering Barbara Fedders likening the process of submitting a manuscript to going naked in public. This was *not* something I could allow to happen to Angela Skyler, a woman who'd lectured my boyfriend on etiquette and morals. I looked up and smiled as I saw Renee return through the far door.

"You're assuming Angela's book is that bad?" Marie raised her dark brows, her gray eyes giving me that judge-not-lest-you-be-judged look. The fact was, that my best friend and her partner, Carol, knew way too much about judgmental crap.

"What I'm *assuming*," I explained, "and based on evidence, which includes a disgusting glob of bird poop, is that dealing with Thea Kenyon can be a real roller coaster ride. She can be generous one moment then—*wham*—vicious as a rabid dog. I mean, what if the battery in her laptop runs out and she goes completely ballistic? Why take that chance?" I nodded my head. "Especially if there's another option."

"I don't know, Darc'," Marie said, brows furrowed. "Carol says that Kenyon is the best and—"

"She's the kind of woman who incites threats," I said, prodding Marie's shoulder with my finger. Maybe even *death threats*. Who knows?"

Marie snorted and rolled her eyes. "Oh come on! Barbara didn't say that note was a death threat." She nodded her head. "And besides, we've seen plenty of violence in the ER *and* heard all the motives. People kill people because of disputes over drugs, gang territory, road rage, or because of ugly love triangles." She shook her head. "Not because someone dissed their favorite author. I *live* with a writer. Trust me, it's not that exciting." Marie's eyes swept upward as the overhead address system hummed loudly and then crackled. There was a page asking security to report to the galley, followed by a short series of signal tones.

I nodded as Renee and Vicky returned a pair of pantyhose to our table, and then I turned back to Marie.

"Security to the galley? I wonder why they'd need—" I stopped short as Renee interrupted, her voice an excited whisper.

"The chef called them," she said, cheeks flushed. "I just heard it from my friend in the Purser's office." She nodded solemnly. "There was a problem after the galley tour."

"Problem?" I asked, idly wondering about breaches in sanitary precautions.

"A couple of the chef's big knives are missing."

FIVE

"Pure coincidence, Darc," Marie said, squeezing a lime wedge into her bottle of Corona. She settled back against the blue canvas deck chaise and tugged at the hem of her turtle-print Jams. "No one knows better than I do how fast you jump to conclusions, so I'm going to spell this out for you." She reached over and tapped her finger rat-a-tat against the brim of my green sun visor: "The missing...galley knives...have *nothing* to do...with a phony threat against Thea Kenyon." She tapped one last time, harder. "Period."

"Hmmm. But—"

"I am *not* hearing that," Marie said, raising her voice over the steel drums of the reggae combo now competing with shouts and splashing from the Lido Deck pool. "Don't get started, Darcy." She grabbed her stack of glossy brochures to keep them from getting splashed, and then nodded her head at me. "What you *should* be thinking about is which shore tours we're taking when we dock on Grand Turk tomorrow." She adjusted the brim of her battered Yankees cap and scanned a pamphlet. "I was thinking that we could take the Aqua Boats to the coral reefs, or maybe that great dune buggy trek."

"How exactly does a chef *lose* knives?" I stopped dabbing SPF 30 into the crocheted keyhole of my lime tankini top, and squinted over at Marie. "I mean you've always told me that they run these ships like the friggin' military, right? So could an Army commander lose …" I wrinkled my nose and decided against the comparison, reminding myself not to discuss foreign affairs with the very Republican Mrs. Skyler. We were meeting for tea in about an hour. And there was no doubt in my mind that this well-bred Southern woman had been doing the military ball circuit while my mom was dodging teargas canisters and carrying Vietnam protest signs. Only a moron would lose the bet on which woman's mug shot appeared in the local papers. Barrett women didn't break the law.

Marie handed me my tropical martini. "Drink," she ordered "I'm sure the knives were misplaced or, more likely, *borrowed* by one of the other galley staff. Chefs are notoriously territorial about their stuff; he shouldn't have called security so fast." She rolled her eyes. "I heard he even complained that someone fiddled with his spice racks, too. Are you going to start worrying that someone will get lethally salt and peppered?" She shook her head. "Trust me, those knives will show up." Marie held up her palm as soon as I opened my mouth. "And I meant in the *kitchen,* not stuck in someone." She shook her head. "I should never let you give stabbing demos." Her lips curved into a teasing smile. "And, speaking of murder, what time is your tea with the Queen Mum?"

I moaned and took a frosty sip of coconut rum. "Three," I said, beginning to smile. "And, really, I'm glad to have another chance to talk with her. I'll be more diplomatic this time, but somehow

I've got to convince Angela to scrap that appointment with Thea Kenyon. If I didn't already have a bad feeling about it—after she got insulted by that champagne fiasco—I'd definitely be worried by that threatening note to Thea."

I bit softly into my lower lip and sighed. "I don't want to have to explain to Luke that I got his mother mixed up in some dangerous mess. It's better to avoid Thea Kenyon all together. And if there's a chance that I could hook Angela up, instead, with—hey, *bingo!*"

I grinned and nodded my head toward where Keven Brodie, still wigless, thank goodness, stood just a few yards away, surrounded by an openly admiring circle of women. I recognized one of them as Sarah. But why waste my time looking at her when...*whoa*. My gaze swept from Keven's bare feet to his muscular thighs, low-slung black tartan swim shorts and flat belly, up to a wide expanse of tanned chest. One sizeable bicep was tattooed with a ropelike Celtic symbol. He ran a hand over his short, dark hair as he turned our way, then caught sight of me and waved. My jaw dropped. "Holy macaroni. I guess that answers the age-old question."

"What question?"

"'*What's under a kilt?*' of course," I said, shaking my head with amusement at Marie's totally unimpressed expression. "Ooh. And here he comes." I took a swipe at my impossible hair and sat up tall enough to prevent too much skin from showing through the key-hole cutout in my swim top. "Let me do the talking, okay?"

"Uh. Sure." Marie shot me a sideways look. "Frisk the Highlander for knives if you want."

"Shh."

I smiled as Keven sauntered toward us and then watched him straddle the chaise beside me, his thighs stretching ridiculously taut.

He had to have learned the pose in modeling class. He leaned forward on his palms and grinned. "Hey there, Darcy Cavanaugh. Where've you been ... *all my life?*"

I pretended I didn't hear Marie exhale like a punctured balloon. "Hi," I answered, quickly. "That's Marie. We're teaching that workshop together." I waited while they did the mutual head-nodding deal, and found myself noticing Sarah again, now sitting opposite us across the pool. The petite blonde, in a great metallic lizard halter and hipster skirt, was talking intently with one of the uniformed security staff. I saw her cross her arms and shake her head back and forth. What was that about?

"So," Keven said as I turned back toward him. His dark-lashed eyes swept slowly over me and I fought a ridiculous blush. "Do you really think you should be risking that?"

For godsake. "Risking what?" I asked, resisting the urge to fold my arms across my sun-crisp keyhole. I reached for my martini instead.

"Teaching people how to commit murder." He smiled and his teeth gleamed white against his tan. "Maybe you should think twice about it—on this cruise." He glanced around at the people sitting on lounges under the sun umbrellas surrounding the Lido pool. Several of them were from our workshop, and I recognized a few from the head shots of authors, agents, and editors posted on easels in the Promenade Deck atrium. Keven chuckled. "Might be dangerous. With so many egos onboard, I mean. Probably more than a few would like to kill off the competition."

I took a sip from my martini and raised my brows. "You're kidding, right? This is *writing*, not a presidential campaign or the Olympics or ..." I scrunched my brows, trying to think of something that I would kill for. My Grandma's dignity maybe. But the look on Keven's face was completely serious. "The competition is really that tough?" I asked.

Keven nodded, the muscles along his gorgeous jaw tensing for a moment. "Finding an agent is incredibly tough. The ones I work with receive maybe a hundred queries per week. That's nearly five thousand a year. We agree to sign about twenty-five of those writers." He shook his head. "And we'll find publishers for half of those the first year. If we're lucky. What's that make the statistical chances for a writer … maybe a quarter of one percent?"

"*Whoa,*" I said, completely stunned. I turned my head and looked once again at the people gathered in groups around the pool. I picked out the familiar faces … seeing them in a numbing new light. Vicky, Renee, and the werewolf writer—carrying her fur-trimmed manuscript tote—Gertie, and so many others. I couldn't help but think of what Barbara Fedders had said this morning about "seeing dreams come true." Good Lord, no wonder she got excited. With statistics like this, seeing a writer succeed was like glimpsing Halley's comet. I turned back to Keven, still boggled. "Then how do they cope with …"

"Rejection?" He asked, handing his ship charge card to a steward who'd stopped with a tray of drinks. He took a beer and signed the tab. Keven took a sip and smiled slowly at me, his dark eyes making that slow, sexy sweep again. His voice lowered, teasing me. "You've never been rejected, Darcy Cavanaugh?"

I lifted my chin, refusing to take the bait. "You know what I mean. Professionally, not personally."

Keven laughed sharply. "Trust me, no matter how many times a writer's told that the rejection isn't personal, it still feels that way. You can count on that."

I nodded, remembering how Barbara had said that thing about going naked in public, that writing a story filled with thoughts and feelings felt that way. I was suddenly darned glad that my passions ran more along the lines of 10K marathons and smacking the be-jeebers out of a punching bag. I peeked over at Marie and smiled. Her weekend passion was napping, obviously.

Keven took a long swig of beer, wiped his mouth on the back of his hand, and then I saw his dark eyes light with amusement. "Some writers get really creative about coping with rejection, though."

I raised my brows. "What do you mean?"

He shook his head. "I swear I heard this is true, but I've never seen it." His eyes widened. "There's this site on the Internet that will print your rejection letters on a roll of toilet paper."

"No."

"Swear. Costs like ninety bucks, I hear." He laughed. "And it's the one-ply stuff but, hell, it might be worth it, right?" Keven winked. "They advertise with something like, 'Use this to put your bad news behind you.'"

I grimaced. "*Eew.*"

He smiled and then raised his dark brows. "So you see what I mean about teaching writers how to murder? Desperate people take desperate measures."

"Hmm, well, I—oh damn," I said, glancing down at my charm watch. "I have to meet someone in the dining room, and I've got to change my clothes first." I rested my hand lightly on Keven's arm.

"But there was something I wanted to talk with you about. It's sort of a ... favor. Can I meet you somewhere later? Maybe in the Crow's Nest after dinner?"

"Sure—*great*," Keven said, putting his other hand over mine and looking into my eyes. Oh jeez. I could tell that this man had the whole thing wrong, but I didn't have time to explain. I needed to meet Luke's mother for tea. It had been my brilliant idea to fix her up with the Kenyon appointment in the first place. But now that I knew the Judge's wife had a 99.975 percent chance of going naked in public and being rejected, *I* was suddenly the *desperate* one. Desperate to make certain I wasn't jump-starting Angela Barrett Skyler's new collection of custom toilet paper.

* * *

High Tea was served in the Vista Dining Room at linen-covered tables made even more splendid by glittering conch shells filled to brimming with tiny roses, baby's breath, and pale pink sweet William. Steaming pots held offerings of Earl Gray, Prince of Wales, Darjeeling, and oolong—no Lipton in sight. Piled high on silver trays were crustless sandwiches filled with piquant tuna, egg salad, and cream cheese with walnuts, along with caviar puffs, and miniature Cornish pasties. There was an unimaginably beautiful array of sweets, including apricot scones, chocolate raspberry rings, brandy snaps, classic shortbread, fresh berries, and—oh boy—golden toasted macaroons. I'd have to figure a way to discreetly smuggle a couple of those coconut wonders back for Marie; the woman would wrestle wildebeest for them.

A formally dressed harpist plucked away on the carpeted mezzanine above us, and our table steward, in waistcoat and white gloves, was gracious enough to ignore my instinctive grimace at the offer of clotted cream. But apparently it's a traditional tea thing, nothing like the medical reference at all, safe, and very very British. I watched him spoon a dollop of the cream, along with a small mound of glistening red jam, onto the plate next to my scone.

I tucked a loose strand of hair back into my upsweep and stretched tall, smoothing the empire waist of my floral sundress. Then I lifted my teacup, took a breath, and gathered my wits. For Luke's sake, I needed to try to connect with this woman, *somehow*. Especially since, ironically, it was I—who didn't know clotted cream from a medical condition—who had to implement the plan to save this snooty woman from herself. I was hooking her up with Keven Brodie, even if it killed her.

"This was a wonderful idea, Mrs. Skyler, thank you for thinking of it." I smiled warmly at Angela over the porcelain brim of my oolong.

As usual, she looked perfect. Her ash blonde hair was sort of Diane Sawyer casual, makeup understated, her eyes the exact gold-flecked blue as Luke's. She wore clustered pearl earrings that I'd bet were generations old, and a wheat-colored woven check jacket that had to be Armani Italian and as new as last week's visit to Neiman's D.C.

I tried, just for a moment, to picture this woman at a Cavanaugh clan gathering. The usual Sunday scene: Chinese take-out boxes stacked on the sink, Dad's pest control goggles drying on the dish rack. And Grandma Rosaleen counting koi pellets into snack-size Ziplocs to dispense as "medication" to her various neighbors. Mom's latest biker beau would arm wrestle Willie who'd do his Goofy-on-Steroids act, hoping to impress the newest Snow White recruit. I'd shout in vain to shut them all up, so we could catch a few more seconds of the hopelessly garbled and blurry webcam transmission from my big brother, Chance, at his Galapagos research camp and … *aagh!* Hopeless. The Cavanaughs and the Skylers had nothing at all in common. Except for the fact that two of their offspring were sleeping together; and that was only once every four to six weeks, which, in itself, was pretty pathetic. *Jeez.* I wondered if I could get the bartender to slip a shot of something in my oolong.

"It's my pleasure to have you join me, Darcy," Angela responded, smiling back at me as she stirred her tea. "Of course this isn't nearly as grand as our teas back in Charlottesville." She clucked her tongue. "My dear friend, Melanie, gives the most marvelous annual 'Orchid Tea' for our garden club. You should see it; every detail is so *per-fect* … the orchid motif embossed on her silver, dozens of exotic blooms on the tables … salmon and caper sandwiches cut into the shape of fishes, mango pastries, scones with pomegranate jelly and Devonshire cream … ah, it defies description." Angela's hands rose to her hair. "And she always loans each guest a vintage hat from her collection; last year I wore the Audrey Hepburn pill box—with the veil, a peach rose, and those pale velvet leaves … I wish you could have been there, Darcy."

I smiled. Somehow. *Umm. Right. Vintage hats.* Who was going to tell this woman that when I wasn't pumping stomachs in the ER, I spent my Saturday afternoons in the gym, wearing sweaty Nikes and boxing gloves? For godsake, where was that bartender?

Angela turned to wave as the Prices, that artist couple, took seats at a table adjacent to ours. Then she turned back to me and sighed. "Anyway," she continued, "I do love the ritual of afternoon tea. It's so civilized after a rigorous workday. Don't you think?"

Rigorous workday? I managed not to choke on my mouthful of tea, but I'm sure that my eyes widened. No way was I going to start comparing the Cavanaughs' gritty trench work to Skyler days spent in mahogany-paneled judges' chambers, but I would concede that Angela's efforts to birth horses required more than a little elbow grease. You had to admire that. Not to mention the fact that her son, my lover, packed a big-ass Glock for the FBI. Plenty of rigor there. I nodded and then did my best to segue tactfully.

"Absolutely," I said. "And I'm sure you need some R and R after spending all those long hours writing your book." I raised my brows. "I can't even imagine how difficult that must be, and now I'm learning that the effort it takes to actually get something published is ... well, grueling." *And can make you crazy enough to spend ninety dollars on a roll of one-ply toilet paper.*

Angela sighed and set her cucumber sandwich down. "That's right," she said. "Most people *don't* realize the work involved. Researching, writing, revising, sharing with critique groups, searching for agents to target, sending out carefully worded query letters—"

"Letters? You've *done* that?" I blurted, not wanting to interrupt but completely surprised that she'd already been hunting for agents. And so relieved. My mind started to whirl: this was great. Because if she'd been doing that, then *of course* she'd already been rejected and one more rejection from Kenyon, no matter how ugly, would be just that: one more rejection. It wouldn't be like Angela were some dewy-eyed virgin.

"No," Angela said, her face infusing with what I could have sworn was a girlish blush. "I guess you could say I've been saving myself for Theodora Kenyon. I've always believed that she would be the one to really appreciate my book." She smiled and shook her head, and I was shocked at the vulnerability I glimpsed in her eyes. "The truth is that I was working up the courage to contact her, when Luke told me about your connections to Writers Afloat. And the next thing I knew, you'd made arrangements for my agent appointment." Her manicured hand glided past a plate of Cornish pasties and took hold of mine. "I don't know how to thank you, Darcy."

Oh my God. "Well, I …" *should just jump overboard and drown myself.* My stomach fought the oolong and I could find nothing coherent to say. Maybe I could find her a deal on the bath tissue.

"And I hope," Angela said, patting my hand and then sitting back in her chair once more, "that you'll understand why I chose to give that appointment to someone else."

My stomach settled and I prayed my hearing wasn't failing on this crazy roller coaster ride. "You gave your agent appointment away?"

"Yes, but for a very good reason," Angela explained all in rush. Her blue eyes were taking on an excited gleam. "I found out that I could submit the first several *pages* of my book to Theodora instead," she explained, nodding head up and down like she was willing me to understand. "This is so much better than just telling her about my book, Darcy. Having her read the pages is tantamount to skipping a step in the whole submission process! A real coup. And it brings me that much closer to seeing my dream come true."

I was still a little confused, but hopeful, even if Angela's use of the "dream" word was bringing back that whole conversation with Barbara Fedders. "So you won't have to meet with her to hand it in?"

"No. I already turned the submission in to her assistant, Barbara, this afternoon. Thank heavens that I brought the manuscript along. I'll have to wait a few weeks to hear anything, I suppose. But that's okay." Angela laughed suddenly and lifted her teacup. "Let's be honest, Theodora Kenyon may be the best agent in the country, but she isn't known for her well-bred manners. A private read will be fairer to me and," Mrs. Skyler's blue eyes twinkled mischievously, "I won't be tempted to smack that tacky broad."

My jaw dropped and then I started to smile. Big time. *Wahoo!* I didn't have to worry about Luke's mother going naked in public, I wouldn't have to beg the Highlander for favors, and I'd somehow managed to sneak three macaroons into my purse. Even the harp music seemed suddenly festive—hot damn, things were looking up after all!

I reached for another scone and grinned at the Judge's wife, completely surprised by a sudden warm sense of camaraderie. "Pass me the clotted cream, would you, Angela? I'm starting to like that stuff."

* * *

"Hey, I forgot to check out your feet," I said, pulling our cabin door closed and stepping out into the carpeted corridor behind Marie. I glanced down at the cuffs of her tuxedo. "What's the latest in sock bling?"

Marie grinned, hiked up a pant leg, and then pointed the toe of her patent leather Birkenstock. "Winnie the Pooh and Piglet glitter, compliments of my buddy and your brother, Goofy." She raised her brows. "By the way, did you get chummy enough with the Judge's wife to spill some of the more interesting Cavanaugh family quirks?"

"God no," I said, laughing as I tucked the key card into my beaded evening bag. "I want to keep sleeping with her son." I pulled at the strapless bodice of my cinnamon satin gown, being sure that no "quirky" shamrock showed. "But actually, I was surprised that Angela wasn't as snooty as usual." I nodded, sending my crystal chandelier earrings swaying, as we started off toward the amidships elevators. "Especially when she tossed in that great line about being 'tempted to smack that tacky broad.' There must be something about this writing business that brings out a person's primal instincts."

"Yes, well, the only primal instinct I'm thinking about right now is *hunger*," Marie said, as we passed between the parallel rows of G-Deck cabin doors. "Formal night means lobster, and I'm sure I can eat two. And still have room for that great chocolate—hey, that's Gertie's cabin."

Marie stopped in front of the door just half-a-dozen or so down from ours. "Why's it propped open?" She pointed to what looked like a pink-feathered slipper wedged under the door. The other slipper lay, upside down, in the doorway.

"I don't know," I answered, noticing that the transparent plastic "mailbox" outside her cabin was stuffed full of the daily programs and inevitable two-hour-sale brochures from the Galleria boutiques.

"You okay in there, Gertie?" Marie shouted, rapping her knuckles against the door. "We saw your door propped open … are you in there?" She listened for a moment and then turned to me, scrunching her brows. "Maybe the cleaning people left it—" Marie halted and nearly fell in, as Gertie swung the door inward. She was dressed in a black strapless bra drooping low—nearly belt-level low—a half-slip and high heels. She was holding a *Cosmo* magazine. She kicked the loose slipper aside and grinned as she recognized us.

"I'm fine, girls," she said. "Just sittin' on the pot." She pointed down at the slipper wedged under the door. "My roomie forgets her key card and comes and goes … so I just leave the door propped open for her, in case I want to nap." She pointed back toward where her clothes were laid out on her twin bed. Beside the bed was a compressed-air nebulizer unit, breathing treatments for her emphysema, probably. "I'm still getting dressed; running late 'cause of all that nonsense with security."

"Security?" I asked, protectively leaning into the doorway to provide some cover for the half-naked senior as people passed in the hallway outside. Gertie, apparently an exhibitionist, waved her *Cosmo* in a greeting over my head.

"The missing knives," Gertie explained. "They're questioning the folks who took the galley tour. The few of us they could locate anyway, since there wasn't a signup list. They basically contacted those of us who stood out enough to be remembered." She winked. "Something memorable about *my* face, I guess."

"Who else got called in for questioning?" I asked, suddenly curious as I remembered Carter's fan, Sarah, talking to the security guy poolside.

Gertie squinted, her sparse brows drawing together. "A couple of the historical writers, that man who's writing the terrorist thriller, that painter, Frankeen Price, Miss Cantrelle, Sarah, Keven … Oh yes. And that woman who kept fussing at the pastry chef about the pecan pies—had to be *dark* corn syrup, not light syrup if you wanted *authentic Southern*, blah, blah. A real pain in the pa-toot." Gertie tapped me with her rolled-up *Cosmo*. "You know who she is; that judge's wife."

Marie grumbled at me all the way to the glass elevators, then called me "compulsive and overly responsible" on our four-story ride up to the Dolphin Deck, and continued the lecture all the way down the wallpapered corridor toward the ocean-view verandah suites. If Angela needed my help, she would have asked for it, Marie explained. No reason to check on her, our lobster was waiting, and so on and so forth. She wasn't convincing me, especially since it was my bright idea to suggest the galley tour to Angela in the first place. I just wanted to be sure she hadn't blown a gasket over being questioned by security. I'd made some progress with her at tea, and I wanted to keep moving in that general direction. Getting her frisked for knives could definitely work against me.

We passed Cantrelle's door, then the suites occupied by Thea Kenyon and Barbara Fedders, and checked the cabin numbers against the number on the note that Angela had given me. Marie had just begun a rerun of cautions about minding my own business and letting sleeping dogs lie, when we rounded a turn in the corridor and heard an excited buzz of voices. And deep gasps. Followed by screams.

And then we saw her, one of the workshop presenters—Carter Cantrelle's editor, Ellen—staggering forward, rubbing her hands together, face milky pale and ... *oh God.* She was covered with blood.

SIX

"STAND BACK!" I ORDERED. "*Please.* And someone keep an eye on that elevator. If you don't see the medical team in two minutes, page them again."

I grabbed a fresh towel from one of the bystanders and knelt back down on the carpet beside the unresponsive Ellen. Her face, pale and glistening with sweat, was speckled with a fine spray of red blood; alarming, no doubt, to the small clutch of anxious on-lookers. But it was in no way near the volume of blood that was on this woman's palms—the source, it appeared, of the far scarier trail of red smears across the front of her ivory satin gown. *What happened here?* I rubbed at the sticky mess on the editor's hands and then shook my head. There were no wounds. Then *where* was all the blood coming—"Oh," I said, seeing the woman's eyelids flutter. "That's good, Ellen. Open your eyes. I'm here to help you."

I patted her face, feeling reassured as she took a shuddering breath and the color returned to her cheeks. It was looking far more like she'd fainted than fallen into shock from blood loss. Good. But we still needed to know what had happened here. I glanced down to where Marie, squatting on the opposite side of our victim, was dabbing at the woman's foot with a terry towel. "Find anything?" I asked.

Marie frowned at a bloodstain on the cuff of her tuxedo and then nodded at me. "A laceration. Maybe about a half-inch long. Top of the foot, located right over the—*oops!*"

The bystanders groaned and Marie leaned quickly away, as a thin spray of bright red blood shot upward, spurting like a low-budget horror movie. She repositioned her compress to staunch the flow. "Right over the pedal artery," she explained, raising her brows. "Nice little pumper. Remind me to carry Handi Wipes next time you're my dinner date." She shrugged. "But no other wounds that I can see. Chest is fine, abdomen clear."

Marie kept one hand on the terry towel and reached for something with her other hand. She lifted a shoe, an ivory satin pump dotted with pearl accents and blood clots. "Shoe pretty much says it all. Except for what the devil she cut her foot on. Something sliced through her pantyhose." Marie glanced toward Ellen's face. "Hey, maybe we can ask our patient now."

Ellen raised her head, her eyes wide with obvious confusion as she peered up at the circle of faces overhead. One of them was Keven Brodie who, though gorgeous in his tuxedo and tartan vest, was every bit as pale as the downed editor. Jeez, the last thing we needed was to have this squeamish Highlander topple onto us. *Suck it up, cover-guy.*

"I'm so embarrassed," Ellen mumbled and then licked her lips, smiling weakly at me. "I guess I fainted. I'm not good around blood. And it kept spraying out of my foot." Her pupils dilated with the memory.

"No problem," I said, smiling as I reached for her wrist. Her skin was less damp, her pulse picking up to a healthier rate. Recovering, definitely. "We've got the bleeding controlled now, and the doctor will be here any minute." I raised my brows. "But how did you manage to cut yourself out here in the hallway?"

"Well, I…" Ellen rose up on her elbows and grimaced at the bloody hand smears on her gown. She shifted her hips, rocking side-to-side and looking down at the carpet beside her. "Where is it? Oh dear… am I lying on it?"

She tried to sit up and I pushed her gently back, knowing she'd faint again if she got up too quickly. "Where's *what*?" I asked, noticing for the first time that the editor had been lying on a stack of brochures and daily programs, as if she'd just emptied her door-side mailbox. "Do you mean your other shoe? It's here. Marie slipped it off."

"No," Ellen said, her eyes dilating again. "I meant the *knife*."

There was a collective gasp from the onlookers, and a ripple of, "knife, knife, *knife*…?" And then I heard authoritative voices in the distance. Security and the medical team, thank God. Keven sprinted off, waving his arms overhead to signal them.

"Knife?" I asked after shooting a sideways look at Marie.

"Yes," Ellen said, allowing us to take her arms and raise her very slowly toward a sitting position. "I pulled those papers out of my mailbox—it was overflowing with shopping brochures and tour information—and then I felt something heavy fall out and…" her eyes got big again and I reminded her to take a deep breath. "It stuck in the top of my foot. Right through my stocking."

"Easy does it, Ellen," I said, helping the woman scooch sideways on the carpet. "Be careful. If there's something sharp under you— are you sure it was a knife?"

"Yes," she said, pausing for moment as Marie changed her grip on the foot compress. Ellen groaned and then inched sideways again. "A knife with a black handle. I was horrified and the pain was awful, so I grabbed it and pulled. And that's when the blood started spraying up into my face. *Ooh, see?*" She rocked her hips and pointed to something shiny on the carpet just below her buttock. "There it is."

Before we could move enough to get a good look, a trio of security staff, wearing purple latex gloves, stepped silently through the crowd. One of them produced a plastic bag and knelt onto one knee beside the editor. He smiled politely—and then carefully retrieved the large, forged-steel chef's knife.

* * *

Fortunately, nurses are good at dodging blood, so it didn't take us long to spiff up and dash to the Vista Dining Room in time for Marie to net her lobsters. Her stomach had growled through our entire trauma nurse performance and I knew, as well as I knew the ABCs of CPR, that if she'd had access to a cold slice of pizza, Marie would have munched with one hand and compressed that artery with the other. I'm serious. Add a Styrofoam cup of hours-old coffee, a two-minute potty break, the wail of incoming sirens, and you'd pretty much have a snippet of our everyday life back in the ER. You can bet that Marie wasn't about to let a minor mishap with a pointy object interrupt our rare, leisurely dinner. As for me, I was far more interested in seeing what effect the news of the grisly incident had on the folks who'd already been questioned once about the missing knives. Like my boyfriend's mother, who was sitting right across the table from me and frowning after the newest flurry of knife-related speculation. *Jeez.*

"It's utterly ridiculous," Angela said after the waiter refilled her wine glass, "for security to think that any of the *writers* would be involved in a prank like that."

Vicky poked her fork tines against the hollow red shell of her lobster and chuckled. "Don't be so sure, Angela. The large majority of us are mystery and suspense writers, after all. Maybe it was some-body's misguided idea of research. That's Gertie's theory, anyway."

I smiled, thinking of the plucky old woman who'd propped her door open while reading *Cosmo* in her undies, and how last night in the bar she'd claimed, *"Nothing scares me anymore."* I believed that of Gertie, but I wasn't so sure about Angela. She seemed a lit-tle nervous to me. I caught her eye.

"So you think the knife showing up in the editor's mailbox was a prank?" I asked casually, kind of feeling things out.

"What else?" Angela asked quickly. Her gaze—blue eyes en-hanced by the periwinkle shade of her stunning jacquard gown—swept across the faces at our table. And then darted quickly toward the sea of faces at other mauve linen-topped tables. "Does anyone really think someone *intended* to harm that poor woman?"

Barth, Keven's golden counterpart, dipped a chunk of lobster into drawn butter and shrugged his big shoulders. "Don't know. Never heard anyone say anything bad about Ellen. But people can have mixed feelings about VIPs like agents and editors and authors and ..." He grinned and straightened upright in his chair. I swore I could see him flexing his chest muscles right through his tux shirt. "I've had my share of stalkers, too."

"Stalkers?" Renee asked, her brows drawing together. She fiddled with a cameo brooch on the bodice of her gauzy empire-waist gown and her face paled. "You think there's some *cuckoo* at this conference?"

Aw... man. I heard Marie struggle to contain a snort, and I gave her ankle a little warning tap with the heel of my T-strap crystal slide. We were in a minority here and we needed to remember that. Even if we *did* think that ninety-dollar rolls of TP and questions about fangs were as cuckoo as any bird in a wooden clock.

I turned to smile at Renee and my gaze settled, instead, on the face of Sarah Skelton, seated beside her. She looked more than a little tense, and I realized, for the first time, that she must feel like a minority at this table, too. Double-minority, actually: a reader among writers, and now one of the galley gang, too.

"I only threw that stalker theory out," Barth explained, "because, if you think about it, the whole Dolphin Deck corridor, where the knife showed up, is nothing but muckety-mucks: that promotions bigwig, three editors, the e-book publisher, that artist couple—the Prices—Thea Kenyon, and her assistant. And Carter Cantrelle..."

Barth paused and shook his head, and I watched Sarah bite into her lower lip and glance away. Carter definitely had a supporter in this girl. "Can you believe they put Cantrelle and Kenyon in rooms across from each other? Not too smart. But anyway, like I said before, the only people in those cabins are VIPs or people rolling in frickin' dough. And—" the cover model's face flushed as he caught himself. He smiled at Angela. "Oops, no offense."

"No offense taken," Angela said, her voice sincere. "My stateroom is lovely, and I welcome any of you to stop by. But I promise you that just because it's located along *that* corridor, it doesn't mean that I know anything more than the rest of you. I still think the knife episode was a boorish prank, and not anything in the least bit sinister."

I nodded and smiled to show Angela that I absolutely agreed and supported her 100 percent. These people should just get it into their right-brained heads that this whole bit about the knife and the cut was some freak accident, completely unscripted and—*oh no.* My mouth sagged open and the lobster started to rumba in my stomach as a perfectly horrible thought hit me. *No. Not possible. Couldn't be . . .*

"That's right!" I heard myself suddenly chirp, in a voice so ridiculously perky that I didn't blame Marie for eyeballing me. But all of a sudden, a couple of things were starting to freak me out. Facts. Things I hadn't really thought of until right this moment and . . .

"And the *important* thing is that Ellen is perfectly fine," I continued, determined to settle this whole discussion. "Small cut. Couple of stitches, and she's good to go. No worries." I nodded my head up and down, forcing myself to stop obsessing about those *two damned facts.* "Actually," I said, forcing a nervous chuckle, "Ellen said she'd meet us at the Crow's Nest tonight, even if she has to 'prop her foot up on the bar.' Miss Cantrelle offered to bring a pillow to do that. So see? Angela's right. Nothing sinister. Just a prank and a minor cut and—" I saw Vicky's brows shoot up and had a bad feeling that she was about voice one of those pesky little facts that I didn't want to think about. *No, don't—*

"Good thing it wasn't a cut like you showed in your *stabbing* demonstration today, Darcy," she said. "When you drew those gross diagrams of the human body, then took that knife and *jabbed* it right in." Her brows shot even higher and her lids blinked a bunch of times. "Hey, wasn't that right before the *galley tour*?"

There was murmur of voices around the table and I heard Marie clear her throat softly, like she was putting the facts together herself. *This fact and that other scary one.*

"Yes," I said, trying to keep the perky deal going with my voice … and really failing. "Wow, I hadn't thought of that. But, hey, Marie and I only had those little pink plastic—"

"Damned right, Vicky!" Barth said, shaking his head and sending his blonde mane swirling across his shoulders like a lion on the hunt. "Good point. And don't forget that there's *another big knife still missing.*"

Bingo. That other creepy fact.

* * *

Thank goodness for booze and the grislier-than-a-knifing tales of writers' manuscript rejections. After twenty minutes in the Crow's Nest Bar, that earlier hint of a connection between the Nurse's Guide to Murder workshop and the foot-stabbing incident had been replaced by hotter topics. In fact, just minutes into my own lemon drop martini, I admitted that it was highly likely I'd "jumped to conclusions" again. Much to Marie's smug pleasure. Things were cool, and I was now convinced that there was nothing in the least bit ominous going on. The biggest proof had to be the healthy and carefree smile on our former patient's face.

Editor Ellen had indeed kept her promise to join everyone. With her foot in a compression bandage and propped on a chair, she'd generously sprung for the first round of drinks. Her author, Carter Cantrelle, hovered protectively, while—discreetly behind—Reader Sarah hovered over Carter, all in all making a strange little three-some. And it looked to me like these impromptu "Cocktails and Craft" sessions were destined to become the favorite late-night gathering of the literary crowd; a place to unwind after the workshops, trade rejection stories, share tips, and metaphors, and...rub elbows with the bookish "muckety-mucks," as Barth would say. Or at least Sarah Skelton was doing her best to place her own elbow in geographic proximity to Carter's elbow. I watched as the agile blonde slowly inched her chair across the dipping floor of the ship's bow lounge. Agility and stealth; you had to admire this fan's determination. Cantrelle's books must be darned good. Obviously I needed to expand my own reading beyond *Runner's World*, *RN Magazine*, and the Neiman catalog.

I twisted in my chair to get a better look, and then reached for a pretzel, nodding at Marie. I pointed my pretzel past the heads of Vicky, Renee, and Gertie. "See that? Sarah's making her move."

"Yes," Gertie said, nodding. "I don't think I've ever seen such a loyal fan. She showed me something she's planning to present to Carter, an 'Altered Book.'"

I scrunched my brows and Gertie explained, after pausing to take a hit from her inhaler.

"I had to ask about that one myself," she said. "Apparently it's when someone takes a book—in this case, the sixth in Carter's Atlanta Allure series—and creatively 'recycles' it into a work of art." Gertie spread her hand as if opening a novel. "It can be re-bound, painted, gold-leafed, rubber-stamped, collaged…drilled…" She nodded. "All as a tribute to the author. And apparently Sarah's done that for Carter. She said she's been working on it for over a year." She smiled and shook her head. "All that remains now is for Sarah to summon the courage to present it to her. The poor thing's terrified."

I glanced over at the little blonde who was watching her favorite author with rapt attention. "Whoa," I said, raising my brows and turning to Marie. "Ever do that whole star-struck groupie thing?"

Marie rolled her eyes like I was crazy, then smiled slowly over the foamy brim of her beer. "Trekkie thing."

"*No*," I said, my eyes widening. "You mean—"

"Spock's autograph right on my calf. I pulled down my Klingon knee-highs, gave him a Sharpie marker and—" Marie suddenly whipped her head sideways, sloshing her beer. "Holy moly, what's *that*?"

"What?" I asked, and then caught sight of Barbara Fedders moving through the doorway. Artie was perched securely on the shoulder of her linen jacket, wearing something on his head that looked like… "Uh, it's a sort of round, plastic ball. Only more like a little cage or—"

"Beak bubble," Gertie said, leaning forward over her piña colada. I scrunched my brows, trying to decide if the old girl was talking bird accessories or penis euphemisms. But then she pointed at Artie and nodded with confidence. "A muzzle for birds. He tried to take a chunk out of the first mate this afternoon. It's the only way they'll let that bird in the public areas now." She laughed. "Which means I'm safer when I have my appointment with Kenyon tomorrow afternoon."

I nodded, watching as Barbara and Theodora, wearing a matte jersey tunic and slacks with an artsy tooled leather belt, joined Barth and the promo team at a table by the window. Artie squawked and fought his beak bubble and I was reminded of how glad I was that Angela had opted out of her appointment with that circus act. "Yes," I said, turning back to Gertie. "Although, if you wanted 'safe,' I guess it would be best to take that option to turn your manuscript pages in to be read later. Like Angela decided to do."

Gertie laid her hand on my arm and opened her mouth, but Renee spoke up first.

"Oh dear," She breathed, peeking over at the agent who was already sipping her first mai tai. Renee looked back to me, eyes wide. "Angela's risking a 'Chop or Shop'?"

Huh? My mouth went dry and Marie plunged ahead for me.

"'Chop Shop'? What the hell does that mean?"

"'Chop *or* Shop,'" Gertie explained. "'The Chop or Shop Critique.' Thea's been doing it for months on her Internet blog, critiquing anonymous submissions from writers. It's been wildly popular. For the thick-skinned or suicidal among us, that is." She half laughed, half coughed, and then took a sip of her drink. "Picture Simon from *American Idol*—on steroids. Thea doesn't exactly hold back, honey. She'll tell you outright whether your work is something that an agent would want to 'shop' to publishing houses, or…" Gertie's arthritic hand did a quick karate slice inches from my nose. "Chop to pieces."

Renee shivered and glanced toward where the agent sat, now tapping away on her laptop. "Did you see that leather belt she's wearing? See the carved markings on it, all along the edges?"

I nodded, taking a closer look at the interesting, hand-tooled motif, and wondered why we were suddenly talking about belts. "Yeah?"

"Notches," Renee said, her eyes widening. "People say that there are little notches carved into that belt. You know, like those old gunslingers who notched their belts for people they've shot?"

Gertie licked the rim of her glass. "Or chopped." She rolled her eyes. "But that belt thing's a load of crap. Nothing but urban legend. Bottom line is that Thea's Chop or Shop is a valuable free service to writers."

"Some service," Marie said, grimacing.

I fought a wave of unease. "So, these submissions that Barbara Fedders has been collecting onboard ... ?"

"On the chopping block tomorrow night," Gertie said. "A live, in-person critique, with Barbara reading the submissions aloud and Thea giving her verdict. Or so rumor has it; it's not actually on the program sheet. But we've heard that Thea's planning a 'surprise' at her workshop. So my best guess is that anyone who's submitted manuscript pages better be prepared for—" Gertie clamped her hands over her ears as the parrot's voice shrieked across the bar.

"You write *craaap!*" Artie screamed through his beak bubble. He lurched side to side on Barbara's shoulder, whistled, and then cut loose again. "Burn it ... goddammm *triiipe!* Re-jeck-ted, re-jeck-ted ... *aawwk!*"

I looked at Marie and moaned. Luke's very-proper mother was headed for the Chop or Shop. Missing chef's knives paled in comparison. I needed some air.

* * *

The best thing about jogging on a cruise ship is that not a lot of other people are doing it, especially at midnight when the buffet is cranking up poolside on Lido Deck. Face it: the fare-paying folks had coughed up good money to square off with mounds of gua-camole, chilled pink shrimp, mini-quiches, a fifty-pound Gouda wheel, and fruit kebobs. Add a three-foot tall ice sculpture, a bub-ble-making machine, and a Jamaican doing Barry Manilow, and you've got a guaranteed crowd. Which meant lots more room for me and my pink Nikes on the Promenade jogging track that cir-cled the deck below.

And right now, running— even if it was in circles around a 951-foot ship moving at twenty-four knots—was just what the doctor ordered. I'd had more than enough of the potty-mouth parrot and the literary gang, and I was avoiding the phone message back in my cabin. Luke. Expecting me to answer his clever question: "Have you got Mom headed for the bestseller list yet?" How could I tell him that all I'd done so far was put her in the lineup to become a notch on a belt? I couldn't. So that's why I was running out here in the dark, with the sea-scented tropical breeze against my face and the teak decking squeaking under my Nikes. It felt great. Even if the footing dipped down and then rose up...and tipped a little side-ways and... *whoa, easy there.*

I rounded the foreship stretch, leaning into my uphill Nike to avoid drifting toward the rail with the ship's motion. I glanced down at my watch to estimate my distance. Eight minutes per mile meant...I squinted in the dark at the dangling face of my bracelet watch. Three miles. Not too shabby. I smiled as I passed Bill Price and his wife Frankeen—wearing a hot pink gown, her dark hair in an elegant upsweep—standing at the rail with their arms around each other's waists. Then I picked up my pace, sucking in the humid air, enjoying the responding stretch in my quads, and feeling that first floaty wave of endorphins rise, promising to lift me away. From everything... and everyone. Writers and editors and agents and—*oh crap!* A voice was calling my name from behind. I continued on for a few more strides, my feet slapping right-left, right-left against the sea-damp teak, trying to pretend that I didn't hear it. But then he shouted my name a second time, and it was impossible.

"Darcy! Hey, wait up!"

Ahh... I slowed to a half-jog and turned, feeling a rivulet of sweat trickle between my breasts. So much for solitude and escape.

He paused under the deck lights and smiled. Then jogged on toward me.

Damn. Forgot. I told him I'd meet him.

Keven the Highlander.

SEVEN

AND IT MADE PERFECT sense that a romance cover model would go jogging in a ... *G-string?* For godsake.

Okay, maybe it wasn't a exactly a G-string, but when Keven Brodie came to a halt beside me, all I could see in the soft glow of deck lights was a wicked expanse of sun-bronzed muscles—calves, thighs, belly, and chest. If there was a scrap of fabric somewhere in between, you could have fooled me. Oh Lord. I kept my gaze safely riveted to his face.

"Hi." Keven smiled and his teeth glowed in the dark like the Cheshire cat. "What happened to meeting me? Did I get that... wrong?" His breath escaped in a half puff, and sweat glistened on his neck. I saw his dark eyes move quickly over me, taking in my heather-pink Lycra shorts, my sports bra, and my run-wild curls. "Or are you one of those coy women who likes to be ... chased?"

I gave an unladylike snort and narrowed my eyes. "Right." I wiped my fingers across a trickle of sweat on my jaw and then shook my head. "Sorry, Keven. I completely forgot that I'd asked to meet with you." I smiled at him. "But then things got a little crazy this afternoon, if you remember."

Keven cleared his throat and hesitated, and I thought I saw a replay of that same queasy expression I'd glimpsed at Ellen's stabbing—*accident, dammit*—earlier. Only this time he wasn't so deathly pale.

"Yes," he said, his expression brightening. "That was wild, wasn't it? You sure looked like some kind of hero back there." He tapped his knuckles against my bare shoulder. "But I think everyone's blowing that whole incident out of proportion. Ellen's fine." He glanced upward toward the source of faraway music. "I saw her in the Crow's Nest before I started jogging, bought her a chocolate martini as a matter of fact."

"Great." I smiled and relief flooded through me. Hot damn, this half-naked cover model was validating my whole position. The editor's wound—along with the still-unaccounted-for chef's knife—was in no way related to the Nurse's Guide to Murder workshop. "And you're right about people being too quick to think the worst," I added. "I mean, regardless of how the knife got in that mailbox, it's not like someone *stabbed* the woman, for godsake."

"Right," Keven agreed. "If she hadn't tried to grab that whole stack of mail at once, it wouldn't have fallen and—"

"Exactly!" I said, suddenly realizing that, in my enthusiasm for our Zenlike harmony, I'd taken hold of Keven's arm. His bicep, tattooed with the Celtic design, was firm and warm beneath my fingers. Keven's eyes moved from my hand to my face and he smiled, pure masculine confidence gleaming in his eyes. I pulled my hand away and cleared my throat. "So," I said, nodding once or twice too many times and fighting a stupid blush. "I guess we've settled that. I should probably go rescue the casino from Marie."

Keven took a step toward me. "Wait, Darcy. You never said why you wanted to hook up tonight. Something about a favor?"

Favor? The only favor I wanted from this guy was to stop looking at me like that.

"This afternoon," he continued, reminding me, "at the pool. You said you needed a favor."

"Oh," I said, stunned for a moment that I'd forgotten so quickly. But then High Tea with Mrs. Judge seemed like light years ago now. I took a step backward, hugging my arms around myself. "That's right. It was about my … friend. She's a writer. A sort of virgin writer." I smiled a little sheepishly. "Truth is, I was going to try to talk you into listening to her book spiel. To save her from Thea Kenyon."

Keven raised his dark brows. "She has an appointment with Thea?"

I sighed and then frowned. "Had one. But now she's opted to turn in her pages instead."

Keven clucked his tongue. "Chop or Shop?"

"Oh God," I said, grabbing at a hank of my hair. "It's true, then? She's really doing that heinous thing tomorrow night?"

He faked an innocent shrug. "You didn't hear it from me." The look in Keven's eyes turned genuinely sympathetic. "But I'm guessing that, virgin or not, your friend must have pretty thick skin to risk submitting anything to Thea. She has to have heard about her reputation."

I scrunched my brows, wondering how Angela's skin—nourished by nine pints of Southern blue blood—could possibly be thick enough to survive what Thea had planned. Barbara Fedders has said submitting work was like "going naked in public." I had a feeling that, regardless of how thick her skin, Angela Barrett Skyler would rather die than be caught naked.

"I don't know her that well," I said, truthfully. I saw the confusion on Keven's face and decided, especially since the Highlander had somehow managed to take hold of my hand, that it was time for the whole danged truth here. "You, see," I said giving Keven's hand a friendly little squeeze before slipping my fingers from his grasp. "She's my *boyfriend's* mother and this is the first time I've ever really spent any time with her." I hurried ahead, ignoring the quick scrunch of the man's beautiful brows. "And the fact is that I finagled the appointment with Thea Kenyon, to sort of impress her."

"Well that's the shits," Keven said, chuckling quickly. I couldn't tell if he was acknowledging my unlucky choice for impressing Angela, or the fact that I had a boyfriend. But, regardless, I was relieved to have confessed both facts. "You're really worried?" He asked.

"You mean about having her eaten by a parrot, or the part about her becoming another notch on Kenyon's belt?"

Keven laughed. "The story about the belt's a crock. It was her father's belt. Thea had it cut down and re-designed. To honor him, I guess."

I had a fleeting thought of Sarah Skelton cutting, pasting, and gold-leafing Carter's book. Some people had strange ways of honoring their heroes. "But what about the 'notches' on that belt?" I asked, crossing my arms.

Keven shook his head. "You mean those marks everyone's so paranoid about?" Keven extended his forearm to expose the dark scabs still visible from his tangle with Artie, and frowned. "The damned bird's probably been gnawing on that belt for thirty years. Now *he* is something to worry about. Someone ought to wring his neck."

I smiled weakly. "You know a lot about our infamous agent." I glanced up for an instant, as the music grew louder from the Crow's Nest Bar a few decks up. The Cocktails and Craft party must still be going strong.

Keven shrugged his big shoulders. "I hang out with Barbara here and there at these events. I buy her a drink and we talk. The woman's a gem—hell, if there were a way to lure her away to work for me, I'd be giving Thea's agency a run for the money."

I smiled. "Maybe you should ply Barbara with chocolate martinis."

"Nope." Keven shook his head. "Charles Krug merlot, that's all she drinks. And sparingly. Amazes me. If I had to deal with Thea and Artie, I'd be swilling gin by the bucket." He nodded at the Prices passing us on the rail, and then grinned back at me. "But, seriously, despite her ego, Thea Kenyon is an icon." Keven lifted a dark brow. "Why do you think Carter Cantrelle's own daughter submitted work to her?"

"That's true?" I asked, remembering Gertie saying that same thing.

"So goes the rumor mill; I can't get Barbara to confirm it. But can you imagine how it would gall Carter, to have her daughter's work publicly…dissected?" Keven shook his head and then shrugged. "But maybe the daughter's got a viable manuscript." He smiled at me. "Maybe your boyfriend's mother does, too, Darcy. Thea's got a sharp eye for talent. Don't sell your friend short; maybe she's got talent." He nodded and the deck lights danced in his eyes. "Or at least a great *hook*."

I must have looked as confused as I felt, because Keven laughed and explained.

"A hook is the tease that tells us the story has a fresh twist. Something in a book pitch that immediately grabs our interest, intrigues us, and makes us *need* to know more. That's how you land an agent." Keven's voice lowered and he reached out to trace his finger along my forearm. "For example, like right at this moment, you've got me hooked to find out how serious you are about this so-called boyfriend of yours."

I shook my head and laughed. Even though I didn't respond to his hypothetical question, I suspected Keven knew the answer. But what I still *didn't* know was how this would all fare for Angela at the Chop or Shop. "I don't know if she has a 'hook,'" I said. "I guess it's a crapshoot tomorrow night. No one can guess ahead of time what Thea will do."

"Only Barbara," Keven said.

"You mean because she knows Thea's taste so well?" I smiled to myself, thinking of the irony that only a reserved Merlot Woman could truly understand a Mai Tai Monster. "She can predict Thea's reaction to the manuscripts?"

"And because she reads them all first."

She reads them? Hmmm.

"So," Keven said, tipping his head and smiling boyishly down at me. "Boyfriend, huh? Dammit. Guess that means all I have to look forward to is watching you demonstrate murder techniques." He raised his brows. "What's first tomorrow? Let me guess: poisoning, baseball bat bashing, or are you going to set some poor slob's hair on fire?"

"Fire?" I groaned. "Nah, we crossed fire off the outline." I shrugged. "Safety codes. But you're welcome to join us for a cup of cyanide." I stifled a yawn. "Jeez. Sorry. I'm pooped. And Marie and I have to get up early to get our shore tour on Grand Turk. Don't know yet if we want to do Ultimate Snorkel, parasailing, or maybe that 4 × 4 safari along the beach."

Keven touched a fingertip to one of my rogue curls and smiled. "I should have known you're the adventurous type." He rolled his eyes. "Barbara's doing that 'Sea Tracker Helmet Tour.' Guaranteed not to get your hair wet."

I raised my brows. *Barbara. Who reads Thea's manuscripts ahead of time. Who likely already knew if Angela was getting shopped or chopped. Hmmm.*

Keven walked me back toward the elevators. I couldn't help but smile at the looks on the faces of the women we passed in the hallway. Obviously the kilt and sword were just frosting on the cake for this tall, bare-chested Highlander-turned-agent. I said good night, stepped through the brass doors of the elevator and pushed the button for G-Deck. I yawned again. It was after two AM, and we'd be in our first Caribbean port not long after sunrise. Sun, white sand, and palms—I loved the whole idea. I chuckled to myself, remembering what Keven had said about Barbara's 'Sea Tracker' Tour, "guaranteed not to get your hair wet." Merlot and safety—no taste for adventure in her choices, obviously.

At the cabin, I pulled my key card from the pocket of my running shorts. My gaze turned to the clear plastic mail file mounted beside the door, and I noticed that Marie had filled out our room service breakfast menu. She must have gone to bed. In a few hours, the stewards would retrieve the menu and replace it with the coming day's newsletter, special announcements, and tour information. I tried to push the image of Ellen's mailbox—and the razor-sharp chef's knife—from my mind. The mailbox, the blood, and the knife. But the fact remained that there was still another one of those galley knives missing. It was as undeniable as the fact that tomorrow night Angela Skyler would face the Chop or Shop. My stomach did a little delayed elevator dip as I thought of Luke's phone message: *"Have you got Mom headed for the bestseller list yet?"*

It wasn't like I could *do* anything about any of this, right? I mean, what could I do? Nothing. There was nothing to do. Period. *Stop obsessing, Darcy.*

I sighed and slid the key card into the slot, heard the lock whir and saw the green light flash. The door opened into darkness and I smiled as I saw the warm orange glow of my best friend's Lava Lite, and her peacefully snoring silhouette. Dreaming of our exciting upcoming adventures, probably, and … then the idea came to me. Brilliant really.

Yes. I'd simply convince Marie that the dry-hair 'Sea Tracker' Tour was as cool as Mr. Spock's autograph.

I needed some alone time with Barbara Fedders.

*   *   *

Grand Turk and Caicos, according to the brochures, are a cluster of tiny islands "strewn like party confetti" off the southern end of the Bahamas—remote, romantic, and "deliciously desolate"—where lucky visitors may catch a glimpse of the "famous endangered pink flamingo." Marie and I got our first view of the island via its brand-new port, which boasted an eight-hundred-foot white sand beach, swimming pool, cabanas, and Jimmy Buffet's "Margaritaville" bar and restaurant. Impressive. And we *did* see that endangered flamingo: silk screened onto at least a dozen Hanes tee shirts, stretched across the droopy breasts of the gray-haired women standing in line for the Sea Tracker Helmet Tour. Unfortunately, glimpses of elusive Barbara Fedders proved far more rare, which was the direct impetus for the evil look that Marie was shooting my way.

"Hmmm." Her gray eyes narrowed as she watched our group's first elderly adventurer descend the schooner's ladder into the warm and incredibly blue sea. When the woman was shoulder deep in the water, our senior-age Sea Tracker guide lifted a seventy-pound dive helmet, complete with a really long air supply line, over her head and her owlish bifocals. He explained how to equalize ear pressure and then demonstrated the appropriate hand signals to use underwater, in the very unlikely event that she experienced problems like trouble breathing, sudden claustrophobia, or wet hair.

Marie turned back to me and, by the smirk on her face, I was sure she was thinking up her own uniquely expressive hand signal.

"Great," she said, "I just paid eighty bucks to helmet up like Buzz Lightyear, pull on a pair of rubber booties and take a slow walk in the water—following a waist-high safety chain. Hope my heart can take it." She snapped the shoulder strap of my jade racer-back swimsuit. "So where's Fedders?"

"Ummm," I said, scanning the other groups of Sea Trackers again, and basically stalling. Because the truth was that only minutes after we'd joined the large group of passengers boarding the ex-rum-running schooner transporting us to the diving platform, I'd begun to doubt that Kenyon's assistant was here at all. And, now that we were at the reef, I was almost 100 percent certain. Not that I had the nerve to confess that to Marie. Especially after the Buzz Lightyear crack. I was pretty sure now that it wouldn't help if I sprang for a souvenir photo.

"She's not here, is she?" Marie asked, groaning softly and pressing her fingers against her eyes. "Admit it. We've jumped onboard one of your overly-responsible crusades to try to …" she shook her head. "Remind me again why I'm not parasailing?"

"The Chop or Shop," I said, glancing for a second over my shoulder as I heard a vaguely familiar laugh. *Who … ?* I couldn't see the laugh's source, but it didn't sound like Barbara, blast it. I turned back to Marie. "I thought that if Barbara's read the manuscript pages, maybe I could schmooze her a little, get an idea of what was in store for Angela. And somehow prevent—" I whirled my head around, as that raucous, braying laugh split the air again. Sounded just yards away. A little nasal and sharp and … "Who is that back there?" I asked Marie, while trying to peer between two endangered flamingo tee shirts.

"Don't know. And we don't have time to find out." Marie gave me a little shove forward. "You're up, Buzz."

Wow. I was, and the next thing I knew I was pulling on a pair of blue diving booties and easing myself down the ladder into the reef cove, feeling the warm water lap against my thighs. A flower-scented breeze lifted a tendril of hair from my ponytail, and the sun warmed my shoulders … hey, pretty nice. I smiled up at our leathery and square-jawed instructor, thinking that even if it was corny and old-lady safe, this little excursion could actually be—

"Show me the shark signal, doll," the man said, reaching for the humongous white dive helmet. Oxygen hissed as he tested the line.

Library name: BRO

Date charged:
6/27/2014,15:58
Title: Gambit [DVD]
Item ID:
31035160461256
Date due: 7/7/2014,
23:59

TO RENEW
914-337-7680
914-674-4169
www.
westchesterlibraries.
org

Shark? I opened my mouth and stared up at the man, over at Marie, and then back at the man. "Shark?"

"Gotcha," the man said, laughing and exposing gold bridgework as he settled the huge helmet over my head. "Just kidding. Here you go. Just show me your distress signal, young lady, and you're good to go."

I stared back at him, through an expanse of bubble-shaped Plexiglas, feeling a lot like I was going for a ride in my grandma's old front-loading washing machine. It smelled faintly musty, and maybe a little like... *Cheetos?* No. Impossible. But, hey, I could breathe fine, my hair was dry and—I extended my arm, palm out and raised it like I was asking a question—I knew the diver's distress signal. Like the man said, I was good to go.

Our dive-instructor-slash-comedian gave me a thumbs-up and rapped his knuckles on my helmet. I descended the stair rungs, awkwardly tipping my helmet-heavy head back to grin up at Marie through the Plexiglas. Water droplets made her face look strangely wavy, but I was pretty sure she was smiling back and... *hey, that woman behind her looks sort of like*—A wave-swell raised the water to eye level, distorting my view and then the clear briny water closed in over my head.

Whoa, weird. I was on a space walk under the ocean. No, *better*, I was Jacques friggin' Cousteau! I waggled my fingers—comically magnified by the bubble glass—in front of my face, then planted my dive booties into the sugar-white sand and took a few surprisingly springy steps along our designated undersea track. I turned my head slowly side to side, expanding my view, and suddenly there were huge, craggy pillars of fiery-orange coral, clusters of pink-tentacled sea anemones, lacy purple sea fans, strange tubular neon green ... oh my gosh! This was *so great!*

I laughed out loud and the sound bounced around in my helmet as I turned—not easy in spacewalk slow-mo—to see if Marie was underwater yet. I swayed in place, holding onto the heavy-link guide chain, and squinted at the helmeted person following several yards behind me. Hard to tell ... nope. Not Marie's turtle-print Jams. Some woman in a red one-piece suit with skinny legs. Blast, she must have been sent in ahead of Marie somehow. Then I smiled as I caught sight of the familiar turtle Jams just beyond.

I held onto the chain and leaned outward to peer around the looming red-suit woman who was beginning to obscure my view. Marie flashed me an enthusiastic thumbs-up, and I raised my hand to do the same and—*hey, dammit, that woman's poking me?* I tilted my head backward ... too close to her now to see more than a pair of flaring nostrils and—*ouch!*

Her second vigorous nail jab answered my question and I turned quickly, bouncing a curse off the inside of my helmet as I moved on, and out of the red witch's reach. Some people had no patience, even on vacation. But, then, I guess I was holding up the line. *Ooh, man, fish!*

I inched forward grasping the chain, following the people in front of me; and despite the contentious woman behind me, was enthralled by the magic of it all. Yellow fish, striped with electric blue, hovered in place in front of my helmet, fins swirling as they curiously peered in at me, then darted away to be replaced in an instant by more. A long, thin one—bright purple with yellow fins and tail—glided lazily into view, then disappeared as a school of larger fish, flashing like polished silver, swept by. Then they turned in unison and changed direction again. Fins tickled my ankles and I giggled inside my helmet, the sound combining with the comforting hiss of infusing oxygen. About four people ahead of me, I saw a tour guide, in his own helmet, holding up what looked like a pink lobster, and I remembered that the brochure had said that there were also puffer fish and sea turtles and starfish. It was incredible and—even with dry hair—a true adventure.

Man, I wished I were closer to Marie, so I could see the look on her face. Because there was no way that she wasn't as thrilled as I was with this sea trek. Even if it started out as a scheme to get close to Barbara Fedders to try and do something about that damned Chop and—*oh, jeez, she's poking me again!* What was this woman's problem?

The pointy fingernail stabbed me from behind, and then a full set of fingers gripped the back of my arm. The hand squeezed hard enough to bruise, loosened, then slid down to my elbow, grasped my hip and fumbled down my thigh before letting go. What was this, an undersea grope? Completely pissed, I planted my booties and turned around and—*whoa*, what was wrong?

The woman was kneeling on the sand at my feet, obviously agitated, arms flailing like an octopus. I saw Marie let go of the chain and jog-swim forward, arms outstretched. She nodded her helmet up and down and we both sank to our knees beside the woman, sending a swirl of white sand drifting outward, clouding my view. I did my best to signal to our nearest comrades—raising my palm in that diver distress signal over and over—praying they'd get the guide or find the scuba diver overseeing our tour. Because, even though we were in barely ten feet of water, this woman could still be in serious trouble. People can drown in a bathtub, for godsake.

97

I reached through the gritty swirl and felt my hand connect with the woman's shoulder, then tried to catch her arm as she clawed at her helmet. Marie grabbed her other arm, and my mind ticked off a rapid assessment of the situation: helmet delivered more than three times the required oxygen, tubing was connected, helmet looked intact, her skin was pink and—*oh my God!*

I moved closer, staring wide-eyed through the bubble of Plexiglas at the face of the grabby, panicky woman in the red swimsuit. Theodora Kenyon.

EIGHT

WELL, HOT COCOA WASN'T going to ease the grouchy aftermath of Thea's panic attack, that was for darned sure—unless it came with a healthy shot of Jamaican Rum and a paper umbrella. The Sea Tracker team could learn a thing or two about resuscitation.

I patted the agent's damp shoulder with my polka dot beach towel and smiled my best nursey encouragement. "Feeling better now?" I asked, widening my stance as our brightly painted schooner rose, dipped, and continued its return to the dock. Somewhere up toward the bow, limbo music had begun in earnest and I had no doubt that Marie was first in line. You haven't lived until you've seen a woman hunker under a bamboo pole with a cigar pinched in her teeth.

"Better? Hmph!" Kenyon grumbled, frowning at the mini-marshmallows congealing on top of her chocolate. "Only if there's a Valium floating somewhere in this revolting shit." She shot me a withering look. "And only if you're *not a writer*."

"Me? God no—*swear*," I said quickly, crossing my heart and leaving a streak of coconut tanning lotion across the front of my swimsuit. But I was relieved to see that the agent had stopped trembling, and that her shoulders had relaxed an inch downward. Cocoa therapy aside, Thea Kenyon already looked far different than the woman I'd seen flailing and scrambling on the ocean floor twenty minutes ago. "Really. I can barely text message," I said, smiling sheepishly and blinking into the sun.

"Good." Thea tossed her Styrofoam cup over the side of the boat, and then brushed her fingers over her silver blonde hair; dry, per Sea Tracker guarantee. She frowned again and I noticed that her forehead remained Botox smooth; her phobias didn't include needles, obviously. She chuckled. "Glad to hear that. I was sure you'd written some seven-hundred-page, slobbering memoir that I'd be forced to take on because you saved my life."

"*Saved your*—oh, no," I said, raising my palms like I was stopping traffic. "Wait. I didn't do anything that big, Miss Kenyon. You had plenty of air and—" I stopped short when she poked me in the hip with a red-lacquered fingernail.

"It's *Thea*. And I panicked like a goddamm sissy, and you know it!" The agent growled and prodded me once more for emphasis. Her steel-gray eyes fixed on mine, then rolled upward as she sighed. "Whatever possessed me to let that moron put a glorified goldfish bowl on my head, when I'm too claustrophobic to ride in the back seat of a Manhattan cab ..."

"*Why* then?" I asked, trying not to wonder if Angela Skyler's manuscript was seven hundred pages long, or contained any puddles of slobber. And how ridiculously ironic it was to have been stalking this agent's assistant only to end up within poking distance of the Real Deal herself. Not that I'd have the nerve to discuss Angela with her, or tonight's Chop or Shop. No way. I'd rather limbo with a stogy in my lips. I raised my brows. "So why *did* you do the Sea Tracker Tour?"

"Good question." Thea hailed a deck hand carrying a tray of drinks and barked a mai tai order, then turned back to me. "It was *Barbara's* ticket," she explained with a heavy sigh. "She'd been yammering on about the stupid tour for days and then needed to run an errand at the last minute and had to miss it. Her own fault, of course." Thea repeated that creepy Botox frown. "I still can't believe she forgot to pack my spare battery pack. The one I'm using won't hold a charge for more than an hour—what am I supposed to do, go around looking for the damned electrical outlets?" She clucked her tongue and pointed a scarlet fingernail toward a line of palm trees and thatched roofs in the distance. "And that's exactly why I snatched her out of the line for this tour. She needs to find a new battery or get the damned thing repaired."

Jeez. I bit my lip before I could say that the chances of finding a computer repairman on this island were probably as likely as her own nomination for the Nobel Peace Prize. I watched her take a mai tai from the offered tray and began planning my exit strategy. There really wasn't anything more to talk about here. My nursing responsibilities were over, I wasn't a writer, and I was too much of a chicken-shit to bring up the subject of the impending workshop massacre. I'd chat a minute more, wish her Godspeed and ... "So you used her Sea Tracker ticket," I said idly, beginning to fold my dotted towel.

Thea laughed ruefully. "Seemed practical. I was already in line."

Riiight. I caught myself before I snorted since, according to Marie, the woman had elbowed her way through that line and squeezed in right up front. Which is how she'd ended up getting in the water behind lucky duck me.

Thea took a long swig of her umbrella-topped drink, then tilted her head and peered at me like she was seeing me for the first time. Her eyes widened. "Wait a minute. Now I remember. You're that *nurse.* Yes, Cavanaugh. The one who's teaching the murder class everyone's talking about." She took another sip of her mai tai, threw her head back and brayed like a rabid donkey. "Oh my God, I *love* it! The woman who saved my life is the same damned woman who inspired that *hit* on Carter Cantrelle's editor. Shit, is there any more poetic justice than this?"

Hit? I froze like a deer in headlights. *Everyone's talking?* I stared at the finger-poking agent with my mouth wide open. "Hold on a minute, Thea," I said, despite the fact that my stomach had started a limbo of its own. "Our workshop is in *no way* connected to Ellen's accident."

"Accident? Acci—*hee...haw...*" Thea's words dissolved into a second raucous donkey bray. I flinched and weighed the benefits of jumping overboard. Good Lord, what was going on here? I watched mirthful tears slide down the agent's face, and prayed.

"Surely you don't believe..." I began, holding my dotted towel in front of me like a shield.

"Wait." Thea Kenyon stood and wrapped an arm around my shoulders, splashing me with sticky droplets of fruit juice and rum. She smiled and her gray eyes glinted brighter than the steel on a chef's knife. "All I'm saying, my *dear* Darcy Cavanaugh, is that you

102

have my gratitude and I am in your debt. You saved my life today. Now what can *I* do for *you*?"

Do for me? *Oooh.* My mind whirled. I managed a smile and a few coy bats of my eyelashes. *Luke's mother, the Chop and Shop, and...* "Well, Thea, I don't know of anything that I really need, or—"

"Bullshit. Everybody wants something. You'll meet me for drinks tonight. And we'll talk," she said, downing the last of her cocktail and nodding like it was a done-deal. "I have a small block of time available after my appointments and before..." she did the wrinkle-free frown, "I have to crush the dreams of a half-dozen writers."

Crush dreams? "Hey, ya gotta do what you gotta do," I said, finally—sure that I was going to be struck by a righteous bolt of lightning. And then Theodora Kenyon pulled me against her in a conspiratorial squeeze. God. She gripped as good as she poked, and—okay—I'm *certain* that it looked to anyone watching like I was throwing in with the enemy, but...

I leaned against her and smiled. Because for the first time in days, I was now just as certain that I could save Angela Skyler's ass. Hell, maybe I'd even hoist that tushie onto the bestseller list after all. Who knew?

* * *

Marie insisted on wearing her *Let's Limbo, Mon!* tee shirt and her first-place medal to our murder workshop. From what I'd heard, there was plenty of video proof that even at forty-one and packing a few extra pounds—and while crooning "Day O" around a cigar—the woman was as agile as ever. I wished I'd been there, but I wasn't sorry that I'd spent my time schmoozing Thea Kenyon because, in the end, it was going to score me big points with Luke's mother. And with Luke. I was tingly already, just imagining how deliciously grateful the big guy would be. Meanwhile, Marie's fifteen minutes of celebrity had snagged us quite a few new workshop attendees. I rescued my nametag before it could slide from my rose-stripe tailored blouse and scanned the crowd.

"I hope I brought enough fake cyanide," I whispered, after Marie had handed out the last of my little jars of almond-scented potpourri. "I can't believe how many people showed up." I nodded my head toward the rear of the crowded room. "Even Carter Cantrelle again. She doesn't have murders in her books, does she?"

Marie shrugged. "Don't know, but her groupie's here, too." She nodded toward where Sarah Skelton sat sniffing a jar of potpourri. "Although maybe," Marie added, with grin, "she's transferred her loyalties to our cover model, instead."

It was true. Sarah, wearing a purple tube top and a short, flowered skirt, was sharing the poison—à la Romeo and Juliet—with a very attentive Keven Brodie. Apparently an afternoon ashore had eased the torture of not being able to have me. *Brother.* I rolled my eyes as he slid an arm around her sun-pink shoulders. Not that I was insulted by his quick turnaround, but public, tacky displays of—Marie nudged me toward the microphone. "Huh?"

"Oh, sorry," I said, shifting my gaze to where Vicky was waving her hand. "Question?"

"Yes," Vicky said, rising from her seat between Renee and Gertie. "How fast does cyanide work?" There was a rustle of paper as folks flipped through the pages of our handout.

"Depends on the type of contact," I answered. "Inhalation of powder or fumes is the fastest, but ingestion—drinking or eating the poison—can lead to impressive symptoms pretty quickly, too." I lifted an index card. "Weakness, confusion, bizarre behavior, and headache. It's similar to the effects you get from climbing a too-high mountain, where the air is thin. And, as we've shown you with those jars, the victim's breath smells of bitter almond." I moved aside as Marie joined me at the podium.

She nodded and leaned toward the mike. "What happens is that the cyanide stops the cells of the body from being able to use oxygen," she explained. "So an acute cyanide ingestion can have a dramatic and rapid onset. The victim is short of breath, develops heart complications, vomits, froths at the mouth, has seizures, and collapses." There was a crescendo of moans and "ughs," around the room, and Marie gave a quick, teasing smile. "Which is not nearly as ugly as falling on your ass under a limbo bar, folks."

I rolled my eyes and then took hold of the microphone again. "So that's the quickie review of what we've presented the past two days: choking, bludgeoning, suffocation, stabbing, and poison." I glanced down at the workshop schedules and then back out at our crowd, trying not to think about how many of them would attend Thea's event later this evening; *going "naked in public," to be chopped.*

I cleared my throat. "We want to leave time for you all to visit the vendor booths they've set up out in the foyer. Tee shirts, writing books, website designers ... very cool stuff; someone's even doing henna tattoos." I winked at Gertie. "If you ever wanted the likeness of Harry Potter down on your ..." I smiled. "Seriously, we'll take a couple more questions and then you're out of here. You'll have plenty of time for everything you want to do." I glanced toward Sarah just in time to see her squeeze Keven's thigh. No doubt in my mind what *she* wanted to do with her time. Maybe she'd "alter" a copy of the Kama Sutra for him afterward.

Marie took a last question regarding the symptoms of smoke inhalation, and then I started to gather my index cards and notebooks. I was anxious to get to my own "date," which involved far less sweat and heavy breathing than Sarah's, of course, but was not without its own pulse-sparking intrigue. Drinks with "Chop or Shop" Kenyon. It was going to be great.

* * *

Except that she arrived late. And was apparently sticking me for the tab.

"No problem, I've got it," I said, reaching for the drink ticket, after waiting innumerable moments for the "grateful-you-saved-my-life" agent to make her move. *Great.*

"Fabulous," Thea said, raising her mai tai and then waggling a finger at the Crow's Nest waiter. "And just keep Darcy's tab running, would you? I'll be having another one of these."

Hmm. Not that I'm one to exaggerate in order to toot my own horn, but it looked like I at least needed to get my money's worth here. I tugged a strap of my teal and blue sundress and then cleared my throat. A little reminder wouldn't hurt.

"So, no ill effects from your awful *near-drowning* this morning, Thea?" I asked, noticing, as she removed her jacket, that she was wearing the infamous "notched" leather belt. "The more I think about that, the more I realize that it was such a blessing that I happened to be there."

"What? Oh, *that*," Thea said, a small snort escaping through her nose. "No, I'm fine."

106

She glanced around the bar, nodded at several of the patrons, then turned back to me and drummed her fingernails—tickety-tick like a cab meter—on the tabletop, making it obvious that she had better places to be. "Now, what were we meeting to discuss?"

It was becoming fairly obvious to me why this woman received ugly threats. I took an orangey sip from my Cosmopolitan and smiled, undeterred. I was on a mission. "You told me, on the schooner this morning *after that awful incident,* that you wanted to 'do something' for me." I waited for a moment and tried again. "You insisted, actually. You said that since I'd saved your life, you owed me a favor."

Apparently I hit a nerve, because she suddenly leaned forward across our table and narrowed her eyes. "You're not a wri—"

"*Not* a writer!" I said so loudly that several heads bobbed upward at the bar behind us. Most of which, I'm sure, belonged to writers. *Jeez.* "Sorry," I said, lowering my voice. "I just meant that we already talked about this and, no, I'm not a writer. And, I do appreciate," I added, smiling as graciously as I knew how, "how pressured you must feel at conferences like this. The last thing I'd want to do is take advantage of your generosity by—"

"Enough prologue already," Thea said, poking her paper umbrella stick against my wrist. "Cut to the chase. What do you want from me?"

I hesitated while some wimpy seed deep inside me began to blossom into self-doubt and cowardice. What could I possibly accomplish with this, anyway? And why did I think I needed to protect Angela Skyler, when it was perfectly obvious that she could stand on her own two feet?

"Well, then," Thea took her second mai tai from the waiter and glanced down at her watch, "if there's nothing I can do for you, then I'll take my drink with me." She summoned that too-smooth frown and stood up, adjusting her infamous belt. "I've got to go make some notes before my workshop tonight. I need to look through those manuscripts and start dividing the chaff from the wheat, so to speak." A short, braying laugh escaped from her lips, and her hand made a little chopping gesture in the air.

"Wait," I said, quickly. "I *do* need something. A favor. For a friend." I took a quick gulp from my Cosmopolitan and then plunged ahead like some trembling Girl Scout hawking her first box of Thin Mints. "You see, she's my boyfriend's mother, actually. And, naturally, I wanted to make a good impression—I've never been able to do that with this woman—so I told her I could get her an appointment with you. And then, she decided to submit—" *Huh?*

I stopped short, realizing that I was babbling away to Thea's backside. She had whirled to peer at two beautifully dressed blonde women—almost like bookends in the bar's diffused light—who were entering through the Crow's Nest doorway. One was Carter Cantrelle, and the other was...

"Well, I'll be damned!" Thea said, sloshing her mai tai as she set it back down on the table. "If that doesn't make perfect sense." She turned back toward me and pointed over her shoulder. "Do you see that? It's Cantrelle with *that woman*. They look like goddamned twins!" She sneered and planted her hands on her hips and I could swear that one of her fingers was rubbing the notches on her belt. I tipped my head to see around her, to see who Thea was so fussed about, but...

"It's her, all right," Thea said, stepping aside and pointing again. "See?" I squinted and made out the two figures, backlit by the doorway. Carter and—

"It's that pushy *bitch* that tried to bribe me with the champagne," Thea snarled, just as I recognized the second blonde.

Angela Skyler.

* * *

I downed my drink—nearly choking on the lemon twist—and then breathed a sigh of relief that Thea had left without a confrontation with Carter and Anglea. I doubted it would be of comfort to her that their side-by-side appearance in the bar's doorway was simply a coincidence. Each woman had moved to opposite ends of the bar not long after the disgruntled agent made her exit. I was thinking of getting out of there myself—toying with the idea of hitting the gym, and its punching bag—when Barbara Fedders appeared from out of nowhere beside my table. Her shoulder was parrotless, her cheeks were flushed, and her eyes sparkled. *Sparkled?*

"Hi, Darcy." She smiled and reached for the chair that Thea had vacated. "May I join you?"

"Sure," I said, noticing that the change in this woman's looks likely had everything to do with a spa visit. She'd had the works. Hair, nails, facial, brows ... makeup, too—a deft stroke of blush across her cheekbones, carefully lined lips and lids. Even Barbara's suit was different from her usual pinstripes and drab navy; a dove gray jacket this time, with a shawl collar, mauve underpinnings, and a touch of lace. "Hey, you look *great!*"

"Thank you," she said, barely stifling giggle. "Big night tonight. Thea's workshop starts in less than two hours." She smiled and the gleam spread to her eyes. "I'm doing the oral presentations, reading the manuscript pages aloud. All twelve submissions. I've been practicing in front of the mirror to be sure that I give each writer's words my most…careful…" She paused and raised her freshly manicured fingertips to her throat and I could swear that I saw them tremble. Good Lord, this woman was dedicated. I mean, I already knew how she felt about "seeing dreams come true," but right now she was so wired she could topple off the damned podium. She needed a drink. Hell, I could use another one myself after that fiasco with her boss. I didn't want to think of what Thea might have in mind for Angela at the Chop or Shop. But then, wait…maybe I should. And since Barbara had read the entries, she just might be nudged into sharing a little insider information. *Hmmm.* Back to Plan A.

"How about a drink?" I asked, giving Barbara a reassuring smile as I reached into a small bowl of goldfish crackers. "I was going to order another one myself, and a drink might help you to sort of mellow out before your big event." I glanced around the crowded room and then back at the barstools packed shoulder-to-shoulder with patrons. Gertie—with her penis colada, no doubt—Keven and Sarah, Carter, Angela, Vicky, Renee, the Prices, and… "Merlot, right?" I asked, waving to a bar steward headed our way.

"Yes." Barbara lifted some crackers from the bowl and laughed. "I'm always the only person who doesn't have an umbrella in her drink. Boring, I suppose—but I stopped at the bar on my way over and ordered my merlot already…ah, he's got it right here." She smiled as the steward set the glass of wine down and then took my order. "And you're right," she said, laughing, "I probably do need to mellow out. It's been quite a day, although not as exciting as yours.

I can only imagine how panicky Thea got in that diving helmet, and how grateful she must have been for your help."

Yeah. Two mai tais' worth. Good thing she wasn't more grateful or I'd have to take out a loan. I nodded. "So did you get her laptop fixed?" I glanced toward the bar as Sarah and Keven's voices rose in a chorus of laughter.

"No, I got an extension cord." Barbara lifted her glass halfway to her lips and then set it back down and sighed. "And you can guess that she wasn't happy. But I did find the bath salts she wanted, and I'm just hoping…" the sparkle I'd noticed earlier came back into her eyes, "that she'll find a marvelous new client as a result of the workshop readings tonight. That's what Thea lives for, finding some talent that she can champion."

"And will she?" I asked, shifting in my chair as the steward set my cocktail down. I pinned Barbara with a look. "You've read the submissions; how many are shops and how many are chops?" I watched her brows lift and took a quick sip of my Cosmopolitan, determined to get my answer. "I mean, just between us girls, any big winners there? Or"—I wrinkled my nose—"any real stinkeroos?" I tried to look only casually interested, but something in this assistant's expression told me that she'd caught on. She was looking at me like I'd just asked her to dope a racehorse. "I mean…just curious, of course."

Barbara traced her fingertip along the rim of her wineglass and smiled slowly. "You submitted a manuscript, Darcy?"

"Me?" Why did everyone think I was a writer for godsake? After everything I'd seen aboard this ship, it was the last thing I'd ever want to be. "No." I sighed. "Okay, fine. I'm going to be honest with you, Barbara." I smiled and glanced toward where Angela sat at the far end of the bar. "My boyfriend's mother submitted some work. It all came about because of my bright idea." I groaned. "And now I'm sort of worried."

"That she'll end up as a notch on Thea's belt?" Barbara asked, shaking her head and smiling sympathetically. And exactly like she'd heard this worry a gazillion times before.

"Pretty much," I admitted. "And I thought that since you'd already read them, that maybe you could forewarn me, or…" I groaned again. This was hopeless.

Barbara hesitated for a moment and then reached over and patted my hand. "Okay, you didn't hear this from me. But what name does she write under?"

I opened my mouth, closed it, and scrunched my brows. "Name?"

"Pen name. Or does she use her real name? I would remember the entry by the title, or maybe by the writer's name. I assign numbers to the submissions, because Thea prefers not to know the writers' identity. She likes it all completely anonymous." Barbara lifted her merlot to her lips.

Anonymous chopping? Kind of a twist on those medieval executioners in the black hood. Jeez. But a title, pen name?

"I don't know," I said reaching for my own drink and lowering my voice to a moderate whisper. "Her real name is Skyler. Angela Skyler." I watched Barbara's face as she took a sip of her wine, grateful she hadn't recognized the name from that champagne bribe scenario.

Her lips puckered as if she were thinking. "Yes, I think I …" Her brows drew together.

"Or it could be her full name—maiden name, too," I offered, "Angela *Barrett* Skyler."

"Barrett?" Barbara asked, half-coughing and eyes suddenly wide. "Barr-rr—" she coughed again and then gagged, the purple-red wine, dribbling indelicately from the corner of her mouth. The wineglass tipped in her hands and her face went pale.

What the—"Barbara, what's wrong?" I asked, jumping to my feet as Kenyon's assistant set her glass down and began spitting into her napkin. She coughed again and sputtered, face red and eyes watering. I moved quickly to her side, thinking: inhaled cracker, choking, Heimlich Maneuver. She wasn't holding her hands to her throat in the universal choking signal, but—"Can you still speak?" I asked, realizing that several people had gathered around us. "Are you choking, Barbara?"

She looked up at me, eyes wide. "No, No, I'm sorry, it's just that something's wrong with this drink. It doesn't taste right. It's ... here," she explained, handing me the glass. "Smell it."

I lifted the glass to my nose. Sweet, cloying, and nutty almost ... *Oh. No.* I stared at Barbara Fedders. "Almonds?"

She stared back at me, the fear in her eyes intensifying with the rising rumble of voices around us, repeating "*almonds... almonds?*"

Then I dropped the wineglass as Renee shouted out loud, "Oh my God, it's cyanide!"

NINE

Barbara Fedders was a saint. I would've started swinging after that third medic leaned close, sniffed my breath and said, "Yep, almonds, all right. Feeling twitchy, lightheaded… *want to vomit*?" What was that, a frigging invitation? Marie and I had been standing watch at the foot of Barbara's infirmary bed so long now that *I* wanted to vomit. Of course, that might have everything to do with the dozen mystery writers huddled outside the door murmuring, "stabbing, cyanide… ooh, what's next on their outline?" Or the fact that we'd just learned that ship security was coming to interrogate us.

"Dammit, Marie," I whispered out of the side of my mouth after patting Barbara's foot for the umpteenth time. Thank heaven, she was showing no symptoms after a full hour of observation, except for the smudging of her spa-perfect makeup by the oxygen tubing and an understandable weariness of having everyone poke their noses in her mouth. I turned toward Marie. "You don't think security really believes we have anything to do with this, do you?"

Marie glanced to where Barbara's cardiac monitor blip-blipped in perfect sinus rhythm, seventy-eight beats per minute—as completely normal as her blood pressure readings, oxygen saturation, and initial toxicology screening. I knew full well that it was only because Marie had worked aboard this ship that we were allowed in here at all. Otherwise we'd be pacing outside with the inquisitive literary crowd. She tapped her open-toed Birkenstock against the wheel of the gurney a couple of times and then looked back at me with a shrug.

"What do you want me to say, Darc'? That it doesn't look suspicious that we were hawkin' cyanide?"

"*Potpourri—sshh*—it was potpourri!" I nodded my head up and down faster than Fedders's heartbeat as I glanced toward the lookylous at the door. "And plastic knives, toy baseball bat—props. They were just *props*. Try to remember that, okay? Big difference."

Marie ran her fingers through her short curls. "Ellen's bleeding foot was *real* and Barbara's drink *was* tampered with, and two people have ended up on these gurneys, babe. I don't know what security wants from us but," she glanced over at Barbara who seemed to be resting comfortably, "the good news is that Barbara looks fine." She smiled ruefully. "I think you remember—from a certain murder workshop—that the symptoms hit fast with that ugly poison. If someone had actually slipped her any cyanide—*uh oh. Heads up!*"

I turned toward the door in time to see the arrival of a uniformed security officer, the Crow's Nest bartender, a bar steward, and Theodora Kenyon. Kenyon? Great, what was *she* going to do, remind everyone about my "hit" on Carter Cantrelle's editor? I think I must have groaned out loud, because Marie nudged me with the webby toe of her Spider-Man sock. Fortunately, Thea wandered off in search of the medical staff, while we followed the beckoning trio of men to a corner of the infirmary.

The security officer, a fortyish man with huge shoulders and an oily Steven Seagal ponytail, immediately produced one of my ribbon-tied jars of potpourri. He was wearing too-tight latex gloves, and his other beefy hand held a Ziploc bag containing what appeared to be Barbara's shattered wine glass.

"Is this jar what you presented at your workshop, Miss Cavanaugh? Miss Whitley?" He removed the lid to sniff the dry, twiggy contents, and the ribbon slipped off the jar and fluttered downward to his huge steel-toed boot. My face flamed. For godsake, a *ribbon*? What was I, the Martha Stewart of Murder?

The security guy looked back up at us, raising his brows. "I understand that you used this to demonstrate the scent of cyanide poison."

"That's right, sir. Almonds." Marie nodded and stepped forward, planting her Birkenstocks and Spidey socks square in front of his boots, in a show of calm bravado. I could have kissed her. She crossed her arms, lifted her chin, and looked him directly in the eyes. "But both Darcy and I promise you that there is no connection—" She stopped and frowned as the bartender, also gloved, thrust a small, brown bottle just inches from her nose. Its label was partially torn away and the cap appeared to be missing. And—*oh boy*—I could smell the pungent odor of almonds from three feet away.

"And this?" The security man asked, his eyes scanning our faces. "Was this bottle also part of your presentation?"

Marie and I looked at each other, which—as anybody who watches *Law & Order* or *CSI* knows—is the same as confessing, and then we both started to babble at once.

"No, *no*," I said quickly, "never saw *that* before."

"We're *nurses*," Marie added quickly, "not felons, so maybe you need to check—"

"Hold it!" The ponytail man said, raising his big palm fast enough to send bits of potpourri sailing. "We're not accusing you ladies of anything. We're simply gathering facts." He glanced toward Barbara Fedders, who, I noticed, was now sitting in a chair beside the gurney and smiling, without the aid of oxygen tubing. Thea was beside her, tapping at her watch. "I'm only confirming some information about this bottle, which was found in a Crow's Nest Bar wastebasket. Empty." His tone softened. "Look, if it makes you feel any better, several people from your workshop confirmed that you didn't use a bottle of liquid for your demonstration."

"Then ... ?" I closed my mouth, not even sure of what I was asking. Mostly I was just hoping that the other ugly subject of injuries and weapons wouldn't rear its head. Too late.

"But the facts remain, ladies, that, directly after similar content in your workshops, there were thefts from the ship's galley, a knife injury, and now what appears to be an intentional—" He broke off and turned, as we all did, at a loud commotion at the doorway of the infirmary.

The crowd of Writers and Readers Afloat grumbled, as the galley chef, a small, wiry man with an apron, red bandana, and a Pillsbury Doughboy hat over long, dark curls, elbowed his way through. His eyes were wild as he sputtered something that had to be an Italian curse. He waved his fist as he marched forward, and I hurried to pull Marie a few safe steps back. *Now what?*

We watched as he reached for the little brown bottle and then cursed again as the security officer restrained his arm, warning things about "evidence" and "gloves" and "potentially dangerous exposure."

"Dangerous? What? You *fools!*" The chef bellowed, a vein standing out on his temple. "First you allow someone to steal my knives and pilfer my spice racks, and now you tell me I need *gloves* to recover my own precious bottle of *be-au-ti-ful*, imported Greek . . . almond extract?" He glowered and crossed his arms, his dark eyes closing to mere slits. "No more baklava for you!"

*   *   *

I was tempted to try Luke's Styrofoam cup / cabin microwave / macaroni and cheese idea, but Marie convinced me that ice cream was just as good an antidote for a cyanide scare. And I had to admit it was working. The Creamery Carib, on the Promenade Deck, consisted of a few tables with wrought-iron chairs, all gathered around a huge ceiling-high sculpture of monkeys' tails linked and holding colorful triple-scoop cones. All in honor of a glassed-in counter stocked with the requisite sweet, frozen cholesterol, of course.

The passengers were sparse, most of them still attending the seven o'clock theatre performance or hitting the bars for some liquid courage before Thea Kenyon's Chop or Shop. With Barbara's clean bill of health, that literary holocaust was still on the docket. And I was facing the fact that I'd accomplished nothing that would keep Angela's head from rolling. How was I going to help that woman?

I squeegeed another frigid spoonful of Mayan Chocolate across the roof of my mouth and watched Gertie tackle her banana split. I could see by the pile of shopping bags that she'd hit the Writers Afloat vendor booths in the corridor beyond us. I could also tell by the henna tattoo of Captain Jack Sparrow on her neck.

"Nice tattoo," I said, squinting against a jab of eye-freeze from spooning too fast. "I've seen quite a few people with them. Something for everyone, huh?" My fingers instinctively hovered over the real-deal shamrock on my left breast; trust me, it had taken far more than a pint of Häagen-Dazs to get me up onto that table in New Orleans.

Gertie's laugh ended in a faint wheeze. "Well, not for *everyone*, apparently." She pulled out her inhaler and took a quick hit. "That Southern-belle judge's wife had a thing or two to say about the kind of women who get tattooed. She was in quite a state."

My eyes widened and I felt Marie nudge me with her Birkenstock.

"Oh, yeah?" I said, easily imagining the holier-than-thou look on Angela's face as she'd made her pronouncement. But then Gertie didn't know my connection to Angela and I didn't want to embarrass her. I'd play along, no problem. "Pretty snooty, huh?"

"My guess would be more like scared spitless," Gertie said with a quick wink.

"Scared?"

"About Kenyon," Gertie explained, biting down on a maraschino cherry. "Mmm. 'Scuse me." She swallowed and daubed her lips with her napkin. "I was telling Angie about my appointment with her this afternoon—which went very well, by the way—and she told me she was doing the Chop or Shop tonight. Well, Vicky explained to her how it all works and ..." Gertie whistled softly.

I set my spoon down, knowing I'd been fooling myself that ice cream would make up for this mess of a day. Missing Barbara on the Sea Tracker Tour, rescuing Thea and then getting nowhere with her in the gratitude department, followed by that whole cyanide fiasco. And now the Big Chop. I might as well bare my tacky shamrock to Angela Skyler and kiss Luke goodbye.

"But I think I cheered her up," Gertie said with a nod. "We got to talking about grandbabies."

"Grandbabies?" I scrunched my brows. "She doesn't have any. Or, uh, so I heard. I mean, her daughters aren't married yet."

"Her *son's future* babies," Gertie said, smiling. "That's her big dream, 'a Skyler heir.' Guess all the men in that family have Roman numerals carved on their asses."

Marie kicked me again and I think I made a stuttering noise, but no words would come. I stared up at the monkey sculpture, pressed my palms over my ovaries, and tried not to panic. *Grandbabies? Heirs?*

Gertie laughed. "Tell you the truth, the judge's wife was talking horses at first, thoroughbreds, blood lines and breeding programs, and it took awhile for me to realize she'd moved on to her *son's* breeding program." Gertie's eyes widened with a wicked gleam that belied her age. "A strapping young lawyer. Saw his picture. Good God, now that's a *stud*! Blue eyes and dimples. He looks like that actor. You know, uh ..."

"Matthew McConaughey?" Marie offered, while dodging the toe of my Manolo.

"Yes, that's the one. Anyway," Gertie said, unsuccessfully stifling a yawn. "Angie's apparently on that grandchild quest like a bloodhound on scent. She's got it all scheduled out. The boy runs for Senate, wins by a landslide of course, and then gets hitched."

"Hitched to—" Marie stopped short as my shoe finally connected. I stared at my melting ice cream, letting this information whirl around in my head. Was it possible that Luke had said something to his mother about some upcoming plans? And maybe Angela was more accepting of me than I thought?

"No," Gertie said, reaching for her inhaler again. "I have no idea who the lucky girl's going to be."

The inhaler made a fizzy whoosh as she closed her lips around it and sucked inward. Then Gertie coughed and smiled. "Ah, much better. All I know is that Angela's fancy lawyer son got involved with some 'nobody' out in California, and now she's relieved as hell that he's back on the East Coast where he can find a 'proper wife.' She said she was going to see to it; has some Junior League former debutante all picked out." Gertie winked. "Tell you what, it didn't take me too far into that conversation to figure out that Thea Kenyon's met her match in Angela Skyler." She tossed the inhaler into her tote and began to gather her shopping bags. "So it looks like that whole mess with the almond flavoring was just a harmless prank, huh?"

"Uh huh ... guess so. Ah-hemm-mm." Marie mumbled and then cleared her throat. My guess is that she was trying to figure out the right thing to say to the tattooed *nobody* sitting stone-faced next to her—doubling up my fists like Rocky.

"Because everyone's just going on like nothing really happened," Gertie chirped with a quick nod. "Security has stopped questioning people. Barbara Fedders is fit as a fiddle." She stood, yawned again, and glanced at her watch. "And the Chop or Shop starts in a little over an hour. You ladies heading that way?"

Chop or Shop... Angela... "nobody"... Luke's heirs... Junior League debutante?

"No!" I said, leaping to my feet and smacking the table hard enough to make the monkey sculpture quiver.

I watched Gertie's eyes blink and then forced myself to take a breath and smile. "Oops, sorry about that. The fact is that I suddenly don't give a rat's ass what happens there."

* * *

I slammed my red leather Everlast against the gym's heavy training bag with a hook that sent it swinging sideways, and when it whirled back I hit it with a second hook and a stiff jab. *Oh yeah!* Sweat dribbled onto my lips and I sputtered, forcing myself to concentrate on the boxing combinations: One-two jab, straight right, left hook, right hook—*California nobody... the kind of women who get tattooed?* I shifted my weight and delivered a vertical uppercut and my dripping ponytail whipped against my neck. Take that, Angela Barrett Skyler! *Aagh.* As if I'd even *want* to reproduce her judgmental, clotted-cream-eating, stick-up-your-ass kind of genetic protoplasm. I jabbed the bag again, then jumped as someone tapped my shoulder from behind. I whirled, glove raised.

Marie raised her hands. "Yipes! Easy there, Cavanaugh, cyanide is way more subtle." She shook her head as she gave me the once-over. "You're sweatin' like a beast, kid; about done here?"

I lowered my gloves, glanced around the empty gym, and sighed. "Guess you knew where to find me."

Marie laughed and reached for the zipper of her fanny pack. "You mean, do I know where you go to let off steam?" She pulled out a cigar and pointed it at me. "Hell, that's a no-brainer. One of three choices: jogging the decks or punching the crap out of one of those bags ..."

"That's only two."

Marie smiled slowly. "Luke's not on board."

I groaned and pressed the smooth, padded bulk of the boxing glove to my forehead. "Oh God. Don't remind me."

"Hey," Marie said gently, picking at the cellophane on her cheroot. "Take off the gloves and let's go outside, so I can smoke. And give you the benefit of my vast wisdom."

I unlaced the gloves, patted my face with a towel; then followed Marie out the door onto the Sports Deck, smiling as I saw the flowered patch Carol had embroidered onto the butt of her faded Levis. The sun was finally gone and the breeze was just humid enough to remind me that we were only a twelve-hour sail from our next tropical port, Half Moon Cay. Good. If I didn't get off this ship soon, I'd wear out their punching bag.

I watched Marie flick her Volkswagen lighter, touch the flame to her cigar, puff-puff for a moment, and then take a long drag. She was quiet for a while before she looked at me out of the corner of her eye.

"Angela's wrong, of course," she said, exhaling and sending one of her perfect smoke rings to drift out over the teak rail. "You are anything *but* a 'nobody.'"

I tried to think of some cocky remark, but when I opened my mouth all that came out was a soft growl. I shook my head. "It's not really *what* Angela said, so much," I tried to explain, not entirely sure where I was going with it. "I guess it's just so frustrating, you know? Making the decision to invite her in the first place, pulling strings to get her that appointment, and then busting my ass to try and save her from Kenyon..." I adjusted my sports bra to cover the topmost leaf of my Mardi Gras shamrock. "I mean, she's Luke's mother, for godsake, so I felt like it was important to—"

"Get her to accept you?" Marie asked very softly.

I turned to peer at her through a haze of cherry-scented smoke, and knew she was about to go Yoda on me. "Well, I..."

"Look," Marie said, her gray eyes holding none of their usual teasing. "I've been with Carol going on eleven years now, right? We've bought a house, we share a dental plan, we host our neighborhood Fourth of July block party... and my mom still tells all her Bunco cronies that I live with this great guy named 'Carl.'"

Marie watched the orangey glow of her cigar for several seconds, and then sighed. "My dad's turning seventy in November. Mom's throwing this big party. I know that if I go, I'd have to go alone. She keeps calling to see if I'm coming, and I've been avoiding the calls and..." Marie shook her head. "I wish it were different. But it doesn't make what Carol and I have together any less special. You know?"

I struggled for something to say, but before I could, Marie blinked a couple of times and the impish twinkle returned to her eyes. She gave me a little jab with her denim-clad elbow and did her best Jedi Master nod. "You, kid, are the *somebody* that Luke loves. He's wild about you *and* your banshee tattoo. Screw the Judge's wife!"

I laughed and slid closer, slipping my arm through hers. "Not necessary," I said, lifting my hand to peer at my dangling charm watch. "Thea Kenyon's going to do it for me. The Chop or Shop's starting in thirty minutes."

Marie raised her brows. "Tempted to go watch? Or you wanna hit the casino with me? The Prices are doing an art demo there—I want to catch it."

I looked at her like she was nuts. "Art? Since when are you interested in painting?"

Marie grinned. "Not paint. My man Bill is a *metal* sculptor—you gotta love any art that involves a hammer and blowtorch." She nodded her head. "You game?"

"Sure," I said without hesitation. "Definitely. And I'll buy the first round of drinks. We're celebrating, after all."

"Celebrating?"

"Sure," I said watching a second smoke ring rise in the humid darkness. "Our workshops are over, we'll get to soak up some island sun, and all that crap about the knife and cyanide turned out to be nothing but stupid-ass pranks. We're in the clear!"

We stopped in the gym to grab my gloves and bag, and then took the glass elevator that would get us back down to our cabin on G-Deck. I picked up my pace as we passed through the pink-carpeted foyer to follow the starboard cabin corridor. I'd take a quick shower, change my clothes—maybe wear my jeans skirt and that lime crochet tank and beaded shrug—and then we'd hit the casino. Watch the sculpture demo, then do some serious gambling. Hell, I cut my teeth on blackjack chips, might as well take advantage of it. And then we could stop by the Purser's office and pick up our tickets for the Stingray Adventure tomorrow and—*whoa!* I barely stopped in time to keep from running into the back of Marie. She'd halted abruptly about ten cabins down from ours, cocking her head to the side.

"What's the matter?" I asked, peering around her to see.

"Smell that?" She asked, taking a step forward. "See what I see?"

"Hey!" I shouted as Marie took off down the carpeted hallway at a run.

And then I saw what she was talking about, and started running myself.

Smoke? Oh God, it *was* smoke! A narrow black stream of it, curling upward from a cabin door. I picked up my pace, sucking in a mouthful of acrid, sulphurous fumes as my eyes began to water and sting. Good Lord, what was causing this? Where was it coming from?

I heard Marie shout, just as the fire alarm began to shrill overhead.

"It's Gertie's cabin!"

TEN

I COULD BARELY SEE Marie through the smoke, let alone make out the cabin number in front of us. How could she be sure it was Gertie's? I coughed and blinked my eyes, then yelled over the screeching alarm. "Are you sure … this is … Gertie's?"

"Yes, *look*!" Marie nudged me and pointed toward the bottom of the door, where the smoke hugged the carpet in wispy thin layers, and at a pink-feathered slipper wedged there. "Remember? Gertie props the door open when she naps. Shit, Darcy, she's *in there*!"

"Oh my God!" I whipped my head around to peer down the smoky corridor, making out a few heads peering out from the cabin doors, but no stewards. I flattened my palms against the door, testing for heat, nodded an "okay," and then Marie pushed it inward with her shoulder.

"Gertie!" I yelled as smoke billowed into our faces. No heat, no flames visible, thank God, but—"Gertie, are you in there?" I shouted again, following Marie inside. It was dark, suffocating, impossible to see.

"Damn," I cursed, smacking into a bed frame as Marie yelled for Gertie again. I stumbled on, wincing against the shrill screech of the smoke detector. I could faintly see the floral privacy curtain in front of us, dividing the second bed from...wait, was that Gertie's voice? There were raspy attempts to call out, fits of coughing. I struggled to see through the smoke and prayed I wouldn't see flames. "There, Marie—pull that curtain!"

There was another choked cry, followed by a paroxysm of coughing, and Gertie lurched forward through the smoke, just as we were doused with something cold and wet from overhead. Water? Oh jeez, the fire sprinklers and...*aagh!* Water sprayed onto my arms, head, face, and into my eyes as I moved forward waving my arms until, finally, my slippery hand connected firmly with Gertie's. Voices, then shouts, erupted from the corridor beyond and then flashlight beams sliced the smoky darkness.

"Got you!" I said, slipping an arm around Gertie's waist and propelling her forward. She was shaking, and I could feel the outline of her ribs against her water-soaked blouse. Her chest wall vibrated with her wheezes as she struggled to take in air. "Don't try to talk, Gertie, just follow me." I turned back. "Marie, you okay? You're coming?"

"Right behind you," she yelled. "I'm grabbing the oxygen and nebulizer. Get her out into the hallway. I've got it all now. Go!"

I hugged my arm tighter around Gertie and blinked first against the sprinklers, and then against sudden brightness as the overhead lights flicked on. We pushed our way through a clutch of extinguisher-wielding ship staff and lurched out into the hallway, then hustled down the corridor and out of the smoke.

Within two minutes, I had Gertie sitting on the carpeting outside our open cabin and taking a puff on her inhaler, while we watched for the medical staff. Marie quickly adjusted the flow on the oxygen tank and then plugged the breathing machine into an outlet just inside our door. I threaded the green plastic tubing gently over Gertie's ears and fitted the soft prongs into her nostrils, giving her a reassuring smile. I was glad to see that her skin and lips were pink despite her obvious distress. A moment later, and just as the infirmary medics began jogging down the corridor, Marie snapped open a plastic vial of albuterol mix, squirted it into the nebulizer chamber, and started Gertie's first breathing treatment. Our patient sighed and relaxed a little, leaning back against the corridor wall. The medication and saline mix bubbled and fizzed with an infusion of compressed air, the comforting sound at odds with the continued screech of the overhead smoke alarms.

I tossed Marie a look over the top of Gertie's snowy-white head and she smiled ruefully, reading my mind. Yep, we might as well have packed our hospital scrubs instead of cruise wear this trip and—oh jeez. I raised my brows as the ship's staff arrived beside us, and Marie nodded. She saw what I saw.

Directly behind the medical staff was that big guy from the security team. The one who'd questioned us about the cyanide. My stomach plummeted as the truth struck me. *Smoke inhalation.* That was the last thing we'd covered at our murder workshop.

*   *   *

Marie was right about the casino: blackjack, roulette, and craps were the perfect way to take our minds off the conversation we'd just had with that security goon. I still couldn't believe he thought *we* could have slipped that huge smoke bomb into Gertie's wastebasket. A publicity stunt to promote our workshop? His theory didn't even make sense because we were being compensated by way of a free cruise, not by registration money. And, because today's session was our last, there were no more audiences to "entice" anyway. What the steel-toed flatfoot *ought* to be doing—and trust me, I told him so, much to Marie's angst—is looking for some pimply prankster who shopped at those Texas firework stands. You could buy big-ass smoke bombs, firecrackers, Roman candles, things you'd go to jail for owning in California. My brother, Willie, always had a nice stash—from Mexico via Texas to a sandwich bag hidden in his sock drawer. Not that I told the security guy that, of course.

But the good news was that Gertie was fine, we'd survived the questioning, and although we'd missed the sculpture demo, we were having a pretty good time in the Treasure Trove Casino. My luck at the tables was phenomenal. Amazing, considering that there was a maniacal parrot peering over my left shoulder. I jumped as I felt Artie's wing brush against the back of my neck again. I turned to-ward the now familiar silver-haired port lecturer holding him, and tried to smile.

"I ... I'm not really comfortable with Artie quite so close," I said, after polishing off the last chip in my third plate of nachos. I raised my voice above the chink-chink of tokens tumbling from the silver-and-neon rows of slot machines. "And isn't he supposed to be wearing that beak bauble?" I took a wary step backward, flat-tening the butt of my jeans skirt against the blackjack table. The bird was ogling me, for godsake.

"*Bubble*," Herb Dugdale corrected, glancing affectionately at the creature preening on the shoulder of his flowered shirt. The man smiled and his tidy moustache stretched like a silver caterpillar. "They're called beak bubbles and, as an ornithologist, I have to say that I'm not a big fan of them." Herb reached up and stroked the parrot's cheek with his fingertip.

"Ooh, be careful." I sucked air through the space in my teeth, wondering how I'd jerry-rig a finger tourniquet when that evil bird bit off the end of—*wow, he didn't.* Artie didn't bite Herb. He didn't even cuss. *Unbelievable.* I think my mouth dropped open.

"See?" Herb said, chuckling. "Artie can be quite sociable when he's not stressed."

I took the Long Island iced tea offered by a passing waitress and smiled despite my misgivings. This retired Dr. Doolittle had been the subject of quite a bit of buzz from the senior women aboard, Gertie included. I had to admit that he *was* pretty charming. I took a sip of my drink and watched the seventy-something man whisper to the bird, beak to beak. In profile, the two looked strangely alike.

"Yeah," I said, "Barbara told me that traveling upsets Artie so much that the vet prescribed sedatives. I had no idea there *were* birdie 'downers.'" I shrugged. "I'll be honest with you, Dr. Herb, I'm not much of a pet person. I have trouble keeping my grandma's old goldfish alive."

Herb nodded, his bright eyes not in the least bit judgmental. "Not everyone has the patience. Or the time." He smiled. "That's why I offered to watch this old fellow. Otherwise he'd spend the evening in the cabin, picking out his feathers and worrying. I've already taped my lecture for tomorrow, so I have plenty of time to bird-sit. Barbara wanted to take care of a few things before she went on to Miss Kenyon's workshop."

Chop or Shop. My stomach rebelled against the nachos, and if I'd had feathers I would have yanked a few myself. Half the reason I'd followed Marie to the casino was to keep my mind off of Angela's impending slaughter at the hands of Theodora Kenyon. Even if she'd called me a "nobody," it still was hard to imagine Luke's mom on the chopping block. Where was Marie, anyway? I glanced toward the craps table next to us. The only familiar faces were Sarah Skelton and Keven Brodie. The cover guy looked gorgeous as ever, of course, in a white linen shirt and snug jeans, his dark hair shower-wet and combed back. All of which was being fully appreciated by our Reader Afloat.

"I'm keeping you from your friends," Herb said. "I'm sorry. Artie and I will mosey along now, young lady."

"Oh, no," I said quickly. "Really, I was just looking for Marie. Don't run off."

"Well," Herb said, his cheeks flushing. "The fact is, that we're going to go play some pinochle with Gertie. Keep her company. She had quite a scare earlier. Of course, you know that better than anyone." He reached out and patted my arm. "You were quite the heroine, I heard."

Before I could protest, Herb's silvery brows scrunched. "Do you really think these incidents are pranks? The chef's knife and the cyanide scare? And now Gertie?" He shook his head. "I hate to think of what might have happened if you and your friend hadn't found her."

"I..." I looked into the old gentleman's face and my heart squeezed unexpectedly. Maybe there was something about his eyes that made me think about my grandma, or remember the countless elderly patients I'd seen who had been admitted after falling victim to malicious abuse. I turned as a loud whoop and round of applause distracted me.

Keven Brodie swept Sarah up in his arms and swung her around as the other craps players hooted and applauded. I had no doubt that if the cover model had access to his sword, he'd have been twirling it over his head like that guy in *Braveheart*. Apparently he'd gotten lucky in more ways than one. I turned back to Herb Dugdale, noticing that Artie was treading anxiously in place on his shoulder, head tipping side to side and then sort of upside down. A guttural hum rumbled low in the bird's throat.

"Look, Dr. Herb," I said honestly, "I don't know whether all of those incidents were random, or if they were somehow related. But as Marie and I explained to the security team, the only reason that we presented those crime methods was to aid the research of fiction writers. It was never our intent to have our murder workshop be used as some sort of *guide* to actually *harm* people or ..."

My voice faded off as I watched the ornithologist's brows raise and then I realized what I'd just said. Had I really said that? That I thought someone *was* using our workshop outline to scare people? Threaten people maybe, hurt them, or even ... I thought of Gertie's raspy breathing, her painful struggle for air. *Kill them?* Oh God, was it possible that Marie and I had actually had a part in—there was a sudden loud screech from the PA system overhead, and then a microphone clicked several times. Artie lifted his wings and fanned the air, partially obscuring Herb's face as the page finally blared overhead.

"*Security, please. Security Team B report to the Pirate's Annex Conference Room, Promenade Deck. Security, please.*" The PA screeched again and I turned to see that Marie had arrived beside us. She was puffing and a little breathless.

"Did you hear that?" She asked, after shooting a wary glance at the clearly agitated parrot. "It sounded like they said the Conference Room—" she stopped short and then stared, along with me, at Artie as his voice erupted.

"*Daaamn it to hellll!*" The bird garbled low in his throat. "*Shiiit. Aawwk!*"

"Oh dear. Pardon us," Dr. Herb said with a sheepish smile. "So sorry."

Marie turned back to me just as the page repeated overhead, louder this time:

"*Security needed. Conference Room C. Pirate's Annex, Promenade Deck.*"

"See? They *are* paging for that room, Darc," Marie said, staring overhead and then back at me.

"Conference Room C?" I asked, confused. "What do you mean?"

"*Goddamn hack,*" Artie screeched, "*Ya write shit! Shiiit. Flush it, flush it! Aawwk!*"

Marie grabbed my arm, her gray eyes wide. "That's where..."

"Oh no," I said, shoving my blackjack chips into my skirt pocket and grabbing my purse. "You're right. That's the Chop or Shop. Let's get over there!"

We took off at a jog, Artie's scream fading barely a decibel as we left him behind us.

"*Re-jeck-ted, re-jeck-ted... aawwk! Gimmee a daaamned mai tai!*"

* * *

The Pirate's Annex Conference Rooms were on the same deck as the casino, but aft and all the way to the stern, which is a pretty decent jog when you're wearing three-inch JLo wedges and your skirt pockets are bulging with casino chips. But we made it there in time to see the security staff escorting a man—whose godawful fumey breath gave me an instant ER flashback—out from the open doors of Thea's workshop. We heard loud cheers and then applause explode from inside, but the forty-something drunk was still waxing poetic despite the burly security officer on each of his arms.

"Ye-ea-ah, well, what all you women *need* ish-sh a *real* man in your beds!" he shouted back over his shoulder. "Then you would-d-n't haff the time to write all that ro-man-tic *crap*. All I wa-sss trying to do, was o-ff-fer my servi-shes." He struggled against the officers and threw his head back laughing. I pulled Marie back a few steps. "Oh, wait. I get it," he cackled as they finally propelled him down the carpeted corridor, "you're all god-damned *les-sh-bians!*"

I shot Marie a look and grinned. "Hey, he's makin' that look pretty good to me." I nodded toward the open doors. "Want to have a peek inside and—" I stopped short as Renee appeared at the doorway and beckoned to us.

"C'mon in," she whispered, "there's a couple of seats next to me." She shook her head, smiling. "You should have seen Barbara Fedders handle that drunk. Man, she's great." She waved her hand again. "C'mon. Thea's finishing up the last few submissions. Only a few paltry flesh wounds so far."

We followed her through a doorway decorated with crossed pirate swords and into the conference room, then settled down into fabric-covered folding chairs arranged in half circles around a single-step stage and a podium. I noticed, right away, that Thea's laptop, sitting on her presentation table, was plugged into an outlet via a long extension cord. But otherwise, it looked like things were all-systems-go with the Chop or Shop.

Barbara, in her gorgeous suit and obviously cyanide-free, held the microphone and smiled warmly at the assembled writers. Theodora Kenyon, holding a red thermos and wearing the notched belt over a sharp black jersey pantsuit, stood behind a wooden chopping block, sporting a huge stainless steel ... meat cleaver?

"Oh my God," I whispered, staring in disbelief. "She actually has a cleaver?"

Renee nodded and laughed. "Great, huh? There's been a digital photo of a cleaver on her Chop or Shop blog for months, and what *fun* that she arranged to have this one set up just for us!"

I looked sideways at Marie and back at Renee, wondering anew about these nutso literary folks. *Fun?* If chopping blocks were fun, then what were razor-sharp chef's knives, cyanide scares, and smoke bombs? Disney World? Maybe Marie and I made one *huge* mistake in agreeing to this workshop gig.

"Look," Marie whispered, as Thea led one last round of applause for the security team's handling of the heckler. "There's Angela, right up front."

She was; sitting a few chairs down from ... Carter Cantrelle? Kind of surprising to see her here. I switched my gaze back to Angela. She was wearing that great oyster-gray Chanel, and her eyes were riveted on the huge projected screen behind Thea Kenyon. Her anxiety was obvious, and I had no doubt about the cause of it. The titles of the remaining three manuscript submissions were projected in foot-tall letters: *Bare-ly Legal, My Garden Gone Wild,* and *Last Dance Last Chance.*

I looked from the screen to Angela's face, to Barbara, who held the submitted papers, and then over at Kenyon, who had begun to smile eerily over the rim of her red thermos. I scanned the chairs holding maybe sixty people. Who was on that chopping block besides Luke's mother? And which title was Angela's? My pulse kicked up a notch and I wiped my clammy palms across the side of my skirt, sending a casino chip clattering to the floor.

"I don't think I can take this," I said to Marie as Barbara stepped up to the microphone. "Maybe I'll go now. I should write a postcard to my grandma, or—"

"Shh, please," Renee said, leaning forward as Barbara began. I sank down in my chair, gritted my teeth, and tried to pretend that I was anywhere else.

I think I was actually holding my breath until Barbara got to the sentence about a nude, shape-shifting dominatrix-turned-space cop...and then I relaxed. *Bare-ly Legal,* though wonderfully read by Fedders, could have absolutely nothing to do with Angela Skyler. Even if her only son was a federal agent—kind of a cop—nudity was not her thing. And I soon noticed that this particular work of fiction was not Thea Kenyon's thing, either. Obviously. *Oh jeez.* Was she really picking up that cleaver? And saying...*oh man.* I grimaced and resisted the urge to cover my ears. No way I could be a writer; this was way beyond feeling naked in public. This was abuse. I tried to catch the look on Carter's face, but no luck.

"And," Thea continued, after stopping to take a big swig from her red plastic thermos. "Word of wisdom, my little Choppees? Just because you're sending me something about damned green...space aliens, doesn't mean you can use formatting from some other frickin' galaxy!" She took another sloppy swig from her thermos, walked a few swaying steps toward the giant screen, and waggled her fingers at it. "Good God, what *is* that? Baby-shit-colored Crayolas in Wingding font?"

I grimaced and stared at the back of Carter's immobile head. But Thea wasn't finished.

Kenyon whirled back to face her audience and nearly stumbled over the laptop extension cord, sending the notched belt sliding sideways around her narrow hips like a hula-hoop. She wiped at the front of her pantsuit where her thermos drink had spilled, and made her way awkwardly back toward the chopping table. Her nose and cheeks were red, eyes bleary.

I looked sideways at Marie with my best *you thinkin' what I'm thinkin?* look.

"Whoa," she said, dark brows scrunched. "What's in that thermos?"

"Comes with an optional paper umbrella. Bet you ten bucks," I whispered, starting to have a very bad feeling. Especially when I saw the reaction of Angela Skyler: arms crossed, back rigid, and eyes narrowed. There was no doubt in my mind that the Judge's wife was on to what was powering Theodora Kenyon. And it was pissing her off. She was, after all, the woman who'd tucked notes about morals, etiquette, and decorum into her college-bound son's suitcase. She wouldn't sit back and condone public drunkenness and—*Oh Lord*. I gasped as Angela began waving her hand in the air.

"Uh-oh," Marie whispered, giving me a sideways look. "What's she doing?"

"I ..." My words faded away, as I watched Barbara Fedders catch sight of Angela, raise her brows, and then shake her head with an obvious dismissal and a barely discernable frown.

She took the thermos from Thea's hand, set it on the chopping block, and picked up the microphone, smiling brightly and summoning a laugh. I'd bet ten more bucks that she'd done this before. Plenty of times. I glanced back toward Angela and caught a glimpse of Carter Cantrelle ... and maybe a flash of a smirk on her face.

"Good point, of course, Thea," Barbara said quickly. "And all joking aside, formatting is important." She touched the lacy neckline of her blouse and glanced over at the agent, who'd picked up the thermos again. "Our writers' guidelines are posted on the agency website, but ..." her eyes darted toward Kenyon again, "I brought some printed handouts. Just contact me after the—"

"Next!" Thea barked, interrupting. "What's next? We don't have time for handholding if we're going to finish." She straightened her belt and peered out at the audience. "You came here for critiques, right?" She raised her hands, beckoning to the crowd. "Am I right?"

There was a hesitant smattering of applause, which gradually increased, and then someone near the front called out, "Chop or Shop! Let's do it, Thea!"

Barbara shuffled her papers. Angela's hand shot up. I gritted my teeth.

"Excuse me," Angela called out, "but perhaps it would be best to end this now?"

"No," Barbara said quickly, cutting her off. "No comments, *please*." She picked up the next chunk of manuscript papers. Thea raised her thermos. *Oh jeez.* I squeezed Marie's arm as Angela stood.

"Miss Fedders, I have to insist that this workshop end at this time. It feels most inappropriate to continue, considering—"

"No," Barbara warned, grasping the microphone. "Please sit down."

"I'm sorry, but I must object to—"Angela repeated, raising her voice.

"*Sit!*" Barbara shouted, inducing the microphone to send a deafening screech across the room. "Sit *down, Miss Barrett!*"

My jaw dropped. The crowd murmured. Angela gathered her purse and marched along the wall toward the back of the room as Barbara hit the computer keyboard to project the opening page of *My Garden Gone Wild.*

I think I was stunned. Yes, I *know* I was, because I barely heard Barbara's reading of the next manuscript or much of Thea's half-slurred remarks. I kept my eyes on the back wall of the conference room where Angela stood just yards beyond me, occasionally looking up while making calls on her cell phone. At one point she stepped outside the door, and I saw her speaking with a security person while pointing back toward the conference room. I was sure that she was complaining about Thea's behavior but, frankly, I was glad she'd stepped out since I was fairly sure that one of these last manuscripts was hers. Written under the pen name of Barrett, obviously, since Barbara had just screamed it out to the whole crowd. So much for anonymity. But at least Thea, if obviously snockered, wasn't intent on spilling blood at the moment.

But it all changed when Barbara read the second page of *Last Dance Last Chance.*

My first clue was the ear-splitting whack of the cleaver.

ELEVEN

THEA WHACKED THE CHOPPING block a second time, and I thought that Barbara Fedders was going to faint. Her face and lips went fish-belly white, and her skin, in the glare of the overhead lighting, glistened with what I'd bet was clammy-cool perspiration. She lifted the slim stack of manuscript papers and held them against the front of her jacket, eyes on her employer. I was pretty sure that her hands were trembling.

"Wait, wait. Read that last page again, Barbara," Thea ordered, pointing the cleaver first at Barbara and then swinging it in a dramatic arc toward the assembled writers. She smiled with what looked like smug satisfaction. "I've just had an *epiphany!*" She reached for her thermos, waited a moment, and then frowned at Barbara. "Read? *Now?*"

I nudged Marie and scrunched my brows, wondering if she was as worried about Barbara as I was. The assistant's face wasn't as white as it was a moment ago, but there was still something so vulnerable, or maybe just hopelessly tired, about the look in Barbara's eyes. For godsake, it was understandable. How many years had she been running interference for this high-visibility bully?

"No worries," Marie said softly, "Barbara's a trooper. See, she's getting it together now."

She was, thank God, and I felt a new rush of admiration for the woman as she turned back to the previous manuscript page and prepared to read it again. A soft click made me turn, and I saw Angela slip back into the room to stand against the wall behind me. I tried to catch her eye, but she seemed to be completely absorbed in the unfolding melodrama.

Barbara cleared her throat and smiled. She glanced for a second toward the projected page on the screen behind her, neatly typed paragraphs that looked darned perfect to me. She began reading from *Last Dance Last Chance* with such practiced and sensitive inflection and fluidity that she sounded more like an actor than a reader. Even to my untrained ears, the passage sounded beautiful, compelling. Impressive, really. I saw Carter Cantrelle smile and nod her head, so maybe my impression was right on the mark. Then I glanced around the rest of the audience, and covertly over my shoulder at Angela, thinking that whoever had written this submission should be damned pleased with the way Barbara was presenting—

"*Enough!*" Thea screeched, pointing the cleaver again. "Stop right *there!*" She crossed her arms and I grimaced, wondering if she were going to accidentally hack into her own elbow. "Did you *hear* that?" she asked of the crowd. She frowned when there was no response and then stepped close to the edge of the stage, within a few yards of Carter Cantrelle. "Well, Choppees? Have I taught you *nothing*?" She pointed her cleaver to acknowledge a woman's raised hand.

"Um, 'passive voice'?" The woman asked tentatively, and then flinched back into her chair as Kenyon's voice exploded again.

"Passive? Oh God, that's rich! How about frickin' *wimpy*? How about worthless?" She laughed. "How about the egotistical *balls* of someone to think that because they can string a few vignettes of … slobbering, self-indulgent college memories together that it will become a book that anyone would want to actually *read*?"

Thea strode to the chopping block and slammed the cleaver into it with a loud thwack, leaving it lodged upright. And then she crossed her arms and laughed again, looking directly at Carter Cantrelle. My stomach sank to my sandals. "Not that *some people* aren't making the New York lists with that kind of tripe. I still don't understand that one."

Somehow, Carter remained expressionless, despite that ugly reference to her work. She was amazing. But there was no way I could summon the courage to look back at Angela; this *had* to be her manuscript and she must be dying of humiliation. All I could think of was getting the hell out of here. I took one look at Barbara's face—frozen and immobile—and knew she was thinking the same thing. But I saw her move toward the microphone in what had to be one of her well-practiced attempts at intervention. Thea was having none of it.

"Do you realize," Kenyon said, pressing her fingers against her forehead, "how many times I'm forced to read this kind of thing? For how many years?" She took a step forward and wobbled a little. "For crissake, people," she pleaded, "can you at least be *original*?" She pointed toward the screen and shook her head. "I could swear I've read this *same* damned story a dozen times—" she stopped, eyes wide, as Angela Skyler began to shout from the rear of the room.

"Stop this now!" the Judge's wife ordered, smacking her cell phone, gavel-like, on the top of an empty chair. "How *dare* you do this! Do you think you can get away with promising to *help*, only to engage in nothing short of vicious *slander*? Do you really think you can get away with that?"

The crowd began to rumble and whisper, some rising to their feet, but Angela continued, despite the fact that two of the security officers had slipped through the door behind her. One of them reached for her arm and she brushed him off. I slid from my chair and made my way quietly toward her.

"I'm promising you," Angela shouted again, "that I *won't* let you treat writers this way ever again. Other agents don't, and you have no right to." She pointed her cell phone like a sniper taking aim. "I'll use every influence I have, do everything possible to see that you are stopped, even if I have to—" Angel halted mid-sentence, and I wasn't sure if it was because the security man had taken one of her arms, or because I was tugging on the other one. All I knew was that she did stop and managed a very polite smile at the man, nodding as he dropped her arm. And then she turned to me.

"I'm finished with this dreadful farce, Darcy. Will you leave with me?"

"Uh, sure," I said, after glancing toward the stage one last time. Thea Kenyon was calmly coiling the extension cord of her laptop and putting it away. Barbara Fedders was gone. The crowd had begun to file toward the front exits. I gave a little nod to Marie. "Absolutely," I said to Luke's mother, summoning a smile. "Maybe a nice cup of tea would help."

"Tea?" Angela Skyler looked at me like I'd lost my mind. Then she laughed and reached for the door. "I'm drinking Jack Daniels— neat. Think you can keep up?"

*   *   *

An hour later, I wasn't sure that I *could* "keep up." Luke's mother was certainly no Baptist.

We'd made a mutual decision to avoid the Crow's Nest Bar— Angela because she "couldn't abide the sort of spineless, lily-livered attitude of people who tolerated unadulterated abuse by that arrogant, tacky, rum-swilling Yankee agent." And my decision was based on the fact that I didn't want to risk her repeating that ugly mouthful in public. Obviously.

So we'd plopped ourselves onto navy poplin chaise lounges on the deck outside the Crow's Nest, far enough away that we didn't have to hear the Chop or Shop postmortem gossip. And close enough that the bar steward could "keep them coming, darlin.'" Which he did. And which Angela, unlike a nameless rum-swilling agent whose life I'd saved, graciously paid for. And now, an hour into our soiree, I didn't know for sure who was more swacked; but I did know Jack Daniels better than I did before. Way, way better. *Lord.* I had tickets for the Stingray Adventure tomorrow. Would I even be able to pull a swim mask and snorkel onto this fuzzy head? The ship rocked very gently and I clutched the sides of my chaise to keep from falling off.

"So," I said, a tiny bit alarmed to see Angela's face revolving above the buttons of her Chanel, like tumblers on a slot machine. "Feeling better now?" I tried to pat her sleeve and missed. "I mean," I added with a reassuring smile, "Kenyon's opinion is only *one*, for gaaawd-shake." I grimaced, licked my lips, and repositioned my tongue. "I

145

thought Barbara read your manuscript beautif-fully, Angela, and I even saw Carter Cantrelle applaud. So, to me, it sounds like that was *damned* fine writing in *Last Dance Last Chance.* I don't think you should let anything Kenyon said about it bother you."

"Not mine," Angela said, lifting her whiskey tumbler to eye level in the pale moonlight. She tipped it side to side, while the warm night breeze lifted a wisp of her blonde hair.

"Huh?" I scrunched my brows, remembering Barbara calling Angela by that pen name, Barrett. I'd simply assumed …

"That wasn't my manuscript that Thea butchered," Angela explained. She took a sip and turned toward me, smiling. "Oh. You thought all that was about defending my work?"

"Well, I …"

"Of course you did," Angela said, with a sigh. "Along with everyone else, I suppose. But that doesn't matter." She sat up in her lounge chair, back straight, chin lifted, and blue eyes so intense that for some crazy reason I thought about Scarlett O'Hara defending Tara. Though I doubted this haute couture woman would go so far as to wear the Skyler curtains.

"What *matters*," Angela said, finally, "is a person's sense of integrity, dignity, and self-worth. *Individuality*. No one has the right to attack that. You agree, don't you, Darcy?" Her eyes connected with mine with such power, that I started to nod as fast as I could, managing to slosh the JD out of my glass and into my low-cut tank top. *Ugh.*

I forced a smile as the whiskey dribbled between my breasts and sluiced over my shamrock tattoo. Dignity. *Uh huh.* Self-worth. *Absolutely.* Individuality…. *individuality? Hmmm.* I pressed my fingers discreetly to my left breast, using my tank top as a blotter, and

146

listened to Angela's impassioned rant. *Mm-hmm*…while my new friend, Jack Daniels, began tempting my feisty Irish ego down a very slippery slope. Individuality, dignity, self-worth…*California nobody?*

"Perhaps it's a result of being surrounded by lawyers—judges, for heaven's sake. Or because Granddaddy Barrett was a damned *Demo-crat*," Angela said with a slight grimace. "But the very idea of someone venomous enough to attack freedom of expression by using personal slander is simply intolerable for me."

She raised her glass and her gold charm bracelet shone in the deck lights. I saw the glinting silhouette of a pair of baby booties and wondered if they were engraved with Luke's birthdate. My bleary mind whispered, *"heirs, grandbabies,"* and I tried to quiet it with a cough-inducing chug of Jack D. *Don't Darcy…don't you dare.* I cleared my throat and smiled again, even though my lips were completely and totally numb.

"Thea Kenyon r-r-really pissshed you off, Angela," I said, showing my heartfelt, if lispy, support for her opinion. I was going to *do* that, dammit, even if my tongue wasn't cooperating. "You're so *right*. Thea Kenyon stood up there and ripped up somebody's *dreams*. Some wriiiter daring to go *naked* in public, for godsake. She told that writer that she was a 'frickin' wimpy'…"

I struggled to sit up on my lounge chair and recall what other horrible things Thea had said about the author of *Last Dance Last Chance*. "Yeah, and 'worthless,' like a 'slobbering'"—I jabbed my finger in the air while I searched for the perfect word that refused to come to mind. What was that word I was trying to think of? I hesitated, searched, and then my new friend Jack whispered it in my ear. "'Nobody,'" I said suddenly, "like she was just a *nobody*."

I stopped for a second, realizing the drunken, cosmic signifi-cance of what I'd just said. I weighed the wisdom of shutting the hell up against the sudden righteous sense of wah-hoo that was now warming me far more than the whiskey. Then I plunged ahead with what was probably a huge, huge mistake.

"Angela," I said, sitting fully upright by some miracle. "First, I've gotta say thank you for the drinks. You are *verrry* generous. Too generous." I nodded my head and lifted my palms when she began to voice a well-bred demur. "No, really. Thank you. But you know the *best* part of tonight? Of this chance to get to know you a little better?" I tossed her a bleary smile. "Just me and ... my Luke's be-loved mommy?"

Angela smiled over the brim of her glass, and I thought for a minute she looked wary, but that didn't stop me. Jack and I were on a roll.

"The very best part," I explained, "is finding out that you and I are totally on the same page about such an *important* issue." I nodded about four times and went right on. "The most important damned thing someone can have *is* just what you said, a sense of integrity, dignity, and self-worth. Individuality." I scrunched my brows and realized they were numb, too. "You did say individu-*al-lity*, right?"

"Yes, I did," Angela said, setting her glass down and looking definitely skeptical now. "Darcy, dear, maybe we ought to get some coffee or—"

"Nope, not finished," I said, raising my palm again and smiling. "The point I'm making here, Angela, is that you may not realize that all of *this*—what we were talking about—is practically a *creed* for my family. For the Cavanaughs. And I'm damned proud of the fact that we are *very* individual. And original." I raised my brows and then slipped in a quick addendum: "Not that the Skylers aren't. Of course they are. It's just that ..." I reached for my drink and polished it off. "Okay, here it is, Angie. Bottom line: Dad traps rats and Mom was a nun until she ran off to Vegas. They're divorced, but still sleep with each other on major holidays. My brother, Chance, is digging up bones somewhere in South America ... we think." I squeezed my eyes shut, took a big breath and blamed my pal Jack for a sudden prickle of tears. "Grandma Rosaleen is being sued for feeding koi food to her neighbors, and my little brother is the *best* damned Goofy that Disneyland has ever seen!" I paused and looked her square in the eye. "We're Democrats, Catholics, and Californians. For generations now. Oh, and one more thing ..."

I smiled, shrugged, and then reached for the neckline of my tank top.

* * *

"Holy shit—you flashed Angela Skyler?"

"Oh God, just kill me now." I groaned and rested my forehead on the cool marble surface of the café table, rolling my head sideways to peer up at Marie. "It's only because I've had four cups of coffee that I'm able to confess this to you at all."

"Five," Marie said, pointing to the cluster of ship's logo mugs near my right ear. "You've had five cups in the last hour. I'll probably have to defibrillate you." She sighed and reached over, patting the top of my head. "Hell, kid, it was high time you stopped tiptoeing around that woman. Thank God Luke didn't inherit the same tight-ass attitude."

149

"*Aagh*," I groaned against a rush of caffeine-induced heartburn. "*Luke*." I squeezed my eyes closed. "I keep replaying this awful image of Angela eyeing my shamrock, starting to do that judge's wife smirk, and then her face dissolving into this look of pure *horror* as she put two and two together about the name painted on her son's sailboat. Oh shit." I opened my eyes and saw Marie struggling not to laugh. "You think this is funny?"

Marie rolled her eyes. "C'mon, Darc'. So you have a tattoo and Luke named a boat after it. So what? What I *think* is that everyone has something they don't want—pardon the expression—'flashed' around in public. I think we've *all* got skeletons." She raised her brows. "You really believe that Angela Skyler can't relate to that?"

I raised my head from the table. "You mean, do I think she's going to have this great awakening now? Like, tell herself, 'Hey, why fix Luke up with some rich, WASPy Charlottesville deb, when I could breed a whole new line of half-Irish, Democratic, redheaded, tattooed—'"

"Oh, you're *breeding* now?" Marie asked, lifting her brows over the rim of her brandy-laced coffee. "News to me. Seems more like Luke's the thirty-six-year-old with the ticking biological clock and *you're* the one hiding eggs faster than the Easter bunny." She tapped a fingertip to her temple. "Guess I imagined all that panic last spring when you thought he'd bought an engagement ring."

"Okay, okay!" I sat upright, surprised that my head was no longer swirling. The caffeine had done its job, chased Jack D. back under that rock he'd crawled out from to throw a monkey wrench into my life. I sighed. "You're right. I don't care what Angela says about me. Besides," I reached over to break off a corner of Marie's cranberry scone. I smiled. "The dreaded Chop or Shop is over now. And since nobody actually *died* ..."

We both looked up as several people walked into the Java Café: Renee, one of the paranormal writers, Barth, followed by Gertie and Herb Dugdale—without Artie the parrot. I glanced at my watch. Eleven thirty; these folks were probably killing time before the Dessert Extravaganza at midnight. I was going to pass on that event, not sure how dangerous it might be to chase whiskey with chocolate truffles and cream-filled éclairs. Climbing into bed was sounding pretty good.

"There's my girls," Gertie said as she and Herb settled at the table next to ours. She raised her hand, palm down and fingers extended, to prove she had no residual shaking after the back-to-back albuterol treatments. She grinned. "Steady as a rock and breathing like a champ. Thanks to you." She lowered her hand, and I noticed that Herb took hold of it. *Well, well.*

"Glad to see it," Marie said. "And glad that you're off bird duty, Herb."

Herb nodded. "Artie's safely back in his cabin. Not that I don't enjoy him, but I did want to play a little ... pinochle." He squeezed Gertie's hand and I swear I saw her cheeks flush.

I took a sip of my lukewarm latte and thought of poor Barbara, forced to do bird chores after the stressful Chop or Shop. "Well, I hope Barbara's put him to bed."

"No," Gertie said quickly. "She's been at the spa. Renee just came back from there and said Barbara was doing laps in the pool." She took a deep breath and then exhaled, and I was glad there were no wheezes. Apparently Herb was good medicine, too. Gertie raised her sparse brows. "Guess Barbara needed a break after the Chop or Shop. We heard there was quite a brouhaha?"

I frowned. "Yes," I said, shaking my head. "That's one way to put it, I guess."

Gertie, lowered her voice. "Actually, I heard that Thea was drunk as a skunk and got into a shouting match with that judge's wife."

I opened my mouth, searching for the right words, but Gertie kept going.

"And I heard from our little Sarah," she said, "that Kenyon managed to insult Carter, too." She shook her head. "Let me tell you, honey, that little fan of hers was plenty pissed. It's a good thing Thea went straight to her cabin."

"She did." Herb nodded, and this time I saw his weathered cheeks blush. "To take a bath," he said. "I offered to cover Artie's cage for her, but Miss Kenyon said ... um, no, that she, well ..."

Gertie laughed. "What Thea said was, "'Hell, no, I'm getting buck naked and that damned bird's coming in with me.'" Gertie shook her head, eyes sparkling wickedly. "And then she said that Herb could hop in the tub too if he wanted, because she'd never managed to train the parrot to scrub her back—" she stopped as the ornithologist quickly handed her a cup of coffee.

"Let's just say," Herb finished for her, "that Miss Kenyon asked me to call for the bar steward and extra towels. She asked me to leave her door ajar for the steward staff, and that she seemed quite content with her plans for the rest of the evening."

"More content than the judge's wife, that's for sure," Gertie said after blowing on her coffee and taking a sip. "Herb saw Mrs. Skyler in the Dolphin Deck VIP lounge, complaining to the conference coordinator about Thea's workshop. She was insisting that money be refunded, and then she threatened to call her 'husband the judge,' and start a class-action suit."

Herb put his hand on Gertie's arm and cleared his throat. "Really, Gert, I don't think it's prudent to repeat any of that." He smiled at me and I got the feeling, from the discomfort in his kind old eyes, that he was struggling against an ingrained sense of decorum. "I believe it's safe to say that emotions have been running high, and … er … shall we say that drinks have been flowing freely? Mrs. Skyler, in my opinion, may simply have been under the influence—"

"She was *drunk*?" I asked, interrupting. "When was this that you saw her?" I looked down at my watch, thinking that Angela had walked away from our own little drink-fest far more sober than I had, and that had been … what, an hour ago?

"Why, not twenty-five minutes ago," Herb answered, after retrieving his pocket watch from his jacket. "And, truly, I didn't mean to imply anything detrimental to the woman's character. I only meant that she appeared a bit unsteady on her feet and, as I said, somewhat overly emotional." He blinked as I quickly rose from my chair.

"Excuse me, Herb, Gertie," I said, nodding toward Marie. "But I forgot that I told someone I'd meet them, and …"

"Oh," Gertie said, with a knowing smile, "you're off to the Dessert Extravaganza."

"Uh … yes," I said, as Marie stood up beside me, her brows scrunched. "So, have fun, you two. Nice to see you. Bye."

I headed for the Java Café door, forcing myself not to break into a trot. Marie fell into place beside me once we cleared the doorway.

"Dessert?" She asked, trying to pull a cheroot from her fanny pack as she hustled to keep up with me. "Are you nuts? You know what banana cream pie and whiskey tastes like when you barf them up together?"

"Stop it," I groaned, heading toward the mid-ship elevators. "We're not going to the buffet. We're going up to check on Angela."

"Angela? Why?" Marie asked as we covered the stretch of carpet leading toward the elevators and stairs.

"Because she wasn't drunk when I left her, and now I'm worried that she hit the bar after I rattled my family skeletons and—" I stopped at the brassy row of elevator doors and jabbed the Up button.

"And?" Marie asked, stepping into the elevator beside me.

"And because," I said, feeling my stomach do a little dip that had nothing to do with the elevator, "I'm starting to have this really *bad* feeling."

The doors opened onto the Dolphin Deck, and we'd passed the empty VIP lounge and turned down the corridor toward Angela's cabin, when we heard the screams. We broke into a run, our feet thudding against the thick carpeting, and then hurried toward a female cabin steward standing at the open doorway of a cabin. A stack of towels lay in a heap at her feet. She screamed again, dark eyes wild, and then caught sight of us, and began waving frantically.

"Oh please, oh please … *Madre de Dios!* Help, please. Miss Kenyon—I think she's dead!"

TWELVE

I NEARLY SCREAMED, MYSELF, when we entered the agent's bath-room. *What... how... oh dear God!* My stomach lurched as I strug-gled to make sense of the grotesque scene in the bathtub.

Theodora Kenyon was naked and submerged nipple-deep in water, a paper umbrella tucked behind one ear, eyes glazed, and mouth gaping wide. Red, fluid-filled blisters dotted her chest just above the water line, stretching from armpit to armpit. One of her arms, pale and flaccid, was draped across a corner of the marble tub rim crowded with overturned cocktail glasses, discarded swiz-zle sticks, jars of glistening bath salts, and—*oh no!* My hand shot out, snatching Marie's sleeve and stopping her in the nick of time. "No! Don't touch her. Look at that!"

Marie tensed, then swore softly as she saw where I was pointing: the laptop computer, its surface bubbled and blackened, bobbed just beneath the surface, and a long extension cord stretched across the tile floor from the tub to the suite's bedroom beyond. Marie nodded quickly, brows scrunching. "Right. Okay then. You go pull the plug. And on your signal, I'll drag Thea out and ..." She frowned and whirled toward the steward who'd begun to wail anew. "Hey, *stop screaming*, would you? Call the operator and have her page the medical staff. Now!"

I'm not proud to admit that it took me two tries to pull the scorched extension cord out of the wall. Completely irrational, I know, but after watching my brother Willie shove Dad's toenail clipper into one of our dining room outlets ... let's just say that I have a healthy respect for volts and ohms. So much so that, trust me, when I'm in charge of the ER, even first-day student nurses learn damned quick how to man a defibrillator. Not that I can't rise to the occasion. I gritted my teeth, yanked the plug free, and shouted to Marie. Then I hustled back into the bathroom as the first emergency page shrilled overhead—and just as Marie laid our patient, face up and soaking wet, on the tile floor. I took one look at the unconscious agent and groaned. It didn't take a triage nurse to predict that there wasn't much hope for Thea Kenyon. But, by God, we had to try to save her. "What've we got to work with?" I asked, pushing up my sleeves and joining Marie on the floor.

I held my breath as Marie lifted the woman's chin and then leaned close to check for respirations—looking for the rise of Thea's chest, listening for the sounds or the feel of any exhaled air. *Breathe, Thea.* Marie shook her head and frowned, and I rose onto my knees, positioning my hands to start cardiac compressions. "Any pulse?"

Marie gave initial rescue breaths, watched Thea's blistered chest rise and fall and then pressed two fingers into the side of the woman's neck. "No. And, her eyes look bad, too, Darc'—pupils big with no reaction at all. I think we're screwed here. But the water was still lukewarm, so maybe she hasn't been down that long ..."

"Let's do it!" I interlaced my fingers to link one hand over the other, rocked forward on my knees, and pressed my palm deep into Thea's slippery-wet sternum, counting aloud. "One and two and three and four and ..." I glanced over at Marie and saw her grimace. "You okay?" I asked while continuing to rock my weight onto the agent's chest. A second page sounded overhead.

"I'm fine." Marie nodded, pinched Thea's nose, breathed into her mouth, and then grimaced again. "Ugh. Sorry. It's just that awful *smell*," she said. "You know, from—"

"Burned skin, or maybe plastic from the scorched laptop and extension cord," I said, nodding and counting my compressions silently, "and—"

"Wet feathers," Marie said, pinching Thea's nose again.

"Huh?" My eyes widened. "*Feathers?*"

"Artie," Marie explained, lifting her chin toward the tub. "He was floating in the tub behind Thea's arm. Barbecued now, I'm guessing. Poor little booger."

"*Aagh ...*" A shameful part of me wanted to scream something nasty about idiots who bathed with birds, people too damned drunk to remember Benjamin Franklin's kite and all those friggin' lightning experiments. But the nurse part of me just kept going. Counting compressions, feeling the burn blisters burst beneath my palm, and watching Thea's ribs rise each time Marie exhaled air into her. And all the while, that hopeful Catholic part of me—as always—prayed to beat the band. *Live, Thea. Please, God.*

It seemed like forever, but was probably only minutes, until the medical team arrived, toting oxygen, Ambu bag, portable defibrillator, IV setup, and drugs. And it was only a few more minutes before the doctor made it clear that Thea Kenyon had likely swung that meat cleaver for the last time. Asystole—that dreaded "flat line"—showed in three leads of the cardiac monitor and, despite high-flow oxygen, the only splash of color on this woman's body was the rumpled pink paper umbrella tangled in her hair. They'd continue CPR, move her to the infirmary's ICU, run through the advanced resuscitation protocols, but I knew the truth. Thea was already dead.

I gave Marie's hand a squeeze and swallowed hard, thinking of the bitter irony that, just this morning, Thea had been thanking me for saving her life on that silly helmet dive and now—we turned at the suddenly agitated voice of a ship's officer behind us. Clipped, with a British accent, and obviously flustered.

"What should I … em, ah … *do* with this bird, exactly?" He asked, holding a towel and peering into the tub, past the clutter of mai tai glasses and fancy bottles of bath salts.

A second officer stepped toward him. "What do you mean, Haverson?"

I squeezed my eyes shut, thinking for the first time of Barbara Fedders. In just a short while, the assistant would learn about her employer's tragic accident. And Artie's demise.

"I mean, look there, man," Haverson said, pointing into the tub. "The bloody thing's *swimming*. Think it bites?"

* * *

I was definitely having some sort of night-shift flashback. I'm sure it had everything to do with the fact that it was nearly two AM and my knees ached from doing CPR on a wet tile floor. And that I was hunkered down a rolling stool in a corner of the ship's infirmary, breathing in the all-too-familiar odor of iodine and surgical soap. With Marie snoring on my shoulder. I don't think she's ever made it through a night shift vertical.

"Hey," I said deciding not to wait until the stool slipped from beneath her butt, "wake up. You're drooling on me. And you're about an inch from sliding onto the floor." Marie mumbled and I glanced toward the curtained cubicle in the distance. "Besides, I think she's here now, and I don't want to be stuck explaining things by myself."

Marie sat upright, squinted, and rubbed her sleeve across her mouth. "Umph ... who? Who's here?"

"Barbara Fedders. Someone said she's had a sedative, but I just saw her walk behind the curtain with the doctor. You know, where they have Thea—" I stopped, when the night nurse, Glynnis, approached us from behind; short, forty-something and big-busted, with ship-issue navy slacks and a white shirt sporting a pink, enameled breast-cancer pin. She had a box of Kleenex tucked under her arm. *The Kleenex sign.* I'd done that same thing enough times myself to know exactly what it meant. Bad news.

Glynnis was also carrying more coffee, thank goodness. She was an old shipmate of Marie's, which meant we'd get the inside scoop now. I was glad, since we'd been in a strange limbo ever since we left Kenyon's cabin, straddling the awkward status line between being considered mere passengers and involved medical professionals. As first responders, we'd had valuable information to share with the ship's medical staff, but as non-ship personnel and non-relatives we were kept frustratingly clueless about what had happened since. I'd seen no overt evidence of continuing resuscitation, but no one was saying one way or another. Glynnis would spill the beans, nurse-to-nurse-to-nurse.

She handed us the coffee, smiled, and then shook her head at Marie. "I see you're still a wuss, Whitley." Glynnis hesitated for a moment, and then reached up to brush a lock of graying hair away from her forehead. She sighed, her hazel eyes turning serious. She set the Kleenex box down on a table beside us. "Sorry to keep you both in the lurch, but I'm sure you guessed there was nothing left to do for Miss Kenyon. We gave her a couple more rounds of epinephrine, considered a pacemaker, but..." the nurse shook her head. "She'd been down too long. There would be brain damage. Doc said that if we'd caught her heart while it was still in fibrillation from the electricity, then maybe she'd have had a chance. But..."

"So it *was* an electrocution, then?" I asked after taking a sip of the strong coffee. "From the laptop?"

Marie looked at me like I'd lost my mind. Her dark brows scrunched. "You didn't notice the blisters?"

I narrowed my eyes, and then decided to let it slide, considering my grumpy pal's whole not-a-night-person thing. "I *meant*," I explained patiently, "that I've heard it isn't that easy to get electrocuted in a bathtub. And even though it happens in the movies all the time, tap water just isn't that great of a conductor."

Glynnis nodded. "That's exactly what the doctor said. But then he explained that electricity flows much more easily through *salt* water, so—"

"Sal—?" I was starting to ask, when Marie poked me with her finger.

"Salt," Marie said, nodding her head up and down. "Bath salts? We saw them all around that tub, Darc'. Remember?"

I did. And I also remembered how insistent Thea had been about being able to use that laptop; and how very pissed that the battery wouldn't hold a charge. That's why she'd yanked her assistant out of the Helmet Dive line that morning, sent her on that wild goose chase to get it fixed and—*oh no, here she comes.* I nudged Marie, and we set our coffees down.

Barbara was walking, zombie-like toward us, hair disheveled, mouth slack, and still wearing her swimsuit and terry cover-up. I tried not to imagine the dual images of Barbara swimming peacefully at the spa, and her boss sinking into that tub, downing mai tais and then tapping away on that deadly laptop. My breath hissed inward between my front teeth. Oh jeez, Barbara was carrying the crumpled paper umbrella from Thea's hair.

Glynnis handed Marie the Kleenex box, and walked slowly back toward the nurse's desk, pausing to pat Barbara Fedders's shoulder on her way. Clearly, Marie and I were now in charge of manning the tissues and coming up with something to say to this grieving woman. What the hell would that be? I reached for a handful of tissues as Barbara came closer, and then changed my mind. She wasn't crying.

"Marie … Dar … sh—Dar-cy," Barbara said, her voice obviously thickened by the sedative. "I …" she stopped and looked down at the pink umbrella in her hands. "I …"

I jumped up, threw my arms around her, and Marie stepped close, clutching the Kleenex box. "Barbara, we're so terribly sorry about this," I said, hugging her terry-clad shoulders. "If there's anything that we can *do* for you. Please let us know."

Barbara stiffened and stepped away. She licked her lips and blinked slowly. "For … me? No. I have my w-work … and the calls to make. To Thea's mother and …"

161

Barbara's face contorted with obvious pain. "All those years that she smoked, I watched so carefully to be sure she didn't leave one burning at night. Then I made sure she didn't drive when she was drinking." Barbara's face paled and her pupils grew wide. "Thea made me buy that extension c-cord, but I didn't th-think she would—"

Marie spoke up quickly. "It was an *accident*, Barbara. No one would guess she'd make a mistake like that."

"Right," I agreed, anxious to back Marie up and do anything I could to derail this woman's obvious sense of guilt. Comfort her some way. Any way. "And," I said, trying to muster an encouraging smile, "it *is* good news that the bird doctor, Herb, was able to save Artie."

Barbara's brows scrunched together and then her jaw dropped. The paper umbrella fell from her fingers. "A-artie? He—"

Oh God, I was an ass. She obviously didn't know that Artie was involved. "I'm sorry, Barbara," I said quickly, "I thought you knew that he was … uh … with Thea. But he's okay. I promise you. Doctor Herb is taking good care of him. He's a little groggy, but he's going to be just *fine*."

I could tell by the look on Barbara's face that she didn't believe me, and that I'd just managed to add one more grisly detail to this woman's ugly, ugly night.

* * *

The three AM atmosphere in the Crow's Nest Bar was nothing like the usual Cocktails and Craft writers' gathering. Oddly, it felt more like that scene in *The Wizard of Oz*, when the Wicked Witch of the West is lying squashed under the farmhouse and the Munchkins are swarming excitedly.

"So ... then I guess she won't be publishing last night's 'chops' on her blog," someone mumbled, a few barstools down from where Marie and I were sitting. Someone else snickered.

For godsake. So much for respect for the dead. I tossed Marie a look and she rolled her eyes in agreement. On the other side of me, Renee shrugged and took a sip of her Brandy Alexander.

"Guess that *is* the 'bright' side to all of this," she said. "Not that anyone should say it out loud, of course. I think we're all finally facing the fact that Thea's been losing it for a long time now. Your friend, Angela, was right at the Chop or Shop—agents usually treat writers with far more respect." Renee sighed, her buxom chest stretching the fabric of her embroidered caftan. "So I can understand that Angela would have mixed feelings about this tragedy." She grimaced. "After all, Thea really bashed her book."

"*Wrong,*" I said, sitting up so quickly that I sloshed my own brandy onto the sleeve of my favorite old white Oxford. I'd showered and changed into comfort clothes, my jeans, topsiders, and a men's-style shirt and, lacking the energy to cook up the mac and cheese, had settled for cheddar crackers and a stiff shot of brandy. I blotted my sleeve with a napkin and turned to Renee.

"That *wasn't* Angela's manuscript," I explained. "She told me so herself, and said she only spoke up because she wanted to defend the other writers in there." I nodded to make my point. "People like you, for instance," I added, maybe a bit too defensively, but I didn't like the implication in Renee's remark. And I hoped no one else was making that sort of callous assumption.

"Oh," Renee said, touching my arm. "Then I guess everyone just jumped to the conclusion that Mrs. Skyler wrote *Last Dance Last Chance.* I hope you didn't think I was being disrespectful or anything, Darcy. She's a lovely woman. Really." Renee's pudgy hand patted my sleeve. "How's she taking all this bad news?"

I wished I knew. The truth was, I'd stopped by Angela's cabin a couple of times since the failed resuscitation, and knocked on her door; I was certain she couldn't have slept through the commotion. But there'd been no answer. I tried not to think that she hadn't heard all the pages and screams because she was passed out cold, driven to that state because I aired the Cavanaugh's dirty laundry and flashed my shamrock. *God.* "I'm not sure Angela knows about Thea's accident yet," I answered casually, reaching for my brandy again. "She was ... um, not feeling too well, I think. So she went to bed."

Renee's dimples framed a knowing smirk. "Oh, I'm so sorry to hear that. Poor thing." She turned on her barstool and glanced toward the tables. "I see Keven over there. And without Sarah, for once; can't believe it. Maybe now I can get his attention long enough to find out if he knows anything new." She turned back to me, the excitement in her eyes unmistakable. "I heard that the media's found out, and that they've been trying to contact Barbara Fedders. And even Carter Cantrelle. Can you imagine?" She pressed her hand to her chest. "I'm dying to know what Carter had to say."

Actually, I'd been wondering about that myself. How had Carter reacted?

Renee hefted herself off the stool, gathered her cocktail and napkins, and made a beeline for the tables at the far side of the bar. I turned to Marie, in time to see her rest her head on the bar and close her eyes. I tossed a cracker into her hair. "Hey, stay awake long enough to walk back to our cabin, okay?" I shook my head. "Can you believe these people? Bunch of vultures."

Marie's eyes opened half-mast and she raised herself up on her elbows. "No secret that there wasn't a lot of love lost on Thea Kenyon, Darc'. A lot of people hated her." She counted on her fingers: "Like Carter, Carter's editor Ellen, half the ship's staff that she's offended, probably all of the folks she 'chopped' last night, Angela—"

"Don't say that!" I whispered, grabbing Marie's fingers and glancing down the bar. "Angela wouldn't take part in dissing dead people, for godsake. She's—"

Marie raised her brows. "Far more comfortable calling her son's girlfriend a 'nobody,' and bashing women with tattoos?"

"Touché," I said, with a sigh. "Still, even if Kenyon was the Bitch Supreme, I hate it that everyone's behaving like this."

"Could be worse," Marie said, yawning.

"What do you mean?"

"We could've taught *electrocution* at the murder workshop. And then everyone would say Thea's death wasn't an accident." Marie frowned, picked the cracker out of her hair and flicked it back at me. "C'mon," she said, sliding off her stool, "I can't be expected to swim with stingrays with no sleep."

We left the bar and headed aft and, though I tried, I had no luck convincing Marie that we should check on Angela one more time. She was probably right. Everyone in his or her right mind—or anyone sleeping off a drunken state precipitated by a conversation with an offensive 'nobody'—would be in bed now. And, by the look of the empty corridors, that was true.

We'd made it to the mid-ship elevators without seeing anyone but the occasional steward pushing a carpet sweeper, when we caught sight of a trio of men in dark uniforms headed for the staircase. I turned to Marie. "Hey, aren't those security guys?"

"Yup." Marie nodded as she pushed the elevator's Down button. "And look, there goes the guy who had issues with your almond potpourri—and wanted to frisk us for smoke bombs."

She was right. It was that big lug with the ponytail, and he was hustling. What was going on?

"Wonder where they're going in such a godawful hurry?" I asked, stifling a yawn as Marie pushed the button to G-Deck and the brass doors began to close. Bed was sounding like heaven. I'd kick off my shoes, slide out of my jeans, and sleep in my old shirt. "Oh, wait," I said quickly. "Push the Hold button, Marie. Someone wants to get on."

It was Doctor Herb, and he looked as tired as we were. Maybe more tired.

"Thank you, ladies," he said, smiling as he stepped aboard the elevator. "G-Deck for me too, please." He smiled again. "I promised Gertie I'd stop by once more before I go to bed. She's still pretty upset."

I nodded and then sighed. "About Thea."

"Yes." Herb cleared his throat. "And, understandably, there's also some related disappointment about her book, of course."

Marie raised her brows. "Her book?"

The ornithologist nodded his head. "The Erotica Romance, as she calls it." Herb's faced turned pink and he cleared his throat again. "Gertie was very encouraged by her appointment with Miss Kenyon yesterday and now..." He shrugged. "Bad situation all around, it seems."

"Except for Artie," I offered, realizing that I had developed a tendency to make that nasty bird some sort of phoenix rising from the ashes of this ill-fated cruise.

"Yes," Herb said and then frowned. "Although now his situation appears to have opened a whole new can of worms."

"Worms?" Marie asked, squinting her eyes and leaning back against the wall of the elevator as we bumped to a stop.

"Soap, actually," Herb said, and I strained my tired brain to understand.

"I see no reason not to tell you," Herb said, his voice dropping to a near whisper as we all stepped out of the elevator onto the carpeting of G-Deck. "Especially after your heroic attempt to save Miss Kenyon."

"What's all that got to do with soap?" I asked, scrunching my brows.

Herb glanced up and down the hallway and then looked at both of us. "In my attempt to treat Artie, I found something most peculiar." He frowned. "A sliver of soap—ship issue, I believe—was wedged inside his beak." He raised his snowy brows. "Forcibly. There was a good bit of blood on his little tongue from the trauma. Poor fellow."

"Huh?" I said, not sure if I was getting this right. "You mean..."

"I mean that someone tried to kill that parrot," Herb said with conviction.

My mind scrambled to sort out the ridiculous and repulsive thought of someone attempting to murder a bird, and I completely missed the obvious. Until Herb said it out loud.

"Which, I'm afraid, also makes it possible that Miss Kenyon's electrocution was not accidental."

Marie and I stared at Dr. Herb and then at each other as the elevator doors slid closed behind us. *Oh my God.*

"So, unfortunately," he continued, "I had the unpleasant task of informing ship security of my concerns. They're conducting an investigation as we speak."

His lips tightened. "I believe that they've gone to interrogate Mrs. Skyler."

THIRTEEN

SURE ENOUGH, THE DOUBLE doors to Thea Kenyon's suite were being guarded by a small platoon of security officers who confirmed that Angela had been taken to their offices belowdecks. I didn't like the knowing look on the face of one of the officers as Marie and I turned to walk back down the Dolphin Deck corridor.

"For godsake, did you see that?" I hissed as we headed back to the elevators. "You'd think that Angela was actually a suspect or something."

I waited for Marie to jump in, waited some more, and then finally grabbed the sleeve of her denim shirt, stopping her. "Hey. Why aren't you disputing that? Why aren't you saying, 'hell yeah, these guys screwed up *big time*'?" I think my voice squeaked a little on the last couple of words, because all of a sudden I was getting nervous. Very nervous. "You don't actually think—" We came to a halt outside the Dolphin Deck VIP lounge, and Marie pulled her arm away, frowning. She fumbled with the zipper on her fanny pack, and then pulled out a cigar.

"No, Darc," she said, finding her Volkswagen lighter. "I *don't* think Angela shoved that piece of soap into Artie's mouth, if that's what you're asking." She flicked the lighter's wheels, touched the flame to her cigar and puffed her cheeks, making the end glow in the corridor's dim lighting. "And," she said, exhaling a waft of sweet cherry smoke, "I don't believe she's a murderess. But..." She peered into the darkened VIP lounge and then looked back at me.

"But what?" I asked, feeling my stomach argue with a dubious diet of snack crackers and whiskey.

"But you have to remember that a few hours ago, right there"— she nodded toward the lounge—"Doctor Herb and at least one member of the ship's staff saw Angela ranting about Thea. And what about the people who witnessed that ugly scene she made at the Chop or Shop? You heard Renee wondering about Angela's re- action to Thea's death." Marie's voice softened. "I'm only warning you that other people may be thinking about that, too."

It dawned on me that not only was Marie right, but that one of those curious people was, well...me. My mind whirled. How *had* Angela reacted to news of the grisly incident a few doors down from her own cabin? Had she heard the commotion, asked for details, or been confused when the security officers came to her door? Maybe. She'd been sleeping soundly enough not to hear my knocks, after all. Sure, she could have been as completely surprised by the news of Thea's death as she had been by... my flashing the source of the name painted on her son's sailboat? I groaned under my breath, cursing for the umpteenth time my stupidity in think- ing that this cruise could be a bonding experience with Luke's truly uptight mother.

"Let's get going," I said heading toward the elevators again.

"You bet. I'm beat; nothing's going to feel as good as that cabin bed."

"Yes," I agreed. "Afterward."

"After what?" Marie stopped at the elevator and raised her brows warily.

"After we go down to the security offices and see what's happening with Angela."

"No, Darc," Marie said, stepping aboard the elevator and then attempting to bat my hand away from the floor buttons. Cigar ashes speckled my sleeve. "We should *not* butt in on this investigation. And, besides, I'm sure they're not allowing anyone down on the service level decks. For crissake, Thea's dead in the infirmary, they've had a soap assault on a parrot, Barbara Fedders is under sedation, and—*hey!*"

She batted my hand again, missed, and groaned as I successfully punched the button to the service deck. And then, as the doors opened, we both realized that she'd been all wrong about security. They hadn't managed to keep the curious people away; in fact, it looked like the whole darned Cocktails and Craft bunch had moved en masse from the Crow's Nest Bar to here. Carter Cantrelle's editor Ellen, that marketing guy from Dolphin Deck, Bill and Frankeen Price, Gertie and Vicky, the blonde cover-guy Barth, and ... "Jeez," I said, wading into the crowd milling along the corridor, "you'd think they were calling bingo down here. Why is everyone on cell phones, and—*what the hell?*" I raised my palm as Renee, a pencil wedged over her ear, shoved a glittery pink cell phone toward my face. "Quit that, for godsake, Renee! What are you *doing?*"

"Pictures, Darcy. Smile. Oh, c'mon, you want your mom to see you on CNN looking like that?" She clucked her tongue and raised the phone camera again. "Look this way, girls. Can you lose that cigar, Marie? Well, just smile then ... okay, suit yourself, *spoilsports!*"

CNN? Marie and I pushed past her and then stopped and stared. Unbelievable. There was a sea of home video cameras, digital cameras, and cardboard disposable cameras. Electronic flashes bounced rapid-fire over countless people taking notes, several people on laptops, and a few holding tiny microphones. People were standing on tiptoe to see past a barricade of chairs stretching across the hallway and leading to the infirmary and the security offices. Some were shouting out questions while jockeying for a closer spot toward the front of the crowd. It was as if every writer onboard—and dozens of non-writers—was intent on becoming a freelance journalist. Snagging the scoop story. No. Worse. It was as if someone had heaved a freshly butchered side of beef into a school of hungry sharks. This was a feeding frenzy. It made our late agent's Chop or Shop look like High Tea.

"Oh Lord," I said as people milled past us, "Angela's part of this ugly circus?"

Marie shook her head and smiled ruefully. "And she probably has a dozen Virginia lawyers flying in by chopper, Darc'. She'll be fine. Let's get the hell out. There's no way we could help here anyway."

Stubborn as I was, I had to agree that Marie was right. All I wanted was to get as far from this mob as I could, and to distance myself from the nagging sense of déjà vu her words had conjured in my mind. *Virginia lawyers flying in by chopper.* Luke was a Virginia lawyer, and—since joining the FBI—he was all too familiar with that whirlybird mode of transportation. Had Angela already called him? Did Luke already know that my big "favor" of hooking his mother up with a famous literary agent had landed her smack in the middle of what might turn into a murder investigation?

"You're right," I said, pushing forward through the crowded corridor. "Let's go back to the cabin; this whole thing gives me the creeps. We need some space to think. We'll order room service, some shrimp and cheese tapas and those Buffalo wings you like, and..." I turned sideways, to slide past two elderly women in bathrobes, "we'll do some brainstorming. We'll come up with a plan to handle this thing with Angela. Absolutely. No problemo." I reached for the elevator button, nodded confidently at Marie, and then stopped cold as a big, beefy hand covered the Up button. A hand attached to the hairy arm ... of that ponytail security guy. *Oh shit.*

✳   ✳   ✳

Thirty minutes later, I was on a first name basis with Ponytail Paul, and dealing not only with acute starvation, but the queasy reality that I might be incriminating Angela. I had no idea where they'd taken Marie. I squirmed in the metal folding chair and pressed my clammy palm against the waistband of my low-rise jeans to squelch an embarrassingly loud stomach growl. "Sorry," I said, "I didn't eat much for dinner." I might possibly have followed those words with a couple of damsel-in-distress bats of my eyelashes. The feminist code of honor is weak at four AM.

Paul, unblinking and obviously no Lancelot, flipped through his notebook again. "Yes," he said with a smug twitch of his thick lips, "you had several cocktails on the deck outside the Crow's Nest Bar." His brows lifted. "Jack Daniels—straight up. And then five coffees at the Java Café, where your friend, Miss Whitley, ordered a

173

cranberry scone. And then you had a brandy just after three AM in the Crow's Nest Bar. Is that correct, Miss Cavanaugh?"

I think I just stared for a minute, my reportedly pickled brain conjuring up one of those *CSI: Miami* images of a medical examiner ID-ing stomach contents. I began wondering if Ponytail Paul knew exactly how many cheese crackers I'd eaten and ... then I got mad. Punching-bag mad.

"Look," I said, sitting up tall in the chair and flipping my hair off my shoulder. I crossed my arms and scanned the cramped, dank hole of an office equipped with a computer, a well-aged coffeemaker, and a bookshelf with several volumes of Maritime Law. Then I looked longingly at the metal door before focusing my attention back on my interrogator. "Can you tell me," I asked, narrowing my eyes enough to make a point, "why any of *that* is in the least bit important?"

I lifted my chin defensively. "I've already answered endless questions about our workshop, and I've told you every detail about my attempts to revive Miss Kenyon. It's nearly dawn and," my lids narrowed another dangerous millimeter, "*as you know*, I haven't had a thing to eat since—"

"Since you were drinking with Mrs. Skyler," Paul said, every scrap of smile gone from his face. "Who, a witness reports, called Miss Kenyon a," he pressed his huge thumb against the pages of his notebook and then looked back up, "'lily-livered ... tacky, rum-swilling,' uh ..."

"'Yankee,'" I said, supplying the word before I could stop myself, but not before my memory wrestled with the identity of this "witness." The bar steward who'd brought our drinks? And, even scarier, I began to wonder if maybe there'd been video surveillance. What if this security jerk had seen me baring my shamrock?

God. "But, look, she was just letting off steam," I explained quickly, refusing to be tripped up by this badge-toting voyeur. "It's not like Angela was making…"

"Threats?" he asked, pursing his lips and raising his brows.

I opened my mouth and closed it, my hollow stomach churning as he flipped to yet another page of his notebook.

"You were also present at Miss Kenyon's workshop, earlier last evening?"

"I … uh … yes." Oh man, where was Marie? This was not going well.

"Where Mrs. Skyler took objection to the proceedings and, according to the taped recording of that workshop, told Miss Kenyon that she would …" He ran a fingertip across the sheet of paper, "'use every influence, do everything possible to see you stopped, even if I have to …'"

Paul looked up and into my eyes. "Do you think that last statement might be inferred as a *threat*?"

What I thought—what I damned well *knew* by the look on this man's face—was that I'd done nothing to help Angela Skyler. And, instead, my performance in the bowels of this cruise ship had done everything to seal my fate with Luke's mother. And to make damned sure that her grandbabies would be mothered by that nameless Charlottesville debutante. Ponytail Paul was determined to treat Thea Kenyon's electrocution as a murder, and to put Luke's mother on the tossing end of that lethal laptop.

When Paul made a last cryptic entry into his notepad and then showed me to the door, I was more than glad to get out. I was glad, too, that Marie was waiting for me outside. She'd already lit another cigar and I could tell that she was as frazzled as I was. We glanced down the corridor at the now-thinning crowd and then walked on to the elevator. Marie mumbled something about Lido Deck Early Bird Breakfast times and pressed a deck button.

"So," she said, after the doors closed. She exhaled, smoke drifting upward. "What are you thinkin'?"

"The same thing I told that security guy," I said, leaning back against the cool brass wall of the elevator. "That Thea Kenyon was very likely drunk, plugged in her laptop because the battery was faulty, then accidentally knocked it off into the tub."

"Yeah. And it flipped a piece of soap—like a little tiddlywink—right into her parrot's mouth."

I pressed my fingers against my forehead and groaned. "Dammit. What is with that soap deal, anyway?"

Marie watched the deck numbers light on the elevator wall beside her. "Herb thinks it was an intentional attempt to kill him," she said after sighing. "By choking him, I guess. He said there was blood inside Artie's beak, remember?"

"Herb could be wrong," I said, with what I knew was a pathetic stab at optimism. "That bird's a freak, face it. Maybe he *eats* soap. Maybe we should ask Barbara about that. Maybe..."

"Maybe you should call Luke," Marie said softly, watching my face for a reaction.

"No," I said shaking my head. I squeezed my eyes shut for a second and then bit into my lower lip. "Not yet. There's no reason to jump the gun; Angela's not going to take any of this lying down. She's educated, she's savvy, and she's tough as nails, for godsake." I nodded my head, pretty sure that I was convincing Marie and, actually, starting to feel a whole lot better myself. "I mean, I'll know more when I get a chance to talk with her, of course, but I'd bet a million bucks that this penny-ante security questioning had no effect on Angela Barrett Skyler, and— "

And then the doors opened onto Lido Deck. Where Angela stood, Chanel suit rumpled, hair in wild disarray, skin pale—and her blue eyes wide with fright.

*　*　*

"I'm sorry," she said, as we eased into the brightly patterned booth in the empty Lido Café. "I hope Marie didn't think I was rude to want to talk with you privately, but ..." Her voice trailed off and she reached up to pat her hair. "Oh dear, I'm such a mess. I must have dozed off in my clothes, and when those security men knocked on my door, I ..."

She sighed, and I caught a whiff of what I'd bet was Altoids combined with brandy fumes. Jeez, were we the classy pair or what? I handed her a pizza rollup, tore at my congealed pork bow, and deposited half of it on her plate. "Don't worry about Marie," I said, summoning a smile. "She's probably already asleep. And," I picked at a pepperoni smudge on my Oxford shirt, "I'm not thinking that fashion and personal grooming are the issue here. Right?"

"Right," Angela agreed, stretching her hands around her coffee cup. She sighed.

"Riiight..." she repeated again, slowly, like she was trying to forestall the inevitable. She sighed and then peered at me over the rim of her cup. "They were taking photos," she said, finally.

"Photos?" I asked, not sure what she was getting at.

"Of me," Angela said, tugging at a button on her jacket, her eyes widening. "So many people down there in the corridor. You know, with those phones that can send, ah ..."

"Digital images?" I asked, supplying the words and then seeing too much of the whites of her eyes. I thought of Renee and her pink glitter phone.

"And they can be sent by way of computer, can't they? To friends, or even the media?" Angela set her coffee cup down so hard that it slopped onto the surface of the table. "Oh dear God. This can't happen. We *can't* let this happen! You have to help me, Darcy."

I turned at the distant clatter of dishes—the galley crew starting breakfast—and then leaned toward Angela. "Of course," I said, as gently as I could. "But what exactly did they say to you down there? The security people, I mean. Were they questioning you about Thea's accident?"

"Accident?" Angela said, half-choking and her tone bitter. "They're investigating it as a possible *murder*. A murder, Darcy!" Her eyes pierced mine. "And I'm under suspicion. Me. A murder suspect." Her hand flew to her mouth and she moaned behind her fingers. "This will ruin the family's reputation." Her lids squeezed closed. "Luke's future bid for Senate would be compromised and ... oh dear God. My son ..."

My boyfriend. "Did you call him?" I asked, praying she'd give the answer I needed to hear. The one which would buy time to do a few things like ... I held my breath.

"Of course not. I can't have Luke involved in this."

I fought a rueful smile at the thought of this mother protecting the big, Glock-toting Special Agent. But my breath escaped in a relieved whoosh. "Good," I said, reaching out to pat her hand briefly.

"Because nothing is concrete yet. From what I understand, security is questioning several people. And it's still an internal investigation; meaning that they haven't called in other authorities."

"But I got the impression," Angela said, relaxing enough to take a sip of her coffee, "that they think I was the one with the most motive to ... harm that agent."

I agreed, but it wouldn't help a bit to let Angela know that. "Maybe," I said, patting her hand one last time. "But let's do some thinking about this, okay? Let's try to recall some of the things that happened. Make some notes—look at the angles with fresh eyes."

She furrowed her brows for a moment and then blinked her eyes. "Do you mean, do our own investigation?"

It sounded sort of crazy to say it out loud like that. Coming from the mouth of a conservative Southern judge's wife, who also happened to be the mother of a federal agent, and especially since she was saying it to a Tattooed Left-Coast Nobody. But when I saw the hope that sprang into those Skyler blues, I knew that I had no choice but to go forward with the so-called investigation. The hardest part would be convincing Marie.

"All right then," I said, after swallowing the last greasy mouthful of pizza roll and glad to see that Angela had eaten hers, too. Shit, we were light years from oolong tea and clotted cream. "First on the agenda, is grabbing some sleep." I glanced down at my charm watch. "The ship doesn't dock at Half Moon Cay until after ten. And since it's not an official murder investigation at this point, I doubt they'll stop us from going ashore." I wiped my fingers on my napkin and patted my lips. "We'll hook up on the island and do some brainstorming, okay?"

"What excursion are you taking?" she asked.

"Stingray Adventure," I said, thinking how Marie had joked that the stingrays were less dangerous than the literary bunch. It had been that first night, when Artie had pooped on the bar in front of Carter Cantrelle, when he'd been swearing like a sailor and everyone had been so shocked. And then Carter confronted Thea, making that crack about her father, and saying that someone ought to wash the nasty parrot's mouth out with—*oh my God*. My mouth dropped open.

"I'm going to that same beach," Angela said, oblivious to my "aha" moment. She wiped her mouth and straightened the front of her jacket, smiling. "Luke bought me a very nice snorkel set, but I won't be jumping in with stingrays. That sounds far too dangerous." Angela's smile faded. "I'm afraid I have more than enough trouble to contend with here."

Soap. Carter Cantrelle had said that someone ought to wash Artie's mouth out with *soap*. Who else heard that?

"Maybe you're not in as much trouble as you think, Angela," I said, suddenly itching to get my hands on a pencil and paper. To start my Suspect list. "Maybe not."

* * *

I walked Angela to her cabin, glad to see that the squad of security people had left the corridor. All that remained on Thea's door was an official "Do Not Enter" sign, and a security seal over the key card entry slot. Otherwise, all was quiet as the gently swaying ocean beneath us. I yawned and had started off toward the elevators, when I heard a door click behind me. The voice, soft and slightly slurred, called my name before I could turn.

"Darcy?"

Who? Oh, of course.

"Barbara," I said, walking back toward her cabin. "Have you been able to get any sleep?" I stepped closer to the half-open door and my heart squeezed when I saw her face. She looked awful, her nose and eyes red, lids puffy, and forehead creased with obvious anxiety. God, I hoped it was true that the ship was finding her another cabin. Being so close to Thea's suite had to cause more than a few nightmares.

Barbara raised her hand to the neckline of her cotton pajamas, her fingers trembling. "I'm..." She swallowed. "I heard voices, and I th-thought it was the steward." Her lids dipped heavily. "I'd ordered some warm m-milk and..."

"I can go get it for you," I said quickly, without a clue as to where I'd find it, but hating to see her like this.

"No, s'all right. They'll come," Barbara said. She glanced down the hallway. "I saw you with that...woman." Her breath caught with what looked like a fresh stab of pain, and then she reached through the doorway and grabbed my arm, hard. "They...think someone *killed* Thea," Barbara whispered, her pupils dilating dark and wide. "Security does. They mentioned all those awful things that happened at Thea's workshop and..." she glanced down the hallway toward Angela's door again. "And that *she*—"

"No—oh no!" I said loudly enough to make Barbara flinch. She swayed on her feet, put an arm against the doorway to steady herself, and I felt instantly guilty. "I'm sorry," I said softly. "I just mean that Angela had nothing to do with Thea's...accident." I nodded my head, feeling worse as I watched fresh tears swim in Barbara's eyes. "It was a sad, tragic accident, Barbara. Nobody's fault."

"They questioned her," Barbara said, the tears halting without spilling over. "Everyone's saying that she hated Thea." The assistant's eyes narrowed. "And that Angela Skyler is rich and spoiled, and has the kind of ego that couldn't take—"

"They're wrong," I said, interrupting and realizing that I was walking a damned awkward line between these two distraught women. "And in fact," I continued, "Angela and I have some ideas that we're sort of . . . mulling over." Something told me I shouldn't be revealing this, but somehow the rules get fuzzy at four thirty in the morning. And maybe I'd inherited my grandma's need to fix things, but for whatever reason, I kept on going.

"I mean, just in case security does go forward with a case for . . . well, murder. We—Angela, Marie, and I—are going to talk with people, make notes, try to recall pertinent facts about things that happened since the cruise began." I nodded my head when Barbara's brows drew together in obvious confusion. "Angela calls it our own 'investigation.'" I nodded and smiled to reassure her, "I don't know about that, but I do know that we aren't going to stand by and do nothing, Barbara."

I reached out and patted her shoulder, not in the least bit sure that I'd done anything to help, and then turned at the sound of footsteps approaching. The room service steward was coming our way. "Good," I said, smiling at Barbara. "Your warm milk is here. You'll be able to get some more sleep." I nodded. "And I promise you, Barbara, I'm going to see to it that the truth comes out. All of it. Don't you worry."

I watched her take the glass of milk and close the door, and then I padded back toward the elevators. For godsake, my brain was being nourished by Jack Daniels and pizza rolls, and I'd just made promises to unsnarl the troubles of two women. How the hell was I going to do that? Marie was right—stingrays were going to seem pretty friggin' tame.

FOURTEEN

THERE'S NO BETTER CURE for a pirate-size hangover than sinking your toes in the sugar-white sand of an island refuge for those same rum-sodden swashbucklers. Half Moon Cay is private, breathtakingly gorgeous and was a godsend—after one hell of a queasy, up-and-down tender-boat ride to shore, that is. *Aargh*. Though Luke and I once put a musty lifeboat to deliciously inventive use, I was darned glad to be settled into a beach chair in front of the island's "Wish I Could Stay Here Forever Bar." Beyond my chair, glistening sand waded into the surreal blue of the Caribbean, while a warm breeze carried scents of coconut and flowers, and vibrated with a Don't-Worry-Be-Happy mix of steel drums and xylophone. But beside me, Marie growled like Blackbeard. Apparently she had more than a few issues with my new agenda.

"An *investigation*?" She asked for the second time, after slathering Banana Boat SPF 30 below the hemline of her turtle Jams. "You told Angela that we'd investigate Thea's electrocution?" She frowned at a blob of lotion on her cigar, and then grumbled again. "What are you, Darc', a masochist?" She nodded toward a shell-strung booth next to the bar. "If you want pain, you could just trot over there and have your hair pulled into a thousand teeny braids. See that woman? She'd do it for fifteen bucks. Maybe having all those beads smackin' you in the head will knock some sense into you."

She slid her Garfield sunglasses down from the top of her head to cover her eyes. The orange cartoon tabby moved side to side as she shook her head. "You've got to be nuts, sitting there making lists of 'clues and suspects and suspicious incidents,' like you honestly think we're going to be helping with a *murder* investigation."

"Shh," I said quickly, glancing toward the lemon-yellow cabana a few yards from us, "Angela's right over there. Don't say 'murder'; she might hear you." I leaned out from my chair to see if Angela was still stretched out on the striped chaise lounge below the swirling palm fan and misting apparatus. She was, and I could also see that her attentive cabana butler was busy carrying her towels and snorkeling equipment from the dune buggy.

Marie peered over her sunglasses at Angela. "She doesn't look too worried to me."

"You didn't see her last night—um, wait, that was this morning." I groaned. "God, what a hellish night. I'm so glad to be off that ship and away from all those whacked-out people." I adjusted the rhinestone peace sign on the top of my aqua bikini, then glanced around and sighed. "Not that most of them didn't follow along, like rats off a you-know-what." I nodded toward a woman wading into the ocean. "Isn't that Carter's little minion, Sarah?"

"Yup," Marie answered, "and I saw that she finally got the nerve to talk with her hero, too." She pointed toward the orangey Mango

Cabana two doors down from Angela's. "Cantrelle and her knife-juggling editor are holed up in there, working. I saw Sarah helping them carry their things in." Marie leaned close and frowned as I underlined a name on my Suspicious Incidents list. Carter was definitely someone I needed information on. And if Sarah had talked to her, maybe she knew something and …

"*What*?" I asked, defensively, as Marie began clucking her tongue. "You don't think it's suspicious that Carter told Thea—right out loud in front of everybody—that someone ought to wash Artie's mouth out with soap?"

"Maybe," she said, tapping her finger against my list, "but then again, I was thinking how much I'd like to wrap some duct tape around that beak myself. If I'd said it out loud, would I be on your list, too?"

I opened my mouth, and Marie held up her hand. "If," she said, "and I do mean *if*, Thea's death wasn't an accident, then what you need to think about is *motive*, Darc'. And Carter Cantrelle—"

"Was insulted over and over by Thea," I insisted, pointing the pencil eraser at my friend's nose. "In the bar that night, and then at the Chop or Shop."

"Not good enough," Marie said, fishing around in her fanny pack. "According to Carol, Carter's books are on every bestseller list in the country. Consistently. Hell, I think she's been a guest on Oprah. *Oprah*, Darc'. Thea's insults are doing nothing to hurt Carter's career. You think she'd risk having to write from a prison cell?" Marie pulled out her Volkswagen lighter and tapped its miniature wheels against my paper. "Same goes with your off-the-wall suspicion about the ship's theatre crew. Even if they have access to special effects stuff, why would they want to put a smoke bomb in Gertie's wastebasket? And what's that got to do with the alleged murder of Thea Kenyon? It's just like I said before, Darcy: *no motive.*"

She flicked her lighter, the flame rose from the little Bug's hood, and for a second I thought she was going to set my lists on fire. To tell the truth, I was starting to think that wasn't such a bad idea. I was no detective, and it had been stupid and impulsive to promise Angela that I could do some investigating. I groaned softly. Not just Angela. I'd made that promise to poor Barbara, too, and—*oh jeez.* I set my list down and nudged Marie as she began to raise the lighter to her cigar. "Look," I said pointing my pencil. "It's Barbara Fedders. I can't believe she came out here."

It was true, though. She was heading toward a cabana, the green Kiwi Cabana between Angela's and Carter's, walking zombie-like with shoulders slumped and wearing a terry robe and dark glasses. Herb Dugdale was alongside her, holding her elbow like he was keeping her from sinking into the sand.

"That was supposed to be Thea's cabana," Marie said after taking a drag from her cigar. "Barbara must have been as anxious to get off the ship as we were. Couldn't be easy being in the cabin right next door to Thea's, sedatives onboard or not. It's good they're moving her to that other deck this afternoon." She shrugged. "But a beach hut's a good place to sleep in the meantime, I guess." Marie raised her brows. "If Herb can get her in there, that is."

I saw what Marie meant. Barbara had stopped in her sandy tracks to stare openly at Angela Skyler, and I knew, from our hallway conversation early this morning, that Barbara was thinking about what security had told her. That Thea's death may not have been accidental. And that Angela Skyler had what Marie insisted that no one else on my list had: a motive for murder.

187

I'd started to stand—to do God knows what—when Angela rose from her chaise and Barbara immediately turned away and walked into the green-painted cabana. And then the Judge's wife headed our way, bare feet sinking in the sand as the warm breeze lifted the sheer hem of a black pareo, printed with a red hibiscus to match her swimsuit. Her makeup was flawless, her hair looked freshly styled, and I wondered for a minute if the cabana butler did double duty in the spa. I glanced sideways at Marie, who'd heaved an audible sigh. She saw it, too: Angela was carrying a notebook and a pencil. Apparently our investigation was moving forward as planned.

"Good morning, Darcy…Marie," Angela said, after glancing around for another beach chair and frowning slightly. She glanced from Marie's face to mine and then tucked the little notebook behind her back. Her blue eyes caught mine and, despite the artful makeup and hairdo, it was obvious that she was still as anxious as she'd been in the wee hours of the morning. "Would you like to come over to my cabana? It's quite comfortable, and the butler went to get some lovely sandwiches. There are cold drinks, and perhaps, we could…talk?" Her brows furrowed, asking a silent question.

"Marie knows," I said, holding up my own papers. "She knows we're looking into the facts surrounding Thea's death and," I squeezed my eyes shut for a second and took a risky leap, "she's willing to *help* us."

Marie coughed around her cigar and her eyes widened.

"Oh thank God," Angela said, sinking to her knees onto the edge of my beach towel. "I can't tell you how much that means to me." She glanced toward the Mango and Kiwi cabanas. "I'm sure I'm not imagining the frosty reception I've received since that horrible

188

interrogation by security. And I simply cannot expose my family to—" She squeezed her eyes shut for a moment, exhaled softly, and then forced a smile. "But I've made some notes." Angela flipped to a page in her notebook. "I've talked to Renee, Gertie, and Vicky."

Marie tried her best to shoot me an evil look, and I avoided her eyes. I nodded my head at Angela. "They're all onshore?" I asked.

"Yes," Angela circled an entry in her notebook. "Gertie's meeting Herb for lunch at the Food Pavilion, and I'll get more time to talk with them then. Renee and Vicky are on the Glass-Bottom Boat Tour and—"

"Oh blast!" I said, sitting up so fast that my chair sank and tipped me backward. I lifted my sun-pink arm and squinted at my watch. "We're supposed to be over at the Stingray Adventure right now, and I wanted to arrive early to make sure I could get a decent mask; it's so hard to adjust them over this pile of hair." I grimaced and reached for my backpack. "The masks always leak, and I'm really not up to a noseful of salt water. But I guess I'll have to deal—"

"Use mine," Angela said, quickly. "Really, Darcy. Luke said it's the best brand, and I've never used it."

"But ... won't you need it?"

"Absolutely not," Angela said, shaking her head. "I'm not going anywhere near the water. Please take it. It's right there on the other side of my lounge chair; and my cabana's on the trail to the Stingray Pool."

I hesitated long enough for Marie to give me a little shove. "Thank the nice lady and take the snorkel set, Darc," she said, giving me a look that I knew meant I was currently on her shit list.

Marie was completely silent as we followed Angela to the Lemon cabana, picked up the very cool Apollo Pro gear and said goodbye.

Something told me it wasn't going to be easy to convince her to be Watson to my Sherlock, but maybe if I—*oh, hey*. I stopped on the sandy trail and tugged at Marie's sleeve.

"What?" She grumbled.

I nodded toward where Frankeen Price—under the shade of an umbrella—was seated at an easel, paintbrush in hand. Just yards beyond her lay Reader Sarah, stretched out facedown on a leopard-print towel in front of Carter's cabana.

"No way," Marie said, moving her arm away from my grasp. "I am *not* helping you question anybody."

"C'mon," I said, scrunching my brows. "If Sarah helped Carter and Ellen carry their things into the cabana, then you know *someone* said *something* about Thea's death and—"

"And it's none of my business," Marie said emphatically. She pointed toward the Snorkel Cabana down the beach, just beyond where Barth and Keven were tossing a Frisbee. "I'm not investigating anything, unless it's swimming directly in front of my dive mask." She studied my face, sighed, and then tapped her watch. "Meet me down at the Dive Cabana in ten minutes."

It didn't take me more than thirty seconds to learn that Sarah was in no shape to cooperate with my amateur investigation—frankly, she looked more shell-shocked than Angela. And so very different from the woman who'd been laughing and partying with Keven in the casino last night. She sat up on her towel and slid her sunglasses to the top of her head as I knelt on the sand beside her. The Reader's hazel eyes were red-rimmed and her blonde hair stood up in little wisps, reminding me—for some reason—of a baby sparrow I'd rescued and kept in a box one summer when I was a kid. Not too smart in a house with three cats.

"I hope I'm not disturbing you, Sarah," I said, smiling. "Just wanted to say hi." My gaze dropped to the ornate hardbound book on the towel beside her. It was open, and the pages were embellished with dried flowers, bits of shells, lace edged ribbon, and— *oh, the gift for Carter.* "Wow, that's gorgeous," I said. "Did Gertie say it was called an 'altered book,' or something like that? And that you made it to honor Carter, because she's your favorite author?"

"Yes," Sarah said, softly, glancing toward Carter's Kiwi cabana and then back to me. I noticed, again, the dazed look in her eyes. "And she was my mother's favorite author, too," Sarah added, touching a fingertip to one of the book's gold-edged pages. "This is Carter's sixth book in the Atlanta series. *Faded Flowers.*" She smiled, the look in her eyes suddenly faraway. "Mom read it over and over." Sarah's smile disappeared, and she swallowed. "And when Mom got too sick to read it herself, I read it to her. It kept her mind off the pain; it made her smile when nothing else could. I was reading it to her in the hospital … the night she died."

Oh boy. I opened my mouth to try and say something comforting about tributes or memories, or … but stopped as Sarah's eyes narrowed and an ugly frown twisted her delicate features.

"Carter's books have helped so many people," she continued, "and for anyone to criticize her work, *insult* her … or threaten to hurt her family …"

Hurt her family? I squinted in confusion. "Are you talking about Thea Kenyon?" I asked.

"Yesss," Sarah whispered, her voice emerging in a soft hiss. "And even if Carter's being gracious and sympathetic about that … accident, I still think …" Sarah's voice trailed away and she left the thought unfinished. She slid her sunglasses back down over her eyes and closed the altered book.

It was all I was going to get. And stingrays were waiting.

*   *   *

I treaded water and peered through the face mask once again at the creature below me: slate gray, flat as a pancake, big raised eyes, pearly white underside ... tail like a possum on steroids and—*ooh, jeez.* I tucked my thumbs inside my fists as the thing undulated by me, then lifted my head, looking for Marie. All I could see were the back pockets of her Jams.

I wasn't sure why they called wading in waist-deep water an "adventure," unless it was because you had to sort of float above the bottom so you wouldn't accidentally step on a sting-ray tail. And, come to think of it, that would have been way too much adventure for me, considering how much I'd wailed when my brother tossed a dart at my big toe at the '82 Cavanaugh Family Reunion. But, the good part of this dubious adventure was that Marie was ecstatic, and had completely forgotten that she was pissed at me for involving her in the so-called investigation.

"Ooh, man," she said, eyes bugging through her face mask as she lifted her head, "look at that big boy down there, Darc'. Bet he's three feet across!" She slapped her face mask against the clear, salty water, bent downward with her butt still floating, and then reappeared. "Holy moly, did you touch one yet? Feel its stomach—it's like velvet!"

Yeah, like velvet with a friggin' hidden beak. That can suck your thumb in. Not kidding. It did. Though I wasn't going to admit it, I'd forgotten the guide's warning to keep your hands in a fist—

thumb tucked in—when feeding the "big boys." I think the whole combination of treading in waist-deep water while holding a piece of slippery squid confused me for a minute.

"Yeah, sure did," I said, raising my hand in a thumb's up signal, mostly to assure myself that my finger was still there. But also because I really was glad Marie was smiling again. "Just like velvet."

I floated on my back for a minute, careful not to bump into any of the dozen or so other adventurers in the small, cordoned-off reef and gazed farther out to sea. Beneath a cloudless sky, the Caribbean stretched out in an incredible blanket of blue; all shades of blue, from the deepest cobalt to sort of neon-sapphire, to a teal green, and every shade in between. And the water was clear and warm and ... too darned shallow right where I was floating. And too crowded. I was thinking of slipping past the rope at the edge of the reef and moving out into deeper water, so that I could find some fish like we'd seen during the Helmet Dive. After all, I had this great set of gear that I'd borrowed from Angela and I'd barely used it. The mask worked beautifully, but I hadn't needed the snorkel. Besides, a little distance from people and commotion was exactly what I wanted after what had been going on aboard the ship. I'd trade murder suspicions for quiet and blue and peace any old day. I'd just slip away from the guide and ...

I nudged Marie and pointed toward the yellow plastic rope, making little dolphin movements with my hand. "Follow me," I mouthed as I checked the guide's position once more. Satisfied that he was preoccupied—which had to be the case, since he was actually holding one of the rays aloft for a curious crowd of adventurers—I slithered under the rope with Marie following.

The reef, indeed, dropped away abruptly and the water was wonderfully warm and clear. Already, without the Stingray Adventurers stirring up sand, I could see schools of brilliantly colored fish. I spit into my mask to prevent fogging, rinsed it, and slid it into place. Then I popped in the snorkel mouthpiece, closed my lips around it, and began to swim. I took one look into the depths below me and knew I'd made the right decision; this was unbelievable. Purple fish with yellow fins, slender striped ones, coral, and—my breath caught and I figured it must be the excitement. I swam forward again, breathed in deeply through the snorkel tube and ... no air came.

What the ... ? I lifted my head, treaded water and tried again. No air. How could that be? I spit the mouthpiece out and took a breath, confused. This was weird.

"What's the matter?" Marie asked, swimming up next to me.

"Snorkel's not working," I said, shrugging my shoulders as I treaded water. I glanced back toward the stingray folks a dozen yards back. They hadn't missed us.

"Blow through it," Marie suggested, treading beside me. "That'll clear it." She raised her brows and smirked. "Fancy-ass equipment. Lucky you."

I rolled my eyes and gave a sharp blow through the snorkel. My cheeks puffed as the air met continuing resistance. "What the hell?" I raised the tube and peered into the distal end.

"What're you doing?"

"Something's wedged in there," I explained, my voice rising with surprise. "It's new equipment, so maybe's there's some of those packing peanuts, or ..." I blew again, and then picked at what looked like a piece of wadded-up paper.

"What is it?" Marie asked.

"Don't know," I said, trying to unfold the tightly creased square of paper. "Looks like …" I finally succeed in flattening it in my wet palm, and my eyes widened. "Oh, shit."

"What?" Marie crowded close.

"It's a note," I said, my mind whirling. "A weird note. Look at this."

I handed it to Marie and she read it aloud, her expression just as confused as mine:

"*I know who you are. And soon everyone will know about you and the flamingo.*"

I stared at her and she stared at me, like we were Dumb and Dumber.

"The flamingo?" Marie asked.

"Got me."

"Someone's *threatening* you?" Marie asked, her voice burbling as the salty blue water lapped at her lower lip.

I stared down at the snorkel bobbing in the water in front of me and then back over my shoulder toward the beach. To the tidy and well-stocked Lemon Cabana. Goose bumps rose on my arms despite the warmth of the Caribbean Sea.

"No," I said, not sure why I was suddenly whispering. "It's not my snorkel. Someone's threatening *Angela*."

*   *   *

By the time we made it back to the trio of fruit-colored beach cabanas, Marie and I had a fairly decent plan for broaching the threatening note with Angela. Direct but gentle. We'd gauge her reaction, let her talk … only problem was that she wasn't there. Butler, dune buggy, towels, tiny crustless sandwiches—trust me, Marie looked for those babies—all gone back to the ship. And not long after we'd brushed off the sand and climbed the gangway ourselves, we discovered why: the news was out that a murder investigation was underway. Renee wasted no time in spilling the beans to us.

"They've called the FBI about Thea's death," she said, catching us as we passed the Lido Deck's poolside hotdog grill. She licked a dab of mustard from her lip and checked her watch. "Let's see, it's four thirty now, so I guess it was about… an hour ago. Can you believe it?" Renee's pudgy face was flushed and her eyes glittered. "There's crime tape wrapped all over the door to Thea's suite—you know, like some screenplay Keven wrote for *Law & Order*. I didn't see it myself, but I have that friend in the Purser's Office who tells me everything."

I glanced sideways at Marie and then back at Renee, my stomach doing flip-flops. *FBI? Luke?* If Angela knew all this, she must be frantic. I exhaled softly and tried to keep my voice as casual as I could.

"Wow, I'd love to hear more, Renee, but…" I patted my backpack bulging with diving equipment. *And the snorkel note.* "I need to return something that I borrowed from Angela Skyler. Know where she is?" I held my breath, praying I didn't already know the answer.

Renee smiled, and by the look of it I would have sworn she'd been slathering mustard on a canary, not a hot dog. "Of course," she said smugly, "she's down in the security office answering questions. They radioed her cabana butler and had him bring her in from the beach. Vicky and I followed them back."

I smiled as best I could, mumbled a goodbye and yanked Marie's arm as I took off down the deck.

"Omigod," I said, as we threaded through the poolside passengers and made our way to the elevators inside the Lido Café, "Angela must be going berserk down there. Could they really think she has something to do with Thea's death?"

"Guess so." Marie jabbed her finger against the Down arrow and waited for the doors to open. She took a look at my face and grimaced. "Sorry, Darc', but think of how many people heard her threatening Thea at the Chop or Shop. And now... well, I've been thinking about those things that Dr. Herb reported—"

"Herb?" I stepped inside the elevator after Marie, trying to balance the overloaded backpack. My arms were getting tired, and Angela's snorkel—protruding from the opening—kept poking me in the nose. "You mean that Herb saw Angela in the Dolphin Deck Lounge making complaints about Thea?"

Marie glanced at the half-dozen passengers squeezing in beside us and lowered her voice to a hoarse whisper. "That and his examination of Artie—the soap and the blood in his beak."

I scrunched my brows. "What's Artie got to do with this?"

"He's a bird," Marie whispered.

"So?" I stared at her, wondering if she'd gotten too much sun.

"Maybe Angela has a ... *thing* about birds."

I nodded at an elderly woman, who'd stepped aboard on Promenade Deck, and then hissed a reply to my friend's ridiculously cryptic statement. "'A thing about birds?' What the hell does that mean?" I nudged her when she didn't answer. "Well?"

The doors opened onto D-Deck and Marie followed me out, silent for a few moments.

When the elevator doors closed discreetly behind us, she turned to me and raised her brows. "Flamingos are birds, too, Darcy. That note in the snorkel threatened to tell everyone about Angela 'and the flamingo.'"

My jaw dropped, the snorkel poked me in the nose, and I don't know whether I was starting to choke, or laugh or—"Shit, Marie. Are you telling me that Luke's mother is some sort of serial bird killer?" I stared in disbelief and when she didn't hustle to deny it, I set my backpack down on the carpet and planted my hands on my hips. "Have you lost your mind?"

Marie ran her fingers through her bangs and sighed. "All right, it does sound whacked. Sorry. I guess I'm only trying to make some sense of that note."

I sighed too, and then picked up my backpack. "Okay," I said, as we started walking down the corridor toward our cabin, "I know this sounds strange coming from me, but let's try not to jump to conclusions until we've had a chance to talk with Angela. Nothing's going to make sense until we do that. I'm sure she'll have a very simple explanation for all of this."

Except that Angela was waiting in front of our cabin door, and the look on her face was anything but simple.

"Thank God you're back," she said, her blue eyes wide. "They've decided that Miss Kenyon's death was a murder and they're questioning everyone again. Her fingers clutched at the neckline of her black terry cover-up. "The FBI has been contacted." She shook her head. "I can't be involved in this. We have to clear my name before Luke finds out." She pulled her notebook out of her purse. "So I've made some notes, asked more questions—"

"Wait," Marie said, using the calm, authoritative tone I'd heard a thousand times in the chaos of the ER. "Stop for a minute, Angela. We have a question to ask *you* first." She turned to me and nodded. "Don't you Darcy?"

God. I cleared my throat, squirmed for a second, and then pulled out the sea-damp square of paper. I unfolded the thing and handed it to Angela.

"I don't … understand …" she said haltingly, brows drawing together. She tilted her head and her lips moved silently as she read the words. I think I heard her gasp.

"It was wedged in your snorkel tube," I explained, hoping I was imagining the color draining from Angela's face. Pale. So pale, and she was swaying a little and then—

"Oh jeez—catch her, Marie!"

And then Angela fainted.

FIFTEEN

WE DRAGGED ANGELA, RATHER indelicately, into our cabin and got her lying down pronto. In just moments, her eyelids began to flutter and the color returned to her face.

"You're okay now," I said, hoping she wouldn't notice, like I just did—*for godsake*—that I was sponging her forehead with a damp-ened Spider-Man sock. I shot Marie a what-the-hell-were-you-thinkin' look and then turned back to Angela. "You fainted. But no pain or shortness of breath or anything like that, right?"

"No. And I'm so sorry," Angela whispered. She cleared her throat and tried to sit, but I caught her shoulder and kept her flat. "I have no idea why this happened," she said.

I glanced sideways at Marie and she nodded. We sure knew why. The snorkel note was burning a hole in my pocket, and I was determined to ask more about it. Angela looked pretty good now; couldn't very well faint again if she was already lying down, so … I nodded as she took a sip from the glass of water that Marie handed her. Then I pulled out the crumpled note.

"We still need to talk about this," I said and heard Angela's breath catch as her pupils dilated wide. If we'd had her connected up to a lie detector, things would have been zinging like a seismograph in a California quake.

"I have no idea," she said too quickly. Her eyes focused somewhere above my head and she bit into her lower lip for a moment. "Really, it makes no sense that it would be in my snorkel. I can't imagine the intent of this ... joke."

"The intent," Marie said, very directly, "was to threaten you, Angela. I don't think it was a joke." She picked up the note and Angela's lips tensed. "Do you know what this 'flamingo' part means?"

Angela's lips paled and I reached for the Spidey compress.

"No," she said, sitting up and crossing her arms. "I'm telling you—both of you—that the note means *nothing* to me."

"You fainted after you read it," I said as gently as I could, considering that I suddenly wanted to shake her. "It had to mean *something* to get that kind of reaction."

"It means I need to eat, that's all," Angela said, waving her palm. "The cabana butler whisked me back to the ship so fast that I didn't even have time for lunch." She glanced down at her watch. "And now it's nearly dinner time, and it's formal tonight. I'll need time to contact the valet service to press my gown and—" She frowned at me. "Will you please let me up, Darcy?"

It didn't take a brain surgeon to know that I was being dismissed. I looked over at Marie and raised my brows, helplessly.

"Look," Marie said, stepping aside as Angela stood up. "All we're saying is that we're concerned. For your safety. This note, even if confusing, is some kind of threat. It's one more mess that needs investigating, so ... since there's now officially a murder case, and the FBI has been contacted, there's no sense in—"

"In continuing to waste any more time," Angela interjected, nodding her head up and down. "I wholeheartedly agree. It's more important than ever that we do everything we can to ensure that I'm not implicated." She turned to me and grasped my arm, her blue eyes anxious. "The federal agents won't be coming on board until we dock in Nassau tomorrow. So we have time to talk with people tonight. Someone *has* to know something."

Marie glanced down to where the snorkel note lay on the bedspread. "I'm thinking we should turn this note over to security." She jumped as Angela's hand snatched the note as fast as a striking rattler.

"No," Angela said, curling her fingers tightly around it. "I don't think that's wise. I mean, that it would only confuse matters. Security told me they're turning everything over to the federal agents. Tomorrow." She forced a smile and tucked the note into the pocket of her beach robe. "I'll keep it safe for now." She took a few steps toward the door and then stopped, looking back at us. "We'll meet in the Crow's Nest Bar after dinner. Nine thirty sharp." Her eyes flicked over me in a quick head-to-toe assessment and then she shook her head. "I wish I hadn't cancelled that spa appointment; I could have given it to you, Darcy. I can't imagine how you'll ever manage that hair tonight."

Aagh! I'm pretty sure my mouth was hanging open as she walked out. I know it was when I hurled the soggy Spider-Man sock against the door. I turned to Marie and shook my head. "She insulted me. Do you believe that?"

"Told you. Typical MO."

I wrinkled my nose. "Huh?"

"Of a serial bird killer." Marie smiled slowly. "You think she bumps the flamingoes off and then uses them to play croquet? You know, like *Alice in Wonderland*?"

* * *

I set the crab puff down and patted my hair, checking to be sure that the carved ivory chopsticks—the ones Luke found at that great shop in Chinatown—weren't slipping out. "How's my hair?" I asked Marie, already angry with myself for obsessing over Angela's critical remark.

"Which ones? That wavy piece hanging alongside your chin, or the clump sticking up on top?"

She snorted through her nose as my hands flew upward. "Gotcha! For godsake, Darc', give it a rest. You look great." Marie tapped an unlit cigar against her frosty beer stein, and then loosened the tailored collar of her tuxedo pantsuit. She glanced around the room. "What I can't figure out, is how we managed to get here so early. Or why we didn't pass Angela out in the foyer frisking people."

"Private dining room," I said, fussing with the chopsticks again and then smoothing the beaded halter of my smoky lavender gown. "She's having dinner in the Odyssey Room with Herb and Gertie, making up for not getting to question them at lunch, I'd bet." I took one more bite of my crab puff and then pulled the lists out of my tasseled evening bag. "And you're right, we're here early enough to go over some of this before anyone else arrives." I looked up when Marie moaned. "What?"

"You can't be thinking of continuing this stupid investigation. The feds are coming, for crying out loud, Darcy."

I raised my glass of chardonnay and nodded. "Yeah, well you saw how determined Angela is. We need to make some sort of effort, if only to reassure her until it's officially out of her hands. She's scared about something, Marie." I lowered my voice to a whisper. "And I get the feeling she's lying about that snorkel threat."

"Ya think?" Marie rolled her eyes and lifted her beer. "So all this crap is because she doesn't want to taint the precious Skyler name? I mean, hell, if I were in her shoes, I'd pull every string I had. And hey, she's got one big ball of twine loaded with legal types. Luke would be down here in a heartbeat, if he knew."

I coughed into my glass and squeezed my eyes shut for a second. "She doesn't want him to know," I rasped, after I got my breath.

"And you don't, either. Obviously." Marie shook her head. "You're taking too much responsibility here, Darc'. As usual. Just because you were nice enough to invite Angela to come along on this cruise, doesn't mean that you could have predicted any of this Thea Kenyon mess. I think you should tell Luke about Angela's part in it before he finds out from the Bureau. You know he's going to."

Marie was right, of course. But I kept thinking of that desperate look on Angela's face. I pulled a pencil out of my bag and tapped it against my list. "Humor me, okay? If Luke calls and asks, I'll tell him. Absolutely. But in the meantime, let's just go over this. Please?"

Marie grumbled, but she grabbed one of the lists and I heaved a sigh of relief. I sure as hell wasn't going to tell her that Luke already had called. A couple of times. And I hadn't said anything.

"So," Marie said, scanning the list. "We've got Carter who hated Thea and who wanted to wash Artie's beak out with soap. We've got Herb who was the last person to see Thea alive."

"Only if he threw the laptop in," I said solemnly. "Technically, whoever was in her bathroom saw her last. But I'm thinking we should go over this chronologically. That always helps me think." I closed my eyes for moment, listening to the soft tinkle of crystal and the pianist playing on the balcony above us. "Okay. First night: Angela sent the champagne to Thea. Carter and Thea had a fight in the Crow's Nest Bar. Herb and Keven and Barbara took Artie away." I scribbled notes on my list. "Then Sarah got pissed and followed Carter to her book signing."

"And the next morning we had our workshop," Marie continued, "and Barbara saved our asses when the group got out of hand. Man, remember? She was so organized she could have taught the damned thing herself."

"Right," I said, nodding. "And that's when she told me about Artie needing sedatives and Thea's laptop battery malfunctioning." I jotted that down.

"And that disgusting stuff about Thea bathing with the parrot."

"No," I said after taking a sip of my wine. "Keven told me that. He was saying how loyal Barbara was despite all that weirdness, and how if he could sneak her away from Thea he would."

"How does he know Barbara so well?'

"Writers' conferences." I shrugged. "Said he spends a lot of time with her at those things. Guess she sort of let her hair down about how tough it was to work for the kind of woman that so many people wanted to—*oh jeez*." I set my wine glass down. "I forgot."

"Forgot what?"

"Thea got an anonymous threat," I said, recalling that conversation with Barbara after our first workshop. "Remember?"

"Yeah, that's right. Do you know what it said?" Marie asked after glancing toward a small cluster of passengers arriving across the dining room.

I picked at the cheese on my crab puff. "It was a complaint about Artie, but whoever wrote it threatened Thea, too, I guess. Barbara was furious, but then said it had happened lots of times before. Kind of blew it off, actually."

"Well, a threat sure as hell seems relevant this go-around," Marie said, wiping some beer foam from her lower lip. "Considering that her boss is in the freezer with the baked Alaska."

"God." I set my crab puff down and grimaced.

"Sorry. But it does seem like someone should be putting two and two together with this note deal. Especially after our stingray adventure."

I scrunched my brows, lost.

"The note to Thea. And then Angela's snorkel note? Maybe there's a connection."

"Jeez," I said, "you're right. I wonder if Barbara reported Thea's note to security?"

Marie glanced over her shoulder. "We could ask her ourselves," she said, nodding toward a table a few yards away. "She's over there."

Sure enough, Barbara was sitting alone at a small table in a corner by a potted palm, searching through her handbag. She was dressed in a no-fuss chiffon gown with a square neckline, in a slate gray that did nothing to disguise her pallor and the dark circles under her eyes. If she was wearing makeup, it was minimal. I caught myself thinking of the contrast between the way she looked now and how radiant and happy she'd looked before Thea's Chop or Shop. Man, this *so* wasn't fair. And I hated to bother her, but I had Luke's Mom to think of, too.

Because even if it wasn't Angela's boss in cold storage, she was certainly as undone as Barbara about this whole tragedy.

I decided that it would be less intrusive if I went to talk with her by myself and started off toward her table, but didn't make it even halfway. I was shanghaied by the Highlander, Keven Brodie.

"Hey, Darcy Cavanaugh," he said, taking hold of my elbow from behind and obviously enjoying the way I jumped. "Where are you off to in such a hurry? They haven't even started serving yet."

I was formulating some snarky comeback, but—truth be told— my mind went completely blank as soon as I opened my mouth. I stared, mesmerized by the combination of tan skin, snowy white tux, dark eyes, and enormous shoulders. I finally managed to narrow my eyes enough to prove that his good looks had no effect on me, *whatsoever*, and croaked a witty response. "Barbara. Gonna ... talk. To her." *Brilliant.*

Keven laughed. "Sounds exciting, but," he hesitated and raised his dark brows, "I wouldn't do that if I were you."

"Why?" I asked, curiosity surpassing my shameless fluster. "Why shouldn't I talk with her?"

Keven patted the pocket breast pocket of his tux and nodded toward the door to the deck. "I need a smoke. Come with me and I'll fill you in."

"Uh ... sure." I glanced back toward Marie, caught her eye and did a little explanatory mime. She nodded over her beer stein and then rolled her eyes. I let Keven lead me out to the darkened deck.

The breeze was warm and humid, the decking freshly hosed, and from the darkness beyond the rail I heard the steady thrum of engines and a responding rush of water as our ship sliced through the dark sea.

Keven lit a cigarette and took a drag, sighing deeply as he turned his head away to exhale. "Sorry," he said. "I've been trying to quit, but the way my luck's been the past twenty-four hours, well—"

"Why shouldn't I talk with Barbara?" I asked, my interruption based half on curiosity and half on the desire to avoid hearing what I suspected could be some personal revelations about his budding relationship with Sarah. Where was she, anyway? They hadn't been together on the beach today, and I hadn't seen her at all since we came back aboard ship.

"Because Fedders is on a damned witch hunt," he said, flicking ashes over the rail. "Pointing her bony finger at everyone. I ran into her earlier and I got an earful, trust me."

"What do you mean?" I asked, feeling a smattering of goose bumps rise.

"I mean that someone needs to put that neurotic spinster back on sedatives," Keven said, his tone suddenly hard, caustic—surprising, until I remembered him that way once before. When he was talking about the competitive business of writing. And Thea's treatment of writers.

His brown eyes looked down at me earnestly. "Really. I'm serious. As a nurse, could you suggest some sort of medication to the infirmary staff?" His hand closed over my wrist. "Something that would knock her out for a day or so. Could you, Darcy?"

I was stunned. And I wasn't sure if it was because of his apparent insensitivity toward Barbara, or because I was having trouble imagining the well-organized woman going off the deep end. "Who's she accusing?" I asked.

Keven took another drag from his cigarette and then flicked it over the rail. "You mean who's the latest?" His mouth twisted into a sneer and he leaned to the side to peer through the glass doors that led back into the dining room. "Let's see, does she have her cell phone out again? Because if she's on the phone with security, then…" he sighed. "Okay, the last I heard, she was ragging on Herb, that bird guy. And the maid who found Thea in the tub. Damn, you should have heard that woman wail in Spanish when old Barb accused her of frying Thea."

"She's personally confronting people?" I asked, gripping the rail as the ship dipped beneath us. "Security can't be okay with that."

Keven's lips twitched into a sneer. "No. And you can damn well bet Carter Cantrelle wasn't, either."

"Oh my God. She accused Carter?"

"Oh yeah. And apparently she sounded like she was channeling Kenyon's ghost when she was doing it." Keven gave a sharp laugh. "Or at least according to Sarah."

Ah, Sarah. "Where is Sarah?" I asked. "You two are usually—"

"Don't know," Keven said abruptly. "Probably camped outside Cantrelle's door with a box of donuts and an AK-47, protecting her hero. Sarah's been a total nut job since Thea died. Who needs that? I'm glad to be rid of her." He pulled another cigarette out of his pack, frowned, and tossed it overboard untouched. "Dammit. I'm going to skip dinner and get drunk. Want to join me?" Keven traced his index finger along my bare forearm. "We could grab a bottle of cognac, go to my cabin, get naked, and…"

"No," I said, refusing to blush. But I played it a little coy, dying to know where Angela was on Barbara's alleged hit list. "Not that you don't make it sound tempting, but Marie's waiting for me." I smiled. "You're welcome to join us for dinner."

Keven shook his head. "No. I wasn't joking—I'm finding the nearest bar." He nodded toward the dining room. "But, I mean it, stay away from Fedders." His dark eyes turned deadly serious, and I got the feeling that he was about to tell me the biggest reason that he brought me out here. "Truthfully, I don't give a shit about Carter, or Herb, or anyone else that she's accusing. But I do care about you, Darcy, and"—he extended his thumb and index finger and drew them together—"frankly, Barbara's this close to resurrecting that theory of your workshop outline being related to Thea's murder. Watch out."

"You're kidding," I said, my eyes opening wide.

"I'm not kidding about any of this, Darcy," he answered, looking down, unblinking, into my eyes. "Especially about that sedation for Barbara. Something needs to be done before she's got you in an FBI lineup, too. Think about it."

"I…"

Keven's eyes softened and he leaned down and brushed his lips against my cheek before I could step away. "And rethink the cognac. We could be … very good medicine for each other. I'll be around, if you change your mind."

I watched him walk down the deck, and then I took a few breaths to keep my mind from whirling. Barbara Fedders had gone ballistic? Risen from her fog of grief to accuse Herb and Carter and—*Lord*— even that poor female cabin steward, and … Angela? Amazing. But ironically, it sounded as if Barbara Fedders was doing exactly what Angela Skyler was hell-bent on doing herself: conducting an independent investigation of Theodora Kenyon's death.

I bit into my lower lip, thinking. Then took a few steps backward to peer into the lighted dining room, now filling with passengers and bustling waiters. Barbara was still there, sipping from her glass of merlot. *Hmm.* If, as Keven said, this grieving assistant was on the same mission as we were—as the FBI would be, come tomorrow—then why not approach her now? Team up, share ideas. Clear away, once and for all, any suspicions about Angela...and our murder workshop. Sure. And then I could go ahead and ask her about Thea's threatening message, see what she thought about Angela's snorkel note, and—*whoa!* I jumped as a person appeared at the deck door. Then raised my hand to wave, as I recognized Marie's face. Count on my best friend to check up on me.

I gestured for her to come out, but just as she opened the door I heard someone shout my name from farther down the deck. *Who...?* Marie stepped out beside me and we both stared into the darkness toward a second shout and the hollow tap-slap of hustling footsteps.

"Darcy!"

Angela crossed the expanse of teak decking, racing toward us as quickly as her cobalt-blue taffeta skirt and heels would allow. A sheer, metallic-beaded stole fluttered behind her, like the failing wings of a downed game bird. Her expression, illuminated by the rows of deck lights, was completely frantic. *Oh jeez.*

"Angela, what's wrong?" I asked, my pulse kicking up a notch as she reached us. "Are you okay?" Marie lifted the edge of her stole from the damp decking, and we both waited while Angela caught her breath.

"I...ah," she took another gulp of air and pressed her hand to her throat, and I realized that she was holding her cell phone.

"I got...a...call," she said, and I knew from the look in her eyes that she wasn't talking about a kissy-poo chat with Luke's dad, the

Judge. Marie put her hand on Angela's shoulder as the woman took a few more breaths and fanned herself with the edge of her stole. "About ten minutes ago," Angela added, still a bit breathless. She stared first at Marie and then at me. "Oh God. What will I do?"

"Well, first," I said, nodding as calmly as I could, "you should tell us *who* it was that called you." Simple, logical. But I could tell by the way her chin began to tremble that I'd said exactly the wrong thing. "Angela?"

"I don't know who called," she said, staring down at the phone and then back up at me again. "But they said, something about— *Oh, God, I don't know what to do!*"

Angela's face paled and I started to have flashbacks about snorkel notes and Spider-Man compresses. *Oh hell.* I nodded to Marie and we each slipped an arm around Angela's waist and guided her to the nearest deck lounge. She sat, fanned herself with her stole again, and then nodded. "I'm okay, really. I won't faint."

"Good. But was the phone call a threat?" I asked gently, joining Marie on the lounge chair opposite Angela. And then I cut to the chase. "Like that note in your snorkel?"

Angela was quiet for a moment, avoiding our eyes, and I'd bet Grandma's goldfish that she was scrambling between that cliché rock and a hard spot. But apparently it was cramped quarters because, when she turned back, those blue Skyler eyes were swimming with tears.

"I need to tell you about the Flamingo," she said.

SIXTEEN

I DON'T KNOW HOW we ended up in the ship's chapel, unless Marie was thinking it was the best place for Angela to confess to serial bird killing, but that's where we went—after snagging the cabernet from our dining table. I sneaked a guilty peek at the non-denominational, shell motif altar and tried not to think how long it had been since my last confession. Grandma Rosaleen would have my hide if she knew. But right now, it was Angela Skyler's turn to fess up. I handed her a glass of wine, folded my hands primly in my lap, and started the ball rolling. "So ... a flamingo?" I asked.

Angela took a sip of her wine and then nodded slowly. "*The* Flamingo," she answered, correcting me, and then continued as she saw the confused look on our faces. "The Flamingo Hotel and Casino. In Las Vegas."

I'm pretty sure that Marie and I must have been doing our Dumb and Dumber imitation, because Angela took a deep breath and smiled for a split second before explaining further.

"1966, more than forty years ago," she said, shaking her head. "I was barely twenty. And it was spring break." Angela sighed, and I sneaked a glance at Marie, wondering if her stomach was doing a tandem "uh-oh" along with mine. This story's beginning transcended generational gaps, that was for damned sure. Spring break? *Oh man*... I took a hit of cabernet at the same instant that Marie did. Apparently we were on the same page.

"I was there with my three roommates from Sweet Briar College," Angela said, "We were young and naïve, I suppose, and wanted to get a taste of the 'fast life' far from Virginia." She pressed her lips together and shook her head. "I think I told my folks I was staying with one of the girls' grandparents." Angela looked up at me. "You understand."

Oh brother, did I. I had a shamrock tattoo to prove it. I nodded and smiled at Angela. "And then something happened at the Flamingo? Something... bad?"

Angela swallowed a generous swig of her wine and then laughed sharply. "If you call armed robbery bad."

"Whoa!" I think Marie nearly slid off her chair. She scooted back and brushed a puddle of wine off her pant leg. "You robbed a casino?"

I sat there, sort of numb, waiting for Angela's answer, but I was also having the strangest sense of déjà vu. *1966... Las Vegas... robbery...?*

"I didn't. We didn't," Angela said, trying to explain. "The man we went in there with did—but he didn't tell us beforehand what he was planning," she said in a hurry. "I guess we provided a diversion." Angela groaned and squeezed her eyes shut. "Or that's what the newspapers said. Afterward."

The déjà vu was making me dizzy. Something about that casino and ... "Diverson?" I asked. "How?"

"We were drunk," Angela said, obviously needing to make that important distinction first. "And young and trusting and ..."

"What kind of diversion?" Marie asked, scooting her chair closer.

I saw a tiny twitch begin beside Angela's left eye as she took a sip from her glass. Her hand trembled.

Marie nodded, encouraging her. "Maybe if you say it really fast and—"

"Topless," Angela said in such a rush that wine dribbled from the corner of her mouth and onto her gown. "We ran topless through the casino, while he took a gun and ..."

And robbed the Flamingo of seven hundred and fifty thousand dollars! The blood drained from my head, and my mouth sagged open as the memory finally hit. *Oh my God.* I tried to speak, but no words came. And then Angela continued explaining.

"And when we realized what he'd done, it was too late. The alarms were going off and the police came swarming in. Everyone was screaming. I saw cameras flashing. I tried to find a way out and—" Angela's eyes widened with anxiety, like she was nineteen again and naked and frantic to find an exit. "And all of a sudden, somehow," she said, tears beginning to brim with the memory, "there was this girl, this casino worker standing there. Like some sort of an *angel*. My true guardian angel. And she gave me this big jacket, took my hand, and showed me a back room exit and ... I got out." A tear slid down Angela's face and she wiped it away. "But my roommates didn't. It was all over the news." Angela's face flushed red. "They starting calling us the—"

"Flamingo Titty Brigade," I said before I could stop myself. "And they called it the Flamingo Titty Brigade Heist." I shook my head, in utter disbelief as the memories continued.

"And," I continued—half expecting the overhead PA to start piping "It's a Small World"—"I'll bet that that casino 'angel' was a tall *redhead*, right? And that the jacket she loaned you was a *man's*. Light green. Embroidered with a big—"

"Bug," Angela whispered, staring at me like I was an alien. "Kind of like a—"

"Cockroach?" I asked, nodding my head up and down. I traced my finger across the front of my gown. "And stitched right underneath the cockroach, it said, 'Bill the Bug Man.'"

"Yes. That's right!" Angela's brows furrowed. "But how could you know that?"

"Whoa, whoa, wait a minute!" Marie said, reaching over to place a hand on each of us. "Would someone tell me what's going on here?"

"Mom," I said, smiling at Angela. I took a deep breath and let it out slowly. "Mom told me that story from the time I was a little girl. Your 'guardian angel' was my *mother*." I shook my head and fought another rush of killer goose bumps. "She got *fired* for helping you get away that night, Angela. Not great timing for a woman with her first baby on the way. But she was damned proud she did it, once she heard how you'd been conned." I clucked my tongue. "Mary Margaret Cavanaugh is a total sucker for an underdog. Don't get me started on how much trouble that's bought her."

Angela's eyes kept getting bigger. "Your ... mother ... ?"

I shrugged. "Of course, that didn't keep Dad from being totally pissed about his jacket. He 'spent thirty-four hard-earned bucks' to have his business logo sewn on it." I wasn't able to squelch my smile. "He still brings it up once in a while. And shows us an old black and white Polaroid of him wearing it at some hokey chamber of commerce cookout." I shook my head. "My brothers call that jacket the Cavanaugh Holy Grail."

I'd looked from Marie's face back to Angela's and had just decided to say something clever, about how Angela and I really did have something in common after all, when her cell phone rang. She picked it up, said hello, and was very quiet for a few moments. Then she turned very pale.

"No," she said, blue eyes wide. "Please don't do that. Please." Marie tapped her arm, trying to get her attention, but Angela brushed her off. She stood quickly and walked a few steps away. "Okay," Angela said into the phone. "No, I won't say anything. Wait, don't go. Can't I meet you somewhere—hello, hello?" She tapped her fingers against the phone, groaned, and then disconnected.

I leaped to my feet and crossed over to her, with Marie close behind me.

"Was that another threat?" I asked, hugging my arms around myself and realizing I was trembling. "Was it?"

Angela rubbed at her forehead like she was forcing herself to think. "Pictures," she said, "they've got pictures. From the Flamingo. If I could meet with them ... and talk about—"

"Sit back *down*," Marie ordered, like she wasn't taking no for an answer. "You're not going anywhere to meet anybody."

"That's right, Angela," I said sitting beside her. "Give us more details here. Was that the same person as before? A man or ... ?"

"I can't tell," Angela said, beginning to shiver. "The voice seems muffled or distorted. I can't tell if it's one person or two. But I don't think they're lying. I think they have those humiliating pictures."

Her pupils dilated. "I can't let them do this to my family." She started to stand and I pulled her back down.

"Wait," I said. "Question: no one in your family knows about the Flamingo? Not your daughters … or Luke?" I refused to wonder how Luke would react to the image of the woman who'd counseled him on morals running naked through a Vegas casino. The man had a great sense of humor, but some things are way too sacred. "Not even your husband?"

"The Judge knows," Angela said, sighing, then tossing me a pained smile. "Unfortunately, it's how we met. He was a young attorney then, just starting out. And the Skylers were friendly with the family of my roommate who lived in Charlottesville."

"And he defended you in court?" Marie asked, her brows rising.

"No. No court. It didn't get that far," Angela explained. "Grandfather Barrett sold some acreage and most of his General Motors stock, made some phone calls, and—"

"Bought people off?" I said, before I realized how bad that sounded. But Angela, to my surprise, nodded without taking offense.

"Yes, I'm afraid so. But he got the case dropped against all of us. Even stopped that awful newspaper that was determined to run our names, along with the pictures that gamblers in the casino had snapped."

"So there were pictures?" Marie asked.

"Oh, yes," Angela said. "I never saw them. And my grandfather made sure no one else did, either." She reached a shaky hand to her throat. "Until now."

I scrunched my brows. "But why are these people threatening you?" I asked. "What do they want? Money?"

218

"I don't know," Angela said. "They haven't asked for anything." She grimaced. "They seem to want to taunt me. To play some kind of cruel joke and ..." She stood again and nodded sharply. "I have to stop them. Can you imagine what the media would do with this story?"

I struggled to think of something encouraging to say, but all that came to mind was that awful tabloid photo of the Duchess of York, topless, with some man sucking on her toes. And, frankly, I wasn't sure that Angela Skyler was as resilient as Fergie. I looked helplessly at Marie. Thank God, she rose to the occasion.

"Mrs. Skyler," Marie said, looking Angela directly in the eye. "I think you need to understand something: that note in your snorkel and those phone calls are *not* a simple matter of 'taunting' or 'cruel jokes,' no matter how much you want to believe that. They're blackmail." She folded her arms and nodded again to be sure she had Angela's attention. "These people are *blackmailers*. And blackmailers are dangerous. It's time to turn this—*all* of this—over to the authorities. The FBI is coming on board and—"

"Angela," I said, interrupting in a flash as I saw the woman's face go pale again, "Marie's right about the danger. You can't take a chance there. But," I shot Marie a pleading look, "I'm sure the agents would honor your privacy. There's no reason they can't investigate Thea's death and this threat to you, too, without involving your family." I crossed my fingers behind my back, fairly sure that I was headed for an even bigger lie. "Luke won't find out about it."

"He's coming," Angela said, her voice escaping in a half groan.

"What?" I uncrossed my fingers and planted my hands on my hips, while my stomach did somersaults.

"Luke is on his way," Angela said in a hollow voice. "That's the other call I wanted to tell you about. He's flying to Nassau tomorrow evening."

I opened my mouth, but Marie spoke first.

"He's part of the investigation?"

"No," Angela said, reaching for her throat again. "I don't think he knows about it yet." She smiled ruefully. "He said he was coming to surprise Darcy."

I tried to think of something to say, but all I kept getting was this crazy collage of images: missing knives, that security goon holding the almond extract, Gertie in the smoke, Thea in the tub, the note in the snorkel…and a judge's wife, naked under Bill the Bug Man's jacket.

I reached for the bottle of cabernet, poured all three of us a fresh round, and then raised my glass. "Well," I said, "then here's to surprises."

*　*　*

Artie looked fine, and in the twenty minutes I'd been in Herb's cabin, he hadn't even said "phooey" or "fiddlesticks." Not a single shriek, either. He shifted side to side on the perch near his cage and preened his feathers calmly. It made me wonder if Thea's killer hadn't done one good thing, at least. The soap—or the jolt—had definitely cleaned up this bird's act.

"It's a miracle that he's alive," I said, pretending that I didn't notice that Gertie was wearing the ornithologist's maroon silk bathrobe. "And a big comfort to Barbara Fedders, I'll bet," I added, testing the waters. I peeked at Dr. Herb. After all, Thea's assistant had pointed a finger of accusation at him, according to Keven Brodie. I wasn't proud of it, but I'll admit that it was curiosity about that—and not Artie's health—that had prompted my visit.

"She hasn't wanted to see Artie," Gertie said, offering the parrot a piece of dried papaya. "Even though we offered to bring him to her." She smiled as the bird lifted the piece of fruit and chortled low in his throat.

"Too many painful reminders, I guess," I said, sneaking another sideways glance at Herb. If Barbara had ranted at him the way she'd reportedly done with Carter Cantrelle, the good doctor was handling it well. Or had quite the poker face. "It would be hard to see Artie and not think of that awful scene in the bathroom of the cabin right next door to hers." I grimaced, remembering the smell of wet feathers, and the image of the agent's blistered torso. "I'm glad the ship decided to give her that suite on Carib Deck."

"She didn't go up there," Herb said, reaching out to stroke Artie's head.

"Really? Then, where did she go?"

"Barbara's still in her cabin," Gertie explained. Then she lowered her voice as if she were about to share a confidence. "Actually, I heard that she *refused* to switch cabins, even though security's got that whole end of the corridor wrapped in that awful yellow crime tape, and the FBI's coming and—"

Herb squeezed Gertie's arm gently, and then turned to me. "I think Barbara is simply more comfortable being close to Miss Kenyon's things. The woman, after all, was her employee for many years. This investigation must feel quite intrusive. Even violating, perhaps. Barbara's naturally upset."

I saw an opening and went for it. "Yes," I said, nodding sympathetically, "and I'm sure that explains why she's been so suspicious of people." I nodded again as Herb's brows rose. "Making accusations about possible suspects, I mean. I heard about the ugly scene with Carter Cantrelle."

Herb's silver brows drew together, and I turned to Gertie, sure I'd get confirmation there. All of sudden I was feeling like a kid about to get her fingers smacked by the nuns for gossiping. Why wasn't I striking a chord? Keven had made Barbara's rant sound like a friggin' sideshow act. It would be hard to miss.

"What scene?" Gertie asked. "I didn't hear about that."

"Nor did I," Herb said, sitting down on the twin bed beside Gertie. "Who relayed that information?"

"Keven Brodie," I said, wondering how I could have misunderstood such a thing. "And he said that you'd been accused by her, too, Herb. Because, well, you were the last person to report seeing Thea alive."

"I was," Herb said, frowning slightly, "and I *voluntarily* went to security to report it. As, indeed, I plan to do with the federal agents tomorrow. But as for Barbara Fedders accusing me of murder," he shook his head and shrugged. "I have no such knowledge. And I can't imagine the poor woman doing that."

"I questioned it, too," I said, mostly to make myself sound less like a gossipmonger.

"But he insisted that he'd gotten the information directly from Sarah, who'd been there when whatever happened with Carter... happened." I cleared my throat.

"Sarah?" Herb raised his snowy brows. "Carter's fan?" He continued after I nodded. "I was asking about that young lady just this afternoon. No one's seen her since the beach."

I'd decided not to quote Keven's theory about Sarah standing guard at Carter's door. I was trying to think of something to say instead, when Gertie spoke up. Apparently she had plans.

"Well," Gertie said, after smoothing the collar of her borrowed robe and smiling coyly at the doctor beside her, "it's after ten. We should put Artie to bed, Herb. And we don't want to keep Darcy from her evening plans. I'm sure the young people are going to take full advantage of the delay in docking to stay up late and party."

"Delay in docking?" I asked, feeling the heat in my cheeks as I caught the implications of Gertie's hint. I retrieved my tasseled evening bag and tried not to think of Gertie in her underwear reading *Cosmo*.

"Yes," Herb said, rising to open the door for me. "Apparently there's been a change in plans. I spoke with one of the ship's officers." He cleared his throat. "We'll be taking the longer, more 'scenic' route to Nassau; and not arriving until late tomorrow. You should have an itinerary change notice in your cabin mailbox."

Gertie looked up at me over the pillow that she was fluffing. "What Herb means is that they won't allow anyone to leave the ship before the feds arrive, dear." She glanced over at Artie, still busy with his papaya. "Because we've got a sadistic murderer onboard."

My knees went weak for a split second. *God. And now a black-mailer, too.* But I didn't say that out loud, of course, and I didn't waste any time getting out of Herb's cabin, either. Not just because these seniors wanted to, well ... get Artie tucked in. But because

I wanted to take a little trip up to Dolphin Deck, to see for my-self what frame of mind Barbara Fedders was in. All of a sudden, Keven Brodie's warning didn't make sense.

*   *   *

My confusion was compounded after a few minutes with Thea's as-sistant. In complete contrast to what Keven had suggested, Barbara seemed nowhere near needing emergency sedation. The woman was rock-steady, completely gracious—and wearing lipstick, always a sign of someone playing with a full deck, in my book. In fact, you'd hardly know that a murder had occurred just beyond that ... I sneaked a peek at the door joining Barbara's cabin with Thea's suite. There was a piece of tape over the key slot. I turned my head as Barbara spoke.

"I'm glad you called, Darcy," she said gesturing for me to sit on the twin bed opposite hers. "I was hoping to get to say hello in the dining room this evening," she smiled, "but it appeared that Keven Brodie wanted you all to himself."

"Yes, well ..." *to warn me about you, sweetie.* I paused, watching as Barbara neatly folded a tee shirt and tucked it into the suitcase sitting on her bed. She reached for another shirt, and I decided to get on with my mission. I needed to know if her alleged list of sus-pects included Angela.

"As a matter of fact," I said as casually as I could, "Keven was catching me up to speed on the investigation into Thea's ..." I hes-itated, unsure, but Barbara nodded at me, eyes unblinking.

"Yes," she said, "I've heard that several people have been ques-tioned about her death." Her brows furrowed. "That cabin stew-ard, for one. Poor woman."

Poor woman? I stared at Barbara. Hadn't Keven said that she had practically nudged that cabin steward down the plank? And accused Herb and Carter? Something wasn't making sense here at all. I stood and walked over toward Barbara's desk, near the door to the ocean-view balcony. It was neatly stacked with manuscript pages, folders, a scrapbook, and what looked like Thea's correspondence. I turned my head back toward Barbara and took my best shot.

"You know," I said resting my fingertips on a stack of papers, "I was remembering that note that someone sent to Thea, the threat." I raised my brows. "You reported that, right?"

"I..." Barbara squeezed her eyes shut for a moment, and then sighed. "Yes, but I'm afraid that's going to be useless." She shook her head. "You see, I threw it away."

My face must have betrayed me, because Barbara raised her palms and groaned. "I know. Stupid move. That security man with the ponytail had plenty to say about that, believe me." She sighed. "But if you knew how many of those threats she's gotten over the years ... It felt good to rip it up and flush it down the toilet. So now it's useless garbage, floating somewhere at sea, I suppose."

Mm hmm. Scraps of soggy paper, out in the ocean like... "You know," I was surprised to hear myself say aloud, "Angela Skyler got a threatening note, too." I wanted to bite the words back as soon as I said, them, but they sure made an impact on Barbara. She dropped the tee shirt she was folding and stared at me.

"She did?" Barbara asked. "What did it say?"

Great. Now what? "I'm not sure," I said, backpedaling and hating myself as I thought of Angela's panic over her privacy. "But, just between us, I'm wondering if it could be the same person who threatened Thea?" I watched as Barbara swallowed a couple of times, her eyes moving side to side.

"Anyway," I explained, "I've convinced her to report it to the FBI tomorrow."

I glanced to where my hand still rested on the stack of papers on Barbara's desk, and a manuscript title caught my eye: *Bare-ly Legal.* The Chop or Shop submissions. *Oh jeez.* I looked back up at Barbara, my mind whirling. Something about the submissions was nagging at the corner of my mind and ... I tapped the papers with my index finger. "Barbara, these are the manuscripts for Thea's workshop, right?"

"Yes," she said, quickly, tossing pantyhose into her suitcase. "I haven't put everything away yet." Her lips tensed and she glanced over at her travel alarm clock on the bedside table. "I don't want to be rude, but I really should get a few things done."

"What I mean," I said quickly, "is that maybe it will be important to give a list of the writers to the FBI, too. You know, in case there was some disgruntled writer ..." before I finished I realized how foolish I'd been. How very, very foolish.

"Like Angela Skyler?" Barbara asked, her eyes narrowing.

God. "And ..." I puffed my cheeks out and studied the stack again, "and a lot of other people." I nodded. "Thea wasn't exactly kind that night. So, to be fair, the investigation should include everyone." I pointed to *Bare-ly Legal* again. "These are identified by a number; but you have a list of the writers' names, right?" I frowned as the elusive thought that was nagging me earlier, flitted by again. Something about Carter ...?

I pushed the thought aside and looked back up at Barbara. "You have that list?" I asked again.

Somehow or other, she had stopped folding clothes and had crossed her arms instead. It made me think that I'd crossed something myself—maybe a line that I shouldn't have. And it was then that I noticed, with a little zing of recognition, that Thea's leather belt—with the infamous notches—was draped over Barbara's desk chair. I reached toward it and Barbara spoke up hurriedly.

"Please don't," she said, her voice choking up.

I looked up and saw that Barbara's eyes were filling with tears. I let my hand fall to my side, and mumbled an apology.

She wiped at a tear and tried to smile. "No. *I'm* sorry, Darcy. I shouldn't be so sensitive. It's only that I have so few of Thea's things that I can take back with me ... to give to her family." She glanced toward the locked door to the agent's suite. "Everything else is considered part of that horrid investigation. Thea left that belt here in my cabin after the Chop or Shop, when we had a drink to unwind. If only she'd agreed to come to the spa for a swim with me ..." the tears welled again and I took my cue.

"I understand," I said, crossing toward the door. "And I'll get out of your way, Barbara. It *is* getting late." I reached for the door handle.

She nodded, her relief obvious. "Yes. And we dock so early in Nassau tomorrow."

I looked back over my shoulder. "No, not until late afternoon," I reminded her. "The delay, remember? At the request of the federal agents?"

"Delay? No. God, no. That can't be true." Barbara's face went pale and she sank to her bed alongside her suitcase. "But I'm leaving the ship first thing in the morning." Her eyes darted around the cabin and back to her suitcase. "I'm almost packed, and ..." she looked back up at me helplessly. "They promised. I have a flight to catch. It's all arranged."

I watched Barbara's pupils dilate and thought, for the first time since I'd arrived, that maybe Keven's idea of sedation wasn't so far off. I snatched some tissues from the box on her desk and walked back toward her, explaining as gently as I could. "I think there's been a change in plans, Barbara. They were supposed to deliver notices to the cabins. Herb said he talked to one of the officers, and that the ship was changing its course."

"No!" Barbara said, her voice climbing to the pitch of Artie's squawk. "I need to get off this ship! I *have* to."

She hugged her arms around herself and tears slid down her cheeks. But, there was something far more disturbing than grief registering in her eyes—there was terror, too. The same sort of terror I saw in her eyes when she'd swallowed that merlot laced with faux cyanide. "Thea's dead," she said, finally. "There's nothing I can do to change that. And now they won't let us off? What if … someone…"

Kills again? Barbara's words dissolved in a tortured sob, and I felt the hairs rise on the back of my neck. She was right, of course. Terrifyingly right. We were trapped onboard with a murderer. And a blackmailer, too. And—*oh jeez*—there was still that matter of the missing galley knife. Damn. I wanted off this ship myself. I handed Barbara a tissue and then went straight to her medicine cabinet.

SEVENTEEN

THE BAHAMAS IS A country made up of seven hundred different islands and cays and, trust me, by early afternoon, we'd seen every friggin' one. Twice.

"Look. That's the world's third largest barrier reef," I said, pointing out over the Lido Deck rail and squinting into the sunshine. "Umm... maybe." I glanced over at Marie, wrinkling my nose. "Hard to tell from this far away. I think we're circling again."

"Courtesy of ship security." Marie lowered her binoculars and leaned back against the deck rail, pulling a printed sheet of paper from the front pouch of her sleeveless cargo vest. The daily cruise newsletter—minus its usual colorful borders, graphics, and photos, hastily printed and distributed—was limited to a single sheet today. Changes that had everything to do with the reason we weren't getting within spitting distance of Nassau. Not until we received a thumbs-up from the feds, that is.

Marie traced her finger down the columns and shook her head. "No mention of shore excursions at all," she said. "But there's

Shuffleboard Championships, Bingo Bonanza, a Napkin Folding Demonstration, Skeet Shooting off the Stern—no wait," Marie squinted, "it's stamped 'cancelled' next to the skeet shooting." She raised her dark brows. "You think—"

"That they don't trust any of us to handle *guns*?" I asked, finishing her thought. "Hell yes." I groaned and wrapped my arms across the front of my batik print wrap-dress, fighting a shiver despite the warm, humid air. "I keep thinking of that look on Barbara's face last night. She wants off this ship in the *worst* way."

Marie shook her head. "Nope. The worst way, is the way *Thea's* going off," she said, finishing with a little grimace.

"Ugh." I gave in to the shiver, rubbing my hands against my arms. "You're right. But Barbara *is* scared, Marie. After all, someone slipped fake cyanide into her wine."

Marie's forehead wrinkled. "Are you thinking that's really related to Thea's death?"

I didn't want to answer that. I hadn't wanted to even tiptoe in that direction, but ...

"I'm not sure," I said honestly. "I've been hoping it's not true. Especially since it puts the Nurse's Guide to Murder outline back in the spotlight, but ..." I glanced toward the pool, catching a glimpse of Carter's editor, walking with Frankeen, the artist.

"But what?"

"But those 'pranks' weren't entirely harmless; you were right when you reminded me of that. Barbara had to spend a couple of hours in the infirmary, Gertie's emphysema attack was no joking matter and," I glanced toward Ellen who, though dressed in shorts and sandals, still sported a bulky gauze bandage on her foot, "there's still a knife missing. A big knife." I shook my head and lowered my voice. "This cruise is a disaster. Even without that other little black-mailing issue."

Marie jutted her lower lip and exhaled, sending a stream of air that lifted her bangs. "They're right—skeet's a bad idea."

I smiled grimly. "And a couple of other things are bothering me, too. Want to hear?"

Marie sighed. "Okay, Nancy Drew, I'll bite—but only if you buy me a Bloody Mary."

I wrinkled my nose. "You don't drink those."

"Hey, I usually don't drink at lunch at all; but if I'm going to, a Bloody Mary sounds appropriate to the theme of this conversation." Marie nodded toward the thatched-roof bar across the pool. Next to it was a full-size outrigger canoe filled to brimming with silver chafing dishes, ice sculptures, and towering pyramids of fresh fruit. "C'mon, we'll grab something from the buffet, too."

We'd made it about halfway, when Renee and Vicky accosted us with a volley of yoo-hoos. Vicky trotted forward, sending her earrings—dangling slices of plastic watermelons—swinging furiously. Close behind, Renee, wearing polka dots from head to toe, carried a dripping mimosa and a huge roll of orange tickets.

"Raffle tickets," Renee announced, arriving beside me. "You look like a gambler to me, Darcy." She extended the ticket roll, dribbling mimosa onto Marie's arm. "Great party, great prizes. You could win a Victoria's Secret gift basket, a Brazilian wax, a date with—"

"No thanks," Marie said quickly, frowning and wiping at her arm as she took a step backward. She nudged me with her sticky elbow. "C'mon, Darc."

"Wait," I said, brushing Marie off for a second, and thinking that Luke might like South America—but mostly curious. "What party?"

"Romance Authors' Society," Renee said proudly. "RAS, but you don't have to be a member to attend; we're opening it to everyone involved in the conference. Writers, editors, agents, and the Readers Afloat group, too." She glanced quickly around the pool. "I wish somebody knew where Sarah was. I'm sure she'll want raffle tickets."

Vicky snorted. "Yeah, like she needs to buy a ticket to date Keven Brodie." She winked and nodded knowingly, making her watermelon earrings jitterbug. "That's probably why no one can find her. Anyone try his cabin?"

I watched them giggle and bit my lip, determined not to say what I knew—that Keven and Sarah had cooled things off. Or at least that's what Keven had implied last night. But then he'd also said those wacky things about Barbara Fedders, too. Things that Gertie and Herb couldn't corroborate. What was with Keven? It was one of the things that I wanted to talk with Marie about.

"Anyway," Renee said, waving the tickets. "It's going to be great fun. And it's a costume affair—Renaissance, or paranormal, or anything playful—you can rent one through the theatre if you didn't bring anything. No costume, no entry. But the party doesn't start until eight thirty, so there's plenty of time. Well?"

Marie gave me another nudge, and even if she was half kidding about it before, I was sure a Bloody Mary was sounding better and better to her. Bikini waxes, romance writing, and dates with male models were not subjects that interested my best pal.

"We'll think about it, Renee," I said, hedging a little and taking a step backward. "We're going to get some brunch and—hey, look," I said, catching a movement out of the corner of my eye. "That's Sarah over there and … Herb."

I pointed toward a striped umbrella, where Sarah, wearing a thin white spa robe, was settling into a lounge chair. She glanced around, and then quickly pulled the robe's hood over her hair before sliding a pair of huge sunglasses over her eyes. Man, she'd gone from looking like a pathetic baby bird to the spitting image of the Unabomber. She clearly wanted to be alone, even though Herb was seated nearby at the umbrella table, reading a newspaper. He was glistening with sweat and wearing... I scrunched my brows. "Why on earth would Doctor Herb be sitting out in the sun, wearing that heavy turtleneck?"

"Hickies!" Renee and Vicky blurted at the same instant, then collapsed against each other in a fit of giggles. Renee nodded, eyes glittering. "Gertie tried to cover them up with my concealer, but..."

"*Oh jeez.* No details, for godsake, I—" Marie grabbed my arm so hard that I nearly toppled over. But I was glad. All of a sudden I needed a Bloody Mary myself.

*   *   *

We decided to carry our trays, and our cocktails, inside, so that we didn't have to watch Herb sweat or Sarah hide behind her magazine. Besides, I didn't want to take a chance that any of our very chatty—and possibly homicidal—shipmates might overhear our conversation. We settled into a table in the corner of the Lido Café, behind a potted palm and dangerously close to an artsy display of chocolate éclairs and miniature New York cheesecakes. Overhead, the PA system announced a Tango lesson in the Crow's Nest Bar.

"You think we cured Angela of the urge to... tango with those blackmailers?" Marie asked, pressing the edge of her fork against a slice of chorizo.

"Mmm … maybe," I said as I lifted the celery stalk from my drink. I munched on the end, my brows rising as a generous hit of Tabasco registered. "Angela really believes that Luke's future is doomed if her tatas show up in *The National Enquirer*. Pretty powerful incentive to try and put a halt on things." I fanned my lips and reached for my ice water. "She's at a spa appointment right now, but I'm meeting her later. I'll warn her about all that again. Right now I'm worrying about a couple of other things."

Marie lifted her forkful of sausage. "Okay, shoot."

"Keven Brodie's lying about Barbara Fedders. Why would he do that?"

Marie rolled her eyes. "The guy parades around in a wig and a kilt, Darc'. Why would anything he does surprise you?"

"No, really. This is serious. Keven said Barbara is accusing Herb and Carter and even the cabin maid of murdering Thea. But Herb didn't know anything about it. Don't you think that's odd?"

"Maybe." Marie turned and snagged a couple of cheesecakes from the display and deposited one on my plate. "And didn't he say that she was back to accusing our workshop outline of masterminding the whole murder plot?"

"Yes," I said. "Which is another reason that I wanted to talk with you." I opened my embroidered straw handbag and pulled out the well-worn sleuthing lists. Then I fumbled around in the bottom of the bag, producing a pencil and a few chunky highlighter pens. Marie groaned around a mouthful of cheesecake, but stayed put. I took it as a green light to proceed.

"Here's what I've got so far," I said, picking up a pink highlighter. Marie shot me a look and I explained. "Pink is for Suspects, lime is for Unlikely-but-Noteworthy." I read the expression in her eyes and hurried on before my green light turned red. "Carter Cantrelle, for instance," I said, "is a suspect. I know you think she's too successful to risk it, but her family's hated Thea's for decades—revenge is a powerful motive." I added a second layer of pink over her name. "And she did threaten Artie with soap." There was still something else bugging me about Carter, but I couldn't quite put my finger on it yet.

Marie tipped her head sideways, peering at the list. "Herb's not pink? He was inside Thea's suite right before she got zapped."

I re-capped the pink pen and picked up the green one. "Herb willingly reported that to security. Besides, why would he attack Artie and then save him?"

Marie nodded and then squinted her eyes. "I can't even read that next name. What's the brownish highlighter mean?"

I sighed. "Pink changed to green and back to pink again."

"Huh?"

"It's Keven Brodie. I can't decide about him."

Marie lifted a second sheet of paper. "What's this one?"

"Victims," I said. "Yellow pen." I took a swig of my Bloody Mary, letting the tangy mix of vodka, tomato, and salty Worcestershire sluice over my tongue. "Starting with Thea and ending with ..." My eyes watered as the Tabasco hit again.

"Us?" Marie looked up, eyes wide. "You put *us* down as victims?"

"Well, sort of." I set my drink down and pointed to our names. "See the chartreusey color? That's because I changed the highlighter from green, to yellow, and then back to green, because—"

"Dammit!" Marie grabbed the pens and dropped them into the abalone shell breadbasket. She leaned forward on her elbows, squeezing her eyes closed for a second. When she opened them, she sighed softly and then smiled. "Sorry. But no more pens, okay? Just tell me what you're thinking here."

I forced a smile. "I think our workshop *is* tied to this murder, Marie." I pushed my plate aside, propped my chin in my hands and stared into my friend's gray eyes. "We have to face it: we're victims too, because someone *used* us—by way of our outline—to stage a series of attacks that finally escalated to murder."

"We didn't demo electrocution."

"No. But how can this all be coincidence? We stabbed away, and Ellen got slashed with a knife; we sniffed cyanide, and Barbara's drink got spiked; we talked about smoke inhalation, and Gertie—"

"Survived to give hickies," Marie said, interrupting. "And that's the point, Darcy, those 'victims' all survived. I don't think any of those events were meant to be lethal."

She did have a point, blast it. I bit at my lower lip, wondering if Marie would smack me if I reached into the breadbasket for my pens. My mind was whirling, and I focused much better with the aid of color graphics. But something clicked, regardless, and my jaw sagged open. "Oh, I almost *forgot* something."

"What?"

I reached for my lists and pointed to an entry I'd made. "The Chop or Shop manuscript entries were marked with assigned numbers, to keep things anonymous. But I'm pretty sure that Barbara has the corresponding list of names with her. At least the late entries." I nodded, remembering. "Because Angela entered at the last minute, and Barbara called Angela by the pen name of 'Barrett,' right? When she was yelling from the stage, trying to keep Angela from going off on Thea?"

Marie squinted her eyes. "So. What's this got to do with anything?"

I picked up my cheesecake. "Susth-pects," I lisped, biting into the creamy dessert. "Mmm." I swallowed and nodded. "Thea did a hatchet job on most of those manuscripts. Someone might want to fry her over that."

Marie looked at me like I was crazy. "Yes. Which points right back to Angela. Do you really want to do that?"

"It wasn't just Angela's work that Thea tore into," I reminded her. "Remember the awful things she was spewing about that one entry, *Last Dance*...uh..." I struggled to recall the title and Marie chimed in.

"*Last Dance Last Chance*," she said, rubbing her chin for the same reason that I used highlighter pens. "Hmmm...and Angela said that wasn't her entry. You're right. The FBI could be pretty interested in that information. Was Barbara handing the list over to security first, or what?"

I picked up my Bloody Mary, frowning. "Unfortunately, that's when I blurted out the fact that we weren't being allowed to disembark this morning."

"And you ended up having to dose her with sedatives." Marie's brows rose. "Pretty much what Keven Brodie wanted in the first place. Maybe he was right, Darcy. Maybe Barbara did make those accusations about Herb and Carter. Maybe she *is* losing it."

"No," I said, reaching brazenly into the breadbasket for my highlighter pens. I pulled out my lists and frowned, remembering the sad look on Barbara's face when she talked about returning Thea's notched belt to her family. "Barbara's grieving. And she's scared that someone on board might be threatening her, too. Damned valid, I'd say."

Then I uncapped the Suspect pen and drew a fat pink question mark over Keven Brodie's brownish name. "But Keven's telling lies about her all over this ship. I need to know why." Marie prodded my arm with the celery stalk from her Bloody Mary.

"Ask him, then," she said, nodding toward the doorway of the café. "Your cover model just walked in."

*   *   *

I wasn't sure how receptive Keven would be, considering that I'd pretty much rejected him last night, but he'd apparently done a complete one-eighty mood-wise. He greeted me with a hug that lifted my feet off the café floor, and then whisked me back out to the poolside cocktail hut. I ordered a Virgin Mary this time—no vodka, and a good reminder to get my fanny to Mass when I flew back home. Not because sitting beside a half-naked cover model inspired impure thoughts or anything. I blinked against Tabasco tears, determined to discover if Keven Brodie warranted a pink highlighter pen or not.

"So what's all that?" I asked, as he pulled a sheaf of papers out of his leather briefcase. I wrinkled my nose. "Isn't a Highlander supposed to be toting a sword instead?"

Keven smiled, a flash of white against his tan, and his dark eyes crinkled. "The party tonight is my last stint in a kilt, thank God." He tapped a knuckle against his papers. "Then it's time to put a whole lot of other things in motion. Finally."

I tilted my head to get a peek at the topmost paper, but he picked up his beer and rested his elbow on the stack, obscuring my view.

"You mean with your agenting career?" I asked, and then forced myself to use the opportunity to get my foot in the door. "I suppose Thea's death leaves clients ... available?"

I had to glance away at the last second—chicken-shit that I am—because even if I was dying to know Keven's reaction, I was totally ashamed of the insensitive remark as soon as it left my lips. I held my breath for a hundred years and then finally looked back up, but—*What the hell?* It was obvious that Keven was so absorbed in his papers, that he hadn't even heard me. He'd pulled out a pencil and was making some notes.

"Keven?" I tapped the papers and he looked up.

"Sorry," he said quickly, looking up at me. "It's my novel." Keven smiled and I swear his eyes glittered like a cheesy cartoon hero. "It looks like things are falling into place with it, and—"

"Why did you tell me those lies about Barbara Fedders?" I blurted, suddenly tired of beating around the bush. I kept going even when I saw his smile fade and his eyes begin to narrow ominously. "I talked with Barbara last night," I insisted, "and she didn't make accusations about anybody. Not Herb, or the maid, or—"

"Carter Cantrelle?" Keven asked, his voice suddenly heavy with sarcasm. "Well then, if Barbara didn't point the finger, maybe *you* can explain why Carter's having a lawyer flown in to Nassau. A well-known *defense* attorney?"

I heard my breath suck inward. "Really? How'd you find out about that?"

Keven's lips twisted into a sneer as he nodded across the pool, where Sarah, still hooded and behind dark glasses, lay stretched out in the sun. "Carter's bodyguard. Not that Sarah's the most reliable information source." He shrugged his big shoulders. "But supposedly Carter got called in by security last night—about the galley tour and the knife that showed up in her editor's mailbox." He raised his brows. "And the fact that she attended your murder workshop. *All* the sessions."

This time I know I gasped. "Shit," I said, itching to pull out my lists and a highlighter pen. "They think there's some connection between that and Thea's murder?"

Keven was smiling again, and for some reason it made goose bumps rise on my arms.

"Maybe," he said. "Maybe not. But you have to admit that it's intriguing." He bit into his lower lip and a low chuckle escaped. "Damned intriguing. The perfect … hook."

"What?" I asked, not sure what he was getting at, and not really paying that much attention anymore, since I'd begun to worry instead about being questioned by the FBI myself. And I was starting to wonder, too, if Luke had heard all about this yet. "What'd you say?" I asked again, trying to focus.

"Oh, nothing," Keven said, dark curls brushing his forehead as he shook his head. "Agent-speak, that's all." His eyes did that creepy glittering thing again, and he reached out and tapped his finger against the end of my nose. "Let me buy you a *real* drink, Darcy Cavanaugh. I'm burning that damned kilt tonight. That calls for a celebration and—" he stopped, and we both turned as a familiar squeal split the air behind us.

Renee, holding her pink glitter cell phone to her ear, was trotting toward the Café door as fast as her chubby legs and polka-dot flip-flops would allow. She slowed down as she recognized us, and then squealed again. "Darcy, Keven, hurry, or you'll miss all the excitement!"

"What?" I asked, rising from the barstool. "What's going on?"

"A press conference!" she said, breathlessly. "I can't stay and explain it all, but apparently the news got out to the media about the feds coming on board, about Thea and her parrot, and the awful scene at the Chop or Shop ... and your murder workshop, of course and—"

"What do you mean by 'press conference'?" Keven asked, interrupting. "There weren't supposed to be any reporters until we dock in Nassau. The facts need to gel, and ..." He'd gone pale, his pupils dilating and brows bunching together. "No. There's no way a press conference can happen right now ..."

"One of the passengers is a journalist with some big-deal British magazine," Renee explained, snapping her phone closed. "Traveling with a group of other journalists, I guess, and they have worldwide newspaper contacts. Anyway, it's all via conference call, but they're taking photos and asking for statements, and security's having a hell of a time—look, I've gotta go now. Come see for yourself. In the library."

Renee took off at a trot again, a dizzying blur of polka dots, and when I turned to Keven he was jamming his papers into his briefcase. I swear his fingers were trembling.

Twin splotches of color rose high on his cheekbones, replacing the pallor, and his forehead shone with perspiration. I couldn't read his expression, whether it looked excited or agitated ... or even scared maybe? I wasn't sure, and I still wanted to ask him a few more things about Barbara. I slid my notes discreetly from my purse and cleared my throat, but Keven downed the last of his beer, grabbed his briefcase, and jogged off without saying so much as a paltry buh-bye.

For godsake.

241

I stood there for a few moments like a jilted idiot, holding my Virgin Mary and my color-coded Suspect list and muttering to myself about my pitiful lack of sleuthing skills. No doubt about it, I was going in circles faster than our ship was looping around the Bahamas and—I turned my head as a movement across the pool caught my eye. *Someone running*... yes, Sarah, cell phone to her ear, robe flapping open, making a mad dash toward the deck door. An instant before Angela shouted my name.

EIGHTEEN

ANGELA WAS WEARING DARK glasses—huge, retro Jackie O's—a drab gray sweat suit, and a white terry turban knotted loosely over her hair, its tie ends dangling. She looked like one of those grainy photos on the front page of the *Enquirer*—you know, where some Hollywood star's been caught sneaking out the back door of a liposuction clinic. There was nothing about her that was recognizable as "Skyler"; even her fingers were stripped of their usual multi-carat bling. *Jeez.* It didn't take a colored pen to highlight this as suspicious behavior.

"Um ... I thought we were meeting at four thirty. For tea," I said, blinking my eyes as I watched Angela sneak a peek over her shoulder for the third time in thirty seconds. Every time she moved, the turban ties flopped back and forth across her forehead. "What's going on, Ang—" I jumped as her hand shot out and snatched the list from my hand.

"Good God," she hissed, sliding her sunglasses down to peer at it, "what *is* this?" Her blue eyes darted from the list to my face, over her shoulder and then back again. "What in God's name have you been *doing*, Darcy?"

I stared at her, biting my tongue and wondering if it was too late to defile my Virgin with a double shot of vodka. I took a deep breath. "You know what that is," I said as calmly as I could. "You had one yourself, the last time I checked. It's a list, notes, for our 'investigation.' The one that *you* asked me to help you with?"

"Oh *no*," she said, after turning her neck like an owl for the umpteenth time. "No," she repeated, holding the sheet of paper out with her fingertips like it was toxic or dangerous. "I can't have anything to do with *this*. And neither can you." She stepped close to me and lowered her voice to a pleading whisper. "Darcy, please, all of this must stop immediately. Promise me."

"I ..." I hesitated, confused by her sudden reversal, and then nodded and took the list from her hands. "O-kay," I said, slowly. "But, tell me, does this have something to do with that press conference in the library?"

Angela slid her sunglasses back into place and I couldn't see the look in her eyes, but her lips tightened for a moment and then relaxed as she sighed with what almost looked like ... relief? Frankly, it surprised me. "Does it?" I asked her again, gently.

"Maybe. Sure. Absolutely," she said, pressing her fingertips to her forehead. "Yes." Her fingers touched a dangling turban tie and she gave a sharp laugh. "I guess you can tell that I'm attempting to be incognito."

I smiled, glad to see her relax even a teeny bit, and then gestured to the cane-top barstools. We sat, and when she ordered a straight shot of JD, I pretty much guessed that tea wasn't going to happen, unless it was some Mad Hatter deal. But I was still damned curious. "Incognito?" I asked after she took a swig.

"Yes," Angela said touching the frame of her sunglasses. "You're right about the press conference. Security's trying to put a stop to things, but those Brits are a tenacious bunch." She peeked back over her shoulder again. "They're determined to interview the 'key players.'"

"And they are … ?"

Angela's lips tensed. "Carter, and that bird doctor, *me* apparently, and a few people who took the galley tour, attended your classes … and all the writers who submitted manuscripts to Thea's workshop."

I thought of Barbara Fedders, wondering if she'd slept after the sedative I'd given her, and if she'd located the list of writers' names to turn in to the FBI. Even though I knew she'd be champing at the bit to get off the ship when we docked in Nassau, I couldn't imagine her not doing whatever she could to help solve Thea's murder. And that list of writers' might be … my brows rose as a thought occurred to me.

"Angela," I said casually, after taking a sip of my still-Virgin Mary, "you never said which of those submissions was yours."

"No," she said smiling wanly, "I didn't." She shook her head, sending the turban ties flopping like a drunken rabbit's ears. "But I don't mind telling you now. It's called, *My Garden Gone Wild.*"

I scrunched my brows, embarrassed actually, that the title didn't mean squat. "Uh … and did Thea—"

Angela gave what sounded like a bitter laugh. "No. The irony is that she said very little about my work, and what she did say wasn't half bad." She shook her head. "No praise, mind you. But nothing chop-worthy." Angela flicked her fingernail against her shot glass. "Of course everyone in that room assumed I'd written that *Last Chance* fiasco."

"Well," I said, trying to be encouraging, "that will be corrected as soon as the FBI—" I stopped short as I caught the look on Angela's face. "Angela … ?" I took a sip of my drink and waited, watching her face.

"Luke knows," she whispered hoarsely.

I coughed and came millimeters from shooting tomato juice from my nose. "Aagh! Luke knows about the *Flamingo Titty*—"

"No!" Angela grabbed my wrist, her nails digging into me. "No, no. I didn't mean *that*. Oh … God. I can't let him find out about that. It could ruin his chances for the Senate nomination."

"Angela, wait a second." My pulse kicked up a notch. "You haven't been contacted again by those blackmailers?"

"No," Angela said quickly. "Nothing." She relaxed her grip on my wrist and swallowed hard. "I simply meant that Luke knows about the investigation into Thea's death, that I'm to be questioned. He called me a few minutes ago. He said he'd leave you a message, too."

"Is he still coming?" My heart did that funny flip-flop it always does when I think about Luke Skyler. "He can't be part of the investigation, can he? Wouldn't that be some sort of conflict?"

"Yes, he's coming; probably not until around ten tonight, but he'll be here. And no, he's not part of the investigation. Officially," Angela said, picking up her glass again. "He said he's coming as a concerned son."

I nodded and smiled knowingly. "Who happens to be a lawyer."

She pressed her fingers to her forehead again. "I truly don't know how I'm going to get through all of this, Darcy." She moaned softly and my heart went out to her, despite our sketchy, hit-and-miss relationship. The woman was clearly distraught. And there was something just too darned touching about a woman trying to protect a son who was on his way to protect her.

"I'll be here too, Angela," I said softly, patting her hand. "And maybe," I let my glance linger on the well-worn list lying beside my purse, "some of the information I've already managed to uncover about suspicious incidents will help. I'll tell the federal agents—"

"No!" Angela said, pulling her hand away and removing her sunglasses. "Didn't you hear what I said? You can't ask any more questions *or* volunteer any information. You have to stay completely out of this investigation, Darcy." Her blue eyes riveted to mine. "You have to promise me that."

"I'm only trying to help you," I explained, frustration making my voice whine like a little kid.

"Trust me," she said, putting the glasses back in place and downing the last of her whiskey. "That's the only way to help me and—*oh dear,*" Angela glanced at her bare wrist. "What time is it?"

"Nearly four," I said after stopping the sway of my watch charm.

"Oh—I'm late. Got to go." Angela tapped my arm briskly and turned.

"Wait," I said quickly, "are we still meeting for tea?"

"No tea. No time. I'm late." Angela nodded, her white turban flopped, and she took off quick as a bunny.

"But I thought..." I watched her go, munched the limp celery in my Virgin Mary, and faced the fact that I was even more confused than ever. Even if I wasn't attending the Mad Hatter Tea, the fact was that there was something damned unnerving about Angela Skyler's behavior.

She couldn't have done a better impression of the White Rabbit if she'd tried. What was she up to?

* * *

It took me more than an hour to find Marie and—trust me—if she'd been winning in the casino, I'd never have pried her out of there. But the fact was, that she'd just used all her fingers to count the number of overtime hours she'd need to pay off her MasterCard. Plus, she was out of cigars, so it was relatively easy to prod her into getting into the elevator and heading back up to the cabin with me. It was the small detour that pissed her off.

"Hey," she said staring up at the brass-encased elevator numbers. "Didn't we just pass our deck?"

"Oh, yeah. Guess we did," I said, innocently. "We'll just go up to Dolphin Deck and then take the stairs back down." I patted a front pocket of her cargo vest. "You know, to help us watch our girlish figures."

"Watch your own figure. Mine needs a cigar," she said, her gray eyes narrowing with suspicion. "Okay, spill it. Where are we really going?"

"To check on Barbara," I said as the doors opened onto Dolphin Deck. "I feel kind of responsible. You know, after I broke that upsetting news about the docking delay."

"You mean after you went there to see if she was Looney Tunes?"

"Keven lied about her," I said, shaking my head and leading the way down the carpeted corridor. "And I still don't know why."

"Well," Marie said, slowing as we passed the first door on Barbara's hallway, "if what he said was true about Carter and her attorney, then security's investigation must have made some headway. Whether it was Barbara who aroused their suspicions or not." She shook her head as we passed the door to Ellen's suite. "Although why Carter would want to do something to harm her own editor…"

"Or to harm Barbara," I said, recalling that terrifying moment in the Crow's Nest Bar when I'd sniffed her glass of almond-tainted merlot. "I mean, even if Carter hated Thea, it makes no sense to take it out on her assistant."

"Or on Gertie," Marie added as she stepped around a pile of dishes stacked outside one of the doors. She glanced down the hallway. "You know, I was thinking that the murder workshop 'copycat' attacks targeted only the Dolphin Deck VIPs. But Gertie's—"

"On *our* deck," I said, finishing her statement. "Good thing, too, since we were right there to find her in time." I stopped in front of Barbara's door. "Here we are."

I glanced at the next door—Thea's—now barricaded not only with yellow crime tape, but also wooden sawhorses. Security was keeping people away, until the FBI swarmed all over it in a few hours, that is. I was surprised they didn't have a guard posted, but then again, from what Renee had said, it sounded like every man they had was busy trying to thwart the unauthorized British press conference. At least Barbara could have a little peace and quiet this way.

I tapped on her door softly, waited a few seconds and then knocked harder. When I started thumping with the side of my fist, Marie pulled my hand away and gave me a look like *I* was the Looney Tune.

"Hey, kid," she said, raising her brows. "Is there something you're not telling me?"

"What do you mean?" I asked, turning my head to peer down the hallway when I thought I heard a door click.

"You're pounding like the Big Bad Wolf, for cripes' sake. This is all because you feel bad for upsetting her?"

I sighed. "Okay, I need to ask Barbara if she found that list of writers' names for the Chop or Shop entries."

Marie narrowed her eyes. "Why? To mark it? With pink and green and yellow?"

"C'mon, Marie," I said with a groan. "Can't you tell I'm worried? Angela was trying to hide it, but she's totally freaked about being questioned by the feds. If I could get the suspects diluted a little more, by adding *all* the names from that writers' list, then—"

"Then you'd be going against your promise to Angela," Marie insisted. "You told her that you'd *butt out*, babe."

"I ... *hey, Barbara, open up!*" I yelled, turning away from Marie and rapping the side of my fist against the cabin door again. "It's Darcy. Please open—" I turned as a voice called my name from a few doors down.

"She's not there," Ellen said, stepping across her threshold wearing a ship robe and a towel around her hair. For the first time, her foot was free of the gauze bandage. A neat row of black nylon stitches dotted her instep. "Security's been up twice looking for her, but no luck." She squinted and looked upward as the PA system paged Barbara Fedders's name overhead. "See?"

"Why are they looking for her?" Marie asked, reaching up to lift my hand from where it still rested against Barbara's door.

"Preparations for the FBI investigation, I would assume," she said, shaking her head. "They've been hounding Carter for statements, too, though she's holding off until …" Ellen left the thought unfinished, and there was no doubt in my mind that she meant that Carter wouldn't be cooperating until she was represented by legal counsel. What was it that kept nagging me about her? Something about the Chop or Shop, or …

I glanced across the hall at Angela's door, my throat constricting. "And Angela Skyler?"

"Not in her cabin, either," Ellen said, pulling the towel from her hair and patting the side of her face with it. "Although I did see her waiting in line at the Purser's Office before I came up to shower."

"Purser's Office?" I asked. "For shore tour information?" I wrinkled my nose. "I doubt if we'll be onshore in Nassau in time to make any of those." And I couldn't imagine why anything touristy would interest that frazzled woman.

Ellen sighed. "I know what you mean, but I think Angela was asking about cashing checks or arranging to have money wired to the ship."

"Money?" Marie's brows drew together. "But nobody carries cash; she ought to know that by now. All you need is your ship card, or a credit card ashore. Not safe to—" she stopped short and turned to me, her eyes wide and riveted to mine. Her lips moved silently, *"Oh shit."*

I seconded the thought, and my stomach churned as the word *"blackmailers"* began to swirl in my ears like wind in a seashell. Angela was meeting blackmailing thugs with a roll of cash?

Oh jeez, oh man, oh—I grabbed Marie's arm and she grabbed me back, and we probably did what looked like some pathetic, blathering impression of the Three Stooges. Then we said a hasty goodbye to Ellen, dodged the pyramid of dirty dishes, and took off at a run for the elevators.

*   *   *

An hour later we'd scouted the Promenade Foyer, come up empty at the Purser's Office, and checked around on G-Deck. While Marie stopped into the Smoke Shop, I had Angela paged four times without success. We finally headed back outside, just in time to feel our ship coming to a halt. A halt? I glanced over at Marie as I took hold of the rail and felt my body bob up and down with the movement of the deck. The sun was setting, giving everything around us a sort of a peaceful, rosy-gold glow. But even still, something didn't feel right.

"We're stopping?" I asked, peering out across the blue water, realizing that the port of Nassau was finally visible in the distance— aging buildings of pastel pink, yellow, blue, orange, and lavender, like baker's frostings. Heavy plaster, painted shutters, and colonial ironwork, resting on white, white sand, surrounded by palm trees and … "What's the deal? We're taking tender boats in?"

"No, looks like *we're* anchoring here and *they* are coming in to us."

"They?" I squinted out across the expanse of surreal blue in the direction Marie pointed. Toward a pilot boat plowing through the water full speed ahead.

Marie nodded. "Want to take bets on whether that's full of guys wearing Men's Wearhouse suits, conservative ties, dark glasses, and shoulder holsters?"

I think I groaned; I know I gripped the railing harder, and then I whirled around, scanning the deck once again. "Where is she, Marie? Why didn't Angela answer our pages?"

Marie sighed. "I don't know. I want to think she's simply avoiding security, gathering her thoughts... or hitting the salon to get all pretty for the prodigal son?"

I glanced back at the pilot boat. Damn, there *were* men in suits and dark glasses, but... "Luke's not coming until late; he's got something to wrap up in Boston. He left me a phone message." I squeezed my eyes shut for a second, remembering the concern in his voice and the way he'd said how grateful he was that I was there to watch over his mother. *Oh jeez.* "And we called the salon, remember? She wasn't there. And none of that explains the cash."

"We don't even know if she got that money, Darc."

I peered over the rail, losing sight of the pilot boat as it tied up alongside our ship. I groaned aloud. "But she's got jewelry: bracelets, necklaces, rings—the Skyler heirloom platinum wedding set. What is that engagement ring, four carats? How badly would someone want to get his hands on that? Huh?" I could hear my voice climbing higher, and I was suddenly feeling desperate for solutions far beyond what lists and highlighters could ever handle.

"Do you think we should go to security and tell them about the blackmail?" Marie asked, raising her voice over a dual page for Barbara Fedders and Sarah Skelton. Was everyone AWOL for godsake?

"Aagh," I said, pressing my hands against my eyes. "And have them tell the FBI? So they can discover the whole Titty Brigade mess, just in time to lay it all out for Luke?" I shook my head and it did nothing to stop my pulse from pounding in my ears. "You should have seen how frantic Angela was, Marie. Making me promise to stop investigating Thea's murder and—"

"Stop? Why?" Marie interrupted, her forehead wrinkling. "Angela was so intent on clearing herself, finding other suspects. Hell, she badgered us into helping her, and then kept pushing it. Why the sudden change?"

"Um..." I opened my mouth and then closed it, thinking about what Marie was saying. And thinking of Angela, all nervous and stressed and then bolting off like the White Rabbit. It *was* odd. She'd practically torn those lists out of my hands, and the look on her face had been pure panic. She'd said that neither she nor I could "have anything to do with this." In fact, Angela said the only way I could "help" her was to *stop* asking questions about the murder suspects and—*oh my God!*

I grabbed Marie's hands, my eyes wide. "That's it!"

"What?" Marie asked, brows scrunching. "What do you mean?"

For some reason—probably fulminating paranoia—I glanced around to make sure no one was standing close by, and then I fought to keep my voice steady. "The murderer and the blackmailer are the *same person*." I opened my purse, dug around, and pulled out my lists. "It was here on my timeline and I didn't catch it." I found the list and pointed. "See? Angela's snorkel note came immediately *after* we started questioning people about the events surrounding Thea's murder. The murderer was trying to scare Angela off. Stop her from investigating."

Marie peered at my color-coded entries. "But...he knew about that incident at the Flamingo."

"Yes," I said. "But even if we don't know how Thea's murderer knew about the Titty Brigade, it seems more than a coincidence that he only mentioned it *after* we started our investigation. Right?"

"Right, but—" Marie stopped short as a page overhead instructed, *"All security staff report to security office."*

The feds were onboard.

Marie nodded. "You're right, it does seem like the timing for that snorkel note was suspicious. But I still don't understand why Thea's murderer would stage those other attacks, the knife and the cyanide in Barbara's drink, and that smoke bomb."

"I don't know, either," I said honestly, "unless he wanted diversions." I bit my lip, thinking. "To keep security busy, or ..." I was searching my brain—and my lists—when the sound of approaching footsteps made me look up. It was Renee, wearing the same velvet and brocade Renaissance gown we'd seen that first day aboard ship. Suddenly that seemed like years ago.

She smiled, tapped her watch and raised her brows. "The 'party of the year' starts in less than an hour, ladies," she announced. "And if you're hanging around to get a peek at those FBI guys, don't bother." She giggled. "I already had a look: middle-aged, balding, no sense of humor." She frowned. "On the other hand, if you see our to-die-for Highlander, would you tell him to get his fine, kilted ass down to the ballroom? I've sold one hundred and twelve tickets for a date with him. He'd better show—and be flexing every inch that does."

"Keven's ... missing?" I asked, feeling the hairs stand up on the back of my neck, despite Renee's teasing tone. Marie shot me a glance out of the corner of her eye.

"No," Renee said quickly. "Not missing. Just hanging around the library, trying to see what those British reporters are saying about the clues surrounding Thea's murder. He's been sneaking around there, eavesdropping and taking notes. I swear, it's like he's obsessed." She swiped her hand across her perspiring forehead, and then lifted the hem of her gown to start walking. "I've got to get down to the ballroom. Hope to see you there!"

She started off, then stopped and turned back to look at us. "I caught your friend Mrs. Skyler earlier this morning; she said she'd come to the party." Renee giggled knowingly. "I *know* that woman can afford raffle tickets." Renee shook her head. "My friend in the Purser's Office said she just cashed the biggest check in the history of this ship. Must be nice."

We watched her leave, and for a minute neither of us could think of anything to say. But it didn't take me much longer to realize that it was time to *do*, not talk. I was having a very bad feeling and I had to do something about it.

"C'mon," I said, tugging at Marie's sleeve. "We haven't got much time."

"For what?" Marie asked, her eyes more than a little wary.

"To get down to the theatre and rent our costumes," I said, feeling more certain every second. *Keven Brodie was "obsessed" with the journalists' investigation? Sneaking around and eavesdropping?*

"What the heck are you talking about?"

"For the party. You heard Renee; Angela might be there."

"Yeah, right," Marie said, shaking her head. "Dressed up as a vampire, carrying a wad of cash under her cape. Makes perfect sense. Should have thought of that myself."

"Well maybe she figures it's a good place to hide out from the feds. I don't know. But anyway…" I sighed. "Okay. The fact is, that I need to talk to Keven Brodie. He knows something, Marie. I feel it."

I nodded my head sharply. "There was something so creepy about the way he was talking about Thea's death; how he was saying that things were suddenly 'falling into place' for him now that she's dead. I think he's—"

"Involved with her murder?" Marie's eyes widened. "For godsake, Darcy. Then shouldn't you be telling this to the FBI?"

"Not yet," I said, remembering my promise to Angela. "Not until I know more." I gave Marie's arm a squeeze. "Go along with this, okay? Just a teeny bit longer?"

Marie sighed and reached into her fanny pack for the new cigar stash, muttering under her breath. I could barely hear, but it sounded something like ...

"What'd you say?" I asked, as she flicked the wheels of her Volkswagen lighter.

She took a drag and exhaled, cherry smoke curling upward. "I don't wear velvet. And nothing with tights."

I smiled and nodded. And tried not to think about the fact that the mysterious Keven Brodie would be wearing a kilt ... and carrying a really sharp sword.

NINETEEN

"No. You look good. I swear. Sort of fuzzy and…" I pressed my hand, complete with scarlet press-on nails, against my painted lips, looked Marie up and down again, and suppressed a howl. Howl being the operative word. "And *cute*, really," I managed, my voice squeaking between the plastic fingernails. "For a Disco Werewolf." I hoisted a quick thumbs-up. "And look: no velvet. No tights. No— *nooo!*"

Marie grabbed a ball of sequin socks from her bed and hurled them across the cabin. They bounced off the laced-up bodice of my Wench costume and—before I could dodge—were followed immediately by her spit-covered, plastic set of… "Eeew!"

"I'm not wearing those nasty-ass teeth," Marie said, scowling at me. At least I *think* she was scowling. It was hard to tell with all the glued-on facial hair. And pointy ears.

She raised a furry paw and began counting on her fingers. "Taco Bell Chihuahua, Holstein Cow, Cowboy Waiter… do you know how many costumes I've ended up in since we met? Sweaty, itchy, humiliating costumes? And now, if I smoke, I'll catch my face on fire! And all for—"

"Good humanitarian reasons," I said, nodding my head and sending my huge gold hoop earrings swinging. "And even if we didn't have much choice on last-minute costumes, at least now we can get into that romance party and find Keven Brodie. And maybe gather enough information to get poor Angela off the hook as a murder suspect. Or at least reduce the chances that Luke will find out about..." I adjusted the skimpy, gathered blouse to cover my shamrock tattoo, "his mother's tasteless Titty fiasco." I set Marie's fangs on the dresser and smoothed the layers of my factory-tattered peasant skirt. "So, are we good?"

"Hmph." Marie rolled her eyes. "You want to page Angela once more before we go?"

"No," I answered, reaching for my crochet purse, "security's been doing that for the last half-hour. It'll just freak her more."

Marie turned up the collar on her purple lamé shirt and opened the cabin door, waving me ahead. "You still think she's hiding out?"

I lifted my skirt hem and stepped into the outer hallway, feeling my stomach churn at the thought of Angela with a roll of cash—and so desperate to quash the scandal that might damage her family's reputation. And Luke's future Senate bid.

"I don't know," I said honestly, "but there isn't time to sit and wonder. We've got to do what we can before," I glanced back over my bare shoulder as Marie pulled our door shut, "we get called in for interrogation ourselves. Because, face it, we will." I shrugged. "We taught the murder how-to. No getting around that."

We boarded the elevator and Marie pressed a hairy finger against the button that would take us to the Sky Ballroom, one floor below the Crow's Nest Bar and at the stern of the ship. I smiled at our fellow passengers, and then murmured a "thank you" for Marie when Bill Price graciously complimented her white patent platform boots. From the look in his eyes, I'd guess our resident metal sculptor had spent some memorable hours under the disco lights himself. I watched the illuminated deck numbers, trying to formulate my questions for Keven, and then stepped back as the doors slid open at Dolphin Deck.

Standing outside was a petite green alien. Or, rather, a petite woman in a fluorescent green costume that hugged her tidy curves. And who was wearing a helmet-style mask with huge, wraparound alien eyes. Very Roswell. She stared at us, hesitated, and then began to turn away.

"Hey, wait," I said, waving her toward us, "plenty of room in here. Jump onboard." I nodded toward Marie and smiled. "Doesn't bite—left her teeth in the cabin."

The alien raised her palms and waved them, silently shaking her egg-shaped head and, obviously, changing her mind about joining us. I watched as she padded back down the Dolphin Deck foyer, but the doors closed before I could see which cabin corridor she followed.

"Well. Guess they have issues with disco on her planet," I teased, peering sideways at Marie.

"Or with a known sympathizer of the Kenyon camp," Marie whispered.

I scrunched my brows. "Huh?"

"That was Sarah. Carter's Sarah?"

I did a double take and my earrings smacked me. "What's *she* doing on Dolphin Deck?"

Marie shrugged, lifting purple padded shoulders. Her fur-edged lips curved into a smirk. "Maybe you should highlight that on your list of things to ask the cover model."

*   *   *

Which was easier said than done, considering that Keven Brodie was continually surrounded by no fewer than two dozen drooling women. Including a chubby one, dressed as a winged pixie, who kept dropping appetizers on the floor, just to sneak a peek under his kilt. I almost skidded on a stuffed egg.

I stood on tiptoe and glanced around the Sky Ballroom, picking out familiar faces among the costumed crowd that mingled under yards of purple and red crepe paper streamers and dangling glitter hearts. Affixed to the far wall were silver balloons, forming the letters RAS—Romance Authors' Society. Beneath that, a buffet table, flanked by Renee and Vicky, stooped under the weight of a jillion "genre-themed" desserts. Marie had taste-tested the Renaissance Writers' ordered spread of jam tartlets, puddings, and gingerbread cake ... and then scuttled away—fast as humanly possible in six-inch platform boots—when Gertie grinned wickedly and offered her an Aphrodisiac Nut Bar.

I waved to Herb, sporting his safari vest, turtleneck, and pith helmet, then smiled at Editor Ellen, dressed as Elvira, while continuing to search the faces in the crowd. No Angela, no Carter, no Barbara and ... I squinted at a flash of glittery green back by the chocolate fountain. No. No alien Sarah either. And, I noted as I glanced at my watch, it had been more than an hour since the FBI boarded the ship. Who were *they* zeroing in on? Is that why some of the literary folks were missing? Well, I knew the man that I wanted to question, but—I jumped as warm fingers spread across my bare shoulder.

"Hey, Wench o' my heart," a deep voice whispered in my ear, the words were followed by a brush of beard stubble and then warm lips on my neck.

"Keven—*whoa*," I said, my breath catching with a jolt. My heart thudded up into my neck and made my hoops quiver. "You kind of sneaked up on me there."

I smiled, trying not to think too much about the fact that the bare-chested man towering over me carried a real-as-hell broadsword. And that it was probably fairly stupid to confront him about being involved with Thea's death. But maybe if I were discreet, and used our budding friendship to ...

"Buy me a drink?" I asked, crossing my arms under my breasts and lowering my eyelids halfway—so shoot me; I was on a mission here. "Or do I need a raffle ticket for that?"

Keven chuckled and tilted his head, causing a lock of the long, dark wig to brush his muscled shoulder. Not that I noticed, or ... *are those pecs oiled?* I pried my eyes back to his face, saw Keven's smile broaden and the tip of his tongue sweep just inside his fleshy lower lip. Damned if he didn't look every inch the virile Highlander. Those publishing folks must have made a bundle on this guy.

"Tickets?" Keven chuckled again, low in his throat. "You don't need no stinkin' tickets." His gorgeous brows furrowed as he glanced down at the pixie-woman sliding a tortilla chip along the floor near his left boot. "She, however, needs a *roll* of tickets. And a cold shower." He slipped his arm around me. "C'mon," he said, "let's get out of here. You're saving me from a fate worse than death."

Death? I forced a smile, and then hesitated a moment as I looked at the huge double-edge Scottish broadsword in his fist. "Great. And maybe you could lean that cumbersome weapon against a wall somewhere?"

Keven laughed and lifted the sword. "And have it stolen? Not on your life. This bad boy goes up on eBay right after I burn my kilt—and my modeling contract." That glitter, the one that had unnerved me earlier, reappeared in his dark eyes. "I'm celebrating tonight, remember?" The eye glitter reached disco-ball proportions. "And after all that's happened this cruise, I've got one hell of a lot to celebrate. Let's get to it, Wench!"

All that's happened this cruise?

Keven slid his fingers around my bare arm and I glanced over my shoulder to catch Marie's eye. Where was she? I wasn't sure what Keven had in mind, but if it involved leaving this ballroom, I wasn't going alone and…I spotted her by the chocolate fountain just as Keven gave my arm a little tug.

"No backing out now," he said leaning close. "Something tells me that you're a woman who has no trouble setting a man's kilt on fire."

Oh for godsake. I fought to keep my eyes from rolling back, and tried once more to catch Marie's attention. I saw her look up from a plate of goodies, was pretty sure she saw me, but couldn't read her expression because of the werewolf fur. Then Keven nudged my hip with the hilt of his broadsword, took my hand, and began towing me in the direction of the darkened deck.

He paused at the bar, slipped his sword into its scabbard, and then snatched up a bottle of champagne and a couple of glasses.

Before I knew it, we were outside. The sky was dark and moonless, and all I could do was hope that Marie had seen me because, risky as it might be, I still didn't want to miss this chance to talk with Keven alone. He knew far more about Thea's death than he was saying. I could feel it—just as clearly as I felt his hand grab my ass the second the door closed behind us.

"Hey," I said, sliding away from his reach. "Easy there. The skirt's rented."

Keven attempted a sheepish grin. "And I promised you a drink … first." He set the glasses on a deck table, and eased the champagne open with a soft pop. He held the bubbling glasses aloft and winked. "Forgiven?"

I moved to the rail—glancing up and down the empty deck—and considered my choices. Hightailing it out of here, leaving Keven holding two glasses of champagne and still securely kilted, was the safest, but it was nearly nine o'clock. The FBI was rounding up interviewees, Luke was on his way, and Angela had a roll of cash. I took the offered champagne and downed a gulp. For courage. And then sneaked a peek at the broadsword before plunging ahead.

"You seemed pretty interested in that press conference this afternoon," I said, resting an elbow casually on the rail. "I mean, one minute we were talking beside the pool, and the next—poof—you run off without so much as a 'see you later.'"

Keven gave a quick laugh. A nervous laugh, maybe? "And I hurt your feelings. I'm sorry, Darcy." He shrugged his oiled shoulders. "I have no real excuse, except that—"

"You needed to sneak down there to hide and take notes?" I asked, causing what looked like a twitch at the corner of his eye. "In fact, Renee said that you seemed *obsessed* with what the media was saying about the events surrounding Thea's death."

It was definitely a twitch. And then as Keven's eyes narrowed, I glanced toward the deck door, praying for a werewolf. No such luck. But I couldn't quit now.

"I don't know what you mean," Keven said slowly, after taking a drink from his glass. His voice held none of the playful warmth from just minutes ago. And his lips were tight, tense. "Why are you bringing this up?"

I took a deep breath. "Because you *lied* about Barbara Fedders's mental state, Keven. And you said she was accusing people when she wasn't, almost like you were trying to divert…" I hesitated, remembering something strange. About Keven working on his novel today, and how excited he seemed about things "finally falling into place with it." And then how he got so agitated when Renee mentioned the press conference, almost like one thing affected the other. I scrunched my brows and stared at him. "Wait," I said slowly. "Didn't you say that you used to write crime dramas for TV?"

Even in the darkness, I could see Keven's face go pale. "Maybe. Why?"

"Murder plots *maybe*?" I asked, lowering my voice and taking a step closer. "I'm guessing that would interest the media. The police, too. And *maybe* you were worried that *you* would become the next suspect?" My mind whirled as I watched my words' impact play out in the expressions on Keven's face. And then I remembered something else, and the hair began to prickle and rise on the back of my neck. My eyes widened. "And you took the galley tour. Where the knives—" I yelped as Keven's hand shot out and closed over my wrist.

"Dammit," he growled, pulling me close. His grip tightened enough to make my fingers curl inward. Keven's eyes searched mine wildly. "What are you doing? God. Have you been saying those things to people? To security?"

"Keven, don't ... please ..." I took a step backward and he followed, his huge broadsword rattling in its scabbard to remind me of what a fool I was. I tried to pull my arm from his grip and failed, while fighting the grisly images of stab wounds presented at our murder workshop. *Would he actually ...?* My mind whirled, and I'd just lifted my right knee toward his groin when—wham, and bless her butt—the Disco Werewolf burst through the door.

"Back off, Brodie!" Marie shouted, nearly falling when her platform boot snagged the threshold. She swore, scrambled for balance, lifting her cell phone overhead with a furry paw. "I've got security on speed dial and an inside connection with the FBI." Marie righted herself and strode forward, holding her phone like—for godsake—it was a match against a thirty-seven-inch carbon-steel blade.

I gritted my teeth, gave my wrist one last tug ... and fell onto my butt as Keven let go. I scuttled on hands and knees toward my werewolf hero, and the safety of the deck door. And then, dammit, I pulled myself upright, and got pissed as hell. I planted my fists on my hips and shrieked like a fishwife.

"Tell us the truth, Keven—or we'll go to the federal agents right now!"

I tossed Marie my most grateful look and we leaned shoulder-to-shoulder while we waited for the Highlander to cave or draw his sword. Thank God, he caved.

"Don't," Keven said, raising his palms like we were actually dangerous. "Please. Don't do this to me." His big shoulders sagged for a moment, and he rubbed a hand across his brows. "I'll tell you the truth, but you *have* to believe that I had nothing to do with Thea's death."

Marie pointed her cell phone and cleared her throat. "The Wench believes better when swords aren't an issue."

Keven sighed, unfastened his scabbard and let it clatter to the deck. He looked up at Marie, frowned, and then nudged it farther away with the toe of his lace-up suede boot.

"I didn't kill Thea Kenyon," he said, his dark eyes unblinking. "But I did do the other things. The knives—and damned if someone didn't take the second one from my cabin. If you don't think I haven't been worrying about that..." Keven shrugged. "And I took the almond extract, and planted the smoke bomb." His brows scrunched. "I swear I didn't know Gertie was asleep in there; she was supposed to be at the Crow's Nest."

I couldn't believe what I was hearing. And I sure as hell didn't understand. "Why?" I asked. "Why would you do all that?"

Keven gave a sharp laugh and squeezed his eyes shut for a second. "Promotion," he said, "hype, buzz?" He looked me straight in the eye. "The 'perfect hook'—to sell my novel."

He smiled ruefully and continued. "My novel about a copycat murder...at a mystery writers' retreat. Where the murderer follows a forensic class outline to stage a series of attacks."

"Wait!" I said, getting it—still a tiny bit confused, but absolutely getting the incredible gist of it. "You got the idea for this book on-board the ship, and then did the stunts and started writing..." I frowned, wondering how he could have done this so damned fast. And then Keven spelled it out.

"No. I wrote the book first, and then got the modeling job so I could come aboard and do the stunts. No one was ever supposed to find out about it, of course."

Marie cocked her head and a chunk of fur fell toward the deck. "But the knife and the cyanide and the smoke inhalation were exactly what we taught in our class. How could you—"

"Barbara showed me the proposal that Darcy submitted," Keven said, almost smiling. "At a writers' conference last summer. It was a brilliant plan..." any vestige of a smile left his lips, "until Thea got killed." Keven stepped toward us and we stepped backward. He stopped, his brows drawing together and his dark eyes pleading. "I made a mistake—I admit that—but I swear I didn't have anything to do with throwing that laptop into Thea's bathtub. Why would I do that, when I was hoping she'd represent my book?"

I wasn't 100 percent sure that I believed him, but... I crossed my arms and asked the question that was starting to bug me now. "Barbara gave you our outline so that you could do all of this? She was part of it?"

"God no," Keven said, shaking his head. "She had no clue that I was using the idea. You saw how she reacted to the almond extract. And she is ... *was* so damned protective of Thea." He shook his head. "Which makes it kind of weird that now ..."

"What's weird?" I asked, watching the look on Keven's face.

"I wasn't totally lying about Barbara's squirrelly behavior. She told me that it was her duty to 'protect Thea's legacy.' That she'd rather have the murder unsolved than have the authorities go 'poking around' in Thea's personal papers and 'disrupting the writers' creative processes.' She said she'd burn it all first. I swear, she had all this crap piled up on her bed and—"

"When was this?" I blurted, my hopes sinking as I pictured Barbara destroying the writers' list for the Chop or Shop. And then maybe deciding that she did want to point a finger at Angela after all. "When did you see Barbara?"

"About an hour ago," Keven said, after looking at his watch. "But, hey, I wouldn't—"

"We-gotta-go," I said in a rush, as I grabbed Marie's arm and pulled her toward the deck door. I hauled it open, lifted my skirt, and took off toward the elevators at a jog, with Marie clump-clumping steadily behind.

I heard Keven call my name, saying something about Carter and her daughter. And the Chop or Shop entries... but I couldn't make it out. Marie and I needed to keep going. And it wasn't until we got to the elevators that it hit me what he meant. It was the thing that had been nagging my subconscious all day: that Carter Cantrelle's daughter had submitted a manuscript to Thea. Was that why Sarah was so angry about Thea "hurting" Carter's family and...? No, there wasn't time to think about all that right now. Something was telling me that we'd better get up to Barbara's cabin before she destroyed any more evidence.

And then it occurred to me that there were no guarantees that Keven wasn't lying. And that maybe we'd just left the likeliest suspect free-as-a bird, and packing a broadsword.

* * *

Barbara wasn't in her cabin. We found that out because when I knocked on the door it moved inward an inch, because it was hung up on a bathroom throw rug. Which, of course, made it perfectly okay to go in—out of the goodness of our hearts. I mean, look at what had happened with Gertie, right? I pushed Marie through the door ahead of me.

Barbara definitely wasn't there and Keven wasn't lying about the mess.

"Shit, look at this!" Marie said, scanning the room. "There's stuff everywhere."

It was true. Both beds were piled with clothes, including Thea's metal-heeled Manolos, office supplies, plastic sacks of parrot kibble, and—I walked over to the bed and picked up a big Ziploc bag. "What's this?" I lifted a syringe and a large amber vial of medication.

Marie took the vial from me and squinted at the label. "Vet stuff, maybe Artie's sedative?" She shook the vial. "Must be a pretty nervous bird. It's empty." She watched as I headed for Barbara's desk near the balcony door. "Darcy, hold on. I don't think it's exactly legal to be poking around in here. What if—*eeew*, for crissake, look at that."

I lifted a scrapbook covering the stack of Chop or Shop manuscripts, and looked back over my shoulder. Marie was pointing to a roll of toilet paper balanced atop a pile of clothing.

"So?" I asked. "I take the extra soaps and shampoos home. Barbara takes TP. What's the big deal?"

"This roll's got *writing* on it," Marie said. "Swear to God. Words printed right on the tissue squares, and it looks like—"

Writing? Wait. "Rejection letters?" I asked, flipping through the scrapbook and remembering what Keven had said about that rejection toilet paper gimmick. Some writer must have sent it to Barbara as a joke. But we didn't have time for jokes. Not if I was going to find that list of Chop or Shop authors to give to the FBI. Maybe one belonging to Carter's daughter and—I stooped as loose yellowed clippings from inside the scrapbook fluttered to the carpet.

Marie's voice lowered. "Hey, Darc', these are rejection letters from *Thea*." She turned toward me, her brows raised. "To Barbara." She held the roll out toward me and let the tissue feed out. "Damn, there's dozens of them."

I wanted to look, but I couldn't take my eyes off the paper in my own hands. *Oh my God... it can't be.* I struggled to make sense of it, ignoring Marie.

"Darcy? Hey, look," Marie called, waving the TP. "Isn't this the weirdest thing?"

My heart squeezed with panic as I stared down at the old news clipping in my hands. "Not as weird as this," I whispered, finally, with my heart wedged in my throat. "I think it's ... a topless photo of Angela."

And then we heard the scream from Thea's suite.

TWENTY

I SHOOK THE HANDLE and then shoved my shoulder against the door adjoining Thea's suite. It was locked, with the security tape still in place. Marie called out, but there was only silence from beyond. I whirled away, my heart pounding. "You heard that, didn't you? I wasn't imagining it?"

"No way. That scream was real." Marie nodded her head. "And after everything we've seen in this cabin..." she glanced toward the open balcony door. "Check to see if that balcony connects with Thea's, while I page security." Her lips tightened. "And don't go over there, Darc'. Just check."

I slid Barbara's balcony door open and stepped outside, immediately noticing light spilling onto the dark decking, filtering over from next door. There *was* an adjoining balcony door. And it was open. I peered though it. The shaft of light, from Thea's suite, glinted onto something shiny scattered across her verandah. Broken glass? My breath caught as I heard a groan and a thump from inside Thea's suite. I stepped through the balcony partition, inched up to Thea's open and shattered glass door, peered through and—*oh my God!*

I jumped, startled as Marie arrived behind me; then she gasped as we both stared at the same thing: Angela on her knees beside the bed, with a belt circling her neck. Thea's notched leather belt. And Barbara Fedders standing over her, wild-eyed, ranting, and tugging on the end of the belt as if correcting an unruly dog.

I reacted without an inkling of a plan, shoving the broken door wide, stepping through, and yelling out. "Barbara, no—don't. God …*stop that!*" My heart pounding, I sidestepped farther into the room, flattening myself against the back wall with Marie following alongside.

Barbara jerked her head toward us, her expression at first confused, almost dazed, and then turning angry again as her victim tried to scramble forward on her knees.

Angela's voice was thin, hoarse, and completely terrified.

"Darcy…thank God—*agh, no…pleeaase.*" She coughed, her face reddening as Barbara jerked the belt, stopping her. Angela stared helplessly at me, her mascara streaked with tears. I took a step toward her, and froze as Barbara lifted something off the bed. Shiny metal… *Oh God.* The missing chef's knife.

"Stay back!" Barbara yelled, the huge knife trembling in her hand. "I'm not afraid. I'm not a…weak coward anymore." She stood tall, requiring Angela to sit upright to keep from choking, and I noticed—with an eerie little shock—that Barbara was wearing Thea's pantsuit, the one from the Chop or Shop. "It's all over for me anyway."

Marie shifted beside me, and it took everything I had not to whisper and ask if she'd managed to contact security. *Oh God, please let it be true.* But right now, all I could do was try and reason with ... my stomach twisted ... a woman who'd electrocuted her boss. And was seconds from choking—or stabbing—Luke's mother to death. And maybe killing us, too.

"Okay, Barbara," I said, as calmly and clearly as I could, considering that my guts were doing the mambo. "But it's *not* over. There's a way out of this. I ... we ... Marie and I want to help." I almost added that we wanted to help Angela too, but thought better of it. Obviously Angela Skyler's status was a big fat zero on Barbara's list of priorities—unless she planned to start a notched belt of her own. "I know you've had some tough times."

"Tough times? *Tough ... times?*" Barbara's face twisted into a sneer as she shrieked at me. A vicious yank on the leather belt brought Angela to a squatting position and turned her face alarmingly pale. "I've spent seven years with parrot droppings on my shoulder, I drag batteries around like a pack mule, smooth things over after the ... goddamn *al-mighty* Theodora Kenyon chops the hell out of writers' dreams." She waggled the knife like an accusing finger. "And you dare to call those 'tough times'?"

Crap, she had a point. I was a pitiful negotiator. *Uh oh ...*

Barbara blinked and stared at the blade for moment, as if she were surprised it was in her hand. Then she set it down on the bed and turned back toward us, her eyes filling with tears. "And what about *my* dreams? Wouldn't you think that after all I'd done for Thea, she could care about my dreams? Don't I deserve one last chance?"

Last Chance ... ? My eyes widened as the realization struck me.

I gave the barest of a hang-in-there nod to Angela, said a quickie Hail Mary, and then took a chance myself. "You mean your dream for your own book, *Last Dance Last Chance*?"

I heard Marie's breath escape beside me, but had to keep going. We were running out of time. "I was there when you read from it, Barbara. It was so touching. Beautiful really, and—"

"And that insufferable bitch chopped it!" Barbara yelled, yanking the belt and making Angela sputter and choke again. "Twelve years of work, *twelve years* of pouring my heart into it. It was my life story. And she calls it tripe?" She groaned softly. "Do you know how many times Thea rejected my work before she even met me?"

I shook my head with all the sympathy I could muster; this was no time to mention the fact that we'd read her toilet paper. I needed to keep Barbara Fedders talking. And hope to hell security was on its way. "And then you started working with Thea?"

Barbara nodded and let the belt slacken. "Yes, to learn from her. And I did. Surprisingly, I learned from *all* of them," she smiled and her eyes squeezed shut, forcing a tear down her cheek. "All those writers with big dreams; they taught me so much about risking vulnerability to tell the story of your heart. And..."

I took another big chance. "Angela's a writer, too," I said gently, nodding my head.

Barbara yanked the belt, and I watched Angela's eyes show way too much white before she finally gagged and caught her breath.

"Angela *Barrett*," Barbara spat, "is a spoiled, rich, selfish woman who has the luxury of *dabbling*. She doesn't care who she walks on, or how many people's lives she ruins while she *dabbles*. Writing has never been her livelihood, her only chance for a decent future."

"Like it was for you," I said, feeling the hairs rise on my arms, and remembering the yellowed newspaper clipping: a topless photo of Angela, and that familiar name on the byline. "When you were editing that newspaper in Nevada."

Barbara's brows furrowed and then her sneer returned. "Yes, and I scooped a story that would have gone national. *National.* I had all those candid photos from the Flamingo—paid six months of my salary for them—and then," she glared at the top of Angela's head, "Granddaddy *Barrett* swoops in at the last second to rescue his spoiled progeny. And stops the presses with bags of Virginia cash." She looked over at me and laughed. "The truth is that I never put two and two together, until you mentioned her maiden name, Darcy. *Barrett*—how could I forget that name?"

I think the guilt must have made me groan out loud, but Marie spoke quickly. "That was all so long ago, Barbara. It doesn't matter now."

Barbara nodded. "It probably doesn't—wouldn't have if Thea hadn't … betrayed me." Her voice grew quiet and hollow. "Forcing me to do what I … did. And then Angela had to start snooping around. It was only a matter of time until someone figured it all out. I only pretended to blackmail her, so I could get her to stop. But everything kept getting worse, so I asked her to meet me here tonight … and things kept snowballing …"

Barbara looked directly at me, her expression now remarkably free of anger, almost childlike, and pleading for help. "How will anyone understand, Darcy? Dear God, I *killed Thea.* The one person I admired more than anyone." Barbara's eyes widened, like she was reliving the horror. "She was in the tub, drunk and still ranting about the Chop or Shop. Artie was screaming from his cage, kept biting me when I tried to quiet him. I needed to talk with Thea about my manuscript. Make her read it one more time … and that damned bird kept shrieking." She squeezed her eyes shut for a moment before continuing.

"I got out the bottle of sedative and gave him his usual injection. It didn't work. So I kept filling the syringe with more and more and..." Barbara opened her eyes and stared vacantly toward the door to the bathroom. "And then after Artie stopped moving, I went back into the bathroom and told Thea about my manuscript. About my dreams." Barbara's face twisted with pain. "She laughed at me. *Laughed.* She said I needed to 'keep my day job,' and then she complained about my not getting her laptop battery fixed. That it was my fault that she had to plug it in to use it now, that if I stopped wasting time on 'silly daydreams about writing,' I'd be a better employee. She ordered me to get her another mai tai, and I went for the phone. That's when I saw the laptop on the table outside the bathroom door, with that long extension cord I'd driven all over that damned island to find. Thea started snapping her fingers and shouting for me and... I felt this incredible... *rage* building inside me. I grabbed the laptop and—"

"And you threw it at her," I said, finishing her sentence and feeling my stomach turn over as I thought of the horror she must have witnessed in the minutes that followed.

"Yes," Barbara said in an eerie monotone. "And... afterward... I just felt calm. Peaceful really. I got Artie and decided to put him in with her. And then I saw the soap on the vanity, and I don't know why, but I cut off a piece with Thea's nail file and—" She stopped and stared upward as a page shrilled overhead. A page for security staff. Barbara's eyes blinked, her jaw tensing.

I looked at Marie as the page repeated, and then I thought I heard a muffled voice calling my name from somewhere beyond the wall behind me. From Barbara's cabin or...

"But you didn't have anything to do with those other things?" I asked quickly. "The almond flavoring, and the smoke bomb, and ..." I tried to sound clueless, and tried to keep Barbara talking so she wouldn't hear that voice in the next room. A man's voice maybe, and he'd just called my name a second time. I saw Angela's eyes dart in that direction and her lids squeeze shut like she was praying. Man, I sure was.

"No," Barbara answered. "And not the knives, either." She glanced down at the huge knife, making me realize that I was stupid for calling her attention to it. "Keven did all of that." She half smiled. "It wasn't hard to figure that out. I stopped by his cabin on the way to the Chop or Shop—right after that emergency with Gertie. Keven was nervous and drinking too much, and I could smell the smoke on his clothes ... and then I saw that second knife in the suitcase half-hidden under his bed. All so typically male-sloppy." Barbara shook her head and sighed. "I should've figured it out earlier; Keven was always trying to cook up a perfect marketing hook. It's all he ever talked about. Who was I to stop his dream? Our dreams are all we have." She laughed sharply. "And even if he did slip me that almond flavoring, I decided that I couldn't let Keven get caught. So when he stepped into the other room to take a call, I hid the knife in my briefcase and—" she stopped short, eyes widening, at sounds in the hallway outside the door.

She turned to us, her expression anxious. "What is that? Did you call someone?" Angela whimpered and Barbara yanked the belt.

"No," Marie said quickly. I nodded in support, praying my pal was lying.

"I don't believe you," Barbara said, her gaze darting from the hallway door to the open balcony door and back to us. "Oh God, what's left to do now? It's all over…it's all…" She picked up the knife and my heart squeezed up into my throat.

"Barbara, don't," I said, not far from a panicky whine. "We'll help you, we'll—"

"Stay back! Slide along the wall up toward the hallway door," Barbara ordered, as she began dragging Angela like a dog on a leash. "Do it," she said, pointing the knife first at us, then downward to skim Angela's hair.

We moved, Angela coughed, and Barbara dragged her back to the balcony doors while keeping her eyes on the suite's entryway. Her grip stayed tight on the belt, and Angela's eyes closed, her face growing paler and beginning to dot with perspiration.

There was another noise in the hallway, and before I could think of anything to say to distract Barbara, Marie nudged me with her elbow. I peeked sideways and she gave the barest of a nod toward the balcony door—toward something directly behind Barbara. A movement, a…person?

My mind whirled, my heart hammered in my throat. More than anything I wanted to scream to Barbara to let go of the belt. Angela was losing consciousness fast, her breath coming slower and slower, her eyes beginning to swim. Behind us, beyond the entry door, was the sound of voices.

Then one voice, clear and authoritative—and as federal as I've ever heard.

"Miss Fedders? FBI. Open the door, now."

I didn't know whether to cheer or curse. Barbara's face contorted with pain and panic and then she—*oh God, no.* I leaped forward, arms outstretched, "No, Barbara, don't do that! Let me help you—don't, please."

She'd dropped the belt, letting Angela sink to the floor. Then lifted the huge chef's knife to turn it on herself. She pointed it up high against her abdomen, just under her ribs and her mouth twisted in a horrible, wrenching smile. Tears streamed down her face. "At least I can do *this* right," Barbara said, as the knocking increased on the entry door. "I took your workshop, remember?"

"Don't," Marie said, her eyes shifting from Barbara's face to the darkness of the balcony behind her.

Angela, her face pale and the belt dangling from her neck, rose onto all fours and began creeping toward us. My heart thudded in my ears; there wasn't time to think; I had to get to Angela before Barbara noticed. I crouched, slowly lowering myself down onto the floor as Marie began shouting for all she was worth. Loud, emphatic, accentuating every word—almost like a signal: "Barbara! Don't. Stab. Yourself. With that … *big knife*!"

Then it all happened in a terrifying frenzy: my scuttle across the carpet, my arms closing around Angela, the hallway door slamming open, and six federal agents bursting through the door with guns drawn. At the exact instant that Keven Brodie, plaid kilt whirling and wig flying, launched himself through the balcony window— and tackled Barbara Fedders.

TWENTY-ONE

THE NEXT TWO HOURS were numbing and surreal, a sort of *Law &
Order* rerun. There were below-deck interrogations, written statements, taped statements, photograph annotations... black coffee
and cigars—Marie's, not mine, though if anything might make me
want to chew on a stogy it would have been that bureaucratic mess.
Clearly, mac and cheese wasn't going to cut it this time.

Face it: everyone had questions. Keven's "marketing hook": a
felony or misdemeanor? Was Barbara Fedders a candidate for an
insanity plea? If not, should they screen bird lovers from the jury?
What happened to her manuscript, *Last Dance Last Chance*? Did
one of those British journalists really steal it? What about Carter
Cantrelle's daughter? Was it true that Barbara tossed her entry out
because it was too good? And then there was that question that
still gave me the jitters: how close did Angela Skyler come to being
the first real "notch" on Thea's deadly belt? A thousand questions
and a maddeningly silent FBI made for a boatload of passengers
with insomnia. All of which caused us to end up in the Crow's Nest

Bar around midnight. Not long before the ship's engines began to thrum.

I glanced around at the tables: Vicky, Renee, model Barth, Ellen, the Prices, and—finally huddled together to admire the lovingly "altered" copy of *Faded Flowers*—Carter Cantrelle and Sarah Skelton. Then I looked toward the bar's doorway, expecting to see Angela. She was released from the infirmary more than half an hour ago, completely healthy except for a minor bruise on her neck, so ...

"We're sailing?" I asked, turning back to Marie. I hugged my arms around myself, and the well-worn, man-sized University of Virginia sweatshirt warmed me despite my shower-damp hair. I smiled at a memory, feeling my face warm, too: this was the sweatshirt I'd snagged aboard my first cruise, almost a year ago. The Fall Foliage cruise, my first face-to-face encounter with the FBI and ... Luke. *Federal Agent Luke Skyler who, right this very minute, might be waiting to board ship in—*

"Yup. Nassau, finally," Marie said, after turning her head to direct a stream of cherry-scented smoke away from the table. "But don't get your hopes up, kid." She winked. "I'm thinking it's too late for the Dolphin Experience and the horse-drawn carriages."

Marie grinned and I noticed a sprig of werewolf fur still clinging to her chin. There was no way I was going to mention it. She was in too damned great a mood, considering that she'd spent twenty minutes picking glue and hair from her face, got a nasty heel blister from the platform boots, and then finally called her mother back. Mrs. Whitley had left a minimum of a dozen messages on Marie's cell phone since that plaid-kilt and Glock finale to Thea Kenyon's murder investigation.

I lifted my Long Island iced tea, took a drink, and felt my head respond with a therapeutic wave of wooziness. Then I narrowed my eyes. "Are you ever going to tell me what your mom wanted?"

Marie smiled, her gray eyes twinkling. "She had a question." Her lips stretched wider and the fur sprig stood up like porcupine quills. "A *spelling* question, as a matter of fact."

"Huh?" I watched in amazement as an honest-to-God blush accompanied the gleam in my best pal's eyes. "Spelling?"

"Carol's name," Marie said, shaking her head and sighing. "You know, whether or not there is an 'e' at the end, or ..." She laughed at the confusion on my face, then lifted her beer and grinned at me over the brim. "For the invitations. To Pop's seventieth birthday— damned if Ma isn't inviting *both* of us."

"No ..." My mouth dropped open. "She's including Carol? With all the neighbors and the ... Bunco Club? You mean your mom's finally—"

"Gotten a clue? Accepted reality?" Marie laughed and licked beer foam from her upper lip. "Maybe. Unless ... it was because of the photos."

"Photos?" I asked, turning toward the sound of laughter and the occasional discreet squawk, coming from a few chairs down. I waggled my fingers as Gertie seated herself, followed quickly by Herb and Artie—sans turtleneck and beak bauble, respectively.

"What photos?" I asked again, turning back to Marie.

"On the bloomin' tuuube," she teased in her best cockney accent. "CNN. Those gazillion photos the British journalist took when we were headed down to the security office." Marie groaned. "Megapixel, full color ... *hairy* photos?" She shrugged and shook her head.

"I suspect Ma thinks it's easier to explain a lesbian ... than a werewolf." Then that unmistakable twinkle returned to her eyes. "But whatever the reason, we're going to Pop's party, right?"

"Damned right," I said, grinning and smacking my palm against Marie's in a hearty high-five. I started to laugh, and then for some crazy reason my eyes filled up with tears instead. Because I knew, that even if she'd bravely shrugged it off for so many years, how very important this was to her and—we both turned as the bar rang with hoots and applause ... to herald Angela's arrival. Oh good, I wanted to know how she was. And I needed to ask if she'd heard from Luke. I glanced at my charm watch. *Is he in Nassau?*

"Angie—over here!" Gertie yahooed and waved, and Angela strode toward us, dodging clutches of writers who seemed hellbent on pounding her on the back. She stopped to give someone a big hug—Sarah, Reader Sarah? Weird. But not nearly as weird as what Angela was wearing, for godsake. I tipped my head to get a better view. *What the ... ?*

She was dressed in blue jeans—uncharacteristically casual despite telltale dry cleaners' creases—topped by a bright fuchsia, heart-stenciled RAS tee shirt and feather trimmed logo sun visor. Completing the outfit, was one of the Readers Afloat freebie book bags. No Lovisa, no Chanel—no friggin' way I could believe what I was seeing.

"Like Angie's outfit?" Gertie asked leaning forward on her elbows and peering down the table at me. She giggled as Artie jumped to her shoulder and affectionately nuzzled her ear. "I convinced her to hit the vendors' booths with me ... told her she could afford to lighten up a little, you know what I mean?"

"Um…" I stared at Marie and back at Angela, noticing that her drop earrings were blinking on and off. Little dangling hearts, flash-flashing; battery-operated, probably. I squinted, avoiding her feathers and flashes, discreetly focusing on her neck as she came closer. "Man, that bruise looks awful," I whispered to Marie, my eyes suddenly widening. "Huge, and all black and pink and … sparkly? Sparkly?" I stared harder. "*Oh Lord!*"

"What?" Marie asked, looking up from her beer.

"Jeez," I whispered, which was fairly articulate, considering that I was in shock. And seriously worried about Angela suffering post-traumatic stress, or actual brain damage from that damned belt or maybe… "It's not the bruise. I think it's maybe *covering* the bruise. It's—"

"A *tattoo*," Gertie explained. "Isn't that great?" She wrinkled her nose. "Although I would have chosen something far gutsier than a *flamingo.*"

Holy… Marie and I stared at each other, glanced up as Angela arrived, and then grasped the edge of our table as the carpet dipped beneath us. The engines stopped. We'd reached the port of Nassau.

* * *

For the first twenty minutes that Angela and I were out on the darkened deck, I half hoped that Luke *wouldn't* come after all. I mean, good God, how could he not notice his mother's irreversible brain damage? And not blame me? She was babbling, euphoric, prone to fits of hugging, had cheesy feathers in her hair, and a flamingo stamped on her neck. And then, then finally, my panic subsided and… I *got it.* Finally *got* it. Mmhmm. Oh man. Yes indeedy.

I smiled, and glanced over the rail at the shimmering lights of Nassau. And then I stopped worrying about Luke. I kept one wary eye on Angela's lethal hugging arm, squinted the other to cut down the glare from her blinking earrings, and I simply listened. Like a good nurse, and like a friend, too. Because Angela Barrett Skyler wasn't brain damaged after all; she'd experienced an honest-to-goodness, goose bumpy, cosmic, and life-changing moment—an epiphany, if you will. Okay, inspired by a foursome with a Wench, a Disco Werewolf, and a knife-wielding psychotic, of course—but hell, not every epiphany has to be purely divine, right?

"And so," she said, giving my shoulders another little squeeze, "I even started thinking about how completely ironic it was that"—she let go of me, reached down into her book tote, and produced that familiar bottle of über-champagne—"I began this journey by trying to bribe Thea Kenyon." Her blue eyes, below the feathered brim of the sun visor, caught mine, and she nodded.

"Oh, well, I wouldn't say that you—"

"Pish-posh," she said, cutting me off, "of course I was trying to influence her. I've done that my whole life—created an exceptional *image* ... in order to be *accepted*. Don't you see?" Angela pressed her palms together and glanced heavenward, or as close to that as her feathered brim would allow, and then she lowered her voice like she was about to say something very profound. "Barbara Fedders was right."

Huh? Before I could sort through that one, she continued on.

"About me. I *am* a 'dabbler,' Darcy. I've dabbled my life away to create this perfect socially acceptable *veneer* ... and for what reason?" She raised her palms. "So I can skate by, get a pass, move to the head of the line, while everyone else is out there taking real risks? Exposing themselves to true vulnerability?" She shook her head. "That's what Barbara thought—maybe that's what you think too, Darcy."

I knew enough to keep my mouth shut and assume that question was rhetorical.

"But what if," Angela's voice lowered again, "it's all because I'm a sniveling *coward*?" She smiled ruefully and shook her head, making her blinking earrings blur like a Jedi lightsaber. Then she reached up to touch her temporary tattoo. "What if I let the Flamingo start a lifelong lie... a big, fat cover-up to keep anyone from judging the real Angela Barrett? And perhaps finding her well-dressed, well-spoken, but sadly... lacking."

"Wait, Angela," I said, reaching toward where her hand rested on the deck rail, "don't you think you might be over-react—"

"I thought I was going to *die*, Darcy!" Angela blurted, cutting me off. Then she squeezed her eyes shut for a moment and gave a laugh that was part groan. "Being dragged around like a dog on a leash puts that old topless incident into sharp perspective. Do you understand?"

I nodded, and smiled gently. The woman in feathers had a point.

"All I could think about," she said, "was Lucas—my dear, dear husband—and Luke, and the girls," Angela's eyes shone with tears. "And how I wouldn't see them again. And then I recalled those things you'd said about your family, those *wonderful* things about how proud you were of them—just as they are—and I wondered if my family would remember me that way." She squeezed her eyes shut for a moment, opened them again and sighed. "I'd never have had the courage to do what your mother did that night at the Flamingo. She protected me—a virtual *stranger*—and lost her job because of it. I..."

"Hey," I said, quickly, taking hold of her hand, "you're okay now; we're all okay. You'll see your family; I'll see mine." I nodded encouragement, and gave her hand a little squeeze.

Angela smiled and then reached out to lift one of my curls where it had caught on my post earring—the tiny sailboat, platinum and diamond, from the pair that her son had given me last spring. "It also occurs to me," she said warmly, "that your brave mother did a wonderful job raising *you*, Darcy."

Then, before I could blink or blather, Angela chuckled and moved on. "And," she said, "when I was shopping for clothes with Gertie, I remembered something else."

"What?" I asked, half turning toward voices at the deck door behind us. Marie probably, worrying about me and the brain-damaged Judge's wife.

"I saved that jacket," Angela said, smiling slowly. "All these years."

"Jacket?" I scrunched my brows.

"Your dad's cockroach jacket," she said. "The Cavanaugh Holy Grail."

"No…you're shitting me," I said, with my typical well-bred couth.

The Judge's wife's eyes widened and then she smiled, her expression warm. "*Not* shitting you. Got your cell phone?"

"Sure, why?"

"Tap in your mother's number," Angela directed, like she was suddenly presiding over the Charlottesville Garden Club. "I've got a long overdue thank-you to make."

Well…I'll be damned. I grinned and dug around in my purse for the phone, pulled it out, started to touch the number, then stopped.

"But what are you going to do about that Flamingo story? The feds have Barbara's newspaper clippings."

Angela ignored me and pointed to the phone. "She's Mary Margaret Cavanaugh, correct? And your father is . . . Bill?"

I sighed, hit Mom's speed dial, and handed Angela the phone.

I waited, holding my breath a little, as she struggled graciously through a short dialogue with my sweetly demented grandma, and then finally got my mother on the phone. Then Angela nodded at me and walked off toward the nearest deck chaise, already laughing at something Mom had said. God only knew what. I shook my head and smiled.

Obviously Angela was going to keep me guessing about what she was going to tell her children about her past, but with a friggin' sparkly flamingo tattooed on her neck, I don't see how she was going to avoid a few questions. Especially with her Special Agent son due to arrive at any—

The deck door swooshed open behind me and I turned. My knees went weak and my breath caught like a blushing virgin.

No man had ever looked so good.

"Luke!"

TWENTY-TWO

"Jeez!" I squirmed on the bed and giggled as Luke tipped his champagne glass just enough to drizzle the bubbly, mega-dollar liquid in a steady stream across my bare ... "Aagh, no fair, Skyler!"

I batted a hand at the glass, and Luke, chuckling low in his throat, raised the fluted crystal higher. No doubt about it, Quantico teaches these guys incredible aim. But then again, it wasn't such a bad thing to be the private target of a federal investigation. We'd been in Luke's VIP stateroom for an hour and a half—bed, floor, and shower—and, trust me, I wasn't exactly resisting arrest.

I watched as his handsome head, hair seriously tousled by my fingers, bent over the task at hand; dropping Dom Pérignon, drop by chilly drop, onto—"Okay, you win," I gasped, my abs shivering. "But I'll bet your mother never intended her fancy champagne to be sipped from a Yankee belly button."

"All bets are off. Mother has a tattoo." Luke raised his brows. "And I believe that's exactly what we were just discussing here?" He set the empty glass on the carpet beside the bed, next to the silver-topped dish of special-order macaroni and cheese, and leaned over me again. He smiled, blue eyes glittering mischievously, and then traced the warm tip of his tongue across my belly one more time, making me shiver despite my stubborn resolve. "So," he said, "you've decided to tell me why there's a huge, damned bird stamped on her neck—or must I continue torturin' you mooore?"

"Can't tell everything," I said, secretly loving how this man's voice turned Rhett Butler when he was tired or ... otherwise worn out. Then I continued, my voice completely serious. "Really, Luke. You saw that she was fine, but the rest of the details, including her new wardrobe, need to come directly from her."

I smiled at the confusion on his handsome face. "Let's just say that maybe your mother and I have discovered a common bond after all. And that's a good thing, right?" I'm sure he thought that I meant our tattoos, but it wasn't my place to bring up the Flamingo, or any other details of Angela's epiphany—she'd do that when she had time. After all, Luke had barely planted a kiss on his mother's forehead when she'd handed him the champagne and shooed us away, saying that she was fit as a fiddle. And that she wanted to finish her phone conversation with my mother. Besides, I had no doubt a lot of things would surface as the federal investigation into Thea Kenyon's murder continued. My brows rose.

"Wait," I said, sitting up and causing the champagne on my belly to sluice southward. "Weren't *you* going to tell *me* what you found out at the security office when you first came onboard? Your buddies have been so blasted tight-lipped. I know Barbara's being sent for a psychiatric evaluation, but everyone's been wondering about other things, too, like ... how did Keven know to go to Barbara's cabin?"

"Because of something Sarah Skelton told him." Luke reached to pull up the sheet. "The blonde from that group. Readers ... ?"

"Readers Afloat," I explained, following as Luke scooted backward to lean against the bed's padded headboard. "What did Sarah know?" I settled in alongside him, trying to recall if I'd highlighted Sarah's name on my investigation lists. And what color I'd used.

"Apparently she'd gone to the Dolphin Deck crime scene area to check on that bestselling author, uh ... "

"Carter Cantrelle," I reminded him, remembering that Marie and I had seen Sarah there, outside the elevator, dressed as an alien. It was when we couldn't find Angela, and nobody knew where Barbara was. When we were on our way to confront Keven Brodie. "So what did Sarah tell Keven?"

"That she'd seen Barbara Fedders in that hallway," Luke explained. "And how strange it was to see her wearing Kenyon's clothes. Then Sarah told one of our Agents the same thing—when she went down to the security office and admitted to slipping a hostile note under Kenyon's door a few days back."

Note? The threat. I raised my brows in silent "*Aha*" as Luke continued.

"She said that Barbara was acting strangely and was dressed in the clothes that Kenyon wore to that 'Chop Shop' event." Luke's jaw tensed. "Including the damned belt that she used on my mother." He glanced over at me, his brows furrowed. "The doctor said Mother was fine. She looked okay to me and—"

"She *is* fine," I said, reaching up to touch his face. I smiled. "And you've checked me over—three times now. Stop worrying about us. We're good. But what about Keven? What's going to happen to him?"

Luke laughed sharply. "Damned if he doesn't beat all." He shook his head. "For a man in a wig and skirt—"

"Kilt," I corrected.

"For a man in a plaid *skirt*," Luke continued, "he's damned lucky. My guess is he'll walk away scot-free—if you'll pardon the lousy pun."

I smiled and then scrunched my brows. "Free? But what about the knife, Gertie's smoke bomb, and the cyanide?"

"There's no law against spiking a drink with almond flavoring," Luke explained. "And it seems that neither the editor who got cut, nor the old woman with emphysema ..." he chuckled and raised his brows. "Do you believe she made a pass at one of our agents? Practically grabbed his ass."

"Oh, yeah," I said, nodding, "I have no doubts about Gertie's libido. But what were you saying about Keven's stunts?"

"Neither of the victims is pressing charges against him," Luke explained. "There's some convoluted tradeoff, about Gertie having a manuscript that needs representation, and Brodie being a literary agent ..."

"Oh my God." My eyes snapped wide open. "And Ellen, the editor?"

"Apparently she's making an offer to buy Brodie's murder mystery novel. She kept rattling on about 'the perfect marketing hook.'" Luke shook his head. "These writers are a weird bunch, if you ask me. And after seeing my mother in electric earrings, I'm guessing it's contagious."

I nodded and laughed, then saw Luke's brows draw together.

He tilted his head, then brushed my hair away from the side of my face. Tiny crinkles formed at the corners of his eyes as he smiled. "Speaking of earrings, you're wearing the sailboats."

"Yes," I said, my face warming under his intent gaze. "You like?"

"I ... do," Luke said slowly, and for some reason the way he said those two little words made my breath catch in my chest and my stomach do a strange flip-flop. "Very much so."

Then he took my face in both of his big hands and kissed me tenderly and very, very thoroughly. When he was through, he watched my eyes for a long moment before he spoke. "I liked giving you diamonds," Luke said, still watching me. "But I wasn't sure how you felt about it back then."

I smiled, very much sure of how I'd felt six months ago: damned terrified that the mysterious black velvet jewelry box contained an engagement ring. Frantically worried, scratching at hives, and itching to sail away as fast as I could. And yet I'd been oddly disappointed when I saw earrings in the box instead. Things felt so different now.

It was a matter of timing I suppose, and of growing up enough to trust what my heart tells me—and accepting truths about myself. Big truths. Like the ones I told Angela Skyler when we were slammin' down that whiskey after the Chop or Shop: that I'm Californian, Democrat, and Catholic, proud of my wacky family ... and even of the shamrock tattooed on my breast. And truths that I didn't tell her, too, like the fact that I love being a nurse. Even if it means long hours and gritty realities—with no luxurious respite of afternoon tea. And that I'm going to do my damnedest to help bring as many new folks onboard this profession as I can, because we need them. And because nurses are heroes in my book, going right back to my Grandma Rosaleen. And then, of course, there's the truth that Marie Whitley—cigars, socks, wisecracks, and all—is going to be my best friend forever. Until we're both grizzled, gray, and

"So," Luke said, lifting my chin with his fingertip and interrupting my reverie. "How do you feel about them?"

"About what?" I asked, blinking up at him and realizing that there was one other truth I hadn't told Angela Barrett Skyler: that I'm in love with her son. Completely, no doubts—head over the heels of my eBay Manolos.

I'm in love. Now there's an epiphany.

"Diamonds," Luke said. "Do you like them now, Darcy?"

I hesitated for only the barest of moments, to look deeply into Luke's eyes. But it was long enough to realize that I wanted to be able to do that for the rest of my life.

"I do," I whispered as clearly as I could with my heart wedged into my throat. Then I glanced at the alarm clock, sat straight up in bed, and poked him in the chest with my finger. "Hey, don't you have to disembark, Skyler? They said we're sailing at four AM; we'd better find your pants before—"

Luke pressed a finger against my lips and shook his head. "Not leaving."

"What?" A warm rush of relief made my voice catch. "Hey... *great*," I said, smiling at the thought of the long sail back to Port Canaveral. And how, since he wasn't directly involved in the murder case, he'd have a chance to relax, do a little gambling with Marie; and how we could sneak off to this stateroom whenever we wanted and ... "So when will you go back to Boston?"

Luke's eyes crinkled. "Boston? Don't know—whenever you want to visit there, I suppose. Spring's nice, with the cherry blossoms. Or there's the Cape in the summer, the fall foliage or—"

"*Visit?*" I said, poking him again and scrunching my brows. "What do mean, visit? I'm talking about your *work*. When do you have to be back at work in—" I stopped short as I saw the look on his face. And then my eyes widened and my heart took off lickety-split. "You mean … ?"

Luke nodded, a grin making his dimples deepen. "I'm transferring back to San Francisco. Effective immediately." He brushed the back of his fingers tenderly along my cheek. "And I've taken that purchase option on the Marina apartment. Faxed the papers two days ago. It's mine."

"You're buying … moving …" my voice dropped an octave, "*permanently?*"

He laughed at the shock on my face, and then touched a fingertip to the end of my nose. "Don't flatter yourself so quickly, Cavanaugh. What makes you think this isn't because it's too damned hard to move my sailboat?"

I caught my breath. "But what about … politics? Your run for State Senate?" *And the debutante your mother picked out for your breeding program?*

Luke laughed again, and then reached over the side of the bed to find the glasses and pull the dripping champagne bottle from the ice bucket. "Last time I heard, California could use a little help in that respect. They can't keep electing movie stars."

"Oh Lord help us," I chuckled, shaking my head and thinking of the mixed feelings my parents would have about my part in putting another Republican on the ballot, but how glad they'd be to have Luke available for our crazy Sunday dinners. And how much Grandma loves it that Luke makes her laugh and ... I squeezed my eyes shut and chuckled again, thinking that Angela Barrett Skyler would undoubtedly have similar mixed reactions. I mean, I was pretty sure she liked me now, but could she deal with the possibility of ... redheaded grandbabies? Not that I was going down that road anytime soon, for godsake. But weirder things have happened, right? Angela Skyler had a flamingo tattoo on her neck, Bill the Bug Man was getting his lucky jacket back, Marie and Carol were flying off to a birthday party in New York, and ...

I smiled as Luke handed me a crystal glass of bubbly and then clinked his glass against mine.

And ... I just said yes to the subject of diamonds.

Cheers.

ACKNOWLEDGMENTS

My heartfelt thanks to:

Agent Natasha Kern, acquiring editor Barbara Moore, editor Karl Anderson, and fabulous critique partner Nancy Herriman. Dear friends Ruth and Dick Haas and the staff of Read All About It Bookstore (Boerne, TX) for hosting stellar and laugh-filled launch parties. Bill and Frankeen Price—friends, neighbors, and talented artists—for climbing aboard *Mai Tai to Murder* in generous donation to community charities. Wonderful Tai Chi "princess," Joslyn Crews, for hauling me out of my office chair every Wednesday morning, to "repulse the monkey, grasp the bird's tail, part the wild horse's mane," swirl a fan, brandish a sword . . . and generally keep my Chi flowing. My "sister," Mary Knight, for agreeing to don a snorkel and join my Stingray Adventure research. Readers and lifelong cruisers Clancy and Mary Ann Boyd—yours is a true story of love and adventure.

And to Andy, my real-life hero, always.

Photo by Nigel

ABOUT THE AUTHOR

Candy Calvert is a registered nurse who blames her quirky sense of humor on "survival tactics learned in the trenches of the ER." Born in Northern California and the mother of two, she now lives with her husband in the beautiful Hill Country of Texas. Grueling cruise research for the Darcy Cavanaugh Mystery Series has found Candy singing with a Newfoundland country band, roaming the ruins of Pompeii, doing the limbo atop a jet-powered catamaran, and swimming with stingrays. Visit her website at: www.candycalvert.com.

WWW.MIDNIGHTINKBOOKS.COM

From the gritty streets of New York City to sacred tombs in the Middle East, it's always midnight somewhere. Join us online at any hour for fresh new voices in mystery fiction, book club questions, author information, mystery resources, and more.

Midnight Ink promises a wild ride filled with cunning villains, conflicted heroes, hilarious hazards, mind-bending puzzles, and enough twists and turns to keep readers on the edge of their seats.

MIDNIGHT INK ORDERING INFORMATION

Order by Phone:
- Call toll-free within the U.S. and Canada at 1-888-NITEINK (1-888-648-3465)
- We accept VISA, MasterCard, and American Express

Order by Mail:
Send the full price of your order (MN residents add 6.5% sales tax) in U.S. funds, plus postage & handling to:

> Midnight Ink
> 2143 Wooddale Drive, H074
> Woodbury, MN 55125-2989

Postage & Handling:

Standard (U.S., Mexico, & Canada). If your order is:
> $24.99 and under, add $3.00
> $25.00 and over, FREE STANDARD SHIPPING

AK, HI, PR: $15.00 for one book plus $1.00 for each additional book.

International Orders (airmail only):
> $16.00 for one book plus $3.00 for each additional book

Orders are processed within 2 business days. Please allow for normal shipping time. Postage and handling rates subject to change.